To My Darli...
I'm so glad you share my
love of books! Enjoy, my love!
Always,
Ellen

The
ANGELWALK
TRILOGY

The
ANGELWALK
TRILOGY

by Roger Elwood

ANGELWALK

~

FALLEN ANGEL

~

STEDFAST

Inspirational Press • New York

First Inspirational Press edition published in 1995.

Inspirational Press
A division of Budget Book Service, Inc.
386 Park Avenue South
New York, NY 10016

Inspirational Press is a trademark of Budget Book Service, Inc.

Published by arrangement with Crossway Books, a division of Good News Publishers and Word, Inc., a division of Thomas Nelson, Inc., Publishers.

Library of Congress Catalog Card Number: 95-75105

ISBN: 0-88486-114-7

Text designed by Hannah Lerner.

Printed in the United States of America.

Contents

I
Angelwalk

For Francis A. Schaeffer
—Met Too Briefly But Remembered
for a Lifetime

Foreword

*A*NGELWALK by Roger Elwood is an unusual theme and an unusual treatment of a subject that will fascinate the reader and open new vistas along the line of imaginative fiction.

An angel is faced with the choice of joining Satan in his revolt against God of all creation or of remaining faithful to the One who made him. He is given an opportunity to visit the earth and see and appreciate in advance what the consequences would be if he chooses to follow Satan. His quest is our quest and his experiences our experiences, but what follows the reader will discover for himself as he reads the book. This should whet the appetite of all of us.

Elwood treads in line with the footprints of perhaps the best known writer of this genre—C.S. Lewis, whose *Screwtape Letters* and Narnia Tales have brought him lasting acclaim. For anyone to come near to the heights that C.S. Lewis reached is hard to believe.

Elwood comes as close to duplicating Lewis's achievement as any recent writer has. His background has fitted him well for the task he undertakes. He has a gift for words, a sensitivity to the current milieu, a solid Biblical commitment, and a strong desire to reverse the tide of paganism which is sweeping through the West. He reflects the thesis C.S. Lewis propounded so ably in what I think to be one of his finest works, *The Abolition of Man*.

The reading public will be the final judge of Elwood's effort. And one can hope that his volume will challenge a younger generation of writers to devote their skills to writing fiction in the service of God.

Harold Lindsell

"If Satan himself goes disguised as an angel of light, there is no need to be surprised when his servants, too, disguise themselves as the servants of righteousness"

—2 Corinthians 11:14, 15, JB

I CANNOT AGE, but I do feel somehow old as I sit here, on a mountaintop overlooking the plain where the last great battle of Mankind has taken place. The bodies number into the thousands, and blood collects everywhere—giant, deep pools like a titanic wave over the ground, submerging it. It is possible to drown in blood down there . . .

I momentarily turn away, the odor so strong that it ascends the mountain. I try to close my ears because the cries of the dying are loud enough to form a crescendo that also reaches me—but there is no escaping the panorama below, either in its sights or its sounds.

I decide to leave the mountain and go down to the plain where the old prophecies always had been pointing with devastating clarity.

Some of the dying have had the flesh literally seared from their bones, and they have only seconds left, those that survived at all. They see me, of course—the living do not—but those nearly dead, suspended, in a sense, between two kinds of life indeed see, reach out, beg.

"Please help me, sir," I am asked again and again.

"The pain . . ."

"I know I've been blinded, now, yet I see you anyway. I see—"

Ahead, standing as though on an island uplifted in the midst of a blood-red sea, are several hundred soldiers, but no longer with weapons, their former bodily shells lying at their feet.

I approach them.

"We could not continue," one of them tells me. "All of us asked for God's forgiveness through Jesus the Christ."

"There is no doubt that many of our comrades are doomed," another adds, "because of their allegiance to the Devil. We bid them good-bye . . ."

One by one they ascend. The final soldier turns to me, smiles, says, "We did the right thing."

I nod.

. . . *we did the right thing.*

Yes, they did—all of them—that one group of hundreds out of countless thousands.

They refused the Antichrist. And he had them slaughtered as a result, threatening to do just that once again to any others who might decide to rebel.

And now—

Not one of them bore the scars of how they died—no bayonet wounds, no bullet holes. In their resurrection they had been healed, given the bodies that would be theirs throughout eternity.

But the others share not at all the same end. Every few seconds, more are dying. Bodies piled upon bodies, visible where the blood is not quite deep enough to hide them. I look about, and see hands raised against the sky, like stalks of marsh grass in a bloody inlet. For an instant only. Then cut down.

They also see me. They surround me as I go past, trying not to look at them, their eyes haunted where they yet have eyes. Some do not, seared away, only the empty sockets remain. But they see me just the same. And all turn away, knowing *they* will spend eternity like that—in agony, flames searing them but never fully consuming.

The scene oppresses. I cannot stand it any longer. I leave, not sure of where to go. I have time at my disposal. I can do whatever I want with it, yes, even choose to stay where I am—in this time and place—or retreat through the centuries, their contents disgorged at my very feet.

And yet, in a way that is beyond mere loneliness—oh, how wonderful if it were but a question of being merely *lonely*—I have nowhere to go. An irony that presses me down inflicts on me a weariness that is so pervasive it is as though all of history has become a singular weight from which it is well-nigh impossible to extricate myself. And I think, in tremulous recollection, of all that preceded this moment, this literal battlefield on which I find myself.

Lord, I whisper with prayerful intent against the dissipating sounds of the vanquished. *My dear, dear Lord.*

The beginning.

*W*E ARE SITTING by a crystal lake. A hint of violets surrounds us with its gentle scent.

"Do you know what I used to feel really guilty about on earth?"

The question is asked by a man who had been a show business agent during his mortal life.

"I would be interested in learning about it," I tell him with full sincerity.

He smiles as he says, "When I worked with clients on Broadway, I met plenty of angels, but they weren't like you at all."

We both enjoy the humor of that and then he adds, "My conscience hit me hard, in those days, for two reasons: One, the type of individual with whom I often had to work. I remember the guy who headed one of the studios—one of the most promiscuous homosexuals in a town where being gay was almost an advantage. One day, he invited me to a party given by a producer. I went, against my better judgment. What I encountered was loathsome—open perverted activity, the consumption of illegal drugs, blasphemous jokes, and much more. Many of the offenders were extremely influential in the entertainment business. They had a stranglehold on what the public *saw* in theatres and on television.

"The second area of difficulty was when I had to pass judgment on people, when I had to decide who was or wasn't worthy. Now I know that all of us are worthwhile in the sight of God, that He is concerned about every creation of His, whether a sparrow in the field or a jet pilot or even an agent. But in those days I earned my living in an environment that paid lip service to values and honor and integrity and self-image but in the end created the conditions for the destruction of each of those.

"So there I was, looking at this actor or that one, and I would have to say that one would make it big in the profession, and another might as well quit early. Again and again I played a kind of god game with those kids.

"Actually most took it well, better than I would have, while others did not—but then something happened that changed the whole rat race for me."

"What was that?" I ask.

"I met this exceptionally handsome young actor—tall, attractive and, yes, extremely talented. He was a real contender for the starring role in a potent new TV series. Then someone else came by, and he seemed just right also. I had to choose between them."

"So what was the difference between that incident and any of the others?"

"I had to turn down the first young man. He took it hard, so hard in fact that he shot himself to death less than a week later. He left a suicide note that read, 'I have no worth as a human being. I have nothing. I am nothing. I return to nothing.'

"I was never the same after that. About a month later I accepted Christ as Savior and Lord because I realized that *I* felt very, very worthless at that point, that the only

redemption for me was that which the Lord purchased
with His shed blood at Calvary."

He pauses, looking at the lake, its surface sparkling
like the diamonds described by poets.

"I will never again have to judge another human being.
And I myself have been judged and found acceptable in
the sight of Almighty God."

He stands, smiling.

"I've just arrived, and would like to experience more of
what I could only dream about back on Earth. Would you
excuse me, Darien? That is your name, isn't it?"

"Yes," I say simply.

He walks off, cherubs dancing at his feet.

I wish . . .

The words are unspoken, thought only.

I turn and go in another direction. Soon I am talking to
people born mentally retarded who now have minds like
Augustine or Luther. And the parents who deeply loved
them, who stayed with them, who shared the anguish
because of their steadfast faith that "all things work
together for good"—these parents have been repaid a
thousand times, for what carnal life denied them is fully
realized in Heaven; children with whole minds and
bodies, children who can converse properly and walk
without assistance.

I wish I could accept . . .

"If Heaven offered only that," one mother tells me, "it
would be worth everything."

Those born without limbs or those who lost arms or
legs or hands through accidents are now restored. They
have been "repaired." One woman who had never had
any limbs at all and who remained a human oddity all her
life can now walk about, jumping, running, and shaking
hands with everyone, her face aglow.

Those once blind can see and stroll through the parks
and gardens, looking with astonishment; those once deaf

just sit and listen; those born mute gather in little groups and chatter away.

I wish I could accept all this without . . .

I meet a man known informally as "the Intellectual." He greets me with abundant enthusiasm.

"There was a time when I would have labelled all this as abject nonsense," he admits. "Strolling through heaven! Saying hello to an angel! There was a time when I would have—"

He interrupts himself, saying, "I looked at life as a uniformity of natural causes in a closed system. How could God, if He existed, which, of course, wasn't the case . . . how could God suddenly reach down into that system anytime He desired, and bring about the Incarnation, the parting of the Red Sea, the healing of lepers? No! I said to myself and to others. A thousand times no! Any thought of the supernatural was sheer idiocy and I would have no part of it.

"I lived in a kind of cocoon, refusing to acknowledge that anything at all existed outside it. What I couldn't see, feel, hold, or reason out didn't exist as far as I was concerned.

"And God as a concept simply failed to compute, as I said back on Earth. He threw my entire equation out, and since that was the case, I ended up throwing Him out because that equation and the scientific concepts from which it originated were my life's foundation. That was what I worshipped, not pie-in-the-sky puffery."

"What changed you?" I ask.

"It was the strangest moment, frankly. I owned a private plane. I was out in it one day, alone. Something malfunctioned in the motor. I saw smoke. The plane nosedived. There was no possibility, considering the elevation and how fast it was falling, that I would survive.

"I prayed then. I know, in looking back, how extraordinary that was. Me, the atheist—I prayed! I had heard all about so-called foxhole Christians and I had scorned their weakness, their instability, yes, their hypocrisy. And yet I was doing the same thing.

"Well, I survived, sustaining remarkably few injuries, certainly nothing serious. As I climbed out of the wreckage of that plane, my first thought was about how little pain I felt! I had some cuts, some bruises, but nothing else.

"I was, of course, glad to be alive. But the fact that I *was* alive stunned me. I examined all my safe, scientific theories, computed in my mind the *logical* possibility that I would *be* alive, and yet nothing supported the reality I was experiencing at that moment which was, simply, my survival.

"I remembered that quick, strangely instinctive prayer. Nothing else could have explained what had happened. God had stepped into my closed world, penetrated my humanistic cocoon—and given me a life that, according to the proper computerized readout, should have been wiped out.

"But you know, that wasn't all. I learned something else. I learned the meaning of His forgiveness, the validity of it, the depth of it. I had spent much of my adult life trying to convince others that He was simply a myth and that Karl Marx had had it right when he called religion an opiate for the masses. I *destroyed* the faith of thousands, you know. And yet God chose to forgive me. I was driven to tears as I understood the significance of that. I closed myself off from everyone for weeks. When I emerged from that self-imposed solitude, I became like Saul of Tarsus. The new me was St. Paul, dedicated to the Kingdom, not bent on causing it to crumble."

We talk a bit more, and then he goes off. Isaac Newton is waiting for him . . .

I wish I could accept all this without the questions, one after the other.

Now I am standing beside a golden sea. The waters are pure, clear; birds swoop overhead. No longer is it necessary for them to kill in order to survive. One of them lands next to me, and walks up to me. I run my hand down its back; it chatters contentedly, and then takes off again.

Earlier, I watched as lions played with lambs. (A lamb hid behind a tree and as a lion was walking past, jumped out at it. The king of beasts yelped in mock surprise, and was about to pretend to run when it discovered the identity of the culprit. No roar escaped its jaws; instead it licked the lamb on the forehead, and the two walked off together, the lion wagging its tail, the lamb trying to wag what little it had for a tail.)

I wish I could accept all this without the questions, one after the other, that keep hammering at me. . . .

I think back to when they first started. It was soon after my friend Lucifer was forced to leave Heaven, taking with him a third of all of the angels.

And the great dragon was cast out, that old serpent, called the Devil, which deceiveth the whole world: he was cast out into the earth, and his angels were cast out with him . . . And his tail drew the third part of the stars of heaven, and did cast them to the earth.

Those who remained were told that he had exalted himself too highly, that he proposed to be on a level with God and, in fact, eventually to assume His very throne.

How art thou fallen from heaven, O Lucifer, son of the morning! How art thou cut down to the ground, who didst weaken the nations! For thou hast said in thine heart, I will . . . exalt my throne above the stars of God . . . I will ascend above the heights of the clouds, I will be like the Most High.

I never was able to converse with him about this. The

Casting Out happened so quickly. And since then I have asked myself, again and again, one singular question: What was the *whole* story?

As I remember the moments I did spend with Lucifer, I can see some elements of ego in him, some hint that he was different from the rest of us.

Different . . .

Indeed that was the case—the most glorious of all—with a countenance second only to the Trinity's. A majestic bearing, a power that made him truly stand out.

Others gathered around him. We all listened to his ideas. But as for myself I really never had anything to be discontented about. I yet recall my first moment of existence—from nothingness to awareness, looking up into the very face of God, knowing that though He had created ten thousand upon ten thousand of us, each was special to Him, each as though the only one. God reached down and took my wings and breathed into me the power of life, of flight, the reality of immortality. He first created my very self, and then He gave that self life everlasting.

I was grateful to Him. I came into existence in the midst of a place so beautiful, so good in every way that I had no reason to be discontent. When there is perfection, what could be better?

But Lucifer, I do admit, was not the same at all. Does this mean that God made a mistake? No, He created us—He never dominates us. We are His servants but not His slaves.

Yet was what Lucifer had done so serious, so pervasive that a loving, forgiving Creator could *not* forgive him? And yet later the Father sent His Son to die so that forgiveness was purchased for the rest of time. How could the same God not also forgive Lucifer and give His finest creation another chance, a chance to change, to—?

Always the same doubt—from just after the Casting

Out to the birth of Christ as God Incarnate to His death, burial and resurrection and beyond, to the present. Doubt unchallenged, becoming ever more compelling . . .

Ultimately I decide I cannot endure my inner turmoil any longer. I shudder contemplating what I am about to do . . .

"Are you going to see Him now?" my friend and fellow angel Stedfast asks.

"Yes, I have requested a meeting and He has agreed."

"Do you think, really, that is wise, Darien? Why not just accept, and trust?"

"Can *you* . . . do that?"

"Oh, yes, Darien," Stedfast replies without hesitation. "It is not difficult for me. I see all that has been, and all that is, and what the prophecies promise will be, and I know that acceptance and trust are right and, yes, deserved by God as our response to all that He has done."

"I wish I could accept without question," I say, "as you are doing. I did once, before the Casting Out, but now—"

"Earth, my friend Darien, is where doubts grow. Heaven is where they are put to rest, forever."

Our conversation ends only because it is time for the meeting that will determine my destiny.

In an instant I am with Almighty God, alone, no one to interrupt us. He knew, totally, of my concerns. His plan had been set, I suspect, ever since the Casting Out, He waited only for me to ask . . .

"All around us is warfare, Darien. My prophet Daniel spoke of a ministering angel being late because of having to do battle in the heavenly realm. Satan tries to cause havoc whenever and wherever he can."

I had never been on the front lines myself. Suddenly the strangeness of that fact hits me hard. It is as though God knew I would not be a committed warrior but instead something of a pacifist, not at all certain of the enemy. Yet I had heard, in any event, stories about Lucifer, whispers from the battlefield about a shadowy, almost mythical figure—or at least that was what he had become over the ages as memories of him firsthand faded. The Lucifer I knew had a rich baritone voice and he used it to good effect as he persuaded angel after angel, but certainly he was not a loathsome adversary as would be told by returning warriors, with their tales of contending over the spirits of saints, awful encounters between demonic creatures and the heavenly defenders. I recall in particular an alleged foiling of a plan to storm the gates of Heaven itself; yes, it had brought chills to my very being, and yet I could never decide how much was battlefield bravado and how much was factual.

"I need you with me in this battle, Darien. But I cannot have you halfway. I must have your totality of commitment. You cannot fight an enemy whom you find appealing or whom you think is being dealt with unjustly."

God gives me a choice then: Indeed, I can go to Earth for as long as needed. Since time is not an actuality but merely a contrivance for the convenience of Man, I would be given the ability to go anywhere or any "time" I want. If I felt, at the conclusion, that Lucifer had been dealt with improperly or that perhaps he had reformed, then God would allow Lucifer back into Heaven, along with the others. If, however, the evidence supported the verdict, the justice of Lucifer's exile, then I would in fact return, alone, without so much as a whimper, and in the process forever abandon any notion of following in Lucifer's footsteps.

"Yours is a terrible responsibility, Darien. Your findings will affect all of us forever."

I leave God's immediate presence to ponder just a bit more what should be my course of action. Before that

decision is made, I meet with several more of those in
Heaven who had spent their mortal lives on earth.

One man tells me of being in an airplane, relaxing,
when suddenly a bomb explodes. Directly ahead of him a
six-year-old child is torn out of her mother's arms and
sucked through a gaping hole in the side of the craft. An
elderly woman has the fingers of one hand ripped off on
jagged pieces of metal. The man chronicling this dies as
he goes through a secondary hole that is just barely wide
enough for him; he can feel flesh catching on the twisted
metal and his lungs collapsing as the pressure changes
drastically.

"It *is* violent down there," the man says but without
fear any longer. After all, he is in Heaven where there is
no fear, no sorrow.

I next meet a woman.

"I was attacked and killed while walking home," she
says calmly. "It was at night. Perhaps I should have been
more careful. But I tended to trust people, to think the
best of them while not taking into consideration the sin
nature that is part of every human being on the face of
the earth.

"And, you know what, no one came to help me. I
sensed there were people around, people who heard me
scream, people who even could *see* what was going on,
but they were afraid for themselves."

No bitterness exists—such would be out of place in
Heaven. She is merely recalling the events. If anything,
there was pity for the ones who stood by and did nothing,
her dying agony buried in the corridors of their minds
perhaps for the rest of their lives, like a haunting cloud
always on the horizon.

"I left behind two sons and a daughter as well as my
dear husband. I am so grateful that all of them do know
Christ as Savior and Lord and they will be here, with me,

eventually, and then there won't be any separations again, ever."

She is now smiling, a radiant look indeed.

I talk with others, find out more about life on Earth than I ever imagined could have been true, primarily because I had never asked questions before. My concerns, my doubts are spurring me on. Surely the picture being painted must be distorted in some way. How could it be entirely attributed to Lucifer? How could it be that Lucifer is guilty of stirring up such evil?

"Lord, I *will* go," I say finally.

He looks at me with an expression unfathomable but not unkind. My Lord could never be *that*.

"You go with the prayers of Heaven behind you," He says with great tenderness.

And then it happens. One minute I am in Heaven, the next, my odyssey has begun . . .

*T*HERE IS NO transition period.

It is like stepping from one room to another. I go through an invisible door, and, suddenly, I am on Earth. I have experienced no bursts of light, no swirling gasses, no rolling thunder. I have instantaneously negotiated the void that must be faced by every human being, whether on the way to Heaven or to Hell; whatever the direction it is a journey, yea, destiny inescapable, profoundly inescapable. But I have simply gone in the opposite direction . . .

It starts out well, this journey, for me. The day is Sunday. I hear the sound of hymns. I am out in the country. The sun is directly overhead, the air bright, clear. Flowers are blooming. I walk beside a busy road, automobiles passing by at a steady, fast clip. I begin to feel very good indeed. This is the way I pictured the world. Perhaps there are unpleasant things, things that should never be, and yet not to the extent we all had supposed. Those who went off to fight spiritual battles in heavenly places dealt with the extremes, the fallen angels who had gone over the edge and could never be redeemed. But they are the exceptions—all the old stories of corruption upon corruption simply cannot be true,

I tell myself. *Nothing* could be as bad, as decadent, as pervasive as *that*.

And this Sunday, this cheerful, clear, mellow Sunday, goes a long way toward bearing out my notions. I see many people dressed well, smiling, walking up a pathway to the front door of a country church. It is a white building, made principally of wood, not a garish structure at all, but obviously one made with respect and love, for those who would worship inside and for the beloved God toward whom they would direct that worship.

I join the congregation. The hymn has ended, and there is now a sermon being delivered. The pastor is in his mid-fifties, tall, fine-looking, his voice commanding, encouraging at times, reprimanding at others, filled with the sort of wisdom that can come only from being based in the Word of God. It is a powerful sermon—yes, it talks of sin, it warns of becoming prisoners of the sin nature in each and every human being in that building—but it is a message of hope as well, hope that is the whole foundation beneath the death of Christ at Calvary. Otherwise, that death was wholly in vain, mocking His suffering.

The pastor finishes, another hymn is sung, and then everyone starts to leave. My attention focuses on one family in particular.

The father is still young, in his mid-forties, the mother in her late thirties; they have two children, a teenage daughter and a son in his very early twenties.

Happy.

That strikes me immediately. A solid, happy family. I join them as they drive home. I stay with them as they share a Sunday dinner of roast beef, natural dark gravy, French fried potatoes, green beans, and apple pie. (I almost wish I could know hunger so that such a meal could satisfy me.)

They talk quite a bit—I enjoy the sound of their voices. I enjoy seeing them laugh and hug one another, seeing them express what is wonderful, what is beautiful indeed about humanness. There is a bit of sadness in me as I see but do not participate, as I watch them sharing but must be set apart myself, with them but not of them.

Much time passes. For me, in Heaven, there was no such thing, of course. Time is nonexistent there—that which is forever cannot be measured by seconds or minutes or even millennia.

And yet I *am* in a world that exists on time, that can be tyrannized by it, that at the very least cannot escape it, all the smashed clocks, all the rundown batteries, all the rusty or clogged or spent movements notwithstanding. It is a world where the greatest of rulers, where the most powerful of nations, no matter what the circumstance, all are captive to time.

I shake myself from my musings. This family's day is ending but mine cannot. They sleep, but I am unable to do so. I spend my first night literally not knowing what to do. Others in Heaven, the humans who come in a steady stream, have talked of no longer needing sleep. For many sleeplessness had been a problem. They wanted to sleep, grabbing it in troubled scraps of minutes or hours but not enjoying the refreshment of, as they say, "a good night's sleep." Now, in Heaven, they do not have it at all and they do not *need* it. That seemed to be one of the more astonishing realities for so many.

While the family sleeps, I sit and ponder. They talked of pain, yes: an elderly family member is ill, in fact may be dying in a nearby hospital. The son is upset about his grades at college, from which he is home on vacation. The mother is concerned about her husband working overtime too much, exhausting himself. He himself seems to dislike one of his bosses but does not know what to do about it. The daughter is worried about a relationship with a boy at school.

But these are human problems. After Eden they became regular components of the human experience. They are everyday, commonplace, scarcely of significant trauma. The health of the grandmother seems the most urgent matter.

And they cope. They face everything with a spirit that enables them not to be *unduly* concerned, not to be paranoid, a word I have heard before, as I met with some in Heaven who were relieved that they no longer have any fears, anything *to* fear, their minds clear, free, soaring to the fullest imaginable potential.

I find myself becoming very close to this family, and it is odd that this is the case because whereas I can see them, they cannot see me; there is no interplay between us. As far as they are concerned, I do not exist. While they believe in my kind, they do not know about me.

So I am not prepared for the events to follow, events that will send me from that family out into a world I now wish I would never have confronted . . .

Within one week of the first time I encounter this family, they all are "dead." It is hard for me to think in those terms, for they are not now dead at all; and their present state of being provides that opportunity which could not have occurred in "life," that is, for us to meet at last. For that I rejoice. The wall finally has been broken down and—

But the *way* it occurred, the circumstances that took their earthly presence from them, translating them into spirit, as I am spirit . . .

That way is what appalls me as I think back upon it, as I remember *being* there and not able to do anything to help, an observer of human pain, trauma, looking and feeling but not—

During that week, wonderful, revealing, reassuring, I am constantly amazed by humanness. There is much, I suspect, that is unfortunately embodied in that word "humanness," but what I am seeing is a measure of what

God meant from the beginning—love; patience; joy; a strength together that only the family unit can manage.

Moments of touching kindness . . .

The son, Jon Erik, asks if he can do the lawn for his father who has come home from his business especially weary, and really needing to spend the weekend resting.

"Hey, Dad, you look tired," Jon Erik remarks. "Take it easy for a change. Okay?"

The father, Gordon, smiles, nods, thanks his son.

Moments of a special kind of sharing between mother and daughter . . .

The daughter, Rebecca, is telling her mother about love, this young man at school whom she thinks she does indeed love.

The mother, Lillian, reminisces about her first date with Gordon. They laugh together, Rebecca wondering if her friend is the one with whom she will spend the rest of her own life.

Moments cut short . . .

It happens as all four of them are coming home from a basketball game. Wesley, Rebecca's special one, played as part of the home team. He follows them in his car.

Night-time . . .

Another car speeds through a stop sign, hits the one carrying the family. It is spun around twice, then flips once and smashes into a telephone pole.

Instantly there are flames.

All of them but Jon Erik die upon impact. He manages to stumble from the wreckage, his body afire, his screams heard for some distance, I am sure.

Then he falls just inches from where I am standing. Scarcely a second later his spirit leaves his body. His mother, his father, his sister join him. They look at me, not knowing who I am.

"Can you help us?" the father asks. "We're very confused."

"Wesley!" Rebecca then asks. "Mom—what's happened to Wesley?"

It is then that they look upward. There is a light on them, engulfing them. Their concerns drain away. And then they are—gone.

Wesley tries to enter the flaming wreckage, but bystanders restrain him. He then falls into the arms of a stranger, sobbing.

Why?

They were Christians; they lived imperfect lives, but they tried very hard to please God. Everyone left behind who knew them would be asking the same question, and others related to it, over and over until the shock eases, and even the sad pull of this tragedy on their emotions disappears, and their own lives go on.

Wesley, as devoted as he was, as loyal and loving, and ready to spend the rest of his life with Rebecca, does recover. Not without struggle. Not without tossing in bed many nights afterward. Not without being so overcome with grief at the funeral that he has to be led away by his own family, for he cannot leave the cemetery of his own accord—there is, momentarily, no strength left in him.

He will think about Rebecca for a long time, perhaps to a greater or lesser extent for the rest of his life. He will think about her when he marries another, and they have children, and he wonders what the children of Rebecca and himself would have been like.

But someone else will pay, in a sense, a far worse price: the teenage boy, his system loaded up with drugs, who caused the accident.

He will be committed to an institution, and while there he will be gang-raped, and afterwards he will take his own life . . .

A little more of the world to which I have confined myself unfolds. With my human friends, with this family

of whom I grew so fond, admiring them for their humanity, it seemed, at first, not so bad. Life for them had its
sins, yes—impatience; anger; the threatening thread of
lust between Rebecca and Wesley; moments that arose as
a result of the warfare between flesh and spirit, and not to
be excused, not to be brushed aside as acceptable because
these were indeed *human*. All this, yes, but none so bad,
it seems to me, as the blood on the hands of that teenage
boy who killed them all.

I go to be alone, in a place away from humanity. I do
not really know where it is. I think it might be a park.
There is a pond in the middle, with goldfish swimming
around in it, and a tall, carved-stone fountain and some
pennies hopeful people have thrown there while making
their wishes.

I am absolutely alone. It is early as yet, but the fact
remains that I have seen none of what used to be my
kind, none of those cast out onto Earth.

Where are you? I ask wordlessly. *I want to see you. To
talk, to learn.*

Nothing.

Only the fish. Two robins and a sparrow on the grass. A
squirrel scampering up a nearby tree. The sun is setting,
darkness coming slowly, preceded by a golden light that
reminds me just a bit of Heaven but then is gone, and just
the artificial light of street lamps remaining.

I stay there—how can I judge the length of time when
I have not as yet judged, really, truly, what time is?—and
then leave, walking the night, not knowing where to
go . . .

It is cold that evening. I see people—with their scarfs
and ear muffs and hats—grimacing as they walk. I pass a
theatre with questionable photographs displayed outside.
Next to it is what the sign outside proclaims to be an
adult book store.

I go inside.

I see the pornographic magazines and books, as well as the so-called "marital aids." In the back are booths. And inside are men watching XXX-rated images . . .

I feel like shouting to them about their sin. I feel like grabbing them and shaking them, so repulsed am I by the very idea that a private act between husband and wife should be so degraded.

Am I upset over something minor? Am I overreacting to sexually starved individuals getting release?

No, no, a thousand nos if need be. Because I have been in Heaven. I have seen "life"—the only life, ultimately, that *is* life, not the temporary action of heart beating, lungs functioning, not that life which *must* end after a short time compared to eternity—life lived without lust, life that is pure, life in harmony with God's will.

I run from that place, its awful sounds, stale odors, and ugly yet pitiful sights.

I am shivering as I reach the outside. My whole self is shaking. And not just because of what is on sale inside the shop.

The implications . . .

Yes, the implications that spread far, far beyond that place on that street that cold winter evening.

*I*T IS MORNING.

If I were of flesh and blood, I could say perhaps that I had not slept all night. But not being such, I search for a spiritual equivalent, and find none except to realize that I feel something akin to tiredness. The shock of the events since I came to Earth is having its impact upon me without question.

A police car is stopped in front of a restaurant. There is some shouting. A man comes running outside. Two officers pursue him. They chase him for quite a distance on foot. Passersby jump to one side or the other. One is knocked down. Finally the officers corner the fugitive in an alley. He raises both hands over his head. I see them talking to the man.

"You realize that you have the right to remain silent," one officer says.

My attention wanders to the second officer. He is more distressed than the other.

"You are scum," he shouts. "How many kids have you destroyed because of the drugs you've sold them?"

"Hey, man, I gotta make a buck," the man says as he spits on the asphalt.

31

The second officer lunges at him and has to be re-
strained by his partner.

They take the man back to their car. I go with them,
though, of course, they are unaware of this. The man is
booked, as the expression goes, and put in jail.

I find out why the one officer is so disturbed. His son is
in a hospital nearby, confined there because of a drug
overdose. I listen as the officer and his partner are having
coffee in a diner across the street from the police station.

"Tommy was going to be a computer programmer."

"You refer to him past tense. Is there something you
haven't told me?"

"Yes, Dave, this morning—"

He breaks off the sentence, his face going red.

The other officer is quiet, waiting patiently.

Then . . .

"Tommy really had the ability to go all the way to the
top—be another Bill Gates, the guy at Microsoft, who's
become a millionaire several times over. Or that Steven
Jobs at Apple. Tommy had their brains, once. But not any
longer. It'll be a miracle if he can use an adding machine
from now on."

"That bad?"

"Worse. His mind's nearly gone. As careful as Lisa was!
Giving up the cigarettes and drinking while she carried
him, not even taking aspirin! And that was before all the
reports proving the effect of that stuff on the unborn. We
just used common sense. And Tommy was real, real
healthy when he was born. A big baby! He weighed more
than ten pounds. He felt so heavy to Lisa that we half
thought there might be twins in her stomach.

"But now, oh, he'll 'recover.' He won't be a vegetable.
But he also isn't going to be near what he could have been
if that lousy—"

He bangs a fist on the countertop.

"I hate that guy and his kind so much I—I hope I can

control myself when we come up against the next one. I just hope I don't go over the edge."

His partner pats him on the back, and they leave the diner.

Later, the officer—I find his name to be Henry—and his wife Lisa visit their son.

"Mom! Dad!" the teenager says as he greets them in his room at the hospital.

Lisa and Henry embrace him.

Later, the extent of the damage he has suffered is obvious. His words slur a number of times. He seems nervous, his cheeks twitching sporadically. And Tommy forgets a great deal—what day it is; the fact that his sister is due home from college soon; and he does not remember that the new hard disk drive for his computer had come in the mail, though his parents told him only the day before. And there is the frustration that gradually builds up, apparent in his manner, the quivering of his voice, the expression on his face.

Lisa and Henry know a truth that they have not as yet admitted to their son.

It will never be any different for him . . .

He is going to be the way he is for as long as he is alive, paying for his drugs for a lifetime. And his frustration will continue to build until, one day, he attempts suicide. He survives that attempt, but it is only symptomatic of other aspects of his drug involvement, aspects that will worsen as he gets older until, eventually, he goes on a rampage and kills a dozen people in a quick-food outlet.

Many squad cars are dispatched to the place. Tommy surrenders without a fight. One of the arresting officers is his own father.

Lisa and Henry say good-bye, not knowing, not having the slightest hint of what lies in store, and I am alone with Tommy. He paces the floor, anxiety causing him to perspire excessively, his hospital garb sticking to him.

And then he lies down on the bed in his room, and starts weeping. Soon he falls into a fitful sleep, but even then there is no peace for him as a nightmare fills his mind with terrors that are not very far from the reality already experienced, and which will be repeated, even months later, as he endures the first of a series of drug-related "flashbacks."

At the age of twenty-six, Tommy will die in the electric chair. Not all the legal maneuvering conceivable—even considering the matter of drug damage—will do him any good. Only the date of execution is delayed, in fact prolonging his anguish. He spends more than four years in prison before that final day.

Time which does not exist is no hindrance to me and so I am there, in that chamber with him. The current is sent through him. His body jolts once, twice, then slumps forward. Tommy's spirit leaves that fleshly temple.

"You saw me die?" he asks as he sees me.

"Yes, Tommy, I did."

"Where am I going now?"

In the distance, or so it seems, I hear an eerie sound, like the gnashing of teeth.

Tommy hears it, too.

"I wish—" he starts to say, then is gone.

I feel, for a moment, a singular burst of heat.

And then an hysterical mother's cry that will never, never be forgotten . . .

*T*HE EPIDEMIC HAS spread drastically. Riots are breaking out in a number of American cities. I witness one in Los Angeles. It comes in the midst of a so-called Gay Pride Day parade. (A revelation ranking with the most unnerving of my sojourn is how homosexuals can seriously use the word "pride," when in reality what they practice is intrinsically an abomination. I had never encountered the spirit of any practicing, unrepentant homosexual in Heaven. I did not meet everyone, of course, but at least I would have heard about it. I could imagine that Hell is crammed full of them. Whoever is not in Heaven *is* in Hell. It is one or the other for every human being ever to have lived in the past and any in the future. They may not be able to admit this to themselves because none could escape utter madness if they did. But the question remains: How can they use the word "pride"?)

The so-called festivities begin at the Gay and Lesbian Community Services building nearby and continue on to Santa Monica Boulevard, a street famous for its hustlers lined up at the curb to flag down customers. Police make arrests from time to time to keep up appearances for the benefit of the politicians, but since the whole area is considered gay territory, there is a conscious decision by law enforcement officials to otherwise leave them alone, as long as they keep their soliciting to that one locale.

It is amazing to me that rampant perversion is not only tolerated but supported by the government through hundreds of thousands of tax dollars. Why are these people deserving of "community services"? Many of them will be shocked to find, on their deathbeds, that it will not be Almighty God reaching out to give them any of the services of Heaven. They will perhaps be even more shocked to find their homosexual behavior condemned so strongly by the Lord. But that is the truth, eternal, inescapable truth, however harsh it might seem to the unregenerate mind.

Not long ago, I heard someone say, "Did not the harlot about to be stoned receive the forgiveness of Jesus as He asked those without sin to cast the first stone?" Yes, He told her to "Go . . ." But that was not all He said. He added, "And sin no more." His forgiveness was coupled with the proviso that she give up the sin of prostitution. "But," I heard someone else ask, "Is not the forgiveness purchased at Calvary unconditional?" That it is most assuredly—but, on the other hand, is acceptance of Christ as Savior and Lord truly from the very depths of an individual's spirit if that individual says, in effect, "Yes, Lord, I'll accept You as my Savior and Lord, but don't expect me to give up gayness"?

I watch the convertibles drive by, the flatbed trucks, the people walking in the middle of the street. Some seem, on the surface, quite happy, their faces painted brightly. Quite a number are lifting small bottles to their nostrils and drawing in deep breaths. Others are smoking what is obviously marijuana. A few are dressed in nothing but essentially the lower part of their underwear. There is an abandonment of inhibitions that they embellish with their garish look. Several are kissing not so much out of passion but as a pose for the TV cameras in evidence and, frankly, to shock those not accustomed to things of darkness being played out in the light.

I am amazed to realize that they seem to sense my presence. Several turn and glance and then look away. I suddenly understand why. Only the dying see me. And these people, these men with paint and garish dress, are dying, day by day, their insides . . .

Abruptly, the parade stops, as though the participants have been frozen. I feel the ground shake under me.

"An earthquake!" someone screams.

"No, it's a bomb!" another voice is heard.

Ahead, a column of smoke starts to rise from one of the buildings on the avenue.

A man, probably in his early twenties, comes running down the middle of the street. An arm is missing. He falls at the feet of one of the marchers. He raises the remaining one at the marcher, and shakes his hand, which is closed into a fist, then he falls face-forward on the asphalt.

As he dies, his spirit leaving his body, he approaches me, crying, "I hate them all—the lies, the degradation. My friends and I were free-basing, and it all blew up and—"

Gone.

As instantaneously as that.

The body remains but not his spirit. He has been claimed for eternity.

A riot starts, with people hitting, kicking, clawing one another. I remember a little vignette, minutes earlier. Two men were sitting in a park just off the same avenue. They were waiting for the parade to reach that location.

"It's a glorious day," the older one was saying. "We couldn't have done this a couple of decades ago."

The second man, this one bald and with a beard, was nodding in agreement.

"You're so right. There has been a lot of progress."

But somehow his voice carried no conviction with it; there was an emptiness around the edges. The more he talked, the more obvious it became.

Finally the bearded one broke down and cried, sobs wracking his body.

"I'm dying," he said, trembling.

"You—"

"Yes."

The older man pulled back. He had just had his face close to the other. His bearded companion noticed this sudden movement and looked accusingly at him.

"After all this time, you recoil."

The older man stood up, turned, ran. I noticed something on the lap of the other.

A Bible.

I could read the name on the tan cover, the name of a minister!

Pledged to upholding the Word and yet—

"Oh, God," he screamed. "Oh, God, how could You do this to me?"

He shook his fist at the sky. The Bible fell off and landed on the grass.

Tears streamed down the man's cheeks.

"It's—" he said, in terror, as he noticed a purplish mark on his hand.

He fell into a heap on the grass, his body shaking.

I approached him.

He looked up in astonishment.

"Am I—?" he started to ask.

"No," I interrupted. "You are still alive."

"But I will be dead soon?"

"Yes . . ."

"But why? Why in this manner?"

"You really have no conception?"

"No, I—"

He stopped. For a bit, the truth filtered through the

canvas of lies which he had been draping about himself.
A chill shuddered through his pale, slight frame.

Then—

"God made me this way."

"He did not."

"But I have been this way ever since I can remember."

He recounted some of his experiences. Finally I stopped him because it had become clear that he was not "always" that way but became hooked on the lifestyle, stage by stage, moment by moment, degradation by degradation.

"But I can't change," he protested.

"Do not accept those awful lies with which you have been brainwashed. Look at yourself. You are dying. And yet as you tell me what you have, you are not repentant at all but still fascinated, still hypnotized."

He started sobbing again.

"I can't change. It's too late. The big A—"

He got to his feet and ran. I shouted after him, but he did not stop.

the head downward
the legs upward
he tumbles into the bottomless
from whence he came

he has no more honour in his body
he bites no more bite of any short meal
he answers no greeting
and is not proud when being adored

the head downward
the legs upward
he tumbles into the bottomless
from whence he came

like a dish covered with hair
like a four-legged sucking chair
like a deaf ecotrunk
half full half empty

the head downward
the legs upward
he tumbles into the bottomless
from whence he came.

The sounds of the parade came to my ears, and I left that spot . . .

The riot has spent its fury. And the parade continues! I look at this with disbelieving eyes.

It means nothing to them. Just another experience. The pain almost exhilarating.

I noticed something around the corner of a building. A shape.

Familiar. It's—

Another angel!

I am unable to move at first. He sees me, disappears. I go after him. Down an alley. Across a street. And—

He slows, stops, turns, smiles.

D'Seaver!

A friend . . .

"Darien," he says, looking a little embarrassed.

"I thought I was the only one," I say honestly.

"You have just arrived?"

"Only a little while ago, really."

"What do you think of Earth?"

I fall silent.

"It *is* a shock, is it not?"

I nod.

"I mean, that it took so long."

"What do you mean?"

"You see how weak they are?"

"Yes . . ."

"It took so long to—"

D'Seaver interrupts himself, a strange expression on his face.

"Let me show you a few, well, sights."

I agree to go with him.

First stop is a place with darkened corridors bordered by tiny rooms, each with a single cot. And in the walls between each room are holes.

"What is this, D'Seaver?" I ask.

Most of the doors are closed. I hear sounds. Groanings. A whimper occasionally. Someone cries out rather loudly.

There is a whiff of a chemical-like odor.

One of the doors is slightly ajar. I see a man with his body pressed up against a wall. His head is rolling from side to side. He is naked.

Corridor after corridor.

Men with towels wrapped around them but nothing else. Two in a whirlpool tub, holding one another.

The lighting is almost nonexistent. And in one room there is none at all. It is much bigger than the others. Several men are inside. They—

"D'Seaver, why are we here?"

"I wanted to show you."

"Show me what?"

"What is going on. To actually see and—and—"

"We must leave."

"But—"

"Now, D'Seaver, Now!"

We are gone. It is not difficult to leave. We just will ourselves to do so. We have no bodily substance as such. We can be anywhere we want, as soon as we want.

And we are in the midst of a cemetery.

"All of them will end up here so much sooner than necessary," I say. "Then, for all eternity, they will cry and scream in pain. They will plead for it to end, but it will not. And it will get worse. Every fear they ever had will be fulfilled. Every suffering they ever knew will be revisited upon them tenfold."

D'Seaver, only half-listening, points to something partially buried in the grass near one of the tombstones.

"That is a bottle of amyl nitrate."

"What is that?"

"They sniff it—the heart beats faster and faster—and enormous sexual desire is aroused."

"Why here?"

"I viewed the funeral. Most of the participants had brought such bottles with them. Two or three were talking about opening the coffin and making love, as they call it, to the corpse."

I can scarcely believe what I am being told.

"It is Sunday, according to Man's calendar, Darien. We should go to church."

I agree that we should. Not too far away is a modernistic-looking building. It seems to be constructed entirely of glass, almost in a pyramid shape except that the pinnacle is nearly flat. The sun shining off it makes the glass sparkle in a dozen different colors. People are lined up, waiting to be seated. Altogether there will be thousands inside by the time everyone sits down.

The interior is no less spectacular, with round metal beams crisscrossing the ceiling. Each pew is cushioned with a velvety material. In the middle of the altar area at the front is a huge cross, probably twenty feet tall. At the base, grouped around it, are bright red flowers. The altar seems to have been laid of marble, light-colored, with darker tan veins running through it.

All this is indeed impressive. Choral sounds come from the front, and a hundred men, women, and children sing as they file out and take their places.

Immediately I start to feel refreshed, as though I am about to take a bath to cleanse myself.

We stay in the back of the church. Minutes pass—it is indeed awkward for me to use such a term, awkward to think of anything at all like time.

The choir has finished. There are some announcements. My whole self rises in anticipation. I need this very much. I remember that first service, the family, all the rest.

The minister comes to the pulpit, smiles as he surveys the congregation.

"And, now, everybody turn and shake the hand of someone near you."

The people do this. A feeling of warmth diffuses throughout the hall.

The minister continues, "I want to introduce to you someone all of you have seen on television and in films."

A man with curly hair and a rather rugged face joins the minister. He talks about treating people properly, talks about caring for starving children, talks about being honest at income tax time.

A chill begins to nip me around the edges.

Finally the actor steps down, I think with considerable relief.

The minister beams at the congregation as he says, "There are good people in this world. They think in positive terms. They don't make negativity their god. They can control their own lives and make of those lives what *they* want. I think that's wonderful."

He pauses, then asks, "How many of you agree?"

Everyone claps. I do not. I turn to D'Seaver. He is clapping.

That chill is growing . . .

"And now—"

He holds up a porcelain angel. A nearby television camera zooms in on it.

"This is a gift to anyone who writes and sends in a love

offering," he continues. "It is made of the finest porcelain, molded and painted by hand."

Then a collection is taken up. The minister leaves the pulpit. A black man comes out and begins to sing. He seems a little uncomfortable. And not because he is black. But he does well, with more than a hint of real feeling as he sings, "My Tribute: To God Be the Glory."

I hear someone in front of me whisper, "That's a little heavy, isn't it."

Why? I want to shout. *Why is singing about the shed blood of Christ so "heavy" for church? Why—?*

Several minutes later, the minister returns and begins his sermon.

I listen, with growing alarm, that chill totally enveloping me.

"The epidemic has been described by some as punishment from God. We all know that a loving God would not do that. We all know that that sort of Victorian thinking belongs with all that fire-and-brimstone talk with which some men of the cloth try to frighten the rest of us into submission."

He takes off his glasses, his expression serious.

"We make our own Hell right here on earth. We make life hellish when we forget the principles of upbeat thinking, when we allow negativism to crowd out the positive, the cheerful. And what is Hell but *the most negative concept of all.*"

I can remain no longer.

"We must not stay," I say to D'Seaver without turning to look at him. "We must—"

"Stop it, Darien. This man is good. He is just right, in fact."

"Right about what?"

The minister continues: "My new book, which is an international best-seller, is entitled A POSITIVE RE-BIRTH; it has been made available in the church bookstore for just $12.95, which is $2.00 discounted off the retail. It tackles what has been wrong with the church ever since Billy Sunday and Dwight L. Moody and others of that ilk thundered their protestations of perdition."

He moves with great flair, throwing his hands about, arching his back, his face a mask of exaggerated expressions. His voice raises or lowers with just the right emphasis.

"The time *is* here for a positive rebirth. Away with the gloom and doom!"

He holds up his book, waves it a couple of times before the television cameras.

"Place this book beside your Bible. Read them together. And you will receive a blessing beyond your wildest dreams. You will find your finances impacted very favorably. You can do better with God's Plan for Financial Enrichment than in any bank."

He takes some money from his pocket, shows it to everyone.

"Give to Him 10 percent or more of all that you earn, and He will return it severalfold. God is the best investment you can make. He does not want any of us to be poor. Remember that, my friends. And grab a little of the green for yourself!"

I remember a missionary I had met in Heaven. She had been quite poor during her final years of service. Gradually her support was being reduced by significant percentages. She went back to the United States, leaving the mission field forever. Her husband had died months before, and she was no longer able to handle the strain of the work alone. She got back to her hometown on a Saturday, stayed at a friend's house that night, and drove to church with her next morning. As they walked up to the entrance, the missionary saw the minister park his car and then go inside the church. He had a new luxury model that cost nearly $25,000. She pulled her worn coat around her, asked the Lord to forgive her, turned around and never went inside that church again. In less than a month she was dead. The congregation sent some funeral flowers. But no one attended. There was a picnic that day by the Ladies Auxiliary, a fund-raiser to send the minister and his wife to Hawaii for a week.

No more, I say to myself. *No more in this place . . .*

"Now, D'Seaver, we go!" I say firmly, turning to face him.

It is no longer the D'Seaver that I had known. Something different . . . *something different.*

Demonic.

All pretense is over. No more posing as an angel of light . . .

Instantly D'Seaver and I are outside.

"Lucifer cannot know about you," I say, repulsed by him, barely able to look at what he has become.

His laughter is coarse.

He pounds his feet on the ground, cloven hooves moving with anger.

"You utter fool!" he shouts, slobber dripping out the corners of his mouth. "You act so surprised. You thought I took you to that place, with those men, to lament what they were doing. *That* is The Plan, Darien; *they* are part of it. So is that pompous fool. If he were any more transparent, he would not even *be* there!

"That parade. The riot. More that you may stumble upon while you are here, Darien. It is a real-life script. And it is being played out *exactly* as it should."

I turn and go. Behind me I hear the sound of shrieking laughter . . .

I GO BACKWARD in time, at first enjoying this ability as though it is a kind of toy, something for amusement. And that it is initially. To be able to see the building of the Pyramids! To be there at the American Revolution. To be present with the ancient Aztecs as their civilization was thriving, something that would have been highly coveted by modern archaeologists if it had been possible for them. It was a civilization filled with the worship of false gods, encrusted with heathen practices but undeniably grand in the sense of the knowledge possessed by the Aztecs, knowledge that amazed even twentieth-century scientists. So it was, as well, with the Incas and the Mayans, but even great knowledge, great power lasts, really, for just a season—whatever they knew, these brilliant peoples, more or less died with them, overgrown by the jungles out of which they had carved their cities. The kings and warriors worshipped and feared centuries ago now left only a legacy of ruins and the fascination of those entranced by questions probably unresolvable.

Backward in time, forward as well, through events and places that comprised the history of the Human Race, for good or naught. From the days of dinosaurs to the birth of the Industrial Age, to—

The Holocaust.

I am standing in the midst of Dachau, the German concentration camp.

The sky is overcast; at least that is what I assume until I see the sooty clouds of smoke coming from a giant stack not far away. Floating through the air, dropping down in patches here and there, are specks, thin, like burnt paper, settling on the ground, grey-white.

I walk down one "avenue" between two rows of buildings. Ahead a line of soldiers is standing single file. In front of them is a ditch, and standing just at the edge are a score or more of naked, emaciated men, their faces pale, gaunt.

The soldiers aim rifles, fire, and the men collapse into the ditch. Their bodies join others. This day is apparently being devoted to "thinning" the population of the camp.

"Garbage collection," I hear one of the soldiers say to another, his laughter hoarse, cold.

I want to reach out and throw him in the ditch with his victims. I want to call down all the wrath of Heaven and give him pain and suffering for eternity. And then I realize that that is exactly what he will have. That he and others like him as well as the ones *issuing* the orders will indeed have punishment never ending—it might not come in a year or even a decade, but it *would* come, inexorably.

I turn from that spot, toward the ovens. I see men and women tied, gagged, being put inside. I hear their terror. I feel their pain as flesh is seared by heat, seconds seeming endless and then—

Later, the ovens are emptied, bones not quite powdered put into bags and taken elsewhere. And then more bodies. An endless procession of bodies.

I enter one of the laboratories. A little boy, naked, is

strapped to an operating table. A man, mustached, dressed in a white smock, is—cutting—him—open! No painkiller used—no gas to knock him out—nothing but the "live" operation, whatever it is, for whatever insane purpose.

Afterwards, I hear the "surgeon" talking to an assistant. This is all part of an experiment to see how much pain a human being can take before losing consciousness or dying. They do it again and again, to the young, the older, the elderly. Some of the old ones take it longer than do the young, but most die on the tables—there are a dozen or more of these in other rooms in that same building. A few, a bare handful, survive: some blinded when acid is poured into their pupils; missing arms, legs; parts of their bodies paralyzed because of their brains being poked around in; surviving, yes, surviving those moments of horror and, later, the continuing rigors of the rest of Dachau's daily routine, surviving to the moment of liberation by the Allies and beyond, to live the years left, few or many, in periodic anguish, the residue of being treated as they were . . . then death comes, an anticlimax for many, for they had "died" a long, long time before.

The ovens, the ditches, the "operating rooms" are part of what assaults me in an engulfing torrent. Many others die of disease or malnutrition; many commit suicide; some live with minds that have snapped so that, for them, there is never to be liberation, at least not on Earth.

I visit another camp, this one called Auschwitz. A woman is being brutalized by her "doctor." She falls into a heap on the floor. Her life is almost over. Her murderer stands over her, and she looks up at him, and whispers, "I forgive you . . . may God show you The Way," just before he slashes her throat.

In the blinking of an eye, her spirit has risen from her battered, torn body. She sees me, smiles.

"It is right, what I said?"

I nod.

"Good," she replies. "Is time for me There?"

I rejoice as I tell her that it is.

She is gone . . .

I go back to Dachau. Many years have passed. It is filled with well-dressed people. There are memorial plaques, with names listed on them. The tourists come and go. I wish I could shout to them, about all that had gone on before, a few decades earlier, the buildings, the ovens, the laboratories fairly ringing with the cries of the tormented, the dying.

I see a field next to the camp. It is lush, the grass brilliantly green, the soil dark, rich-looking, flowers vibrantly colored, trees healthy.

I wonder why. The rest of the area is so bleak. And then I comprehend through a veil of revulsion that that healthy, colorful field, so serene on the surface, is where countless numbers of bodies had been buried, human fertilizer nourishing the growth of nature.

But cruelty was never confined to the Germans, I discover. The Japanese had their part in it: the relentless Bataan Death March was just one example. For the veterans who survived, it remains a harsh, awful memory. For me, back in time, it is current, palpable, a living reality.

Thousands are sick, wounded. They walk through mud. In other spots dust is so thick it clogs their nostrils and they cough, deep coughs that, for many, force open further already festering holes, cuts.

I see a soldier drive a bayonet through one of the prisoners, and then two other soldiers join him because the American is not as yet dead, and the three of them stick him again and again with sharp steel, laughing maniacally.

Some men die from previous wounds or malaria or other diseases, their bodies left by the road. (How many would be recovered, and shipped back home eventually? Not a large number, I suppose. They would simply rot where they fell.)

And once again I see something beautiful in the midst of it all, the march of horror that claimed so many lives. I see a man who is a chaplain on his knees, praying, as one of the soldiers hits him across the back of the head with a rifle butt. The chaplain falls but is not quite unconscious. This infuriates the soldier, and he is about to hit the man again, helpless in the mud. The chaplain looks up at him, smiles and says, "Do what you must. I still will not hate you." And I see something utterly, literally incredible. (It is a word I hear often during my journeys, spouted carelessly, a word robbed of any real impact by its cavalier overuse but the only one that does apply, the only one to describe what I see.)

The Japanese soldier seems to understand what the chaplain has said. He hesitates, pulls back the rifle. And immediately, I see a fallen angel beside him, whispering something into his ear. The soldier still resists. I recognize my former comrade to be D'Filer. I see D'Filer go to another soldier, and then this second soldier approaches the first. They get into a fight. The first soldier accidentally is run through by the bayonet as they struggle. He falls, clutching his stomach, just a few feet from the chaplain. The American crawls toward him. The second soldier orders him to stop. The chaplain refuses. The soldier aims his rifle. The chaplain reaches the body of the other soldier, puts his arms around it just as his head is blown open by the force, the nearness of the rifle that has been fired.

D'Filer is not pleased; he knows what has happened.

He is infuriated by forgiveness. This is contrary to everything he wanted. There are two deaths, yes, but the result is forgiveness. He cannot stand that. He goes up and down the long line of American prisoners, driving the Japanese to outbursts of anger in order to vent his own. Prisoners are kicked, spat upon, clubbed with rifle butts, forced to walk faster when they can hardly walk at all . . .

It is now decades later, that same road, a monument being dedicated beside one section. There are scores of Americans and Japanese. Some look warily at one another. But one American extends his hand to his Japanese counterpart. They shake, smile. The American takes something out of his pants pocket. So does the other. They laugh at this. One has a small Bible; so does the other.

"When?" the American asks.

"On my knees a year after Hiroshima. My wife and two children were caught up in the blast. They did not die immediately. They lingered for months. When I saw them, they were almost gone. They had been burned badly, their bodies flaking flesh. My children were both blind. They could hardly talk. I could not even hold them.

"I wanted to kill every American I saw. I wanted to destroy the entire country. And then I remembered Bataan, and the American chaplain I murdered, the dozens of other Americans I killed, beat, spat on, even starved. I remembered that that chaplain may have had a family also. And later, God opened my heart to be forgiven as well as to forgive. If I had never seen that chaplain, never saw him put his arm around Tanaka, and—and—"

He holds up the Bible as he wipes some tears from his eyes.

"This was the chaplain's. It is with me always."

A strange world, largely a kingdom of darkness, a place filled with the ranting and raving excesses of demonic hordes, former angels transplanted to a former Eden, cutting across it a swath of atrocity. And yet a world with such triumph as I had seen, such goodness as I had witnessed, such purity rising regenerated from a giant morass of murder, rape, unfettered passion, unmitigated depravity.

Being filled with all unrighteousness, fornication, wickedness, covetousness, maliciousness; full of envy, murder, debate, deceit, malignity; whisperers, backbiters, haters of God, despiteful, proud, boasters, inventors of evil things . . . Who knowing the judgment of God, that they which commit such things are worthy of death, not only do the same, but have pleasure in them that do them.

And still I could not find Lucifer. Had he been surrounded by a mutiny, and cast off ship, so to speak? If so, where was he? Where was the creature because of whom I had begun my quest in the first place?

I APPROACH A so-called rest home for the elderly. It might better be called a dumping ground for rejects, mothers and fathers left there, like so much worn, excess baggage, to be cared for by hired professionals. An attempt has been made to make the circumstances as cheerful as possible, but for many it is a hopeless charade. Only one thing will lift the burden—the love of families that seem instead to have rejected them. This is the end of the road for the bulk of the people inside, a final prison, and a death sentence.

From the wonder of birth to the passion of youth, on to the achievement of middle age; and then the wrenching, awful waste of years spent as those in the rest home are spending theirs—a game of cards, an evening in front of a television and, occasionally, a letter from the family but coming like a single drop of water to someone in the midst of a desert; a walk on the grounds, a smile from a nurse, some food three times a day, and then to bed, the routine repeated and repeated and repeated until the monotony becomes a noose from which they feel their life is being choked out of them.

I see two women whose circumstances are as different from one another as could be imagined. Millie seems quite dynamic, spending much of her time helping the nurses with the other residents.

"They're my family," she says happily.

It turns out that they indeed are the *only* family she has. Her husband died of a heart attack a year or so before. Her daughter, son-in-law, and two grandchildren all perished in a plane crash months later.

"I was so alone it was ridiculous," she tells a new nurse. "But then I figured I had a friend who would never let me down."

"Who was that?" the nurse asks.

"The Lord Jesus Christ. He's promised never to leave me nor forsake me. Though the whole world reject me, He never will. I have taken all my burdens and put them at His feet. And I am now serving Him more completely than ever before in my life."

She lives her faith, helping to feed Alzheimer's sufferers; those with senility dementia; those so crippled by arthritis that their hands seem more like twisted claws, the pain well-nigh unbearable.

"I can hardly think straight it's so bad, Millie," says one of them.

"Then I'll think for you," she says, smiling. "Let me start right now, dear one . . ."

So it goes, entering the lives of the others, laughing with them, getting them *to* laugh when instead just a bit earlier they had been crying, introducing the lonely to Christ.

And then there is Charlotte. Charlotte sits in her room most of the day, either in bed, or in a chair next to it. She eats a little, cries a lot, refuses to join with anyone in anything.

"Let me alone!" she screams. "Just get out of here. Let me alone to die."

Millie has tried to talk to her about Christ, but Charlotte refuses. Her room is a grave to her; she has already died and been buried in it. Death itself will seem at once anticlimatic to her. As far as she is concerned, life is over.

Two women: one with Christ, one without Him. One lonely, saddened, filled with self-pity, angry and bitter— the other vibrant, contributing, joyful.

"I wish I could do something to reach her," Millie says to a friend.

"Some people are happy in their misery," the other replies. "You are light; she is darkness. You draw people to you; she sends them away. That's just how it is, Millie. Thank God for those like you."

Millie smiles on the last day of her earthly life. I am by her side when her flesh-and-blood body becomes quiet, the heart and lungs still, the brain finally—

"Are you—?" she asks excitedly.

"Yes, Millie, I am."

"Am I in Heaven now? What about—"

She smiles as she looks upward.

"Oh my!" she says an instant before she is gone.

I am at Millie's funeral. It is attended by a hundred or more men, women, and children. Many of those present had once stayed at the rest home, but Millie had revived their spirits so completely that the physical part of them also improved, and they could leave. The children had been brought to see grandmothers and grandfathers con- fined to the home, and Millie had mightily touched their lives as well. There are doctors attending, nurses, more. Millie's legacy of love would be remembered for a long time.

I return to the home. Charlotte is standing in the doorway to her room. She is holding a sheet of paper in her left hand, a note that reads: "I'm going to be with my Savior this day, dear Charlotte. Won't you take Him into your life before it is too late? Let me have the privilege of welcoming you into His Kingdom someday. I love you, dear one . . ."

Charlotte begins screaming, "How can she say she loves me? Nobody loves a mean old hag. Nobody!"

She starts toward Millie's room, sees the empty bed, the vacant closet, the dresser drawers all cleaned out, no toothbrushes in the bathroom, no—

"Millie!" she yells. "Oh, Millie!"

She falls onto the bed, sobbing. But she keeps the note clutched tightly in her hand. Opened on the bed, next to her, is Millie's Bible. She picks it up and starts reading a particularly pertinent verse.

If we confess our sins, He is faithful and just to forgive us our sins, and to cleanse us from all unrighteousness . . .

She had been harboring a whole catalogue of sins, letting her guilt over these eat away at her, turning her bitter, the bitterness manifested in angry and resentful behavior toward others.

She reads other verses dealing with God's forgiveness and cleansing. A few hours later she gets down on her knees and asks Christ to enter her very being and fill the void in her life.

In less than a week Charlotte will have died also. But before then she will have gone to everyone at the home and asked them to forgive her in much the same way as she had asked the Lord. Everyone is amazed at the difference in her.

Charlotte dies quietly. There is little pain. The peace of her death contrasts with the anger and the upset of much of the latter part of her life.

She closes her eyes, and stops breathing. In an instant, Charlotte's spirit, the real Charlotte, of course, sees me.

"Charlotte!" We both hear that voice as though across eternity itself.

"Yes, yes, I'll be right there, Millie."

She turns, winks at me.

"I'll never be rejected or alone again . . . will I?"

"Never."

"Forgiveness for all the meanness?"

"Yes."

She looks serene, a smile lighting up her face.

"Millie's got somebody standing by her side, His hand outstretched. Is that—?"

I need not answer.

As she goes, I hear, for a fleeting instant, the familiar sound of angels rejoicing . . .

SINGER HAS MADE millions of dollars. He is the star of the year, with deals pouring in for all kinds of tie-ins—TV specials, film roles, posters, a dizzying montage, one after the other.

But he cannot sleep at night—because a certain nightmare assaults, tearing open the darkness in bursts of wrenching anguish.

In the dream he is singing before a packed auditorium. The crowd has paid a total of $400,000 to see and hear him. He is at the top of his form, with lyrics that speak of a life of easy sex and growing demonic worship.

Drink the blood of the saints . . .

The words ride on electronic waves into the minds of the young.

Curse the god of your fathers; bow before the New Age Christ . . .

They hear, to leave that dark place and emulate in the soon-spent vigor of their youth, until madness comes on feet of crystal.

Stick your obscene finger into the face of the Almighty . . .

But something else happens in Singer's nightmare, altering in fantasy the outcome of reality. He hears a rattling sound throughout that place, louder, louder, drowning out his music. He stops, peers through the clouds of maryjane and hash, and sees light reflecting off an audience of skeletons. Some have flesh hanging like torn garments from rib cages, others have skulls cracked open, and a few, just a few, show stomachs with the tiny hands of babies grabbing bones like death row prison bars, yelling, yelling, yelling.

He turns to run, screaming, and is confronted by two skeletons backstage, bending over a mirror, using rolled dollar bills to try and snort up the white powder in rows before them, but they cannot because they have no lungs, no nasal passages, no—

Where am I to go? he asks himself in terror. *Where—?*

Behind him the audience is on bony feet, climbing up on the stage. In an instant he is surrounded, the foul odor of decay sweeping over him as—

Awake!

As before. Always the same. Turning on the light. A bodyguard rushing in. Sweat in buckets from head to foot.

And he will fall back to dream again, to scream awake as eventually the night is gone.

Over and over until—

He disappears one afternoon. No notes. No clues. Just gone.

Singer is found one month later, in a distant forest camp, tied to stakes in the ground, heavy ropes on his arms and legs. He has been partially dismembered. Nearby are his heart and his intestines on two alters of still-burning coals.

A diary is discovered; it has been mostly destroyed by flames.

One passage reads:

I found this group today. They seem so wonderful.

They hate the whole lousy world as much as I do. Lucifer is their friend, and so am I . . .

He saw me, Singer did, as, earlier, his murderers carved him apart amid his unheeded pleas.

"I die from my own legacy," he said, "my lyrics my eulogy, is that it?"

"Yes, Singer, that is it."

There is a place for you, for me, where the neon emperor flashes his commands, and innocent blood is the wine of perdition . . .

As Hell sucked him in, across time and eternity, he sang, for an instant, of amazing grace too late . . . too dimly remembered from times of innocence since lost on compact discs and Dolby . . . before the encompassing abyss unending.

THE WANDERING ANGEL is alone, on a vast plain. He stops briefly, looking up at the sky, sighing. To go back there, he says to himself, silent to the nothingness, shrugging wearily.

To go back—

He interrupts himself, a wave of laughter causing him to double over and fall to the parched earth, but with no reaction to his presence, nor would there be throughout the journey, indeed from the beginning of time, a mortal chill perhaps, a whisper of something there, then embarrassed silence, unbelief his scalpel.

How ironic, he remarks, again to himself. *I yearn to return to a place that I have spent all of history trying to convince the Human Race is indeed the stuff of myth, a phantom longing, somewhere that is nowhere because it does not exist.*

He recalls the arguments, so profound, the thoughts planted as seeds, nourished and allowed to spring fullbloom, wreaking the havoc that atheism has been causing over the centuries.

The uniformity of natural causes is a closed system . . .

He repeats the concept with relish, savoring those

words as though they were a gourmet meal perpetually spread before him, and he is being sustained by their nutrients.

A man is sitting in a chair in the middle of a room. He is alone. The chair is his point of integration in a world that is only the room around him. There is nothing beyond that room. There is no God, nothing but the three elements—the man, his chair, and that sparse, limited, very cold world.

"But there *is* more, of course," the angel says aloud to the desert and the sky and the distant horizon. "I fooled millions, yea, hundreds of millions. You all have labored your pathetic lifetimes not knowing that that is but one room in a vast universe of rooms and over it all is—"

He stops, looking around, shivering despite the noonday heat of that baked, arid place.

"Who am I?" you have asked in your agony. "You are machines, I say in return. You live in a barren world, beyond which there is nothing—just machines, that is all. You die as they do, turning to rust and decay and then utter, utter nothingness. The system is closed. God will not reach down into it, ever, because He is just a figment of your cowardly inability to face the reality of your despair."

Then he recalls the students.

"You were ripe fruit ready to pluck from life's tree. I put into your institutions of higher learning professors committed to humanism and nihilism and atheism. They took your minds as potter's clay, remolding and reshaping.

"I went into your churches and your museums and sang the melody of despair. Sometimes I disguised it with god words and sometimes I wrapped it in canvasses of Picasso and Gauguin and Cezanne and others, but it was there, sugarcoated as humanism and existentialism and situationalism. How words fooled you—how they mid-wifed your doom."

The angel sees the skeleton of a man, studies it for a moment, then goes past. Behind him there is no trail, no cloven hoof prints, the sand as ever.

"And this is your handiwork?" I say as we meet, again, an eternity after Heaven.

"Oh, yes, it is," he replies. "Hear the wind—it cries questions without answer. Look at the sand—hope and faith crumbled, through which we walk, undetected."

He casts a glance over the endless miles, parched, with skulls turning to powder, stirred up in patchy little clouds by not-distant cries in the air, wind from the forlorn lost.

"Man," he says without a smile.

"What you have made of him."

"Yes . . ."

And the wandering angel continues on, unable to turn back, past half-buried monuments, with rusty plaques of commemoration, and weapons of war now silent, the bloody stains wafted away, the sun mocking their decay. Toward the lake at the far horizon, its flames rising high.

I DECIDE TO soar. My kind has had that ability since the beginning. There was a time, before the Casting Out, that no limitations existed on our travels. We could go throughout the whole of what was, boundless distances, unimpeded, exploring the wonders of creation.

Oh, what a glorious period that was—Earth had not been created as yet. We soared from one end of the rest of creation to the other, saw the beginnings of life, saw so much that was thrilling and invigorating and—

And then a third of us were uprooted. One after the other left. We were given an explanation and everyone seemed to accept it but me, of course—and now here I am, soaring alone, above a world in the throes of such awful pain, pain of the mind, body, and spirit so intense that it still seems almost unfathomable to me.

I see the millions in famine. I see babies with bellies bloated obscenely, the rest of their bodies bone-thin. They try to get nourishing milk from their mothers' breasts, but there is so little of that. And then they die, though not suddenly, not quickly at all, tiny rattling sounds of agony inside them, some twitching of the muscles, eyes rolling back, breathing in ragged gasps—for hours it is like this, not even to mention the slow draining away that precedes these final moments, a gradual death, worse than drowning, worse than a knife in the heart though, figuratively speaking, it is that as well.

And then the mother, in each case, holds her child, not willing to admit that her flesh and blood is gone. Her womb, a world in itself, protected him for nine months, but the outside world destroyed him.

I see one mother yet carrying a still, limp body hours after the child died—this one was three or four years old—and that body has become hard, one arm frozen in an extended gesture, the fingers stiff, wide apart. Eventually it is taken from her because already, in a desert land, it has begun to smell.

And then I stop in Alexandria, Egypt . . .

It is dirty there. Alexander the Great would be shocked by the place. Dirty is really too polite a word. Filthy comes closer, even though that seems still a bit mild somehow.

Yet I see many, many mothers in Alexandria who are apparently quite happy, tending to their children; feeding them, laughing with them, washing their faces, being with them in the time-honored way of mothers. The striking thing is that since they have known poverty all their lives they have adjusted to it, and they are somehow content to a degree, literally because they have never known anything else.

Children come up to well-dressed and -groomed foreigners, tugging at their sleeves, begging for money, smiling but not in a phony way, not in a flagrant sense of trying to generate pity or compassion, not as a turned-on/turned-off kind of thing, ready at a moment's notice.

They are covered with dirt smudges, their clothes ragged, few with shoes on their feet, and yet a pittance together with a smile, a shake of the hand, a pat on the head makes them nearly ecstatic with joy.

I am now sitting at the base of the Great Pyramid just outside Cairo, on one of the giant blocks, waiting until sunrise. The scene is like the interior of a cocoon, dormant, quiet, only the snorting of an occasional camel discernible, the air rich with the pungent odors of a long-dead antiquity.

The sunrise is rose-red, a flicker, then more, expanding light, the ancient city of Cairo first darkly outlined, then aglow with light, then awash with it.

I see children again. This time they are with their mothers, occasionally with their fathers as well, walking, packs of whatever on their backs. Their bare feet stir up clouds of dust with a reddish tinge, a texture like clay or chalk, and the odor of tombs.

And I see a man with an old camel. They, too, work the roads, confronting tourists eager to gain a little more atmosphere. It is obvious, as I watch, that the man loves this beast. They have been together many, many years. I sense that neither has a home; they live in the open, as countless numbers have done in Egypt ever since the days of the pharaohs, except perhaps for a small tent to help against the sweltering oven in which they find themselves during the noon hours of each day.

Undoubtedly, I imagine to myself, the man will die before the camel does. The animal will probably stand by his body, nudging him without comprehension. Someone else would take it on, and it might outlive the newer owner. But eventually, after decades of wandering, commanded by this man or that one, learning to depend upon each one, even to love each one after a fashion, it, too, would go to its knees one final time, as it did to receive a rider, grunting, and turn over, never arising again.

I cried because I had no shoes
Until I saw the man who had no feet.

I see such among the poor there in Egypt. I see a mother

with no feet; she has her baby in some sort of bag hanging from around her neck; another child holds her hand as she alternately hops or crawls along. There is no man with her. She provides their only hope; they provide her only love, the center of her world. Though the poverty is there, suffocatingly, though often all she can give her baby is the milk from her breasts, she accepts, she goes on, she keeps that family of three together, with no washing machines to lighten her load, no hair dryers, no remote controlled garage door openers, no one-a-day vitamins or nail polish or other "necessities." For her, tomorrow will be another day just the same as today. She and they will survive until the day afterwards, perhaps another week or month or whatever the remaining span, not knowing what the day is or the week or the year, knowing nothing in fact but hunger and dirt and looking up at a stranger for a little spare change until—until the end comes, as it surely will soon, malnutrition and disease reaping a common tragedy.

I get the feeling, as the expression goes, that so long as they die together, so long as the mother can have her little ones around her, their bodies pressed to hers, so long as she does not have to worry about their love, unlike, ironically, mothers elsewhere, insulated from dirt and hunger and disease, cocooned in a world beyond the imagination of that trio on the outskirts of Cairo, who do not know whether their sons or daughters are alive or dead or dying, shot full of drugs, riddled with sexually transmitted diseases, crying out, alone, in some aban- doned, ramshackle place, unlike such mothers, unlike such children, these three may die together as they live, with no one else but themselves, even humming some kind of tune to one another. I hear it from them now, mournful yet lyrical, made up as they go, music created from the very core of their beings—their voices a mutual melody of comfort until one by one the sounds die to a whisper and then silence altogether, except for the cries of the baby, until even that plaintive sound in the darkness, quickly dissipating, is gone, and the world goes on, ignorant of them ever . . .

There is hunger and disease elsewhere, stalking. On the fringes, laughing, I can see the figures of former comrades, gloating as the hungry occasionally resort to cannibalism. How could they? I must ask. How could they, knowing what goes down their throats, knowing what their teeth are tearing, their tongues are tasting?

It has happened before, I know. In my travels through time, I learned, earlier, of the Donner Pass incident, a group of men, women and children, without food, freezing, taking this ghastly step to survive. Or that plane crash in the Andes Mountains, the survivors forced into the same grisly act of desperation.

This is a world once Eden. This is a United States once Puritan. This is a humanity once pure. No place is free of sin. It is only a matter of degrees. And who has committed the greater sin? Those who eat the flesh of others? Or those whose compassion has shrivelled and shrunken, a near-blasphemous mockery of charity, a selfish egocentricity like a wall around their hearts, causing the problem in the first place?

. . . *only a matter of degrees.*

The sin of no charity. The sin of cannibalism. Joined by a vast encyclopedic gathering of others. Sin in rampant poverty. Sin in pillowed, perfumed, pampered luxury. The same, a thread drawn through the gut of each living human being.

Many worship unreal gods; they do despicable things; their practices sicken one's very being. And yet they are ignorant. They have grown up in societies that know nothing else. I think of the Eskimos; they worship survival; it is their god; they worship It in the midst of the worst winters on Planet Earth. And when they live through another one, they feel that their prayers have been answered. The feeble old have no place; they cannot carry their own weight and do not contribute, so they are allowed to leave, no one stopping them, and they go out into the awful blizzards, and die.

The ancient Incas, Aztecs, and Mayans all had sacrifices of their infants, to appease their own gods. Some tribes in Africa consider cannibalism a "holy" honor. And many more, in the past and the present, in isolated places and savage societies committing atrocity upon atrocity, but with ignorance, with no idea whatever that that which they do is a stench in the nostrils of a triune God.

How much worse for those aware? How much worse for the chickenhawk, as he is called, who picks up a teenage boy and they go to a motel room and the man gets his pleasure by forcing the boy to abuse him through countless demonic perversions? And demonic it is. Hovering grotesque beings—my former friends, my former fellow wondrous creations of a God capable of creating the majesty of what they once were, these very ones—I know their names; I came into being the same instant they did!—now propelling His other creation to abominable acts.

How much worse, I shout to the sky and the air and the ground beneath me, to others once like me but now laughing at my shock, my outrage, counting my loathing as pleasure because they exist on such emotions, pain their love, hatred their ecstasy, things whispered in darkness their beacon of light, blinding them, funerals their celebrations, death their domain. Hell their Mecca, and yet they are not satisfied, their gluttonous appetites incapable of fulfillment, bloated though they are with the carrion of their vile imaginings. . . . how much worse, I say, regaining my composure, for those who allow what they know to be so foul that the stench of it gags and sickens and makes anyone with even a thread, a thin, thin thread of righteousness vomit it up in gushers of revulsion.

The next instant, my words a prophecy, I have another glimpse, another layer of Man's sin nature pulled back, revealing the blood and organs and marrow of itself . . .

*T*HE RECEPTION ROOM is rather spartan—white-painted walls, a dark tan carpet, a sofa, two chairs, a coffee table, and a single tall potted plant in one corner. There are no paintings, no plaques, just a no-nonsense "official" appearance. On the coffee table are some magazines.

Very businesslike, I say with no one to hear. The veneer of something quite ordinary, commonplace, yes, mainstream.

But beyond that facade is the opposite reality—a bizarre and grisly slaughterhouse. Oh, even there, attempts are made to seem institutional. Doctors and nurses are running about, some carrying clipboards holding charts, medical reports, whatever.

And it is large, this place beyond the reception area. Corridors spread out north, east, west. Each is lined with doors, dozens altogether, on either side. Behind some, women are undergoing abortions, with saline solution pumped into their uteruses; behind others, babies are being ripped out of wombs, limb by limb. I see a pile of arms and legs and other body parts, ready to be incinerated, and turn away in revulsion. In another, babies are in incubators, with nurses tending them with great care.

I am puzzled. The nurturing of life side by side with the very destruction of it? That one room seems much like any hospital nursery except for the preponderance of incubators.

I overhear a meeting in an office that is rosewood panelled, with leather-covered chairs, and an enthusiastic chap sitting behind a large rosewood desk, facing three other men.

"It's been a wonderful situation, gentlemen," he tells them. "Our receipts have never been so high. This is the best year we've ever had, I can assure you."

"And there are suitable safeguards against any of this leaking out?" he is asked. "None of the mothers have any suspicion at all?"

The man behind the desk replies, "That's right. We have no fears, guys, no worries whatever."

What is he talking about? Angels cannot read minds, as God can, so I could not probe in his brain and find out in that manner.

What is—?

I do not have to wait long to find out.

I leave that office, and wander elsewhere in the building. Much of what I see is bloody. Some babies are still alive as they are pulled from their mothers, but most die seconds or minutes later. The ones surviving are taken to that same big nursery-like room. There is feverish activity as additional incubators are prepared.

"This is so terrible," says a nurse to another. "I don't know if I can continue."

"Me, too. It's ghastly. What if even one of the mothers finds out? They all think their babies are dead."

I pick up other comments as I stay in that place for a long while afterwards, compelled to know exactly what is going on.

Eventually everything jells. The aborted babies who survive are nursed to health and then given out for adoption. The mothers who decided to have the abortions are ignorant of what is happening. The black market operation prospers because they have a ready-made supply being created by the survivors of a million or more abortions annually. (Never mind what damage might have been done to a child, and which may not show up until months, perhaps years later. Couples driven to desperation to have a child, finding obstacle after obstacle to doing it legally, are ripe for such an operation. They have to pay a heavy price, but, for them, the cost is not the important factor. Being able to raise a child transcends everything else. And then, one day, they discover that this little dream of theirs made flesh will be retarded for the rest of his or her life due to the very techniques of abortion, a danger made that much more likely after a second or third abortion on the same mother, the walls of the womb progressively weaker each time. Retardation or leukemia or blindness or deafness— indeed, anything can happen—and no one pays more severely, no one faces more anguish, than the child and the adoptive parents. Those profiting do not, at least in the short term. They run with the money and have a good old time.)

What is supposedly not a living entity but a near-formless blob, surely not a murder victim in any way, what is expendable because it is not yet a person, like jello or a tumor or whatever, that is exactly what is making the perpetrators of this nightmare business quite wealthy, for they have a perfect situation, with no governmental records except that a baby has been aborted, and everyone knows that that is that!

I marvel at the genius of it, while at the same time I cringe at what this further reveals of the depravity of the times. It is a factory, an abortion factory on one level, and an illegal adoption ring on the other. But as awful, as sickening as that is, it is not the worst aspect of what is being practiced in that building. In yet another room, aborted babies, deformed or missing one or more limbs or blinded, are used instead of animals for various experiments.

"It's medically more accurate than using a mouse or a chimp," comments one of the doctors to a colleague who has been expressing some qualms. "As far as the mother is concerned, there is no child of hers alive. And the ones we are using would not be suitable for adoption. It's really a clean, orderly matter. Quite productive, I might say."

His colleague, a young man, nods finally in reluctant appreciation.

"You're right, I must admit. The women are having their abortions anyway, so we might as well turn what is, from their point of view, just dead meat, a memory they want to push into the back of their minds as soon as possible, into hard profit. Brilliant, I've got to admit."

They are chuckling now . . .

I can endure no more. Suddenly what I have seen and heard makes all the protestations about a "woman's right to choose" an even more pitiable distortion of morality, in that context, than ever. The choices of women everywhere are becoming the profit centers of a racket that has to rank with the most infamous in the history of Mankind.

I hear the sound of an explosion. The building is shaken; windows break; a table overturns; some plaster falls from the ceiling.

Abruptly someone yells, "A grenade! They threw a grenade through the front door."

Pandemonium erupts. Bottles containing arms and legs are knocked on the floor, shattering, their contents spilling out.

"Another one!" I hear. "No, two more. They're trying to kill us."

I see flames. A man runs in terror, falls, his white smock on fire. His spirit looks up at me as his body quickly becomes a charred mess.

"The fire was so awful, burning away my flesh. I couldn't stand—"

I say nothing.

"Surely that's not what will happen when—"

His expression is one of unspeakable terror as he disappears in thin air, screaming.

The nursery is untouched. The rest of the structure looks much like a bombed-out building during wartime. But the babies still alive are not harmed. Firemen approach, look with amazement at the sight. And in the days and weeks to follow, the revelations coming from their discovery will captivate the attention of media everywhere.

And what of those responsible for the destruction of the so-called clinic in the first place?

As difficult as it seems to comprehend, there is more outrage over what the attackers did than anything regarding the atrocities at the clinic. Somehow the real truth is muted, if not hidden altogether, for if it were to become widely known, the entire pro-choice movement would be severely damaged.

I "attend" a meeting involving a number of the movement's leaders.

"This could be a disaster."

"Agreed. We must do everything we can to stop the spread of the story. As it is now, we've got a reasonable-sounding explanation—namely, it's a humanitarian aspect of our movement. From time to time babies do live. What are we supposed to do? *Murder* them?"

"But *all* of them? There were so many, Gloria."

"I know, I know. But we've got to try. Too many years have been invested in what has been achieved to date. We haven't let truth stop us before."

How many infant cries must form a deafening roar from garbage cans and city dumps and incinerator refuse buckets before a morally and spiritually indifferent populace rises up and fights through the courts and, yes, as shocking as it may seem, any other means, including civil disobedience, that is necessary to stop a national scandal cold in its tracks? Where is the love of Christ in this? His love has nothing whatever to do with it, but His righteous anger, His intolerance of hypocrisy, His promise of judgment on those who would hurt the very least of His little ones—these have all the relevance necessary.

Reeling, I leave that meeting, wanting to get away from the stench that pervades it . . .

I investigate more of what goes on in other so-called clinics. None of the others seem to have such a racket going on. But then all of them, by doing what they are, find themselves in a grand delusion, a racket of a kind. They have allowed themselves to be seduced by the prevailing notion that a mother's civil rights are at issue—and the Constitution protects them on that score as well as the right to privacy and other considerations.

I am aghast at the specious reasoning people are capable of if it suits their goals. They ignore even the possibility of the agony caused the baby depending so completely on them. They brush aside the slightest chance that "it" is a "he" or a "she" just as surely as the mother herself is, only size and environment the differences. They choose personal convenience above the chance that they are no different than a murderer who takes a gun and shoots a storeowner to death while committing a robbery. When all the niceties, the distortions, the evasions are cut aside, the truth is seen nakedly real and unmistakable, namely, that there seems to be *not* a whisper of a difference between the death of a baby during an abortion, and a drunken driver running down a

child crossing the street. Death is the result; the young
are sent to their grave early.

And yet, on the other hand, a difference does become
apparent—the child killed in an accident will never be
forgotten, will be eulogized during a funeral, and given a
burial, and there will be a headstone to mark the spot.
The memory of moments of laughter and tenderness, of
bright smiles and warm hugs and all the rest—these are
a bittersweet legacy. But nothing of the kind for the
aborted baby—the sooner forgotten, the better—pretend
it never happened—throw the "evidence" away, like a
rejected doll.

After visiting the final clinic, after being numbed by the
vast carnage of human flesh dispatched in the abortuaries,
I am ready to shout to God to take me back. But then I
know He would not, for, later, the old doubts would return.
He knew I would have to be actually confronted with
Lucifer before my mind is ever made up.

In an alley adjacent to the clinic, in the midst of a large
group of trash cans, I find a familiar sight.

Mifult.

One of my closest friends in the days when we shared
many experiences in Heaven.

He is crouched down, in a corner. He looks up as I
approach him. It is clear that he has been crying.

"I look awful, do I not?" he says, full of shame.

"Yes, you do," I reply truthfully.

"You have seen, in there?"

I nod.

"It's been a nightmare, Darien. You have no idea
what—I go through."

"Tell me . . ."

I sit down beside him.

"I am in charge, you know."

"Of what?"

"That—that! It is my assignment—to nurture the

climate for that kind of slaughter, to get people to believe that it is acceptable behavior. D'Seaver, remember him, has helped me on occasion."

That chill—again . . .

"At first I tried to convince myself that there was a reason, that the arguments were valid. Deformed babies, unwanted babies, retarded babies. Why inflict them upon the world? Why inflict the world upon them? Kill them now to save them greater pain later. After all, they went to Heaven automatically. A little pain now, and then it is over. And they have an eternity ahead of them, an eternity of boundless joy."

He stands, starts to pace.

"It was easy at first, you know. The first few were uncomplicated. And then—"

He is visibly trembling, his whole being going through some kind of massive convulsion.

"And then I saw a baby scraped out of his mother's womb, piece by piece. First an arm, then a leg, then bits and pieces of the rest of him. Finally his head, the eyes still closed.

"Oh, Darien, I could hear what the doctor could not, what the nurse could not, what no human being ever, ever could. I could hear his spirit crying out. I could sense the agony he felt, his cries reaching up to Heaven, I know. He had been safe, warm, content. And then his world was literally ripped apart".

Mifult pauses, trying to keep his thoughts intelligible. It is a titanic struggle for him to do so.

"The next time a baby was born alive. The doctor tried to smother him, but that failed to work, though the baby was *nearly* dead at that point. In fact, the doctor thought he was, and threw him to one side, almost absent-mindedly. A couple of minutes later, the doctor turned, looked, saw the little body moving slightly. He then took the baby, broke its neck and threw it into a trash can bag. He—he—"

"Be still, my friend," I tell him. "Let us walk a bit. You can continue later."

Mifult agrees. We come upon an old man and a six-year-old girl. They are playing happily in a park.

"My next mission is to deal with ones like him," Mifult remarked. "We have established the precedent, and now we must carry it to the next step."

"Destroy the old?"

"Yes, Darien. Gas them; poison them; suffocate them."

My mind goes back to the encounter, earlier, at the concentration camp.

"They are as useless as the unborn child. They contribute nothing. They are sick and dying anyway. I must simply hasten their final moment here."

I stop, looking at my old friend.

"And, later, what about the retarded who are contributing nothing?"

His next words somehow seem more terrifying than all the rest.

"Yes . . . they are on the agenda."

We continue walking.

"This world was once different, you know. It was not generally realized, by mankind anyway, that when we were cast out, we found a perfect earth. We ruined it with our loathsome behavior. You see, Eden as such was over the entire earth, a place of transcendent, natural beauty. God started over after that, wiping the slate clean, and established the actual Garden of Eden, its physical, historical location a pocket reminder of what had once been throughout the earth.

"It was God's intention to expand outward after that, for man to have dominion with kindness and with every act honoring Him. But the spiritual battles continued, and when Adam and Eve fell from grace, when they committed the original sin, we all rejoiced with undisguised glee and abandon. We had reclaimed the earth; we had gained an important victory."

I had not realized this. But it makes sense. When Adam and Eve sinned, they were thrown out of the Garden into a world gone from perfection to imperfection, from sinlessness to increasingly rampant corruption. They could never return to the Garden because it no longer existed!

Mifult points to a flower of special beauty.

"The world was once entirely like that ever so fine flower, Darien. And others like it bloomed over the whole earth. There were no deserts. No fires blackened vast acreage of forests. The air was absolutely pure. Any sort of death was unknown. There were no afflictions of pain, disease, unhappiness."

He stops, turns to me.

"*We* brought all that in, Darien. A gigantic, drowning wave of it. Again and again it battered the earth. It continues. There is no letup. Millions succumb. This is what *we* have wrought . . ."

We are approaching a cemetery.

"The bodies rot away and go back to the earth," he continues. "Families are torn apart, many for eternity. And all that is left on this one-time Eden are old pieces of marble or concrete."

He makes a sweeping gesture through the air.

"I have been a part of it all. I have helped with everything that is dank, and unholy, and loathsome. And I yearn to be clean, to look at myself and not turn away in disgust."

"Why have you not forsaken it all before now?" I ask.

"Because there was no one to help. I am surrounded by my own kind. I am trapped the way so many are trapped by their life-styles. You make the first move, and it is traumatic. Leaving Heaven to follow Lucifer was *that*. The rest happens act by act. If one stepped away from the others, he would not remain away. The pull is too strong. He cannot do it alone. So, he goes back, surrounding himself with others like him, cocooning himself in a closed world of those who feel his misery but likewise are weak. And it never, never changes—the blind leading the blind over the precipice."

He shudders again.

"But you are here now. You are not one of us. You—"

A child is coming toward him, with no adult near it. The child is crying. She goes past us, indeed through us, never knowing that we are there.

"Twenty million or more have never been allowed to live as that little girl is living. You saw what was going on back there. I am the one overseeing all that. Oh, look!"

The child's mother sees her, rushes up to her, scolds her daughter for wandering off.

"And there are the others who lived, who were molested, whose minds even more than their bodies were damaged often permanently by what *I* caused."

We stand in the middle of the cemetery. It stretches on for quite a distance in all directions.

"How much ground would be necessary if all the unborn I have destroyed were buried side by side? How many crosses? How much marble? Concrete?"

He sighs with great weariness.

"Darien, may I tell you about a dream, nay, a nightmare I have had for so long now it is impossible for me to trace when it began?"

"Yes," I indicate. "Tell me, please."

"I am very much alone on a plain. It is totally barren— only sand as far as I can see. Suddenly I notice some specks at the horizon. They seem to be moving, though they are still too far away for me to be sure.

"I wait. Closer they come. I begin to see forms, of different sizes. Still closer, Darien. They are now near enough so that I can see what those forms are.

"Babies, and little children. Hordes of them. Almost like bees from a distant hive. There may be thousands, or more, forming a long line extending all the way from the horizon. They surround me.

"One of them approaches, holding out her hand. She says, 'Mister, why did you do those terrible things to me?' And I realize she has been the victim of a child molester.

"A boy comes up, his body covered with bruises. Others as well. Suddenly the crowd parts and I see the most devastating image of all: a tiny body, its arms and legs missing, somehow *rolling* toward me, crying, stopping at my feet. His head is turned toward me, the eyes pleading, the skin wrinkled and blotched and smelling, oh, Darien, smelling of saline solution. The first attempt had failed, so he was pulled apart limb by limb.

"I run, Darien. I run as fast as I can. Abruptly I fall and lose consciousness. I think I come to again, but I am not sure. Suddenly I feel someone tearing at me. There is intense pain. Then more pain. I scream out. But there is no response. I try desperately to fight against someone who is pulling at me, but I realize, I realize, I realize that I have no arms, no legs.

"The next instant I am at someone's feet. Looking up. Pleading. I have become that baby, Darien. *And—I—am—looking—up—at—myself!*"

I cannot say anything initially. What could I offer? He was responsible for nurturing such horrors. He had on his hands the blood of countless millions.

We walk out of the cemetery, both of us silent. Down

the street several blocks, a funeral is taking place. We enter the funeral home.

A minister is praising the deceased.

"He left behind a marvelous legacy. There are going to be people in Heaven because of his witness. There are families still together because of his wise counsel. There is less pain in the world because of him. There is love, more belief in Christ, more—"

The minister pauses, his emotions obvious.

". . . love," he finishes.

Others go to the front of the room. Their words are similar, equally sincere.

Mifult stands and hurries outside. I follow him.

"There will be no eulogies for me," he says. "I have not left love but hate. I have not sown joy but sorrow. I have not eased pain but caused it. There is no light as my legacy but darkness.

"I—I—I cannot stay with you any longer. I must go. The master is waiting, calling."

"But who—?" I start to ask, surprised.

Mifult stops, looking at me disbelievingly.

"You do not realize the truth, Darien?" he interrupts. "You are blind to the central *authority* behind all this?"

"But he could not be that—that—"

"Evil? You were going to say evil?"

"Yes—yes. Just because some of his followers happen to—"

"You fool! You utterly stupid fool! I can scarcely believe that you—"

Mifult suddenly looks terrified.

"I—I must go. Oh, no, please, I must go. I must go. I must go."

He continues to say those words until he disappears from sight, his voice lost . . .

But before he is completely gone, he turns. His countenance starts to change, much like D'Seaver's did, but there is a difference this time, at least for a split second, before his appearance assumes an identical malevolence, the difference of an angel whose expression is one of shame and fear and deep, deep regret, yet regret that is swept away by the habits, the behavior, the entrapment of unspeakable acts committed throughout the centuries of Man's history.

I AM AWAY from the cities now, the soaring, the wars, the poverty. I am in the midst of a forest. I stand and smell the air. I listen to the sounds of life in trees, bushes, a nearby lake. I feel somewhat refreshed, and I wait, relaxing, getting my thoughts together.

Nowhere have I seen Lucifer. Only those who claim to follow him. Only those who claim that he dominates them so strongly, so inescapably, that they are bereft of a will of their own, submitting to him in everything.

If that is indeed the case, then how different from those who follow God, who have accepted His Son into their lives as Savior and Lord. Lucifer's followers, if they are to be believed, are automatons. But with Him, it is free will only, not an enslavement but a dedication, not an obsession but a devotion.

What an answer to the age-old question of why God *allows* certain things to happen. If Lucifer's fallen angels are to be—

If?

That question nags at me. Can the leader be blamed totally for what those with him do? What if all this is without his knowledge? If he has confidence in those who serve him, does he need to check their every move,

86

approve each plan, detail? Perhaps his not doing so, if those in whom he has placed trust betray him, is cause for questioning his judgment in that very area of having chosen them in the first place. But that is another kind of weakness—hardly the same as Mifult overseeing the death of millions of helpless babies; the infamy of those perpetrating the Holocaust. Or—

My musings are interrupted by something carried on the air, it would seem.

The sound, far away, of a piccolo.

I stand, listening more closely.

Yes!

Rather like some of the music heard in Heaven . . .

But where?

I am attracted to it. Enchanted by the gentleness of the notes.

I find the player.

An old man, possibly well into his eighties. He is sitting on a flat rock beside a stream, the sound of the water a faint backdrop to the melody of his instrument.

I stand there, listening, awed by what I hear.

"Well, say something," he says, startling me.

"I—well—I mean—how—?" I stutter embarrassingly.

"You are not very secretive, you know. But then you probably thought you did not have to be. Is that it?"

"Yes, I suppose—"

He chuckles.

"I remember you from the old days. Kind of naive. A little gullible. But good-natured. A dreamer perhaps. But not foolishly so."

"Please, how can you—?"

"See you?"

"Yes? Tell me how."

"Because I came along with them, for the ride. I am the only one who did, of course. The others were quite zealous from the beginning. For me, it was just a matter of curiosity. Though I, too, was cast out, guilt by association, I guess you might say, I have never really joined the others. I have remained uncommitted to their atrocities. But I can never return, either, to the way it once was. God asked for a choice. I made mine, however half-heartedly, and with motives that were substantially different, but it was made just the same. And I am stuck with the consequences, unfortunately."

There is a note of wistfulness in the way he speaks. Underlined by a profound sadness.

"I have counterparts among the human beings of this world, you know. People who want to go along for the ride, who are faintly attracted by the bravado of many of their contemporaries, but torn by the knowledge that they cannot serve two masters—allowing themselves to be beckoned by the one, they end up rejecting the other."

I stand there, still amazed.

"But that old man's body which you inhabit? How?"

"He is the same way. He is unaware, of course, that we are here. He will die soon, and then I must find someone else. It is the same with the others, at least the ones who have been assigned the possessions—they work from within while the rest wreak havoc from without, oppressing with equal vengeance."

"You have been in—inside others?"

"When I choose to be. I have not succumbed to any orders by anyone. I do as I wish."

He pauses, very briefly, then talks with affection about the old hands that are writing down his thoughts, hands mottled with the spots of a liver in distress, varicose veins apparent, nails turning faint yellow.

"I started a journal some time ago. Here it is. See, he's writing in it now."

"And it will be passed on to someone else when you move on?"

"Exactly. There will be new editions when each of the old starts to crumble."

"But why?"

"I am known as Observer. It is what I do."

"But who is going to read it?"

"Those who play host to me. They read it. But they see it only as a collection of myths. They read, oh, yes, they do that, but their understanding is darkened—and, eventually, each will put it aside."

I am eager to know the contents of that book.

"It is to be read only when it is to be read," Observer says ambiguously. "It is a perpetual legacy, left behind by a wandering spirit hoping that, someday, those who have it will indeed comprehend."

I want to pursue this matter further with him, but I know that I will not be at all successful. Instead I content myself with the bits and pieces told to me by Observer as we sit there by that stream, the sun poking through overhead branches, and glistening off the rippling water.

"I have seen The Fall and The Flood. I have been with John on Patmos, at the French Revolution, the Civil War, the two World Wars—from the ancient days to the computer age. And, you know, even I feel something akin to weariness."

He hesitates, then: "You have been around also, have you not?"

I nod.

"But there is a difference between us, my former fellow inhabitant of Heaven. You have sampled history; I have been through it. You have dabbled here and there—I have experienced centuries *as* centuries. In Heaven, time was an impossibility. For Man, it is a necessity. And to a great extent we—the others and I—are entrapped by many of the constraints, the conventions, the limitations of the very creature they—not me, please understand, *never* me—would like to destroy, would like to snatch from the loving arms of a kind and generous Creator."

He begins to sob then.

"I do this often. These are not tears, of course—we are beings of spirit, not tear ducts and blood and nerve endings. But we cry spiritually. We cry with emotion and depth even more profoundly than this old man who wept many years ago over the death of his wife."

Observer/old man stands, walks to a deeper, broader part of the stream, points to some fish there.

"Many will not make it, you know. They will die in that stream or be hooked by fishermen and fried in a skillet and eaten with delight. But they do not know the future. The others and I do. That is why they are so frenzied. That future is always closer, never forestalled. For these fish, it may be the frying pan—for us, it *is* the fire."

He shakes himself with great weariness.

"I cry because I know I am doomed. I know what is in store. I will be there in the lake of torment with all the rest. It is the choice each being makes—of spirit or of flesh—and there by it he must abide for all eternity, in pain or—or in peace."

He turns, sits down again, age readily apparent.

"My host is dying," Observer says simply. "He will see us soon."

The pen drops from the old man's hand as he clutches his chest. The ancient book falls to the ground, amongst some autumn leaves. Lips issue a single cry and then are frozen together, eyelids closed, head bent to one side.

First it is Observer as spirit en toto who leaves that body, and I see an angel much like myself but also very different, wings at half-mast, face pale, the glow of Heaven gone, his lostness apparent in the tragedy of separation from God mirrored in his eyes, the forlornness of his very countenance. And then the old man's spirit, that which is him in actuality, not the disposable cloak soon to rot away, also leaves that fleshly shell.

"You've been with me many years, have you not?" he asks, looking at Observer.

Observer agrees that this has been so.

"I was a good man, kind, charitable."

Observer nods.

"I never engaged in adultery. I lied little."

"That is correct."

"I never cursed any man. I never stole money. I am good, am I not?"

"Yes, you are."

He smiles, but it fades as quickly.

"But why are *they* waiting for me?"

In the surrounding forest are a dozen fallen angels. The sight of them is chilling.

"I have helped the homeless, fed the starving, comforted the dying."

The dozen shapes are beckoning, cloven feet stamping the ground.

"I have served on church committees, raised money for missionaries. I have also planned picnics for the elderly and—and—"

The shapes move from the trees into the clearing.

"Must they have me? Must all my good be as nothing?"

They grab him and take him away, his screams filling the air. One turns, smiles momentarily at Observer. And then is gone with the others.

Observer is shaken.

"I must wait here until the body is found," Observer notes, his voice trembling. "It may not be long. It will be found, along with the book, and I will go along until it passes into the hands of someone else like me, and whoever that is will provide me with pen, ink, and a hand to write. I am called Observer, yes, but I have felt that another appellation was perhaps a trifle more accurate."

"And what would that be?"

He grimaces with centuries of awareness, centuries that weigh upon him like some kind of boulder, pressing him down, sapping away his vitality.

I can scarcely hear him at first, and tell him so. Then he speaks louder as he says, "TuMasters, that is what it should be, would you not agree?" Mifult. D'Seaver. D'Filer. And now TuMasters. What a motley crew, the bane of humanity. And yet there are more, of course, out there among the masses, planting, nurturing, reaping.

"I live under a delusion, you know, as all of us do. Many of the others abort, rape, slaughter. I seem so bland in comparison. I seem to do nothing but observe, hence my title. And that is the appalling reality of my existence. I look; I write down my useless insights through my hapless hosts; but that is all. I interfere not. I stay within a limited circle, insulated, my hosts and I. And we let the world collapse around us."

He has been looking up at the sky, which has but a lone cloud at that time and place.

"When you get back, please, please, please tell Him how very sorry I am."

I start to speak, to say something very evangelical, if you will, to tell him it is not too late.

But he has turned his back on me, and he is sitting by that old, old book, the piccolo lying nearby, and the moment of regret has passed, the door to himself is closed, and Observer will do as he had always done . . .

*T*HE KITTEN IS mewing.

It cannot be more than a few weeks old, the fur still tufted with something like fuzz. A man in a white smock is holding it in his right hand. With his left he is putting little beads of fluid from a dropper into each of its eyes.

The kitten cries louder. The man puts it in a cage with another of its kind, then leaves.

The first kitten cannot stand. Little knives of agony slice continually from its eyes into its brain and then throughout its tiny body. It tries to wash the awfulness away by licking its paw and then rubbing that paw over its left eye, and next the other paw over the right eye. Yet this is to no avail. The pain continues. In fact, it is getting worse.

The kitten starts to vomit, what little food was held in its young stomach spewing onto the newspaper underneath, onto its own fur, and that of its companion.

The kitten can no longer see, its blindness caused by an acid-based dye that has literally eaten away much of the soft material of its eyeballs.

Its body shakes once, twice, its limbs extended out

straight as though frozen in that position. Then it gasps up some blood. And dies.

Its companion walks hesitantly over to the still form, not aware of what has happened, and lies next to it, hoping to comfort what is now beyond that.

A short while later the man in the white smock returns, finds the lifeless body, dumps it into a nearby wastebasket, takes the second kitten, and another dropper with a different solution inside and—

Madison Avenue.

Product marketing meeting.

A tall man, his shirt sleeves rolled up, shows a chart to others in the room.

"It's a great new color," he beams. "I'm calling it luminescent pearl. The women will love it."

The chimpanzee cannot stop scratching its head. It has been doing so for nearly an hour. Its fingertips are bloody, pieces of skin hanging from—

"Last year our best shade was sunset orange," the man continues.

The chimp has blood all over its head, but still it keeps scratching. It does not know what else to do.

"How many units do we expect to sell?" He repeats the question that has just been asked.

He inputs some figures on a calculator in front of him and gives the result to those in the conference room with him.

"That's pretty good, if it's accurate," someone speaks up.

There is general agreement that the outlook certainly is appealing, the more dollars the better.

The chimp is covered with his own blood, for it has continued to scratch itself, tearing more and more flesh. Now too weak to do anything else, it slumps back across one side of the cage.

"How about the testing?" a little man on the left side

of the oak conference room asks. "What about the safety factor?"

"No problem at all," the main speaker replies. "We're finalizing the results now. You know what I always say? Better to kill a chimp than to harm one single hair on a single customer's head. We can always find another chimp, but finding customers isn't always easy."

It moans with enormous anguish several times, then is silent altogether, its eyes rolling upward in its sockets, slobber dripping out of its mouth and down its chin, hanging like dewdrops from the black hairs. And then it dies.

Everyone claps. The mood is buoyant. They have a new color. And sales have never been better.

I am privy to more in other panelled conference rooms in tall buildings along that avenue. Other products are being generated. More dollars coveted. More suffering generated for animals at the mercy of those whose highest ambition, whose most compelling ideal, is additional profit for their companies.

"Who cares if they need it?"

"That's right. We'll create the desire and masquerade it as need."

All the demographics are there. All the convincing marketing research designed to lull the public into an acceptance of whatever the manufacturers care to purvey.

This is not America, I cry out to unheeding ears. It is not the vision of the Pilgrims or the Puritans. They left one kind of domination but not to sow the seeds of another in its place.

And flashing across my vision is a montage of faces, the faces of mothers whose babies are deformed because of cigarettes. Or alcohol. Or drugs innocently taken in trust of a doctor's prescription, only to see a pitiful, twisted little shape coming from the womb, and turning for solace only to hear the shouts of "Abort! Abort! Abort!" all around. You should have killed the thing. You should have—

They are out there in the cities, the towns, the villages. Pumping poison into their systems, through mouths and skinpores and into veins. Poison over the counter, in the midst of shopping malls. Or in a secluded place from a man who profits, chuckling at his fruits. Poison into the temple made by God, graffiti of the spirit, but far more deadly than initials or obscenities or protests on an outdoor wall.

Poison, yes, packaged and labelled and advertised. Poison to color the hair. Poison to prolong the "freshness" of food. Poison to move the bowels. Tested, oh, yes, they test all of it. They reap their profits on the backs of God's helpless ones, the dogs and cats and birds and mice and monkeys and other creatures who wait in their cages for the inevitable, condemned not for crime but commerce.

Present your bodies a living sacrifice . . .

But is a body riddled with the residue of mindless consumption, consumption ignorant of the content of what is being consumed, dictated even among His chosen ones by the latest "discovery" to retard aging, change hair color, take away bad breath, ban body odor, bring on sleep, calm frazzled nerves during the day, give a reason for smiling, is such a body cosmeticized, aromatized, plasticized, artificialized for profit and not a dedication to the betterment of the Human Race, is such a body traumatized by the media, pummelled by sensation at every turn, is such a body indeed truly, truly, truly a living sacrifice or rather a kind of mannequin, dressed up, prettied up, propped up by the merchandising to which it has succumbed? Is there not in that Scriptural admonition at least the implication that those bodies are to be worthy as well as living? Is a gift to a charity of a suit with holes and patches and loose threads and stains and rips in fact a gift? Or, dare I say, an insult instead? Too often, as I have seen in my travels across Earth, a gift is not actually that but instead more like a spent whore, riddled with disease, crippled by exhausted inner drives, drained of energy, worthless in her profession, lying down before God and saying, "Here I am, Lord." That body of that whore has already been sacrificed, but not to God. When a celebrity leaves the glittery world of show business and professes salvation by faith in Christ, is it plus nothing and is it worthy? Or has an illusion been created, the formula now salvation by faith in Christ plus transcendent media attention that revives a slumping career?

But this is the world. The domain of the flesh. What about the get-rich-quick minister steering his congregation on the road to prosperity? Offering them keys to a generously filled bank vault instead of Heaven? The healer on television who claims the name of Christ and then makes a sideshow of purported healing that even the most naive, the most gullible find patently absurd? What about the "Jesus loves me" Ping-Pong paddle peddlers? Those who take sacred verses dealing with Christ being the Light of the World and make that Scriptural truth instead a Jesus night-light to be used in bedrooms everywhere? What about all the rest of holy hardwaredom? Pens and bracelets and bookends and handkerchiefs and endless other products made "righteous" by the name of Christ?

Oh, God, I say, and not in vain—I could never use my Creator's name in vain—this is what has become of America, the world? This is His creation, now, a little higher than the angels? This is Earth, once Eden?

If I had a stomach, if there were bowels within me, I would be in great distress. I would vomit up the sickness that grips me, the slop from within like that which I see without, nauseating and vile.

And even now, yet another wretched truth unravelling, I still see not the creature accused of it all, only those called demons, spirits of the hideous and profane, things that bump in the night, and—
Lucifer.
Not in the abortion mills. Not in the Madison Avenue conference rooms. Not in the gay parties of Hollywood.
Emissaries aplenty, but not Lucifer, my former fellow inhabitant of heavenly places.
Where are you, son of the morning?

*W*HERE AM I to go?

I cannot be seen except by dying human beings on the way to Heaven or Hell. I am as close to desperation as I can possibly be, my inner turmoil so strong that I feel moved to petition to Him to let me back, that I do not really need to find out the truth about Satan because I perceive the truth about the world to which he has been confined for so long. But I suspect God would not allow me to return to His Kingdom under such conditions because, in His wisdom, He knows the old doubts would crop up again later, and—

An idea springs into my mind. If I can just not give up in trying to locate Lucifer, perhaps, upon doing so, I could alert him to what is going on, and together we could make things right. What a triumph *that* would be! And the return of the highest archangel to Heaven would surely be an event of rejoicing without precedent. If we all used to celebrate over the salvation of one sinning human being, what would it be like if Lucifer returned in contrition and with the banishment of all the evil in the world as his legacy?

The possibilities overwhelm me. And I become more deeply committed than ever to the goal of finding Lucifer, for the new reason makes a pygmy of my previous one. Lucifer and I allies! Banishing the perversion, the drugs, the abortions, banishing all the other corruptions that have swept over Earth like the most epochal tidal wave of history.

I ask fallen angel after fallen angel. As before, it is not difficult to find them. A whole horde are at a heavy metal rock concert, infiltrating the audience, backstage with the strange-garbed musicians, and—

No one will tell me. The most I can get out of them is that Lucifer will find me, not the other way around, when he wishes to do so.

I discover my former comrades at a television station during a debate between a minister who claims that the Bible *contains* God's truth, and another who protests that the Bible *is* His truth, from cover to cover. And they also are in the newscaster's booth as he tells a "neutral" story about the Communist takeover of another country in Central America. And they are there as commercials are being telecast, commercials that appeal to the vanity of millions of viewers. They are everywhere at that station, in every department, because this is where their lies, their distortions can be disseminated to a wider number than even they could reach otherwise. But all profess ignorance about where Lucifer is, although at the very mention of his name, they become exceedingly nervous, paranoid.

One in particular seems more upset than the others. His name is Nufears.

"Why do you want to meet Lucifer?" he asks. "Why would anyone?"

He looks from side to side, apprehension growing.

"He is not what you may be expecting."

"But I have to see for myself."

"I must tell you that he—"

He disappears, suddenly, without explanation.

I stand there in a corridor, rock music and interviews and newscasts being spun out all around me. And I am just as puzzled as ever.

More time passes. At different places. In that city. And in others. And I am now in a place where it could be expected that I would find the highest concentration of fallen angels anywhere in America, surpassing even the number in Hollywood.

The President is dying. Gathered around him are his family, two physicians, and three Cabinet members. The rigors of office have taken their toll on the oldest President in the history of the United States.

"He should rest now," a doctor says softly, and they all leave the room.

The First Lady, as though sensing that he will be gone when she returns, whispers, "Good-bye, my love . . ."

The President knows of my presence, so close to death is he by then, and seems not startled by it.

"Almost the moment?" he asks, his voice hardly audible.

"Yes, Mr. President, it is."

"Oh, how I rejoice over that. How I indeed rejoice."

"You have done well these seven years."

"I tried very hard, you know. I witnessed to as many members of Congress, foreign heads of state, and whoever else I could. Many paid no heed, but I hope I managed to reach a few."

"In Heaven there is great anticipation over your imminent arrival."

"Is that really, really the case, my new angel friend?"

"Oh, yes. The President who tried to govern in the *right* way even though that did not guarantee how correct he was from a *political* point of view. You put God first always, and nothing else matters in the long run."

"And I know how much of a miracle it was that I was reelected!"

He coughs, then says: "I once heard a joke. St. Peter welcomes a minister and a politician through the so-called pearly gates. The former is assigned a very nice place to live in for eternity but not especially elaborate. The latter is given a palace, a stunning residence indeed. The politician is appreciative but puzzled. He asks St. Peter, 'But why am I being blessed so mightily while a man of the cloth is treated so humbly?' St. Peter replies, 'It is not uncommon for ministers to come here and stay forever. But it is a momentous event indeed when that happens to a politician!'"

I laugh at the joke, then say, "You must have been perplexed by a great deal of what you have seen, here, over the years."

"Oh, a considerable amount has been ghastly. If ever there was a capital as much for the Devil as for the nation, then Washington, D.C., is it, I am afraid to say."

"Terribly frustrating for you, Mr. President?"

"More than anyone except God Himself will ever know. For example: If I could have established an AIDS quarantine, I would have. It seems suicidal not to have done so. In virtually all other periods of epidemic throughout history, from ancient times to the modern, quarantines have been accepted as a necessity, and this one has perhaps the most devastating potential of all. But certain segments of our society got wind of it, labelled it as a transgression against their civil rights, and, well, as it turned out, they enlisted their cohorts in the media and in the judicial system and I soon had the columnists, the commentators, the judges, and the ACLU against me from the beginning. How blind we have become in this generation. Civil rights my foot! It's a matter of morality and the public health!"

"They would find Heaven a very quarantined place, in

one sense," I say in agreement. "No one is an idolater, effeminate, whoremonger, sorcerer . . ."

"How well I know that verse, how much it and others like it have guided me over the past seven years. The threats I received, many of them in the most obscene terms! That kind of reaction only strengthened my determination, I can assure you.

"In addition, I wanted to get prayer back in schools, but I was ridiculed as a religious fanatic. I wanted to help decent people in other lands to throw off the heavy rule of communism. And I was labelled a McCarthyite because of my oppression to that atheistic government. But the facts are there—persecution of Jews and Christians alike, intolerable conditions for any and all political prisoners. I—"

He interrupts himself, coughing more severely this time, and then continues, "Do you think God, in His infinite mercy, would introduce me to any of the Pilgrims and Puritans in Heaven?"

"I am sure He would be pleased to do so, Mr. President."

"How grand that would be. I want so much to tell them what I tried to do, to rekindle a little of the spirit of what they intended when they landed on these shores. And how ashamed I am of what the nation they died to create has become. Our air poisoned; our morality shrivelling up, an ugly distortion of their ideal; this land with more places of sin than there are churches.

"You know, good angel, I will enjoy eternity for many reasons, of course, but for one in particular."

"What would that be, Mr. President?"

"That I won't have to talk myself hoarse, that I won't have to fight yet day after day, week after week, month after month, year after year for what is good and decent and Christ-honoring. My spirit isn't weary, you must understand, but my mind, my body, there isn't any strength left."

He dies then, this President of the United States, as I stand by his body, and welcome the spirit that arises from it.

"No pain," he says with wonderment.

I nod.

"How old, how very old my body looks. It is true that the Presidency hastens age more than any other job in the world."

"But no longer," I say. "All that is over now. You will not have to prepare for any further battles with Congress, Mr. President."

"Angel?"

"Yes?"

"I hear some music."

And I do as well.

"Oh my . . ."

Against the background melody of an old Thanksgiving hymn, the President of the United States meets his first Pilgrim . . .

Washington, D. C., reacts with official mourning. Heads of government from all over the world come in under tight security. And yet even so a terrorist incident at Dulles International Airport shows that almost nothing is sacred in the atmosphere of this insane world.

A little girl is standing alone near the front entrance to the airline building where a delegation from England is scheduled to arrive.

Dressed in clothes that make her seem a harmless doll, she is holding a rather large handbag. Every so often she looks up at a passerby and smiles.

At the opposite side of the building, a British Airways plane lands. A total of twenty members of Parliament disembark. The Prime Minister and her husband are also on board, but she has had a slight case of airsickness. The others wait at the gate.

"She is supposed to be made of iron," whispers one of them.

"Please, Harold, do not be sarcastic," an associate responds. "You try to hide how much you really do admire the lady, but despite yourself, you cannot."

The other man is silent.

In a few minutes the couple joins them, and surrounded by security guards they head toward the entrance. The Prime Minister seems quite recovered, walking with a sure step.

As the party approaches, the little girl runs up to the first member of the delegation, and gives him the handbag. She is smiling with the sweetness, the innocence of the very young.

"Please, mister, my mommy—!"

She is unable to finish.

An explosion demolishes a large portion of the building, pieces of it scattering for nearly a mile. Most of those directly inside are killed—as well as many more on the outside, bodies flung in a dozen directions.

Several times the number of those dead are injured, blinded by shards of glass, flesh torn by metal, limbs severed, bones broken.

"A war zone!" says the U.S. government official observing the scene.

And that it appears to be. The terminal is in ruins, girders twisted like a toy erector set abused by a very angry child.

Shattered glass is so deep in some spots that—

Cries fill the air. Sirens form a continuous orchestration.

The Prime Minister has survived, but her husband is dead. She is asked by a member of the Joint Chiefs of Staff who has hurried to the airport if she would rather not attend the President's funeral but instead go directly to her hotel.

"Thank you, sir, but the First Lady needs me at this hour," she replies.

As she walks toward an awaiting limousine, she notices a tiny blood-stained dress, red with white lace at the edges, the body it once covered now in scattered pieces.

"Would that be—?" the Prime Minister starts to ask.

"Yes, madam, it is, I'm afraid," the general replies with ill-concealed reluctance.

"Please, sir, would you take my hand? I feel very weak now."

Reports have spread throughout Washington, D.C., with startling rapidity. Some discussion is given to delaying the President's funeral for a day. But that would create more massive security problems than it would resolve.

The First Lady is there. As are the members of Congress. Even the President's political enemies give him praise. One of them, a senior Senator responsible for defeating some of the President's most cherished programs, begins his speech but cannot continue, his grief beyond suppression.

Hundreds attend from scores of countries. The Russians. The Chinese. The French. The Italians. One nation after another, some for the diplomatic necessity of it, others out of a genuine regard for this man, and out of awareness for the fact that life is tenuous, whether it ends "naturally" or through the act of a terrorist group willing to use a child no one would suspect.

The Prime Minister of England now ascends the podium in front of the White House.

"When I left my native land, I had a husband," she says. "When the plane landed just two hours ago, he and I were planning to spend as much time with the First Lady as we could, given the affairs of state back home.

Now, in the midst of this nightmare day, she and I both need to comfort one another.

"Life begins with a miracle bestowed by the hand of God. It ends as we take His hand and He helps us from this mortal body. My husband died in my arms, but he died triumphantly, for his last words were, 'Dear, dear wife, the Savior is waiting, now, for me. An angel attends my way. You must leave me and hurry on, my dearest love.'

"That is in part why I have the strength to come before you now. But it is just a part, however important it is. The other lies in words spoken to me by your President less than a week before his illness claimed him. The words may be familiar to some of you. They are from the Book of Revelation:

"'And he shewed me a pure river of water of life, clear as crystal, proceeding out of the throne of God and of the Lamb. In the midst of the street of it, and on either side of the river, was there the tree of life, which bare twelve manner of fruits, and yielded her fruit every month: and the leaves of the tree were for the healing of nations . . . And there shall be no night there; and they need no candle, neither light of the sun; for the Lord God giveth them light: and they shall reign forever and ever.'

"*That* is the future, ladies and gentlemen, the only one that matters. Right now, as I speak, the President of the United States and my minister-husband are where no bombs can touch them, no lies can hurt them, no pain can sap their strength."

Tears trickle down the sides of her cheek.

"Forgive me," she says as she collapses into the arms of the First Lady.

The next morning, the Prime Minister of England boards a plane with the body of the man she loved for thirty-five years . . .

$*$ $*$ $*$

Even so, government continues on as always, for the better as well as for the worse . . .

I find prayer breakfasts and an organization called Congresswomen for Christ and other such—wonderful to see, encouraging, of course, but along with them, and in greater abundance are the lobbyists for the various industries whose products have caused a great deal of the pain of the world: the liquor lobbyists; the American Tobacco Institute lobbyists; the ones pushing legalization of marijuana; those who favor making prostitution legal. On and on—a veritable sea of them, foaming with the poisons inflicted by their own "doctrines" in opposition to those of Almighty God.

Does it stun me to find the American Tobacco Institute swarming with demonic activity—no real possession, actually, but slavering hordes of oppressors? I overhear several of them discussing a game plan.

"No one can easily make the case that tobacco in itself is evil."

"That may be true, for the moment, but I would not be excessively confident."

"You are too easily upset. The fact is that we have an ideal environment here that has been working out nicely for years."

"Yes, make smoking socially acceptable. Make it commercially profitable. And help form an organization funded to make it respectable, and keep it that way."

"Marvelous! But that has been only the beginning. The *pain* we can inflict, the suffering!"

This one demon is fairly ecstatic with enthusiasm.

"I thought I had died and gone to Heaven—well, you know what I mean—when I saw that chap coughing his life away from emphysema," he continues. "It was wonderful, I tell you. The blood and phlegm and other stuff gushing out of his mouth. And the suffocation he was feeling because of the damage to his lungs. I was delirious for a long time after that, my thoughts jumping ahead decades to encompass all the possibilities."

Says another: "And the retarded children! Wow! What we fail to abort, we can cripple, we can retard, we can do so much else!"

One demon seems to glow as he adds, "And *then* we zap them with *euthanasia*. I do not know about the rest of you, but I want to be there when they kill the first mongoloid idiot legally!"

They are gleeful, planning a whole monstrous tapestry of mischief to be inflicted during the weeks, months, years ahead.

I visit other organizations, each dedicated to spreading its own "doctrine." My next stop is one dealing with freedom of speech and the press.

I encounter a variety of discussions there, in offices, and behind conference room doors. A man who publishes pornography is discussing his chain of adult bookstores. The lobbyists are nodding in agreement.

"It's a free country, you know," the pornographer is saying. "If I want to show some skin, that's exactly what I'll do. This ain't Russia after all, you know. People get their jollies from the stuff in my stores, you know."

"Exactly," a lobbyist agreed out loud.

"Why, you know, I've doubled the number of private booths. I'm providing a real service, you know. I've even had a special deodorizing system so that the places won't smell, you know, like those gay bathhouses. I've got the best line of plastic toys in the industry. And, you know, the aromatics—just great—a cheap high—and my films and books, you know. What more could the stupid public ask for?"

"Yes, yes, absolutely," a Greek chorus responds.

He opens up an attache case and takes out a pile of magazines.

"These are what America is all about," he says.

"I should say so," one of the lobbyists agrees as he leafs through a copy.

"Just good clean sex," the man says, licking his lips. "I mean, where would, you know, that guy from Lynchburg be, you know, without sex?"

Everyone bursts into laughter.

"Look at those," he says, pointing to a centerfold. "Lust, you know, good old lust. That's what makes this world, you know, go around, guys."

I leave though I would rather have disputed everything he said. I would rather have given him the volumes of police reports that indicated that the majority of all violent crime resulting in death had a sexual base. Not to mention the epidemic of sexually transmitted diseases— the disintegration of families—just the kinds of byproducts that his "good old lust" propagated.

Freedom of speech was never meant to bring about the license to engage in any type of lustful, degrading, demoralizing enterprises, allowed to spread their poison because trying to stop this would be "un-American." I can say that from having visited only a little while ago the men who created the Constitution, spending time by their side and hearing all the reasons behind what they would write, what they would desire for the nation.

And further back, hundreds of years, I was with the Pilgrims and Puritans. I heard the essence of what their vision for America was. A country free of persecution but also a country founded on the premise of a new Israel, a land devoted to God, a land that would be free but a freedom with different connotations than the word bruited about in modern times. It was not freedom, they would have said, looking at the United States of the current day, for men and women to be enslaved to promiscuous sex, to violence, to drugs. A law-abiding country was not one in which countless numbers broke moral laws, laws handed down by the Creator. There was *never* to have been *that* kind of freedom or license. In the days of the Pilgrims and Puritans, anyone caught in the sin of adultery or homosexuality would have been dealt with in exceedingly harsh terms. Too harsh, it might be asked? Too unloving? Too judgmental? That which is clearly stated in God's Word, that which is without equivocation branded intolerable should not be overlooked, should *not* be permitted by those who claim the name of His Son, under the guise of not wanting to be judgmental. Oh, what cancers are allowed to run unchecked in the name of non-judgmentalism!

I visit other organizations—set up to serve the elderly, the poor, the homeless. Most are strapped for cash; most have almost to beg for the dollars they need. Yet the tobacco lobby, the gay lobby, the pro-abortion lobby, others of that ilk seem to have no problem finding dollars, for their money is carried to them in sacks on the backs of those dying of lung cancer, and those who are retarded, and those who head for X-rated films instead of being with their families. In a world of evil triumphant, a world of too few good men and women doing too little to stem the tide, to dam it up so that it cannot spread any further, in such a world, the Washington, D. C., lobbyists, sustained by those profiting from the moral degradation, are always going to be ahead, running around like termites eating into the very structure of society, and helped by armies of workers, with banks of computers and millions of brochures and press releases, and unlimited media access, media controlled by those of like mind and spirit.

And where are the Christians? I ask myself, reflecting on that first, fine family at the outset of my sojourn on Earth. Where is the salt of the earth? Salt is supposed to prevent spoiling. Without the salt, there is decay.

I visit some Christian lobbyists who are having money problems, but some others are not, at least not as severe. They are good at raising money. They are good at spending it. And then the other lobbyists, the unsaved ones who would like to see the hastened disintegration of Christian influence in the United States and elsewhere, take the weapon that has been handed to them, the weapon of financial accountability, and fling it back into the heart of Christianity, and those thus wounded cry and scream and raise a fist at the evil world around them.

I stand, amazed, at one ministry in particular. The head of it lives in a home worth $600,000; he has parties in a houseboat valued at $100,000; his wife has a diamond ring worth $20,000; and he just spent $1,000,000 on designing and building a cafeteria so that, to use his words, "my people can eat in style."

That ministry is located not very far from Washington, D. C. Of course, when you are an angel, distance is of no consequence; but I suppose some of the habits, the conventions about time and such that the human beings around me have, are beginning to affect my own thinking.

In any event, I visit the headquarters of that ministry. I see a fleet of limousines carrying guests about.

"They were donated," someone says in response to another's question, the very question I would have raised if I could have done so. But the money was still spent, I would retort; it could have been used to buy less luxurious transportation, and the difference used to support more missionaries or feed more of the poor or given to other needful ministries—the fact that the limousines were donated is irrelevant under the circumstances. (Was the $20,000 diamond ring donated also? I wonder.)

I see the building designed to house visitors, the hanging crystal chandeliers in the lobby, the plush carpeting, the leather-covered sofas and chairs, the imported marble, the hand-carved statues.

"It was bought and paid for through a special fund donated by our supporters," I hear. Some specious reasoning—millions of dollars siphoned away from the mission field, the stomachs of hungry children, the ministries barely able to pay their heating bills.

And I see one little woman, probably in her late-seventies, wandering around, astonished by what she sees, appalled by it as well. She goes into a jewelry store on the premises, sees a particularly fine-looking diamond ring, and finds out that it has just been traded in by the founder's wife who wanted something a bit more elaborate.

She leaves that store, that building. She walks to a bench in a shaded grove nearby. She bows her head, and prays aloud, "Father, take me from this place."

But the vast majority of those present seem joyous. A group of them is singing a hymn back in the lobby. Others are eating a buffet lunch. A mother is holding her daughter, both of them well-dressed. A brass-plated piano is played by someone in a tuxedo.

Getting up to speak is a member of the hierarchy, a vice president of the ministry, who tells of the need for sacrifice, enabling the Lord's work to continue—while not letting you know that his salary is $200,000 a year, and there are others being paid higher sums than that! How much of an abomination this must be in the eyes of God is not lost on me. Many people are indeed sacrificing to keep that ministry going. But just that vice president's salary alone requires a donation of $100 annually from each of 2000 elderly supporters. He lives in a large $250,000 house, so add another 2500 to that number. And he has an expense account greater than the income of thousands of the Christians giving to the ministry. How pathetic! I scream, realizing that I know those figures because the man had told them, earlier, to a visitor-friend, not braggingly, no, not that, but matter-of-factly; which may have been worse actually. Thousands of men and women faithfully giving of their earnings or their retirement incomes, thinking that all this is going for the support of missionaries, for example, and not knowing what is really happening.

Next, there is entertainment. The founder and his wife appear on a stagelike area in the midst of the lobby. Other lights darken, and a spotlight is turned on the two of them. Both are wearing hand-tailored clothes. The founder's wife has more jewelry than just that one large diamond ring; her necklace, bracelet, earrings—all are glittering.

"Everybody enjoying themselves?" she asks.

A roar of affirmation is heard.

Virtually all of those present are caught up in the atmosphere that is, yes, deliberately constructed, a kind of retreat from the outside world.

A truth dawns on me. That is the problem. It is a cocoon of crushed velour and leather and crystal and diamonds and hand-tailored tweed and brass and so much else. But the cocoon is not eternal; it is transitory; from it they must emerge, after a week, even a month, to face that very world from which they have retreated.

"It's a ministry," a guide, beaming, tells one of the visitors.

But to whom? A dying mother from the streets of Alexandria, Egypt—a starving child from the sands of Ethiopia? A missionary from Calcutta, India? And how is it to minister? As an example of what is in store for *every* Christian? Eating in style in a million-dollar cafeteria? Dressing in style? Living in style? Driving in style? Partying in style? The by-products of . . . *faith?*

And what of the times when none of this shields, none of this is there to cling to, to look at, in a sense to hug around the body and the spirit like some gigantic blanket? If this is what faith brings, where is faith when donations drop, when bills cannot be paid, when the diamond ring seems more like a finger raised in a gesture of obscenity?

I leave that ministry sadly. For I sense among those present a kind of substitute for true spirituality. Oh, they are saved, yes, a fact about which I have little question, at least in most of the instances I see, their love of Him obvious. And perhaps this is what really counts, and count it does, but there is more, of course, going beyond the trappings of luxury, that image the world around sees, an image of extravagance, of a Christianity as much based upon the externals of affluence as the internals of salvation, regeneration. Take away the former and there is still the latter, without question, but then it boils down to the quality of life. And how high will be that quality if the externals are eventually gone, replaced by the more mundane, yes indeed, the more typical world known by many more Americans?

I journey on to Atlantic City, a place of glitter in the midst of continuing decay and moral corruption . . .

The man seems old, but he probably is not. His face is so wrinkled that it gives nearly an ancient impression; his hair is straggly, not a great deal of it left. His eyes are bloodshot, his hand trembles as he lifts a soup spoon to his lips. Someone to his right coughs and he mutters something about spreading germs. Finally he finishes the chicken noodle soup and leans back on the folding metal chair, waiting for the rest of the meal. He wipes some specks off slacks that are worn bare at the knees and torn loose from the stitches on the sides. His shoes have served him countless miles of pavement and asphalt pounding, but they will not last much longer. He has 20 cents in his pocket.

The director and his staff do the best they can, but the load is enormous. Each year there is a deficit; each year anxious moments are experienced; each year, the transient population grows, swelling larger and larger, bloated by drug addicts, alcoholics, and those addicted to another pursuit: gambling.

Row after row of cots take up all the space in several rooms. Each one is occupied. A waiting list haunts the director and the other workers.

"We trust the Lord for everything," he says simply to a visitor from out of town, someone interested in helping to support the mission.

The director shows the visitor, a businessman in his mid-forties, around the premises. The work is orderly, effective, but certainly not showy.

"We make the dollars go as far as we can," the director comments. "There is no fat here."

The businessman is impressed. After spending several hours at the mission, he leaves to return home in another state. A short time later, he commits to a regular schedule of donations.

But others, as I find out, are attracted to the glamour of the other ministry and ones like it, caught up in the aura of prospering, and put off by the more basic work of that rescue mission and ones elsewhere across the land.

One man is shaking violently, vomiting over the male staff member trying to help him. The director is called in, decides that they need a doctor for the man. The latter has stopped heaving, at least for the moment. He looks up at the staff member, covered with slop, and at the director and says, his voice hoarse, barely audible, "God does love me even now, doesn't He?" The director replies, "Even as we do."

A doctor comes, gives the man a sedative. In the meantime, the staff member has changed clothes, and the three of them sit in the director's office.

"I don't know how you take all this," the doctor says to the two of them.

"We do it because God wants us to reach out to these men," the staffer replies. "We might *want* to give up sometimes. Throwing in the towel would be easier than cleaning off the stuff somebody has thrown up all over you. But the alternative is to abandon them, and none of us here could live with ourselves if we did that."

The director is obviously, and rightly, pleased at what his staffer has said. He adds only this: "These men have burdens the rest of us will never have to carry. The pain in their eyes is so overpowering with most of them that, well, anyone who is unmoved must be a statue made of stone."

He rubs his chin, an ironic smile on his face as he says, "Periodically the gambling interests offer to help fund the work. From the beginning we have turned them down. Gambling and allied problems are behind what we are seeing here. We can't accept help from those responsible in the first place."

I leave them, and go outside. It is near dusk in Atlantic City. A line of transients is waiting to get into the mission.

But, I say in words unheard by any of them, where are the diamonds?

I feel utterly alone. I have been alone, of course, from the very beginning, at least in the sense of not being joined by others like me, angels who chose not to follow a new leader. But somehow, now, the loneliness is more pervasive, a mournful dirge all about me, the music that of prostitutes soliciting customers on Atlantic Avenue; of chickenhawks cruising near the Boardwalk; of high-

rollers screaming as they lose thousands of dollars; of gangsters in dark corners fixing deals; of the elderly walking the streets because they can no longer afford rents boosted higher and higher by greedy new apartment building owners; of this, and of that, and so much else, a dirge reaching up, I am sure, to Heaven itself.

*P*HILOSOPHER IS DYING.

I hear them talking about that fact. But he himself is smiling, counterpointing their sad expressions.

"I go to be with Him," Philosopher says simply.

Several minutes later, he is "on stage" for his last public appearance, this one in a large college auditorium that has virtually no seats empty, for Philosopher's fame is great. No one in the audience realizes how close to death he is. Only the members of his family and his physicians and his pastor are aware. They had vigorously protested any expenditure of strength on another public meeting, but Philosopher was unyielding.

"There may be one more human being out there whom the Lord wants me to be His instrument in reaching," he told them. "I cannot disappoint my Savior."

And so he sits, in a softly padded chair, looking at the 3000 students, faculty members, and parents waiting to hear him speak.

"I am honored that you are willing to sit and listen to the ramblings of an old man," he says, his voice normally rather thin, and the loudspeaker system has to be adjusted so he can be heard by everyone.

"I want to present only what God allows me to say. I now await His leading."

He bows his head for a moment, and the audience waits patiently.

Philosopher finally looks up again, tears trickling down his cheeks.

"When I was the age of most of you, I did not know what to believe. How could I look at that which was so apparently real and physical, with form and substance, so that whatever it was could be touched and held, and say that a white-haired old man somewhere in the sky created it all by just waving his hands a few times?

"I could not accept any of that, for it seemed to me the stuff of delusion, and I had managed to convince myself that I was smarter than most people, and, as a consequence, certainly less gullible than the 'religious.'

"I started early with this attitude, I must admit. Usually it hits young people later, in college, as some of you can verify, when they are away from the influence of parents."

And he tells them about the years of agnosticism that plagued him, years of careless living, rather like a prodigal squandering everything in rebellion against his father, except in this instance, he did not even believe that he had such a father.

"And then I stood by my flesh-and-blood father's bedside. He had been praying for me all those years. I held his hand, and remember to this day how very cold it was.

" 'Son,' he said to me. 'I have always been truthful with you, have I not?' I agreed that he had. No matter how much I disagreed with my father, I knew he was incapable of lying. 'Will you believe me if I tell you that there is a God and that, right now, my hand is in His, just as my other is in yours?' My whole sense of rationalism rejected what he was telling me. 'Son,' my father continued, 'why have you kept your Bible if you feel that it is nothing but a collection of myths and legends?' I was stunned. How could he have known that? He might reasonably have assumed that I had thrown it away. 'Son, you marked one passage in particular—Revelation 21:4—why?' I could not answer him at first. Who had told my father? A student at college? A professor? But how could anybody have found out, for one thing? No one had access to that Bible except me, because I kept it locked away.

"My father had been crying until then. Yet even as I looked at him, the tears were disappearing, almost as though Someone were wiping them away. He reached up his left hand, and I took it in mine. 'I love you, son,' he said, his voice getting weaker and weaker. He had been in a lot of pain over the month or so prior to that. And a few hours earlier, he had tossed and turned, little cries escaping his lips. But during those present moments, he seemed stronger. His hand gripped mine firmly, resolutely. His eyes sparkled. 'Dad,' I asked gently, 'how did you know?' He replied, 'I didn't.' Then he closed his eyes and never opened them again."

Philosopher stops briefly, the memories still poignant, his own tears glistening under the glare of overhead spotlights.

"As many of you know, that passage of Scripture is as follows: 'And God shall wipe away all tears from their eyes; and there shall be no more death, neither sorrow, nor crying, neither shall there be any more pain: for the former things are passed away.'

"I wanted to tell myself that it was a kind of delusion, that some special mixture of adrenaline and the medicine had revived him temporarily, and the drying of the tears was quite natural. But that still did not explain how my father knew about that Bible and that passage. I had marked it only a few weeks before, long after he had been confined to bed, as a futile hope—at least that is what I considered it to be, an exercise, really—that when my father died, it would not be in a moment of pain, that he would go quietly. We often argued—perhaps debated is a better word—about matters of the spirit, but I loved him deeply, and to have him slip away on a bed of agony would have been intolerable for me. I could not have faced that without going off the deep end, as they say.

"From that afternoon on, I began a slow climb back to faith. A day, a week, more time passed, and I came to believe. Skepticism reared up from time to time, a dragon that had to be fought back constantly. I don't think it is ever really slain. I think it retreats in many of us, waiting for events or circumstances or people or a combination thereof to resurrect it with special ferocity. Becoming a Christian doesn't banish the Devil from us for the rest of our days. It seems to me that the evil one is, rather, driven to a redoubling of his efforts when one over whom he once held sway breaks loose and—"

For Philosopher, there is no doubt that Lucifer is the root of evil, the instigator of corrosive doubt, doubt that builds up a thick, high wall between the sinner and God.

He stops for a little while, sips some water, closes his eyes again, while praying, and then is ready for another segment of the evening.

"I would be very happy to answer any questions you might like to put to me."

An athletic-looking young man near the front raises his hand, and Philosopher asks him to speak.

"Sir, it has always puzzled me as to how God can be in Heaven, and yet indwelling anyone through the Holy Spirit. How can He manage to be in both of these places at the same time?"

Philosopher smiles and says, "I'm very glad we are starting with the easy ones."

There is a murmur of appreciative chuckling in the audience.

"I believe we can approach the matter in this way. Take

a hypnotist—I don't approve of hypnotism and so this example is one with which I am not entirely comfortable, but it may shed a little light on the answer to your question—this hypnotist hypnotizes you, my young friend, and implants within your mind what is commonly called a posthypnotic suggestion. It might be perhaps to eat pickles at midnight or stand in the middle of Madison Avenue and shout, 'The Martians are coming, the Martians are coming.'"

Considerable laughter . . .

"But, whatever it is, that urge is now inside you. The hypnotist snaps his fingers and you are now out of the trance into which he had put you. He stays where he is, which is Fairbanks, Alaska, and you return to your home in Tampa, Florida—many thousands of miles between the two of you. At noon, three days later, you suddenly get up in the middle of chemistry class and announce to everyone, 'I know for a fact now that the world is flat. I almost fell off the edge yesterday.'"

There is no laughter this time because the growing truth of what Philosopher is putting before them begins to become clear to those present.

"There we have it, my friend. That hypnotist is still in Fairbanks, and yet you have just acted upon what his spirit dictated to your spirit. In a very real sense, he resides inside you, and you have just obeyed him."

The teenager continues standing, saying nothing further, pondering the words that have lodged themselves in his mind. He then simply nods twice, and sits down, but he has been reached, indeed he has been reached.

"I will add that in our relationship with Almighty God, the difference is that He actually is within us, whereas only the hypnotist's suggestion has been implanted. And also, I hasten to add, for the hypnotist's subject there is really no choice in the matter—he has been taken over, in a sense. God comes in and stays, true, but He contin-

ues to allow us the free exercise of our will. But this
illustration, which I heard a number of years ago, is
perhaps the closest I personally have ever come to a
comprehensible explanation of what the mystery of indwelling is all about."

Philosopher pauses, a jolt of pain hitting his abdomen.
He feels abruptly weaker.

But he continues, managing the suggestion of a smile.

"Surely there are other questions?"

Another young man, short, bespectacled, raises his
hand and Philosopher asks him to stand.

"You seem to be saying, sir, in more than one of your
books, that Satan and his helpers are spreading their
influence everywhere. But I thought only God was om-
nipresent. Would you clear up my confusion?"

Philosopher responds without hesitation:

"Very simple, actually. Have any of your friends been
experimenting with drugs?"

"But, sir—"

"You do not have to name them—just tell me if any
have done this."

"I suppose they have."

"Where did they get their drugs?"

"Sir, I couldn't answer that here!"

"It is not my intention to have either you or your
friends end up in jail or murdered by some member of the
underworld, not at all. What I meant was, simply, what
sort of person?"

"A pusher . . ."

"Your friends obtain their supply from a drug pusher, is
that correct?"

"Yes . . ."

"And then what happens?"

"I don't understand."

"What happens after the drug pusher leaves?"

"They take the drugs, naturally."

"I must correct you, young man. Taking drugs is never natural. In any event, I assume they do this sort of activity either through a vein or their nostrils or through their mouth. Am I right?"

"Yes, sir, you are."

"Do they generally buy enough of a supply to last a while?"

"Yes."

"As much as they can afford?"

"I guess you could say that."

"How many of your friends are addicts?"

"Sir, I don't mean to be disrespectful, but I fail to see what this has to do with Satan."

"You will, you truly will, and that I promise. How many of your friends are addicts?"

"More than I care to admit."

"It is alarming, is it not, when these friends of yours do become addicts?"

"Yes, sir, it is. They're throwing their lives away. I—I try to help them, but it seems almost hopeless."

"And why is that?"

"They can't break the habit."

"It has a grip on them?"

"Oh, yes, absolutely."

"And yet before they met their pusher, it was not like that?"

"Not at all."

"He does not hang around all the time, does he?"

"No, he—"

The young man pauses, a smile of awareness spreading across his features.

"Sir, you mean that once he gives them the habit, they carry it on themselves. If they don't get the drugs from him, they'll find a supply elsewhere."

"That is precisely what I mean, son. And so it is with Satan. He caused our sin nature from the very beginning.

He can hook those without Christ—and even many so-called carnal Christians—in the same way a pusher hooks a soon-to-be addict. Once the obsession, the addiction if you will, with sex or drugs or money or things is commenced, all he has to make sure of is that there is a supply around to entice, to maintain the addiction. He does not need his demons for that. He himself is certainly not necessary in this regard. People aid his awful designs— the Mafia with its drug and pornography and prostitution businesses, for example. As you can see, so much of what we have around us is inspired by Satan, but he hardly needs to be on call twenty-four hours a day. Advertisers spend billions of dollars to promote so many sinful desires in order to sell their products that I lost count a long time ago. Satan created this kind of atmosphere, the moral, spiritual atmosphere which we breathe today. A brilliant chap, this Satan, this Devil, this Lucifer; his handiwork saves him a great deal of legwork."

The young man thanks Philosopher and sits down. Next, a girl in the middle of the large semicircular auditorium raises her hand. Philosopher indicates that she can stand.

"Sir, you believe, as you have stated in your books, that most of the media are under demonic influence. Have you had occasion to change your mind about that outlook at all?"

Philosopher does not hesitate in replying:

"I have not. And there are many reasons. But one of the most compelling is what the Bible terms 'knowing them by their fruits.' What are the fruits of the media? Promotion of promiscuity is often the stuff of comedy, winking with approval at that which has generated broken marriages, broken homes, diseases that breed insanity, disablement, and death. And we have the modern spectacle that involves the lifting up of perversion as—"

Shouting occurs toward the back of the auditorium. A young man is standing, angrily shouting at Philosopher.

"Son, I cannot hear very well what you are saying. Would you kindly step up to the front or at least a bit closer, would you do that, please?"

The young man climbs over to the aisle and walks up to the stage.

"I happen to be gay. And I am offended that you referred to my lifestyle as perversion."

"Oh, did I?"

"Yes, you did."

"But all I managed to say was a single word—perversion. You seem to have filled in the rest of that on your own."

Someone snickers, then is quiet.

The boy is momentarily flustered.

"But is it not so? Your books apparently make no secret of how you feel."

"You are correct. But I am far from being the originator of that truth. God is. And His Word is quite outspoken on that subject."

"Sir, I feel that you are wrong."

"But, son, that is the trouble. You do not *know* that I am wrong. Nor do you know, as you undoubtedly believe, that the Bible reflects only the mood of the times in which it was written. You know nothing of the sort as *fact*. You only *feel* that it must be so because you admittedly have feelings toward other men, and these feel quite normal and decent to you. Therefore, you conclude, there is nothing wrong with them. You use feelings as your guide, do you not?"

"Yes, that is correct . . ."

"How many times have you been to a dentist over the years?"

"I don't understand the relevancy, sir, of that question."

"Please, would you be willing to humor an old man and provide an answer to my silly little question?"

The teenager nods, then replies, "Half a dozen probably."

"For cleanings, fillings, that sort of thing."

"Yes, sir. Once I had to have a root canal done."

"Oh, my, yes! I have had more than one of those. Simply awful business!"

The boy adds, in agreement, "I remember one time, it was so bad, the pain, I—I thought I was going to die."

Philosopher stands, with effort, and walks over to the edge of the stage.

"You mean, son, do you not, that the pain was so awful, so intense, that you *felt* as though you were actually going to die? And not as a figure of speech, either?"

"Yes, I—" he starts to say.

"But, lo and behold, you are here now, before God and Man, alive. How accurate were your *feelings* then?"

The teenager can say nothing. He stands for a second or two, looking embarrassed and humbled, and turns to walk back to his seat.

"Feelings are wonderful much of the time," Philosopher says. "Feelings can be God's gift. Anyone who has ever loved—and all of us have—knows what a joy it is to love. But not all kinds of love are proper. Can we love money and still please Him? Can we love another's spouse and still honor Him? Can we love to see naked images in a magazine or a film and have God honor that? Genghis Khan loved power; the real Count Dracula loved to impale little children on stakes. A mass murderer named Gacy loved to lure teenagers to his home and seduce them, and dismember them, and bury them all over his property. More than thirty boys died because he loved to hear them cry in pain.

"Love can be grand, ennobling, persuading men and

women toward the finest acts, the most inspiring deeds, the greatest courage, the most honorable intent. But not all that is called love is like that. Can you see this truth? And God has said that those who love wrongly and continue to do so will be punished."

The young man, who has not reached his seat, turns around angrily.

"Sir, surely you are not referring to AIDS?"

Philosopher looks squarely at the questioner.

"Surely, young man, you are not referring to God?"

Philosopher bends down and takes off his shoe, holds it out to the teenager.

"Do you see that?" he asks.

"Yes, it is a shoe."

"It does not fit very well. There is a place at the heel which is rubbing against my flesh. I noticed just this morning that there is a blister."

The young man is silent, a frown on his forehead.

"But I was hasty, wanting to get here on time. While I knew the one shoe presented a problem, I slipped the pair on without really thinking, my haste overriding my memory and, also, my common sense."

"Yes, sir . . ." the boy says a bit impatiently.

"My heel was never meant to have anything rubbing against it in that way. But I have a choice. I can switch to a different pair of shoes, and alleviate the problem, or I can stay with these day after day, week after week, month after month, and at some point I will have worn through to the bone if I haven't caused infection, including gangrene, in the meantime, followed by a spread of that up my leg and eventually throughout my body if I do nothing, even something as desperate, as extreme as amputating my leg. If I keep that pair of shoes, and let the infection spread, and my whole body is riddled with it and, my young friend, I die, is that a judgment from God or the most appalling, wasteful stupidity on my part?

Please do not lay at the doorstep of my Lord and Savior what your own blindness forces you to ignore."

It is obvious that Philosopher is very, very weak. He walks slowly back to his chair, and almost collapses into it. His family whispers to him that he must stop.

"I must go in a little while," he says with great tenderness to the audience, looking out over the thousands listening to him. "I am very grateful that you have come here this night. May we make the next question the final one, please?"

Another student, a girl, raises her hand, and Philosopher asks her to come forward.

"Sir, as you indicated earlier, you once could not bring yourself to believe in God. I cannot now, either. Help me, please."

Philosopher speaks, but his voice is barely above a whisper. He motions her to come up to him. She climbs the steps and approaches him.

"I am dying, my young friend. Let me tell you that there is a God, and even as I speak, He is welcoming me into Heaven."

He looks at her, his eyes wide, a smile lighting up his face. He reaches out his hand, and she takes it.

"Your father says to tell you that he loves you, and is happy now."

Then Philosopher's head tilts to the left, the hand drops, and he is dead.

The girl starts to sob as she turns around to face the audience.

"My father," she tells them, "died a week ago. The last thing he said—he—he said to me was that he prayed I—I—I would—would accept the gift of faith and—and—peace that he wanted to leave behind."

She leaves the stage as Philosopher's doctor rushes to the still, frail form in that chair. But he is no longer there;

that suit of clothes has been shed. His spirit has left his body. Instantly he sees me.

"You have been here from the first minutes?" He asks with awe.

"Yes, Philosopher, I have."

"Are you to take me to my Lord?"

I cannot answer.

He turns, looks upward.

"Jesus," he says. "Oh, dearest, dearest Friend."

And he is gone.

OUTSIDE.

The night air is clear. A great many stars are apparent. Memories flood in on me. I ache to return to my home, for Heaven is my home, my birthplace. I have gone through the centuries on Earth, soared the globe, witnessed a whole encyclopedia of people, events.

It is time to—

"Darien!"

I hear the voice as I am walking away from that college auditorium.

I stop immediately, a thin trickle of dread working its way into me, expanding until I nearly continue on, not daring to turn, not wanting to face—

"Darien! Please listen, my friend."

I turn very slowly.

"Hello, Darien. It has been a long time."

DuRong!

I say nothing at first, unable to speak. DuRong, the angel who was closest to Lucifer in Heaven, stands in front of me—and—and—

"You have been looking for my friend, have you not?" he says, smiling.

"Yes, I have, DuRong. Why are you and the others not inside?"

Hundreds of other fallen angels are gathering in back of DuRong. I see them in the darkness, hovering, almost buzzing like a swarm of bees. Most are pathetic in appearance, distorted and twisted and—

"No one was willing to welcome us in," he says, laughing harshly.

He comes toward me.

"Oh, Darien, there is so much to discuss."

"Yes, there is."

"Glad you agree!"

We walk away from the others. He sees me as I cast an apprehensive look at them.

"You have little to fear from them, Darien," he indicates. "You are one of us, are you not?"

A familiar chill grips me.

DuRong looks little different, still quite majestic—the others have changed with shocking totality but not him, so much like Lucifer. His voice is as nearly as rich, as powerful, like all the greatest opera singers and all the finest public speakers ever born, and yet greater even than that.

I begin to feel a hint of old awe, since DuRong is indeed close to the magnificence of Lucifer himself. While it would be stupid to ignore so much of what I had seen that agreed with all the ghastly stories about Satan, yet other details did not. Why had Lucifer's followers become so loathsome—and DuRong, for one, had remained as grand, as awe-inspiring as ever? Beside him, Michael and the others, including myself, were pallid imitations, reflections in a mirror that had faded disastrously.

"You cannot know how glad I am to see you," DuRong remarks with apparent sincerity. "The others are hardly an inspiration in the remotest sense of the word, but you, Darien, yes, you are very, very different. But, then, I doubt that you realize how very much alike, in every way, the three of us are."

DuRong is casting a spell, I know, but then, like Lucifer he is expert at this, and I am not immune to being drawn to it.

"Let me show you the other side of Earth," he suggests. "I imagine, from the reports Lucifer and I have received, that you have been exposed to the worst that could be seen, the areas where perhaps those serving him may have misunderstood his intentions."

I agree to go with him.

"That *is* wonderful. You make me very happy, Darien, very happy indeed."

The first stop is an opera house. A ballet is in progress.

"That *is* very beautiful," I admit, pointing to the man and woman on stage.

"Both are atheists, you know," DuRong says. "They rejected God a long time ago. That has not stopped them from giving the world discernible perfection in their art. How magnificently they dance! Why not join me for the rest of the performance, Darien?"

The beauty of their moves across the stage is undeniable. Both are in their prime, slim, coordinated, well-trained. Members of the audience gasp at what they achieve in their art, knowing how very difficult it is, appreciating the self-denial indicated by years of exceptionally hard work.

"It comes only after enormous dedication, my friend," DuRong indicates. "They both get up very early in the morning, and stay at it until late at night. Everything is planned with the utmost care—from their exercising to their ballet practice to their meals, yes, everything. And it has *been* like that since they were quite young."

After the performance, DuRong and I leave.

"There is beauty without God, you know," DuRong

says proudly. "In Mankind reservoirs of such creativity, such glorious potential, remain only to be tapped."

After the ballet, we go elsewhere—an opera singer at the Met in New York City; a stage actress giving the performance of her life on Broadway; a gallery in which stunning art is displayed.

"Most of that owes no allegiance to God," DuRong observes. "In fact, a greater number than you can know did their very finest work *after* they shed debilitating guilt, the inhibitions foisted upon them by what *He* demanded in their lives before He would accept them as having any worth at all."

"But, DuRong, that just is not the answer. Is it so wrong to expect them to be moral, to follow the Ten Commandments, to accept His Son into their lives?"

"But the implication *is* that unless they do *all* of that, they are worthless, like worms plowing through garbage every single moment of their lives."

"No, it is not that at all. They have worth; they have genius, creativity, all that is fine and good. But until they take that final step—"

"There is more to see, Darien," he interrupts.

He shows me a home for retarded children. A treatment center for cancer victims. A hospital specializing in reconstructive surgery for burn victims.

"Very beautiful, is it not?" he says proudly. "Could there be anything more loving, more sensitive, more noble than what you have seen? And, Darien, *none* of it can be attributed to God. All of it comes from Man's own instincts. In fact, the home for retarded children is financed by a lifelong atheist. One of the skin specialists at the burn center had studied at one point to be a priest but came to perceive the inherent inconsistencies in Christianity, Catholic and Protestant."

I keep my silence.

There are other places we visit, DuRong showing them off to me with ill-concealed relish.

We pass by a disheveled man in his late thirties. His clothes are torn, his face and hands very dirty, his hair stringy.

"What about him?" DuRong asks. "Where is God's mercy with that individual? Is that how He treats His blessed children?"

I can stand no more.

Lord, give me the words, take upon Yourself my usual ineptitude, make me a channel for Your wisdom . . .

"He ruined his life, that chap," DuRong has continued. "He is rejected, sick, alone. I fail to see God, so-called loving as He is, doing a damn thing for him."

"It is ironic that *you* are the one using that word, DuRong."

"Which word?"

"Damn."

"Surely you have heard much worse while you have been here? Why does it upset you so?"

"Oh, I have. All of those words probably. The difference is that you and the others are responsible for his damnation in the first place. You put temptation before him; you *created* the gun that *he* has placed to his own head admittedly, but without the gun there in the first place, he would have nothing to use. I speak of a gun only symbolically. It is much broader than that, much more perverse. There is no gun, of course; it is simply another word for the alcohol that has eaten away his inside, that has destroyed his mind. God had nothing to do with that."

DuRong laughs hoarsely.

"Show me what He has done to *stop* what is happening."

"God has offered forgiveness through Christ."

"And that is supposed to solve everything, Darien? I

thought you were more realistic than that. If forgiveness means that an Adolf Hitler is going to be in Heaven, I am very glad we left."

"I doubt that Hitler *asked* for forgiveness. But then, now that you mention it, who created Adolf Hitler in the first place?"

"God? Does He not create everyone and all things?"

"True. But what God brought to life was a child He desired to be His own. What made him the Hitler he became was the world you and your fellow demons threw up around him. *You* turned his life upside down. *You* corrupted his mind. *You* twisted a genius into a madman. And Hitler *was* a genius. Few can deny that fact. That his genius became evil, perverted, diabolical is not the fault of God but of yours, of the others—D'Seaver's, D'Filer's . . . of—"

"You still are not convinced, are you, Darien? You hesitate even in saying Lucifer's name."

"I hesitate because if it is true that he is as malevolent as has been claimed through the centuries, then the Lucifer who once was, the Lucifer whom I once—"

"Loved? Is that what you were about to say, Darien? Why would you have loved someone so deserving of such contempt?"

"Not at the beginning. Then he was—"

"Magnificent? Yes, he was magnificent. He—"

DuRong shivers a bit. I sense the slightest change in his demeanor.

"You just said that if a Hitler could get into Heaven, you are glad you no longer remain there. But what if a DuRong, yes, what if a Lucifer could be washed clean, could be forgiven and return to Heaven as angels reborn, what if God were willing to—"

"And we would have to *submit* to Him? Follow His orders? Do what *He* desires?"

"But God has never changed, DuRong. He has always

been willing to forgive. As for submission, what is it now that you are doing? You have submitted to Lucifer's will since the dawn of time. What kind of master has *he* been?"

DuRong is acting with growing strangeness, instability.

"You show me ballet, opera, charities. You point to the beauty of art, the decency that does rest in any motivation to help others. And you indicate that none of those we saw owe any obedience to the Almighty. They have run their lives without Him. And yet you admit that God created each one. DuRong, that which is noble, inspiring, artistic within them was implanted by God in the first place. Talent cannot be taught; it is not a serum injected, a drug ingested, something in the air that is breathed in and takes root. It was instilled even before birth, as a seed destined to grow. Anything good we have seen has come about not because of their atheism but *in spite of it*."

DuRong says nothing. I notice a surge of moaning among the others. They all have been disturbed.

"Just examine the way you all are reacting now. You know truth. You know it better than a missionary who has spent an entire lifetime of sacrifice in spreading the Great Commission. Take a library of all the books of faith ever written and include even the Bible, and yet your knowledge would transcend five hundred times all that!

"Which is why you work so hard to *corrupt* the very universe itself, why many of you also are out there!"

I make a sweeping gesture at the heavens.

"You would like to destroy all of that, and begin anew, fashion the whole of creation in the image of *your* master. Obedience to the will of another is not the problem. Obedience to the One who gave you life *is*—and so you worship a substitute, preferring the demonic to the divine, someone who promises you what that very knowledge of yours knows to be false. You have read the prophecies and know them word for word. If you were to be honest, you would be confronted with the spectre of your own impending doom, and so you cling to the most awful, the most evil, the most decadent lies ever spawned!"

I sense something else at that point. I hear a distant roar, rapidly getting louder, closer. DuRong and the others are cowering, so frightened that if you could say, with any accuracy, their blood was freezing in their veins, then that would hint at how they are now behaving.

"Enough!"

A single word. Just six letters. Spoken in an instant. But spoken with the most traumatic ferocity of any word in history, divine, demonic or human.

"ENOUGH!"

Again. Stronger.

"ENOUGH!"

And in a split second, if time were real, an accurate description, in a split second, there is no ground beneath me, nor sky above, nor fallen angels quavering frenziedly, themselves a blur, nor—

Only . . . around me, vivid, suffocating . . . the reality, the terrifying, monstrous reality . . . of Hell.

At first there is just nothingness. A sound like that of a howling wind sweeps across my consciousness, sweeps through me, causing a chill more profound than any before now. I can still *see* nothing. And I experience an instant of deep, suffocating mournfulness, but even that word does little to describe my state.

I feel what it is like to be in a place without God, cutting aside all the childish rationalism and nihilism of Man, the immature playthings of deluded spirits . . . *experiencing* the inner core of atheism as objective, fundamental *reality* like a vulture swooping overhead, ready to devour.

"Oh, God . . ." I say aloud.

The entire "place" in which I am shudders as though down to its very core.

And then a voice—

"Please, do *not* speak *that* name in *this* place!"

The voice familiar, rich, magnetic, eclipsing even Du-Rong's, a chill edge to it that penetrates to—

Lucifer.

"Where are you?" I ask, trembling.

"Here, there, everywhere," is the reply.

"I do not understand," I admit.

"You are in my breast. I carry you around as a woman pregnant. I spit you out of my womb at my pleasure."

Laughter.

"You have been hunting me over history. And yet you found me almost from the beginning. You have seen me again and again and not known it. How stupid an angel you are!"

I recall the decadence. The pain. The pungent odor of burning Jews assails me.

"Let me now show you something else . . ."

A scene is played out before me or, rather, a montage of scenes, one right after the other. I am in the midst of a gala party. It is in a ballroom. There are crystal chandeliers, and diamonds, and lavish gowns and—

The alcohol flows freely. So does the cocaine.

I see 2000 pairs of shoes, and dozens of Rolls Royces . . .

"I have them all," the voice says proudly. "Because they do *that* while they permit *this*."

A man, dying from hunger, sits on his haunches pleading with passersby for a morsel of food.

Other scenes, spinning, people at the altar of fame, power, sex.

There had been no real warning about the volcano. No

one is prepared. Hundreds die. A little boy runs after a dog whose fur is aflame, screaming for someone to help him until the lava drowns out his thin, agonized voice.

The bodies of many are visible afterwards, some partially covered by the once-red, now-gray molten rock cooling down. Every few feet an arm or a hand is visible among the layer of death, the fingers twisted in pain, frozen that way like Arctic weeds.

A man weaves his way through the hands and arms and other half-buried portions of bodies. He takes off rings, watches, bracelets, puts them in a sack. Some of the bodies are lying on top of the hardening lava. He rummages through their clothes, finding wallets, money belts . . .

"I never caused that natural disaster, but I took advantage of it, Darien. It proved to be an opportunity that I could hardly let pass by, do you not agree?"

The elderly woman is temporarily alone to tend to the family store. Her husband has gone home to get her some more medicine.

Two gunmen blow her head off, and get away with $35.15 . . .

"My workers stayed behind," says the voice. "They wanted to see the husband's expression. It was worth waiting for."

The man is consumed by chills so intense that they seem to infiltrate every inch of his body, every muscle trembling, shaking. His skin is covered with lesions. He weighs barely a hundred pounds.

"Oh, God, why are You doing this to me?" he shouts but never getting an answer—a hundred times a day it seems but only dead, awful silence . . .

"That *is* an achievement, Darien. To get them to blame God . . ."

"Please help me. He's got a knife. Won't someone—?"

"A dozen witnesses, Darien, and no one helped."

In the midst of the town square, a man is blindfolded. Standing before him are five other men, each holding a rifle. The man is clutching a Bible. It falls from his hands, covered with blood.

"Marvelous, Darien . . ."

Image after image, a kaleidoscope . . .

"My world, Darien. Yes, my handiwork. You are coming to stay with me, are you not? To share . . ."

I am shuddering. So all of it is true, any remaining doubt buried under the weight of the evidence surrounding me. God's reasons—all *true*—Lucifer/Satan's exile—*justified* beyond argument. God knew the end from the beginning, and all else. He could *see*—!

Suddenly there is silence.

I feel extraordinary heat.

. . . screaming.

No more blackness. No more—

I knew, from the Casting Out, and beyond, that Hell existed, knew that it was nowhere near Heaven, knew that the evil ones of history were there. But seeing it, being *in* Hell, watching—

Someone on a table. A horde of fallen angels around him. They have knives. They are cutting into him. The pieces are put into an oven. And then taken out, burnt black, fingers and toes in ashes. And still alive, the body dismembered but moving, a charred tongue protruding from lips blistered and swollen, eyes—

"Oh, please, please, kill me, please kill me now . . ."

The voice is German. The man is Hitler. . . .

And then I am confronted by a creature so loathsome that it could not be called human *or* demonic. It is bent over, almost hunchbacked. The face is rotting, wounds raw, open, with pus dribbling out, gangrenous filth spewing forth like geysers of water from a whale.

The thing is holding a baby's body in its hand, a hand twisted with arthritic ravaging.

It is laughing, this creature, shaking the tiny body like some obscene trophy.

"I have won," it cackles.

I am no longer silent. I cannot be.

"You have not!" I shout. "That is only an old suit, thrown away, useless. That baby's spirit is where it belongs—not here!"

The creature spins around and faces me as it tosses the body to one side.

"Fool!" it says, cackling. "You—"

I realize, with electrifying sudden clarity, who this creature is.

I stumble back as the cackling vanishes, and a familiar rich baritone replaces it.

"Welcome to my world," Lucifer says.

He throws his arms about, indicating the vast reaches of Hell.

"The place of my habitation once was very different, as you know."

Incredibly I detect the slightest trace of regret.

"Give it up, Lucifer," I plead. "God may be willing to forgive you. The Cross that is now the symbol of your defeat could become the instrument of your rebirth."

"You speak with great conviction," Lucifer says wistfully, holding up his hands. "But these have centuries of blood on them. These have destroyed the bodies of Jehovah's saints. These have plunged daggers into the hearts of the unborn."

He points to his head.

"My thoughts have invaded the church, the office, the home. My programs are on prime time, on cable, in syndication. My concepts are on stage. In motion picture theatres. Books. Magazines. There is nowhere anyone can turn without being confronted with *me*!"

Gradually that door of regret is closing, as Lucifer relishes his power, his influence, his . . . dominion.

"Return to subservience?" he begins to shout. "Return to sitting at *His* throne? Worshipping Him? You *are* a fool, Darien!"

He spins around and around.

"You probably see how lovely I am now. You probably think how grand it would be if the golden streets of Heaven were once again graced with my beauteous presence."

As he moves, portions of him erupt like giant boils pierced, sending out gushers of poison, green and yellow and smelling of decay and disease.

"This is but one me," he says. "Let me show you another."

He seems to take off that one self and put on a new one, like exchanging a suit of clothes.

"I am a judge. I undermine the legal system by voting to allow abortions. I permit the release of those who have slaughtered others because some technicality of the law has been violated. And when the public finally votes me out, I hide behind my femininity and play at being a coy little devil, if you will pardon the expression."

And—

"Look at me now, Darien."

The change this time is most startling of all, and at the same time, the most obscene.

"This is the guise with which I am most comfortable, Darien."

He is now a tall, handsome, well-built young man, naked.

"This is more the real me, Darien. Why do you think so many followed me out of Heaven? From envy? From respect? You play well the part of a fool, Darien, but I do not think even you are quite that naive."

He walks toward me, flaunting himself.

"Come to me, Darien. Blend your spirit with mine. Have the kind of experience that—"

I run. I know he is behind me, following me. I take flight through the corridors of Hell. I stumble, fall, flames leaping up at me. The spirits of condemned human beings reach out from cells in the walls surrounding me.

"Release me, please!" they cry.

"He has rats eating me. Please—"

"I am being put on a spit and roasted."

"Spiders—no—no—all over me—piercing me with their—"

I am lost. Everywhere I turn, there is horror. I am in an open room, at the end of one of the corridors. Some poor tormented souls cry out in agony. They are feasting on dismembered bodies, oblivious for the moment. And then they realize what they have been doing, and scream in utter despair and terror until *they* are pulled apart and devoured by others who then comprehend what has happened and hold up their blood-stained hands and—

No, no, no! I scream wordlessly. *I—*

Somehow they have heard, and they turn toward me. They cry in unison, *You are an angel. Please relieve us of this torment. Please take us from this place of damnation.*

I try to tell them that I can do nothing. They advance toward me, picking their teeth with the bones of the dead.

I remain no longer but reenter the corridor. On all sides there is screaming, a montage of ghastliness, the odors of—

Finally I can go no further. I have reached a deadend. All around me are flames, rocks glowing red, then turning molten. I trip on a severed head that suddenly looks up at me and laughs insanely—just before it catches fire, the laughter replaced by the screaming of the damned.

I am trapped. It seems I can only wait.

I sense something nearby . . .

Observer!

He is hiding in the shadows.

"For me, there is but an eternity of this," he says in a tremulous whisper. "I have chosen my hell and now I must lie in it. But, Darien, you mustn't do that."

I look about me helplessly.

"Not about, Darien. Not this way or that. Above!"

Ahead I see Lucifer. Gathered around him are a thousand of his demons. As I look, they become one, their forms blending, and at the same time the real Satanic self returns but bigger, even more revolting, red sores erupting onto me, his breath the stuff of cesspools. He raises a hand, commanding Observer, who goes, whimpering, standing before Lucifer, becoming a part of the ungodly union.

And then Lucifer, former comrade of Heaven, now maestro of Hell, turns to me, smirking, his tongue darting in and out of a mouth filled with the tiny bodies of aborted babies being crunched between his teeth.

"Perhaps, Darien, you carry with you the quaint notions that I can be appealed to through an overture to my conscience. Perhaps you think you can reach my heart."

He cackles ferociously.

"Hearts are my fodder, Darien. I enjoy their taste. I wallow in the blood that pumps through them. I add ingredients of my own—some cocaine, a pinch of heroin, a drop of bourbon—that is *my* blood, Darien, and I share it with Mankind!"

He steps a bit closer. I can back away no further.

"Take a look at Observer's book. Examine its pages. He tells all. It is destined to be a best-seller. Millions will read it, *my* millions, when I finally ascend to the throne, and destroy God Almighty!"

He throws the book at me. It lands at my feet.

"You think of conscience. Goodness. Mercy. Silly stuff, Darien. For the weak. My strength is pain, my energy from the bloodshed of wars, my ecstasy from the dying of hope and the birth of despair. Your men of God rant and rave about my punishment sometime someday somewhere. For me, there is no wait. I mete out *my* punishment now. I grow stronger from the cries of starving millions. Plagues are my rejuvenation. I dine on what your redeemed ones call anarchy, barbarism, hedonism. I relish the acts of the homosexual and call them my baptism."

He is very close now.

"Kiss us, Darien," he says. "Kiss us and join us forever . . ."

I have only one act left, the remaining weapon in an arsenal long neglected by skepticism and doubt over the validity of Lucifer's fate. I fall to the molten-red floor of Hell, stirring up the ashes of Eden, and my voice, created by God Himself, cuts through the screams of damnation.

"I claim the name of Jesus Christ, and accept the protection offered through His shed blood."

Instantly Lucifer pulls back.

"You think *that* is enough!" he shrieks. "You think *words* can stop me?"

"Not words alone, Lucifer," I say, gathering strength. "It is what they portend. You *are* doomed. You wallow in the excrement of your foul deeds and call *that* triumph."

He hesitates. His whole being seems to shake to its very core.

"You turn the womb into a graveyard spitting out its dead, and call this a battle won in your war against the Almighty. Your weapons are the bodies of babies with bloated stomachs—your elixir the blood of concentration camp victims mixed with the fluids of perverse acts in dark places of passion. You shout of victory, and yet all you have left is the torment of Hell! Your trophies have become the twisted bones of a demented grotesquerie— your former majesty an eternal mirror held up to the rotting filth that you now call your very being."

My anger is spent. I have only pity left. And I tell my former friend that that is so.

"You are without hope, by your own choice. But as for myself and my destiny, I choose, now, my Creator and yours. Take me back, Lord!"

I feel myself being lifted upward. Through the volcanic-like geysers below, there is for an instant, barely visible, the bent-over shape of a wretched creature falling to his knees and weeping . . .

I AM NO longer in Hell.

But I have not returned to Heaven, either. I remain in some limbo state, still on Earth, still going from place to place, century to century, like someone caught on a perpetual merry-go-round, unable to bring it to a halt, unable to get off, condemned just to stay there, spinning, spinning, spinning. During one turn, the Dark Ages flash before me, filled with overt demonic activity; during another, I see the Civil War in the United States, whole battlefields of the dead and the dying, blood staining dark blue as well as light grey uniforms, often brother having to slay brother; during yet another spin, I witness the birth of the first thalidomide babies, twisted creatures crying pitifully, pain over their entire malformed bodies, while profits were being made on the drug that caused their misery; faster the merry-go-round goes, dizzying, until I tumble off yet again . . .

I cannot age, but I do feel somehow old as I sit here, on a mountaintop overlooking the plain where the last great battle of Mankind has taken place. The bodies number into the thousands, and blood collects everywhere— giant, deep pools like a titanic wave over the ground, submerging it. It is possible to drown in blood down there . . .

I momentarily turn away, the odor so strong that it ascends the mountain. I try to close my ears because the cries of the dying are loud enough to form a crescendo that also reaches me—but there is no escaping the panorama below, either in its sights or its sounds.

I decide to leave the mountain and go down to the plain where the old prophecies always had been pointing, with devastating clarity.

Some of the dying have had the flesh literally seared from their bones, and they have only seconds left, those that survived at all. They see me, of course—the living do not—but the dying, suspended, in a sense, between two kinds of life, indeed see, reach out, beg.

"Please help me sir," I am asked again and again.

"The pain . . ."

"I know I've been blinded, now, yet I see you anyway. I see—"

Ahead, standing as though on an island uplifted in the midst of a blood-red sea, are several hundred figures. I approach them. One by one they ascend. The final soldier turns to me, smiles, says, "We did the right thing."

I nod.

. . . *we did the right thing.*

Yes, they did—all of them—that one group of hundreds out of countless thousands.

They refused the Antichrist. And he had them slaughtered as a result, threatening to do just that to any others who might decide to rebel.

And now—

Not one of them bore the scars of how they died—no bayonet wounds, no bullet holes. In their resurrection they had been healed, given the bodies that would be theirs throughout eternity.

But the others share not at all the same end. Every few

seconds, more are dying. Bodies piled upon bodies, visible where the blood is not quite deep enough to hide them. I look about, and see hands raised against the sky, like stalks of marsh grass in a bloody inlet. For an instant only. Then cut down.

They also see me. They surround me as I go past, trying not to look at them, their eyes haunted where they yet have eyes. Some do not, seared away, only the empty sockets remain. But they see me just the same. And all turn away, knowing that *they* will spend eternity like that—in agony, flames searing but never fully consuming them.

The scene oppresses. I cannot stand it any longer. I leave, not sure of where to go. I have time at my disposal. I can flash forward a thousand years, two thousand, however many. I can retreat in time countless centuries.

But I have nowhere to go. An irony that presses me down inflicts on me a weariness that is so pervasive it is as though all of history has become a weight threatening to—

It does seem as though an eternity somehow has come and gone since I left Heaven. I have seen more than all the human beings since the first two were created by God. Perhaps only the Trinity has seen more.

Can angels become weary? We never sleep, true, but we have consciousness and the very essence of what we are indeed can be subjected to strain, can indeed wear down, can approximate how humans feel. After all, we are not robots without feeling nor batteries that can never run down.

I feel myself spinning again . . .

"I was blind, but now I see!" says the man walking the twisting, winding street. "And my brother was lame, but now he walks."

Not a significant proclamation perhaps; not as momentous in itself as, say, the Holocaust. Nor at all meaningful against the realization that twenty million babies or more have died at the hands of Whim, Convenience or any of the other demons bedeviling those who decide that killing a baby is not murder.

And yet—

I continue walking. I see a centurion with his son.

"You were dead and yet now we walk together," the man says to the child.

I find others, one, two, a dozen, a hundred, a thousand. Healed during just three brief years.

And then . . . Lazarus.

Christ's good and dear friend . . .

Lazarus alive, walking with his family. Speaking of the warmth of the sun on his skin.

People touched by supreme goodness, snatched from ultimate evil, each a victory, one after the other like them throughout history, in Heaven instead of Hell, walking the golden streets, listening to the sounds of angels . . . *singing.*

I sit down on the side of a hill, next to some sheep in that ancient land. Two shepherds are nearby. I overhear them talking about their simple lives, the quiet, isolated place in which they tend their sheep.

I reflect on my journey, recalling everything from the very beginning. I have seen victory and defeat. I myself was almost seduced at the hands of Lucifer.

I indeed am tired. Normally, of course, there is no such thing as being tired for any of the angelic host. We never sleep. We have ceaseless energy for any and all tasks. But this time it is different for me. Along with it is a sense of shame and regret, that I had not simply believed God but, rather, like Thomas had to see and feel the equivalent of the nail-pierced hands and lanced side and mangled feet.

I look about, seeing the sheep, the sky well-nigh cloudless. I remember something God had told me once, about there being warfare all around, just out of sight. Later, in a world of five billion inhabitants, how many would ever be aware of this contest for their very spirits?

Surely, the vast majority scoff at the notion. Angels? How silly! Demons? Nonsense! A creature named Lucifer or Satan or the Devil? How trite and childish! A skepticism presided over by a special council of fallen angels, their job that of fostering the doubt, the sarcasm, all the careless, tongue-in-cheek media depictions of Satan that only enhanced the phony, carnival-like image with which he deliberately surrounded himself.

Of those who believed, how many would follow after Lucifer, not knowing the truth perhaps but instead attracted to him by the veneer of excitement and thrills and seeming fulfillment, beckoned like moths around a consuming flame, its dazzling colors and brightness drawing them in?

A startling insight grips me as though I had a physical body: most of his deluded human followers, seduced by him, would mortgage eternity and be in bondage without ever knowing that this was so, slavishingly responding to his role as corrupt master puppeteer, pulling the strings and causing them to dance to his commands, mixing in huge globs of guilt and regret and much else so that any message of forgiveness is mitigated, unable to get through, unable to become God's knife to cut those strings of Satanic enslavement. Call it humanism; call it gay liberation; call it chemical dependency; whatever the term, it was but another branch on a tree planted by a Machiavellian gardener.

Breathtaking clarity rushes into my very being at that point. The spirit of the age indeed has taken over Earth, and there are now only pockets of the redeemed, a few areas of spiritual oasis—the rest is a desert of damnation.

The net of delusion tossed about by Lucifer and his followers had caught even me by the hem, so to speak, and I had had a glimpse of what total allegiance could have meant, allegiance to one who deserved only contempt.

Something quite astounding happens to me now. I am near Calvary. A storm is ripping the sky apart. I walk up the side of Golgotha, past the time-carved rock that looks indeed so much like a human skull, past the multitudes gathered at the top. Mary, the mother of Jesus, is there, His brothers, a contingent of Roman soldiers, onlookers including Nicodemus. I stand at the Cross, looking at the pain on His face. I am under the crimson flow now, His blood washing over me, all my doubts, all my rebellion flushed away like yesterday's garbage. I look at myself and I am suddenly very white, very pure.

I wander, later, from that place, my mind filled with arresting images. I was at Calvary. I stood beneath the feet of God Incarnate, His blood providing the missing moment in the scenario of my odyssey.

Suddenly I hear a familiar voice. My head has been bowed. I look up.

Stedfast!

Not a fallen angel. Not a demonic perversion of what once was. My friend from Heaven—here on Earth!

"I have been with you from the beginning," he says. "Call me your guardian angel of sorts."

"But I thought—"

"It is all a bit different from what you did think, my friend Darien. Lucifer was actually sad that you ever left Heaven."

"I do not understand . . ."

"You originally were to have joined him, during the Casting Out. You were as close as that. But you held back just a bit too long. It was then Lucifer decided that you would be more beneficial to him actually in Heaven, and he did not try harder to convince you to be by his side, for eventually he thought you would sow the seeds of a second rebellion, acting as his *agent provocateur* in heavenly places. He underestimated your devotion to God, though. You were torn between God and Lucifer, unlike the others who had no compunctions at all about their choice of Satan over God."

"So when God let me go on my journey, He knew what the outcome would be."

"Of course. But He also knew that you would have to discover certain things for yourself."

"And you followed me in case I really did need help?"

"Two angels are better than one, Darien."

"But I never knew . . . I—I never saw you. Nor did any of the—others. How could that be?"

He looks at me, rather like an impatient teacher at an impudent student, fluttering his wings as a telltale sign.

"Darien, Darien, do not put such limitations on the God of miracles."

We walk for a while, talking.

"Earth has turned into a nightmare place," I say at one point.

"Oh, it has—call it the rape of Eden—but even so you have encountered reminders of what could have been if Lucifer had remained loyal, and not allowed pride to entrap him and the rest of Mankind."

That first family, Millie and Charlotte, so many more, redeemed ones for whom the shackles of the sin nature were eventually replaced by the true freedom of being born again.

"You know," Stedfast says, as though reading my thoughts, "so many men and women talk of freedom. They want to have no restraints whatsoever. They want to be free to have sex whenever, wherever, and with whomever they please. And then the sexually transmitted diseases started to put a real dent in *that* thinking, of course: herpes, AIDS, syphilis, and so on. That kind of alleged pleasure brought punishment inexorably along with it. They blamed God, but it was simply the nature of their bodies, the biological realities of being human. Each of them dug their own special grave just as surely as though they had taken a gun to their head and pulled the trigger.

"That is not freedom. That is but a death sentence—they spend the last few months or years of their lives waiting for the execution. The flamboyant piano-playing entertainer, the black ballad singer, the leading-man actor, the rotund veteran TV star, so many other celebrities—the media reports everything. And the message is loud and clear. But, Darien, it is not being heeded, not really. Unfortunately, all of them are under total delusion.

"So there is *no* freedom in *their* freedom, not a freedom that has any validity, for even while it is being shouted from the media as the lifestyle of choice for millions, all of them are in a prison—the bars may not be metal, although sometimes that is the case—and they will go on with that cry of freedom mocking them to the grave and even beyond!"

We wander to Joseph's tomb, go inside, stand by the hard rock shelf on which rests Christ's body. He is passing from death to life even as we watch. Finally He sits up, then stands, smiles at me, and says just five words, "Now you know the truth . . ."

"Yes, Lord, I know the truth," I manage to reply, barely able to say even that, aware of the moment to which I am witness.

A short while later, someone approaches from outside.

A woman.

Our eyes meet.

I find myself saying, "He is not here, the one you seek. He has risen, as He promised."

It is as though the light of Heaven is on Mary's face, her expression sublime.

I watch her go. My whole being weeps with the joy of redemption profound, redemption purchased in blood for all of humanity and which included mercy for a foolishly errant angel.

A voice, rich, kind, familiar . . .

"Darien, are you truly ready now?"

"Yes, Lord, truly . . ."

I AM BACK in heaven, as suddenly as I had left. But whereas I left without fanfare, as though sneaking out, hoping no one except God Himself would see me, I return as the hosts of Heaven stand before me, trumpets sounding.

My fellow angels are spread out in front of me, the assemblage going on further than I really can see. The fluttering of their wings seems so loud that only the trumpets can compete.

Heaven is never dark, no clouds blocking the sun. But in that moment I perceive more brightness than I can remember, an illumination so clear and clean that everything is asparkle.

Moses comes to me, smiling.

Abraham stands before me.

Jeremiah. Peter. John. Constantine. Florence Nightingale, D. L. Moody, Countless thousands of believers over the centuries welcoming me back.

And then the Holy Trinity.

What Man finds so difficult to comprehend is before me in reality, the only reality that counts.

I fall to my knees in humility and shame.

"Arise, Darien," God says. "This is a time of rejoicing.

All of Heaven, angel and human, welcomes you for eternity. Shame is of earth. It has no place here. There is no need any longer."

. . . no need any longer.

How those words wash over me, cleansing me . . .

I am standing next to a woman who seems always to be smiling.

"It's so wonderful," she says, "so wonderful to see that they have no more pain or want or fear."

She asks if I would sit down with her, and I gladly answer in the affirmative.

"There were indeed times when I wanted to give up, the strain was so awful," she admits.

"In what activities were you engaged?" I ask.

"I took upon myself missions of mercy. There were so many of the poor who were dying in the streets. I went to them and bathed them and gave them food. So many children! Their poor little arms were bone-thin. Their eyes were as mirrors of the suffering they underwent. I remember, out of the multitude, one child in particular. His name was Johann. His parents gave him that name because they had a single luxury—a little battery-operated record player and an old scratchy recording of one of Johann Sebastian Bach's compositions. When they could no longer give their son even a crust of bread, they left him by a highly traveled road, hoping some stranger would take pity on him. When I saw Johann, the battery had run down, but the player was still there, the record on it, covered by dirt.

"I held him in my arms and took him to our mission. There was no doubt in my mind that he was dying. The ravages of malnutrition had claimed him too severely for too long. He couldn't even hold food in his stomach. Once he vomited it up over me and my helper. And he was very embarrassed, but I told him not to worry.

"We found a battery for the player and kept the record going again and again. As soon as he heard it, his crying seemed to subside into a low, sad whimper. Finally he closed his eyes, but just before that, he looked at me, seemed to become very much stronger and put his frail arms around me. He whispered just one word in my ear."

"What word was that?"

"Heaven . . ."

She pauses, then: "I noticed something I hadn't before. His right hand had been knotted up, gnarled actually. As the life flowed from him, that hand relaxed and opened, and I saw, lying against the palm, a tiny, tiny cross. The pain was gone from his face, leaving only the most beautiful smile I have ever seen.

"And, you know, I left my earthly home a few years later. I closed my eyes to the poverty around me and opened them to majesty. Johann was waiting for me beside a wonderful lake with a sheen like polished crystal. He was tall, handsome, strong. And he introduced me to his mother and his father.

"If only those who doubt could see what it is that we have here, if only—"

She looks ahead, smiles.

"Johann's calling. Will you excuse me, please, Angel Darien?"

"Yes, of course. Oh, what is your name, dear lady?"

"Theresa," she says.

I see her join a tall, handsome young man not far away. He is not alone. A thousand others have joined him, gathering around this woman named Theresa . . .

I meet others, as I would be doing for the rest of forever. I share their joy, it becomes my own, and we rejoice together.

There is a man named William.

"It was indescribable," he remarks with radiance. "It swept over me like a sudden tidal wave, yet it was quite gentle; rather than knock me down, it lifted me up. My mind soared then, not just my spirit. All the shackles of mortality fell away. It is difficult for me, now, even to remember what hatred was like, to realize that once I was subject to the most unreasonable jealousy and outbursts of temper, that I polluted my body as well as my mind. All lust is gone. All impatience. All anger. Everything else that was a stench in the nostrils of a holy and righteous God.

"All gone. Drained from me like poisons from an unhealing wound. These sins have vanished. To be cleansed before Him, to be as white as snow, to know that I am *acceptable* to my Creator—how magnificent that knowledge, that assurance, that fulfillment of what He has been telling the Human Race for so very, very long.

"And I know, if ever the awareness of such things should reenter, it would be merely in the light of my scorn over them, my astonishment that I had permitted God's creation, my body, to be tarnished with the garbage of man's corruption."

He repeats an ancient prayer that he had read a long time before:

The gates of the sanctuary may Michael open,
And bring the soul as an offering before God;

And may the redeeming angel accompany thee
Past the gates of Heaven, where Israel dwell;

May it be vouchsafed to thee
To stand in this beautiful place;
And thou,
Go thou to the end

For thou shalt rest,
And rise up again.

"I carried that with me, in mind and heart, for many years, thinking about the promise it offered. But, now, the reality is ever so much more . . .

"To stand before my Lord, my Savior, to experience fellowship with Him after all the prophecies in the Bible—and hundreds of sermons, and the anticipation of a mortal lifetime—to have Him call me by name! Do you know what I'm trying to say?"

I answer, with utter tenderness, that, yes, surely I do know what he means.

He stops, then adds, before going elsewhere, "God bless you, Darien."

"He has, my friend . . . infinitely."

God requests that I meet with Him. I am there in an instant.

"There is something I must ask you to see," He tells me. "I know it will not be easy, Darien. Are you willing to join me?"

"Yes, Lord, of course I am."

We stand before what I could call a door except that it is not of wood and metal hinges. It is without actual substance but a door nonetheless.

"I want to show you the future, except for us it is now the present," God says not harshly.

"Yes . . ."

I witness a broad overview of the Battle of Armageddon. I see, again, the lone regiment refusing to continue. They put down their rifles. Ordered to pick up the weapons, they steadfastly refuse. As a result they are shot immediately.

"Even in the midst of such an event, there is redemption," I say aloud. "My own journey now seems more needless, more blind than ever. I gave up nothing but my doubts. Look at *their* sacrifice."

"But that was the whole point, Darien. Those very doubts were the seed of your rebellion. In Lucifer's case, his pride compounded the problem—and the two brought about his doom. Those men gave up allegiance to the Antichrist. You gave up what could have become your eternal commitment to Satan. You fought against what could have been, and won, Darien. I am very proud of you."

And the Devil that deceived them was cast into the lake of fire and brimstone, where the beast and the false prophet are, and shall be tormented day and night forever and ever.

A trumpet sounds. The heavenly hosts sing with great glory. I am allowed to see the final moment of judgment on all the fallen angels—Mifult, D'Seaver, D'Filer, Observer, each and every one on the rim of the lake of fire, and then over the edge. Finally Lucifer himself. He turns, and sees me. The defiance is gone. But not the results of countless centuries of deviltry. His countenance is even worse—however, instead of the flaunting of his powers, the perverse pride in what he has caused, there is only terror as he hears the cries of his fellow angels like a thick fog swirling around him.

"Darien . . ." he starts to say, strangely pitiful. "Even now, God knows even now, I cannot come to Him on my knees and ask Him to forgive me. The same guilt I inflicted on others is like a thick wall between us. I—"

He turns, dancing flames reflected on that cankered face, and then he is gone.

And I saw a great white throne, and Him that sat on it . . . and I saw the dead, small and great, stand before God; and the books were opened: and another book was opened, which is the book of life; and the dead were judged out of that which was written in the books, according to their works. And the sea gave up the dead which were in it; and death and hell were cast into the lake of fire. This is the second death. And whosoever was not found written in the book of life was cast into the lake of fire.

Countless multitudes follow Lucifer—those who obeyed him in life were to share his miseries in the final death. For them all, Hell proved to be just a way station before their ultimate destination . . .

How much "later" is it?

Can such thoughts be answered in eternity?

It is unknowably later, perhaps that will suffice. I stand before God at His beckoning.

"Your walk on Earth was akin to that which many human beings take, from doubt to pain to redemption. It has been so ever since Calvary, Darien. But never before has *an angel* journeyed as you have and come back. Wherever you have been, Darien, the path has been marked. And it will be called Angelwalk, throughout the totality of eternity."

God motions me forward a bit.

"Earth is different now," He says, peering down from His throne, seraphim fluttering.

I sense what is happening. That moment toward which all of history had been heading!

"It is time, is it not, Lord?" I say with thrilling comprehension.

"Yes, Darien. Join us and we go together."

I stand with Father, Son, and Holy Ghost. We pass through the Gate, into the bright, golden sunlight of the new Eden.

Epilogue

*I*N THE TINKLING *laughter of a particular moment amid the journey of that special hour if time were
any longer time, there is found beside that path of legend
called Angelwalk what surely must have been a treasured book of the ancient past, pages nearly gone, lying
near a kindly lion's paws at temporary rest. Only some
meaningless old scraps remain, none displaying anything legible except the last fragile bits of a few lost
words.*

A Bo.k of the Da.s of Obs . . ver, Once an Ang—.

*Then it is gone in dust, trod underfoot by lions and
lambs and bright-faced redeemed led by joyous cherubim travelling Angelwalk toward a golden temple rising
out of the mists atop a majestic mount called Sinai. . . .*

Finis

Afterword

NOW THAT YOU have read *Angelwalk*, how do you feel?

Maybe you feel as I did after I'd finished reading the proofs: like I'd been bruised by something beautifully brutal.

The book is beautiful, no question about that. But chapter after chapter, I found my admiration turning into indignation. One minute I was smiling at a deft phrase, and the next minute I was weeping. I couldn't help it.

I told Roger that *Angelwalk* was like a lovely spider's web—made out of steel cables, charged with high voltage.

If this book has moved us, then there's no escape. We're trapped.

There's only one thing left. It's to ask, "Lord, what will You have me to do?"

And mean it.

Warren W. Wiersbe

II
Fallen Angel

John Long
—*for being the guy who brought us together*

Joey Paul
—*for being an editor who inspires*

And those other
brothers and sisters in Christ
for whom the Great Commission
is not simply money earned
in the work they do

*Foolish [mortals and demons] imagine that
because judgment for evil is delayed, there is no
justice, but only accident here below. [But
it] is sure as life, it is sure as death!*
—*Thomas Carlyle*

Acknowledgments

$\mathcal{A}$ VERY SPECIAL thanks to Joey Paul; when people told me that this man was considerate, intelligent, honest, and a strong believer in Jesus Christ, well, they were hitting the mark precisely.

Then there is Debbie Hannas, Joey's associate, and a remarkably well-organized and wonderful asset to everyone fortunate enough to work with her.

And some other terrific individuals at Word: Laura Kendall who spearheaded the acquisition of the audio rights of the first *Angelwalk* book as well as with this second one; Laura Minchew whose view of quality juvenile publishing is encouraging indeed; Carol Bartley who sees the need for superior reference works for young people; plus Nancy Norris, Patti Daigle and Judy Gill who have been exceedingly helpful to me.

Let me also mention several more: Tom Williams, a transcendantly talented and creative art director who views writers with respect, and whose own talent borders on genius; Charles "Kip" Jordon and Byron Williamson, two heavyweight executives who remain very nice human beings; Jim Nelson Black who provided initial and much-needed support; Noel Halsey, whose own excitement is more than a little appreciated; Lee Gessner, who has been encouraging indeed; Rob Birkhead, a brilliant craftsman; Dave Moberg, who was there early on; and Ernie Owen, to whom I owe a great deal.

And I must voice a sincere debt of gratitude to Sheri Livingston Neely in the final stages of editing the manuscript.

Nor can I forget Jan Dennis without whose help there would never have been *any* book entitled *Angelwalk*, let alone a sequel!

I'll conclude by thanking more than a hundred thousand *Angelwalk* readers; their enthusiasm enabled the publication of *Fallen Angel*.

Foreword

I HAVE TO say that *Fallen Angel*, a sequel to *Angel-walk* is a far superior masterwork. It may be quite unnerving to many readers, and it will certainly prod the consciences of countless numbers of them.

In my own book, *Battle for the Bible*, I named some of the evangelical leaders who seemed to be presiding over the declining numbers of those who hold to the inerrancy of Scripture. In *Fallen Angel*, Roger Elwood does not give us names but goes one step further, by probing the satanic mindset behind the accelerating campaign to tear the Body of Christ away from that most precious and necessary of moorings, the Holy Scriptures, God's Word given to mankind.

You may not agree with every word presented in this gripping work of fiction, but you will be fascinated by an authentic scripturally-sound and rather explosive presentation of Satan as seen through the eyes of his pathetic follower, Observer, for whom we feel the utmost sympathy and whose tragedy is also that of any human being who turns his back on the Living Christ.

There is little doubt that reading *Fallen Angel* could prove to be a greater life-changing experience than would be the case with any other Christian novel in recent memory—and that it will be much discussed over the coming months as Christians everywhere ponder the different characterizations in the book, and wonder how many, if any, are far from being entirely fictitious. I can say one thing: Elwood's uncompromising grasp of the reality of the merchandizing, publishing and commercial side of the evangelical community has in it enough accurate data and clear-eyed truth to warrant those involved taking a hard look at themselves, and starting immediately to correct the imbalances.

Dr. Harold Lindsell

Introduction

"*Y*OUR BOOK CHANGED my life!" The middle-aged woman said as I signed for her a copy of *Angelwalk*. "It alerted me once and for all to the reality of Satan."

I thanked her, and she left—but her words stayed with me.

"Your book changed my life."

Could a writer be greeted with anything finer than that, as simple and yet as profound as that acknowledgment was? Favorable reviews are pleasant and indeed reassuring. Strong sales help perpetuate the ministry of writing. But it isn't until words get beyond the paper on which they are printed and enter a reader's life and have *impact* that the very point of writing, its reason for being, is achieved.

For the Christian who is a writer, all of this is doubly important. The knowledge that what he does can be used by the Lord to enrich the lives of each book's readers, well, I submit the thesis that for the Christian as writer, there *must* be *no* other primary motivation. If his career is *just* to make money, to gain fame, then the Lord may honor the writing anyway because He can always work with the most imperfect of vessels whenever He so chooses. But—and this is a big one—how much better, how much more ennobling if we give back to Him our very best motivations rather than the crumbs from some egocentric desire.

Why go ahead and do another book in what we might call the *Angelwalk* vein?

Because such a story told only from the unfallen angelic viewpoint is not complete. It is one third of the way, but not more than that. So that is why I wrote *Fallen Angel.* I thought it would be potentially edifying if we were able to learn more about the *why* of Satan's fall from Heaven, along with some glimpses of the *how*, that is, how he intends to try to accomplish victory in the spiritual warfare of which he is chief instigator and, ultimately, doomed combatant.

This seemed to be more clearly achievable if told from essentially the demonic point of view, which allows for insights not otherwise possible. It is crucial in any warfare, but especially that which is spiritual, to understand your enemy, and to make sure that you have sufficient armament to defend yourself.

I also feel that Observer represents some of the most frustrating traits of human nature. There are indeed many, many Christians who simply observe the evil around them, moan and groan over the state of the world, and proclaim, "The Lord's in charge. He'll handle everything." What they are saying, in effect, is that they *need not* do anything. In the case of Observer, a fallen angel, the opposite is true. He looks around, sees Satan's power, and assumes that he *cannot* do anything.

As we know, there are people very much akin to Observer, deeply involved in habitual, addictive sin, beguiled by Satan to such an extent that they say either, "I can get out anytime I want," or, like Observer, "I can't break away no matter how hard I try," and believe every awful, corrosive, fatal word.

How much truth has Observer stumbled upon over the

many centuries of his existence? How many falsehoods remain in the corridors of his befouled intellect? And which is which? Does he truly know? Remember, Satan, the master of all those like Observer, is also the Arch Deceiver. Since he is able to deceive human beings, from Adam and Eve onward, would it be at all difficult for him to pull the shroud of deception over pitiable Observer?

These are questions with which readers will need to deal for themselves. They will have to confront each and every word of his story, to discern where divine truth breaks through, and where demonic entrapment runs rampant.

Please note that to fully show the mindset of Satan and his demons, certain words have been used that are quite strong. No Christians speak these words found in the book you are reading—only demonic entities or human beings held in their sway. Sometimes the language we hear from the people around us denotes what they are really like, whom they really serve. So it is, occasionally, within these pages. Please be prepared.

Fallen Angel now begins, entirely from his perspective, this demonic journalist who spins his tale from the Casting Out until that final of all days, when any thought of possible independence, any hope of breaking the chains, will end as he and his brethren continue to play the perverse and awful game of following their leader . . . into the lake of fire forever and ever.

Roger Elwood

A Book of
the Days
of Observer
~
Once an Angel
of Light

In the tinkling laughter of a particular moment amid the journey of that special hour if time were any longer time, there is found beside that path of legend called Angelwalk what surely must have been a treasured book of the ancient past, pages nearly gone, lying near a kindly lion's paws at temporary rest. Only some meaningless old scraps remain, none displaying anything legible except the last fragile bits of a few lost words . . . A Bo.k of the Da.s of Obse . . . ver, Once an Ang—

Prologue

I STAND BEFORE the scarlet flames, others of my kind already have been forced over the edge into this massive lake of fire and brimstone.

(Where are you now, Sunday and Moody and Calvin? Laughing at us from your righteousness? Millions used to scorn your stern messages, crying, in their rebuke, "More love! More love! More love!" and, in the process, sending countless multitudes to hell, that road of infamous damnation greased with the deceptions of an emasculated gospel.)

The cries of my comrades fill the air.

From sitting at the feet of the Almighty to being crushed underfoot!

The end of which they scoffed, and seduced others into doing similarly, that end we relegated to the annals of mere religious myth, now enveloping us for all of eternity.

The dreams we shared!

What plans we had to re-enter Heaven with conquering hordes who would take over and establish a new order.

On the throne of the once-Almighty he was. The hosts of Heaven cowering at his feet. The once golden street littered with the debris of his victory. There was pain now, tears, the pathetic agonies of defeated angels, the dread of redeemed ones from all of history. Satan the victor! His own obscene fantasies now the reality of eternity.

Gone.

Now ashes. Now so pointless . . . diseased imaginings, mocking memories that would accuse us, accuse us all forever.

Forever. . . .

How fair can that be?

(A familiar argument that, the cliché of cynical minds.)

Such a thought is only fleeting, buried by the ravaging images of many centuries, images that project the true truth.

How many times have I stood on the sidelines, watching, often sickened by what I saw, and yet offering no protest?

How many victims from Auschwitz and Dachau and Treblinka have fallen at my feet, and looked up and saw me as they died, asking, "Please, please, do something! Stop the slaughter. For the love of God, do something!"

But I cannot. I cannot. I cannot.

Because I belong to those causing the infamy.

Countless blind humans have asked the same question: If God is just, and loving, and forgiving, how could He *ever* have allowed the existence of Hell?

But I know the answer, truly I do, know the answer in the sight of those gassed or cremated Jews, men, women, and children condemned by captors who were our puppets.

Yet these, as tragic as they are, do not hold the answer in its entirety. Others as well, such as the boys slaughtered by a madman who tormented them unto death, and then made love to their cold, abused bodies and, finally, buried them, thinking they would never be missed or discovered, and that he could go on and on, finding pleasure in abominable ways of darkness.

That question again, yes, yes: *How fair is it for God to condemn anyone to pain without end?*

There is a wretched smile on my face now, a smile without joy, a smile dripping with irony, a smile as I think of those fools so blind to so obvious an answer.

It *is* everywhere, you know, on the front page of every newspaper, on the screen of every television set, everywhere indeed, each time terrorists explode their bombs, each time gangs engage in drive-by killings, each time—

How fair if there were *not* the punishment of Hell for the damned, mandated by countless accusing legions of victims?

Oh, God, I scream silently in my mind, my tormented mind, *oh, God, I know the truth about us, and the unmitigated justice of what You are forcing upon us, their dead, dead bodies like a perverse path on which I step as it leads to the flames.*

I cannot bear the panoply any longer. At the beginning, there was only Cain. And now so *many!*

I turn.

Beside me is Lucifer, his face festering.

"The book?" he asks.

I point to the bits and pieces of my journal on the ground.

It is open to a certain page. Satan glances at this. If he could cry, he would, the tears flowing, but he cannot. There is little emotion left and even now no repentance.

"Leave it behind," he tells me. "Leave it for the useless thing that it is, all it has ever been."

I nod.

Indeed, once mighty arch-angel, Son of the Morning. But what is the use? There is no one left to heed. . . .

"It does not matter anymore, Observer," he says, my expression making the reading of thoughts unnecessary.

He is unsmiling.

"All those prophecies," he says. "We made our victims scoff, we deceived so expertly, cutting into harmless little pieces the great tapestries of divine truth. The tragedy of it is that we became entrapped in our own lies by refusing to heed the same truths."

But not only demons, I say to myself with words he cannot hear because they are unspoken. *Look at so many of the television evangelists who speak of men becoming gods. That is a lie, but they wrap it so tightly around themselves that they and it become as one, and there is no longer any way to separate the two. And so they must go on repeating the deception until it claims their destiny, a destiny they foist upon many of those who look up at them as purveyors of truth.*

Satan turns but briefly, says something I don't quite understand, and then jumps into the flames.

I look in the same direction.

Darien! The voyager treading the path called Angel-walk, facing his doubts, and eliminating these one by one until that glorious moment when all the heavenly hosts welcomed him back into Heaven.

"I could not," I shout to him. "I tried but I could not. His hold was too strong, too—"

I remember so vividly one passage from Darien's journal:

Lucifer.

Gathered around him are a thousand of his demons . . . they become one, their forms blending, and at the same time the real Satanic self returns but bigger, even more revolting, red sores erupting . . . his breath the stuff of cesspools. He raises a hand, commanding Observer, who goes, whimpering, standing before Lucifer, becoming a part of the ungodly union.

"You were right, Darien of Angelwalk," I add in my final words to him. "Your book told the truth."

. . . the final moment of judgment on all the fallen angels—Mifult, D'Seaver, D'Filer, Observer, each and every on the rim of the lake of fire, and then over the edge. Finally Lucifer himself. . . . The defiance is gone. But not the results of countless centuries of deviltry. His countenance is even worse—however, instead of the flaunting of his powers, the perverse pride in what he has caused, there is only terror as he hears the cries of his fellow angels like a thick fog swirling around him.

My book, my book. . . .

A chronicle of all that I am, all that I have seen, all that was wasted, all that could have been but never, never, never was.

It will not be completed now, a fragmented work dropped by the wayside perhaps, and trampled underfoot, eventually becoming just forgotten dust, this pitiable attempt at an overall record of Satan's time on earth, my master's vain and doomed effort at a kind of unholy writ into which all the separate bits and pieces written by my hosts over the centuries would be compiled and made available to the fallen elect.

Fallen elect. . . .

Satan's ravings sing loudly in memory, the sight of massed demons screaming their blood-thirsty approval somehow as vivid as though happening at that very instant.

I shake myself out of that recollection as I see that my familiar former comrade is still so near to me.

Darien.

The wandering angel, filled with questions— uncertain, yes, capricious, perhaps, but not fallen—and finally welcomed back into Heaven to the chorus of angels of light, and the magnificence of the Holy Trinity.

Oh, Darien, where you go soon, along the path called Angelwalk toward Mount Sinai—oh, how I yearn to be by your side.

I wave sadly to dear Darien, my former comrade who wanted nothing but salvation for me. But I was too weak, too—

I step closer to the edge.

The heat touches me!

As everything once more floods back into my consciousness—everything indeed, small and great, no matter how hard I have fought to submerge the recollections, the bits and pieces of the mosaic of all that had gone before—it comes, this tidal wave of infamy, to be repeated over and over as I stand amongst the flames without end.

The faces of my comrades in front of me, their torment so strident as they cry from it—surely I am not like them, surely I do not deserve what they—

Yet surely I do, I know that, Lord, Lord, if only saying. Your name *now* could change my destiny—but I cannot hope for such a miracle, I cannot hope at all because *my* lord stands among the flames.

He reaches out that cankered hand as he sees me. His pus-dripping lips move. He beckons. Only now do I resist for an instant fleeting. And then, as ever—

I come, lord. I come.

And surrender to my destiny.

As I enter my punishment, the memories rage as scornful medusas from the flames to assault me, screeching with demented fury at the failed and evil plans Satan had made so carefully, along with his clever human allies, especially those with their plans for a pivotal assassination, all the way up to that climatic time of confrontation, that final, total Armageddon, and along with these fragments from generations past, there was the foretold anguish.

Foretold. . . .

Oh, yes, it was. We knew the prophecies, we knew the

prophecies so well. For Satan, in that latter part of the twentieth century, before we were banished to the lake of fire, the years that passed were a period of planning. My master knew the end times were coming always closer, the momentum accelerating. He could not relax for an instant. And he drove the rest of us always further, more and more acts of appalling barbarity.

In those final days, he had managed to get a group of communist hardliners, not altogether a difficult task given the atheism that formed the basis for everything they were, every thought, every word, every deed. Now they were planning a grand strategy that would bring power back into their hands, and dispose of Reformer.

Then there were the terrorists, the fanatical Muslims for whom any strike against American interests was pure joy to contemplate, whether it be at oil pipelines in friendly Middle Eastern countries, or at army bases elsewhere, or wherever their utter madness drove them.

Soon these craven minions in allegiance to Lucifer would attack a single target in the western part of the United States itself, causing calamitous devastation.

Satan could hardly wait, could hardly wait to stand among the shards, he and the rest of our demonkind, and hungrily pick off many of the rising souls who then would be flung directly into Hell, their screams the elixir of Satan's psycho-erotic fantasies-become-reality.

But the moment had not quite arrived. There was time, in that final period of history, to think back, to remember, to relive. . . .

Part I

> *Must I do all the evil I can before I learn to shun it? Is it not enough to know the evil to shun it? If not, we should be sincere enough to admit that we love evil too well to give it up.*
> *—Mohandas K. Gandhi*

*J*ESUS CHRISTUS THEOU *Huios Soter.*

I am sitting on the sand in the Sinai Desert. I have left my host back in Jerusalem. But I will have to return to that body later, and feed these thoughts to him in retrospect. This host is one human being whom Satan and I share.

Jesus Christus Theou Huios Soter.

Jesus Christ, Son of God, Savior.

He stands before me, tired, alone, hungry—the physical part of Him, of course—and I look up at this wondrous Man, the sun shining off His magnificent flowing mane.

"You could have been *my* master," I say, my words filled with a pleading acquired over many years of considering the consequences of my actions, the actions of others like me.

"Yes, that is true, Observer," Jesus replies.

He knows that I am with Him, though His death will not come for three years. He knows because He is Who He is, deity and humanity resident as one.

"You could have stood before Lucifer and rejected him," Jesus continues, "but you chose not to do so."

There is in His words a touch of weariness, weariness

in that part of Him which is flesh and blood—and, as well, a prophetic knowingness that can come only from the other aspect of Himself, that which is linked directly with Heaven, and always will be so, the humanity ultimately discarded after the future resurrection and beyond that, the glorious ascension back into the Heaven that we all knew as home eons ago.

He sits down next to me on the sand for a moment.

"Many others will choose over the centuries ahead," He adds. "Many will mock, and turn away, as you did, Observer."

"Oh, I did not mock You," I protest anxiously. "I—"

"Is rejection anything else, Observer?" He interrupts not unkindly, a patient tone obvious.

I want to protest, but the One who is never wrong is right once again.

"Do you *know* what lies ahead?" He asks.

I want to say that I do not, that I have read or heard nothing except what Satan allows, but it would not be truthful if I did that. I have glimpsed on scrolls of papyrus the words of the old prophecies, and they do offer such strong harbingers. But though I serve the Arch Deceiver, the master of lies, how can I stoop to his devices before the Source of all truth? (Such denials would be as ice, quickly melting under the heat of the desert sun.)

"Yes . . ." I reply, all-feeling save the deepest sorrow bled from me by anticipation of the realities to follow.

"The Deceiver deceives himself, and all who have followed," Jesus remarks.

"He tries," I say, "truly he tries. So many of us have been about to break away for a very long time. Perhaps, before it is too late, we will do so someday."

Jesus looks at me, not with contempt but pity.

"The drunkard thinks he can break the shackles of his debauchery, but falls in a stupor before the wine press," He tells me and then drifts into silence.

I, too, have nothing to say for several moments.

Satan has not as yet tempted the Son of Man. That is to come. I have snuck away, to be with Him. Before, I was with Him at the River Jordan, and I saw the Holy Spirit descend in the form of a dove, and God announced the blessed reality of the Savior.

Jesus knew I was there. But it was not only me of whom He was aware. Satan as well. And thousands of fellow demons shrieking.

Shrieking. . . .

Oh, how that sound, heard many times before over the awful years, how it chilled me.

As the flood waters arose, as Noah and his family and the animals were locked in that clumsy old ark, as people beat on the huge wooden door, screaming for refuge, even as they were swept away by the instrument of God's judgment, water which they needed to live, now their executioner—it became clear that Satan had lost this battle.

While being so near to victory, or thus it seemed, he saw the corruption he midwifed spread throughout the inhabited part of the world, men engaging in evil pursuits to an extent unknown until then. Yet those seduced by him finally drowned in a kind of baptism—and wasn't that it, really, the baptism of the wicked. But instead for them it wasn't a ceremony of cleansing—for the world as a physical entity, yes, but not for the students who so eagerly followed their demonic teacher. For them it was a baptism unto damnation. Water that later in the Jordan would touch the body of God Incarnate and proclaim divinity, now sweeping them away, but Satan remaining, to take up again with those who would come later.

Shrieking. . . .

And animals the demons cried, wounded beasts.

And then at Sodom and Gomorrah, when the fire of judgment rained down on those places of depravity.

Shrieking. . . .

First water and then fire and brimstone.

Always the same. God striking back in righteous anger. Satan retreating for a time.

And now—

Another defeat. The most pivotal of all. Not in a moment of spectacular inter-galactic violence, with laser-like swords flying, the wrath of Holiness.

So quiet it was in the human realm, there at the Jordan, unseen by nearly all the world's population at the time.

Multitudes spoke not at all. They stood transfixed by the dove. No one uttered a single word.

But not so in the demonic netherworld, not quiet at all. Leathery wings were flapping. Rage was volcanic. If Satan had had the power, he would have leapt upon the body of the carpenter and torn the flesh off, blood running in the Jordan.

Instead he could only shrink back, cower in hatred. And—

Shrieking. . . .

Jesus knew, of course. As He was arising from the water, the dove settling upon Him so briefly, He looked not at Satan, not at Mifult or DuRong, at *none* of them but me, at Observer, reluctant as ever, Observer who had convinced himself that he was *with* the others but not *of* them. Surely now He was saying that I could cross over, that I could shed the bondage—and yet I saw those eyes of His, moist not from the waters of baptism but tears at once human and divine, and He turned away, toward the beckoning cross three years hence, and I was left behind, my own shrieks part of the cacophony, inseparable.

Yes, I know about shrieking, shrieking that I hear now, for I have proceeded Satan in the wilderness, and he is coming to join us, angry that I got there first, as always paranoid about who might be betraying him, which is not unlike the kettle calling the pot black.

I step back. I think I hear *Jesus Christus* whisper goodbye, and yet how can I be sure? His voice is soft, of such low pitch as to be hardly audible.

His hand reaches out toward me.

Theou Huios . . . Soter.

Oh, Son of the living God, member of triune divinity, were it to be so, were it to be—

I extend my pitiable talon, so deformed that I am ashamed I have nothing better to offer, but He shrinks not. He smiles with such beauty.

Come. . . .

I hear Him. He is actually pleading. He wants me to throw aside—

And then Satan comes between us, in ways infinitely more profound than can ever be expressed through the contrivance of words.

Yet I rebel against my master. I tell him that I have had enough. I reject him forever, and choose another Lord, for Satan is no longer worthy, he has never been worthy, and I tread him underfoot, like dung discarded with disgust, and I reach my Soter, falling before Him as Satan watches, and He welcomes me back into His kingdom . . . immediately I am translated before God's throne, and the unfallen ones issue forth with a chorus of sublime welcome.

No.

I have been with Evil far too long. It is not that I cannot, but it *is* that I do not.

I step back.

Snarling with contempt, Satan orders me to return to Jerusalem to guard our host while he, Satan, tarries with Christ.

The hand of *Jesus Christus* is still extended, still mine to touch, to take hold of.

An instant of time.

Not enough. All of eternity would never be enough.

Farewell, Blessed One. . . .

Soon I am back with our host, back with Judas.

It did not begin then, of course, not there in the wilderness, not at the time of the Flood, not even in the Garden. It began for all of us, for Satan, for myself, for our comrades back before there was a planet named Earth, before there were galaxies, before there was life of any kind but ours, walking the streets of Heaven, singing the praises of Almighty God.

And it would end on a field strewn with bodies, a defeat for all our malignant entities.

But in the meantime, between then and now, oh, what I have had to experience. I have been so close to telling the master that I could not take any more of it, so close—

Always I have pulled back, my disgust buried by the enslavening habits of my kind.

Double-minded. Yes. Yes.

Again it returns, persistent, never far from recollection, that accusatory verse of Scripture read a very long time before: "A double-minded man is unstable in all his ways."

"Not only a man," *I say outloud.*

"What are you babbling about?" *asks a fellow demon, his face contorted in agony.*

"Nothing," *I reply.* "Nothing."

That you would understand.

I WAS THERE when Jesus cast out the demons from the Gadarene maniac, and certain of my kind went into that herd of swine, and then they all plunged over the cliff's edge to their death. Those fellow demons did not die, of course; they and I are spirit, with immortality. But it was a statement by Christ, a statement that when the Holy Spirit moves in, demons cannot remain even though they are legion.

Oh, how they shrieked and wailed and lamented.

"Another defeat!" weeped one.

"One of the worst!" a second joined him.

"But there are other subjects," the first said, bouncing back from momentary depression.

"The Pharisees, the Saduccees!" the second agreed.

"All except Nicodemus," the first added. "He's too wise, too strong. We should not waste any effort on him. We have the others. That is enough."

I was there when Jesus healed those who were blind, who were deaf, who were lame.

I saw their faces, their joy.

I saw my kind leaving their bodies, running scared.

I was in the tomb with Lazarus.

I saw his spirit return to his body. And his spirit saw me.

"You cannot have me as you thought!" he proclaimed.

"*I* never wanted you," I reminded him.

"Are you so sure?" he asked.

Behind him the terrifying sounds of rampaging demons loosed from a dark, damned domain, trying to thwart this greatest of all the miracles.

"Stop him!" they called in unison. "Stop him, Observer!"

"I cannot!" I screamed back to them, enraged at their deception. As if I could stop the very Son of God!

*T*HE *DEATH, BURIAL, and resurrection of Christ.* I was once surprised that I gave so much thought to that unfogettable series of epochal events since they were intrinsically contrary to the totality of my existence, of the existence of all those like myself, in subservience as we were to the Prince of Darkness—and yet those occasional, compelling moments of retrospection, sometimes as though possessed of a resolve, a will of their own seem to *force* themselves to the surface of my awareness, while nothing I do can stem their inexorable advance—yet sometimes they are even *allowed* to return (dare I say summoned?) as I grew weary of all the despicable deeds of which I was part, however oblique that participation may have been, and seek some foolish solace in a personal fantasy to which none of the others has ever been privy, a fantasy in which I learn that that death, that burial, that resurrection were for me as well, that I will not in fact join the despicable damned of the ages, and will be allowed to return to Heaven's glory, washed clean by the same crimson flow—but then reality intrudes, and the fantasy is never more than that . . . yet these moments prove so profound, so unassailable in their supreme display of ultimate love, forgiving love, sacrificial love, love that was so much the antithesis of the very *raison d'être* of Satan's existence— which made my fantasy all the more ludicrous, a fact I had had to face if I were to be honest about him and myself and those around me, and all that was portended for the lot of us, acknowledging that indeed our very existence validified the necessity of what the Son of God endured as the only alternative, the only cleansing act that could mitigate what we had wrought in our wake . . . and so I kept returning to these fragments of recollection, like the proverbial moth fascinated by the flickering shades and shapes of the flames before it—for truly it *was* I, Observer, once an angel, once a being who would have celebrated the foretold act of sacrifice and redemp- tion to which I was intimate witness, it was I who was standing in shame before the Cross as I tried to *will* myself into the same cackling howls of perverse delight that my nearby demonic comrades displayed, wallowing in the conviction to which we all clung, the conviction, fragile, desperate, that this was the end of it, the age-old war between God and Satan for the control of the vast expanse of creation, that all those ancient prophecies were but the vain and deluded ravings mostly of old men . . . and though my fellow fallen seemed to have been seduced by such poppycock, yet I failed, failed miserably in my doomed effort to be satiated with temporary joy at the thought of evil transcendent and triumphant—and, thus, I became instead inexpressibly sad, perhaps more so than the mother of Jesus, or the apostle who loved Him most deeply, perhaps more so than any or all of them, as I, too, looked up into that tormented face, seeing the trickles of blood from under the thorny crown, hearing the groans of pain as the body twitched and shook and wrenched in final agony . . . even so, words of exquisite supplication escaped softly and with infinite tenderness past those pale and twisted lips, a supplication not rooted in condemnation, not seeking the damnation of those responsible but rather a supplication begging God to *forgive* the architects of this infamy—and then that final gasp, a small sound really, hardly audible, lasting only for an instant, that final acknowledgment signifying it was finished for Him that it was indeed over . . . which all of us, the band of fallen ones who attended that moment, took as utterly incontestable testimony to our victory after so long a time, a victory we celebrated gleefully for three wonderful days of unleashed activity—perhaps frenzy would be more accurate—in which we tormented the eleven remaining apostles with crushing doubt and despair . . . relishing this, the pervading ecstasy of it for us, loving every moment of melancholy we midwifed . . . until that Morning, breaking away from the others, when I thought that I alone had visited the Tomb . . . I saw, instead, that I was joined by another, hardly unknown to me, clothed in shimmering radiance—as I once had been but now stripped of it—another who told me that my kind had lost after all, that our jubilation was impetuous and ill-fated, that indeed Christ was not there, that He had arisen, that I should go and tell the others that their awful ravings were as doomed as their ultimate destiny, and as I nodded, my very being shuddering at the gravity of what had been said, stirring up images that I, like the other fallen, had tried hard, oh so very hard, to wipe from our consciousnesses . . . I then saw Mary Magdalene coming forlornly up the narrow pathway to the Tomb, and I whispered, with assumptive despair, "Good-bye, Darien, good-bye, my once-friend," hurrying finally to the multitudes of demonkind, my funereal words of utter and inescapable damnation portended washing over them like a toxic tidal wave, forcing the entire ignoble horde to our knees in a spasm not of repentant prayer—hardly that, of course—but instead the most pervasive futility we had ever known, rising as it did to envelope us like a strange and encompassing shroud, ironically even at the very moment that our master began to exhort us, demanding in his usual Hitlerian tones that we stand, as his followers, his apostles, holding our heads high, and stop acting with such lamentable cowardice, for we are committed, do not *ever* forget that, we are committed to continuing the struggle against encroaching divinity, and, therefore, we have no choice but to fight on, and on, and yet on still.

*H*E WAS CALLED Muhammed or Muhammad or Mahomet or however the devil people pronounced it. Muhammed.

He was my host for many years, from about A.D. 590 until a few years before his death in 632. I generally have not left a host except when the Holy Spirit entered as a result of that host's redemption. With Muhammed it was different. I left, and a demon quite a bit more terrifying slipped in on cloven feet to take over, to drive Muhammed onward with fiercer determination.

But he did write the *Koran* through my guidance. I dictated it virtually word for word—not holy streams of wisdom from the mouth of God, but demonic perversion dressed up to seem noble and profound, a bit silly if it weren't so evil, silly that human beings had the original, and so many of them settled for a counterfeit written by a demon under the remote-control guidance of Lucifer the Magnificent.

I chuckle at that recollection. The *Koran* may well have been my masterpiece. Oh, *The Book of Joseph Smith* was quite good, of course, and so was that tawdry little nonsense which I guided through the hand of Mary Baker Eddy.

But the *Koran*!

Ah, that was the ultimate, truly so, clap-trap religiosity made to seem on a level with God's Word but more like Satan's excrement, droppings from his "bowels" on a stinking dungheap that all of his followers since his death have buzzed around like flies, oblivious to the stench.

And the man himself.

This ludicrous puppet so steeped in his apparent religiosity that he could never realize, not for an instant, that even if the *Koran* were worthy of anything but phlegm from the mouths of any who come in contact with it, if it nevertheless left out the most crucial ingredient of all, it was as nothing, it was as—

Salvation through Jesus Christ and Himself alone.

Not the castrated Allah the Muslims hold so dear. Not the sham religion of Islam that has held tens of millions in its obscene grasp. Not the creepy little men of Libya, Iraq, and Iran, who fight each other as well as their neighbors, and gain near-orgasmic pleasure from tormenting the West, especially the United States, proclaiming their mumbo-jumbo as they turn toward Mecca, those demonic ayatollahs and pathetic Hitlerite dictators and others who are the perfect henchmen of my master, too fanatical, too stupid, too cruel to understand what they *truly* are about, that basically they serve not their countrymen, not the region in which they live, not even the "religion" they profess, but the equally mad ruler of them all.

None of what they profess, none of what they worship, none of what they desire holds any hope for them, for those foolish enough to pay them allegiance.

None of this stinking vomit from hell itself.

Only Jesus the Christ. Only the *real* God made flesh and sacrificed on the cross for the sins of mankind. This same Jesus to whom the rabid and unholy Muslims pay only the most fleeting attention.

I know the right words. I know the right words that could signal my repentance.

I learned them a long, long time ago.

But that is as far as it goes.

And it is not enough.

Not enough at all.

Later, other degenerates guided by Muhammed's lunacy would fit nicely into my master's planning at the advent of the end times, that precipitous moment of infamy in which the Soviets and the Muslims all would be part of the "stew" he concocted. . . .

*I*F MUHAMMED, then why not a pope or two?

My master has always become delirious with the potential of causing the mighty to tumble from their pedestals.

And what more lofty a pedestal could be there than the one on which each pope has rested since the Roman Catholic Church got away from its moorings in the Early Church and became encrusted with barnacles of hypocrisy that until more recent decades made it more often than not a haven for my kind, and in the case of one of the popes, a host for the writing of my journal?

It is fertile fields for devilry that flourish in the tightest secrecy. Few everyday Catholics have *any* idea what transpires in the inner sanctum of Holy Mother Church. Over the centuries, little more than glimpses have been viewed, and these quite fleeting, a flash or two of life at the Vatican.

That was, from the beginning, a formula for "open sesame" as far as my kind goes. How can so-called holy men be subjected to spirit-testing scrutiny if they are unapproachable, hiding behind ornate walls covered with the art of great painters which give literally a façade of holiness but no way of determining the substance thereof?

Many years later, while seeming extravagant at the time, the escapades of the Bakkers would surely be ranked as infantile infamy when viewed side-by-side with the chicanery flourishing in the midst of priceless treasures of paint, gems, and artifacts—but there is a common thread in such matters, a thread of the lack of the pure light of gospel-directed truth acting as an examining beacon, ferreting out all that dishonors and cheapens the pretended holiness.

Can *I*, a fallen angel, be capable of such thoughts? It is a question oft-repeated during my existence, and the only answer: I have them, therefore I am.

There was more than one bad pope, men who allowed the Roman Catholic Church to become grotesquely fat with materialistic embellishments, to become steeped not in spirituality but onerous superstition. During the medieval period, and particularly the time of the bubonic plague, the Vatican's moral character was as diseased as the bodies of many of its cardinals afflicted by the Black Death, along with countless numbers of those peasants and others foolish enough to continue on as loyal worshipers.

Yes, the bad popes, as they have been called through the centuries, chronicled by human journalists in more than one volume, terrible men doing terrible things to and with a vulnerable Catholicism.

But that one, ah, *that* pope!

A man so evil beneath his outer guise of sanctification that it could be said that Satan deserved special praise for his cleverness in disguising the monster's true self.

So evil indeed, but also so pervasive that his thinking held the Roman Catholic Church in its grip for a very long time after his death. One man who carries a disease can die in two days, but those he has infected can infect others, and then those others more still until the chain of death goes on for decades.

The pope, this demon-in-fleshly-garb, took over the writing of my journal. He grabbed it out of my control and went on his own way.

I could only stand by and watch. . . .

He wrote of the most extraordinarily blasphemous images. He revelled in erotic perversions of certain biblical precepts. He took *The Song of Solomon* and turned it into a series of masturbatory fantasies from which he received gratification innumerable times.

But no one outside the Vatican knew what he was like. Only the faintest echoes escaped, at once dismissed—ha, ha!—as a satanic attempt to discredit the Holy Father.

Those who served him, those who put him to bed at night and woke him up in the morning, those who put food on his table and bathed him and dressed him, those who were in his presence day after day after relentless day eventually turned sick inside. And when they would protest, he would accuse them of witchcraft or heresy or whatever; if they persisted, the poor fools would be burnt to death or starved until all life was drained from them— or, in some cases, the good-looking ones especially, they would have the honor of sharing his bed, and then be poisoned at the conclusion of their seduction.

The Vatican was hardly a place of virginal intrigue; it had been steeped in byzantine plots and counterplots for centuries. How Peter the Apostle would have reacted if he had witnessed what became of the Early Church, its simple proclamations of redemption massacred by man-made rule after rule, by men grown obese from the labors of those who could barely sustain themselves but nevertheless gave sacrificially to Mother Church.

After the Hideous Pope died, and was entombed, an

underling found the journal he had been keeping. On one page were the words:

> *To Lucifer,*
> *My One and True God*

The book, written with quill pen on parchment paper and bound in leather, was turned over to certain members of the Church's hierarchy, who were not totally ignorant of the man's "habits," but they were unprepared for the extent of the depraved nature of his writings. They read every page, horrified by its contents—but rather than destroy it, they took the journal to a secret place in the catacombs under the Basilica, where it would rest, unopened, for centuries.

I know the contents, of course. I looked over his shoulder as he penned the stinking words.

A plan.

A plan for Mother Church.

A plan for the long period of history to follow.

A plan to take whatever good happened to remain, the pure water of the Gospels, and turn it into a cesspool of corruption.

His plan was so brilliant, and it was executed by puppets he left behind, men in whom he had inculcated his Machiavellian designs, some quite willing, others not at all.

This was once the Roman Catholic Church, the personification of the Great Whore of Babylon in that final biblical masterwork, the Book of the Revelation. The Roman Catholic Church did become the evil empire that pope had desired, reeking with foul deeds, draining even further the true faith of the early church fathers, until all that remained was not confined within the corporate structure of the Vatican itself nor any of its satellites throughout the world, but the worship of the millions of people who still believed in the goodness of Catholicism, even as those earlier ones believed in the goodness of that pope.

But truth cannot be hidden forever. Assisi, Luther, and others caught a glimpse and it inspired them to greatness. God's Word cannot be destroyed and never return, though that is what my master would like to believe, would like *us* to believe.

And yet, in the meantime, nothing could stop the monolith of the Church from spreading the poisonous dogmas with which it infected the Body of Christ. Take purgatory—as long as I have been a demon, I have never seen such a place or state of existence, if you will. There is Heaven; there is Hell. Period. Anything else is a pure concoction to distract from the truth of God's Word, over which my master rejoices.

And Mary!

Ah, yes, virgin Mary, the woman chosen of God to bear the God-man, Christ Jesus.

She lived as an ordinary woman; she died as one. She was honored by being the mother of Jesus, but she is not as Him. Others have elevated her to goddess, even above the Son. And again, my master delighted in such delusion.

As Mary was dying, years after her son was crucified—the beloved apostle John by her side, heeding the Savior's admonition to take care of her since He no longer could—as Mary's spirit was leaving her tired, tired body, she saw me.

"They will be doing awful things, will they not?" she asked, having had a hint, in some moment between her and Almighty God, a hint of what was to come.

"That is so, blessed Mary," I say, pleased more than words could articulate that she did not recoil at my countenance.

"They will be worshiping me," she added.

"Though they will deny this."

"There will be statues of me in every church."

"That is true, dear Mary."

"And your kind will be responsible."

My shoulders slumped, my wings drooped.

"It is as you say, Mary, Mother of God—"

I could not bite off the words in time.

"They will be saying that?" she asked.

I nodded with regret.

"If only they could realize—" she starts to say, then is gone.

On the body of her flesh, growing cold so quickly, are tears that had started to form in her eyes before her heart had ceased its beating, now trickling down her cheeks, just a few actually, and then gone, like mortal life itself.

"Christ has demolished death and our own will, so that we are saved not by our own works, but by His works. . . . Papal power, however, handles us quite differently. Fasting is prescribed, praying, eating butter. If you keep the commands of the pope, then you are saved; if you don't, then you are given over to the devil."

Martin Luther's words were an arrow at the heart of the way Catholicism was being practiced, at the way it was being *controlled* from the rooms and the corridors and even the catacombs of the Vatican.

Satan hated this man, hated the monk's proclamations. He brought about the martyrdom of such Luther loyalists as Henry of Zutphen, that distinguished preacher in Bremen, and ravaged so many others—but he could not in the end destroy Luther himself.

Luther shot the arrows that wounded Catholicism but did not destroy Catholicism. Later, Satan was nothing less than relieved because without this form of worship, Satan's own plans would have been greatly retarded, with one less cloak with which to disguise himself.

On and on the Roman Catholics once marched without hesitation, dispensing error after error, adding need-less guilt to the minds and the souls of its heedless subjects, ruling with a medieval mentality even into the Industrial Age.

Until the mid-twentieth century.

Until the pope who took a stand and was poisoned as a result, so soon after he became the Holy Father.

Until the man who succeeded him came to grips with what had been eating away at the church's foundation for so long, and sought to reverse the process, to shake up the hierarchy, to cleanse the wounds that had been dripping with gangrenous infections for hundreds of years. Then he himself was the victim of an assassination attempt, but an unsuccessful one, an attempt blamed on Muslim terrorists—but these dupes did not hatch the plot; they would never have gone that far on their own.

They were only the hired guns, nothing more.

One day, alerted by references to it in a very old file that he happened upon, the new pope found the journal so long hidden. He found it, and read it, and prayed for wisdom.

And then he burned it, the old, old pages quickly turning to ash, as he threw his head back, and screamed, "Lord, Lord, only with Thy strength, only with Thy might can this battle be won."

A battle, yes, a battle for the soul of the Roman Catholic Church. Which may yet be won. The men who burned Joan of Arc at the stake were succeeded, later, by those who were at the forefront of the crusade against the murder of unborn infants.

(My master groans at this turn of events; I secretly rejoice.)

And it continues. This battle. It continues in the Vatican and every archdiocese on the face of Planet Earth.

Flames without end.

The lake of fire stretching in every direction for as far as I can see.

But burning in agony for eternity is not to be the totality of our destiny.

Reliving the past.

That is another part of our punishment, the past and everything it had ever contained.

For a demon, that is Hell indeed.

Especially when I remember the children. . . .

My third child was thus deposited in a foundling home just like the first two, and I did the same with the two following: I had five in all. This arrangement seemed to me so good, so sensible, so appropriate that if I did not boast of it publicly it was solely out of regard for their mother. . . . In a word, I made no secret of my action . . . because in fact I saw no wrong in it.
—*Jean-Jacques Rousseau*

CHILDREN HAD BEEN a special target of Satan's for a very long time. He seemed so singularly *devoted* to bringing about their corruption that it could be said with absolute truth that no other group elicited such venomous dedication on his part.

"Be sure you quote me properly," he said at the very beginning of all this. "Be sure you set down every syllable without the slightest error."

"And what is it that you want me to say, master?" I asked.

"They must be attacked at every turn. We can go in so many different directions. But whatever we do, it has to be effective. Destroy children of any given generation and you rob all other generations to come."

He was standing on the outskirts of Eden or, rather, where Eden had been. There was nothing left now, only straggly weeds, burnt tree stumps, a dry river bed, and bodies, so many bodies, of fish and birds and other creatures—death where there had been nothing of the kind, death replacing the sweet odors and beautiful sounds with its own abysmal scents of filthy decay and that cold silence, except for the shrieking of a wind so forlorn that it seemed to have come straight from Hades.

. . . *so many different directions.*

Child abandonment was one. There was a period in the first century after the death, burial, and resurrection of Christ when this practice was so widespread that the church fathers sought to counter it in a number of ways. But they tended to fail rather than succeed because Christianity then was not nearly as influential in prodding the public's conscience as it would become later.

"We send them into the cold streets on feet of despair and rejection," Satan was saying, as I returned abruptly from my private thoughts. "They drift into crime. They become diseased. They cry out their anger but few hear them, few care, and they die in physical pain and the deepest emotional anguish. *It is perfect, Observer, perfect!*"

He planned to initiate this during the onslaught of the Roman Empire and continue through to what would be known as the "Middle Ages" and beyond.

"We were so successful for hundreds of years," Satan would say later in retrospect.

And he was.

There was a point, for a century or so after the birth of Christ, at which the business of prostitution went into a prolonged slump—not because of any sudden surge in moral values but, rather, the knowledge that a swelling percentage of abandoned young girls got work at brothels, staying there for a number of years, which raised the danger that men frequenting such places could quite conceivably end up having an evening of sex with their own daughters without ever recognizing the heavily painted "lady"!

This sometimes casual rejection of children by their flesh-and-blood parents went on for many centuries, all the while my master rejoicing in the misery of those countless numbers of children cast out into the streets of the cities of the then-civilized world. From Rome to Paris to London and elsewhere, the little ones mostly starved to death if they did not become creatures of the night's dark alleys and dirty streets, their bodies available to anyone who would pay for their services by giving them money or food or simple shelter, or else they would, in the awful weather of winter, freeze where they dropped.

Oh, how hard it was to stand there, as they died so slowly, as they became aware of my presence, reaching out their small pale hands toward me, their bloodshot eyes begging, always begging, afraid of the greater darkness that was sweeping inexorably over them.

But in the midst of that ravenous evil pleasure of his, Satan had not anticipated the manner in which God would intervene. His demonic nature had been absorbed so long without seeming rebuke in what he was inflicting on the pitiable innocent through the sin-nurtured insensitivity of their earthly parents and the blindness inherent in the society of those ignorant times—indeed, he assumed that he somehow could go on and on unimpeded, as though God could not see, did not care.

It all happened through the mere kindness of strangers.

How those words skewered the plans upon which Satan had spent so much effort implementing!

. . . *the kindness of strangers.*

After celebrating for so long the mean-spiritedness of a vast majority of mankind, he was unprepared for other than the most sporadic and tentative acts of concern. The change commenced with the first few hospices, foundling hospitals, and orphanages—many of these, especially the latter, imperfect at best, often operated haphazardly, but still not the streets, still not the streets.

More and more of these sprung up as ecclesiastical and civic organizations came into existence for the express purpose of assisting the poor and the homeless. An example was the Hospital of St. John set up in Jerusalem and staffed entirely by Western Europeans—its sole purpose: caring for abandoned or, as they called them in those days, "exposed" children.

For a time, the number of cases of children thrown out of their homes actually increased because parents could deposit their offspring on the doorsteps of these institutions and not be afflicted quite so severely with attacks of guilt or "conscience," since they had the assurance that helpless boys and girls were not automatically being condemned to death.

But the Christian sensibilities that made better care of such children inevitable also led to stricter penalties against the abandoning parents. Finally there were not only fewer cases but better treatment of those that did occur.

So, Satan gave up for hundreds of years, and turned his attention elsewhere.

But then the latter half of the twentieth century presented him with new opportunities. Drugs were introduced to such an extent that hundreds of thousands of young people experimented casually, or so they rationalized, then became hooked, with some addicts as young as nine years of age. He was able to generate a whole industry dealing in child pornography, and he got special satisfaction in this area.

"It is a slow form of death," he told me as he watched three children expose themselves in front of a 16 millimeter movie camera. "We destroy their minds, and they begin a long period of suffering, then they move out into society and explode their frustrations on others. Perfect, Observer, as perfect as can be!"

He was right, of course; but such measures of pure evil all were eclipsed by the one that was his proudest accomplishment, if pride can be considered the right word

Abortion.

It pleased him for a variety of reasons. First, tens of

millions of babies were condemned to death—but many would be born alive, only to be strangled in minutes or else nursed back to health and sold out the back doors of numerous abortion clinics to couples so desperate for children that they wouldn't hesitate to go the black market route. Second, abortion would divide a nation, pitting the pro-choice adherents against the pro-lifers. And third, ah, yes, this was a stroke of genius on Satan's part.

"If they only knew what would happen when they finally *want* to have children," he said. "So few understand the fate their actions force upon the babies which are next in line."

I nodded in reluctant understanding, knowing that there was a 40–60 percent greater chance for mothers with a previous abortion to give birth to a retarded child or a child afflicted with blood, bone, or other diseases.

To the delight of my master, to the delight of the entire demonkind. . . .

It was on such occasions, among many, when revulsion welled up most violently within me. There I was, watching, chronicling, lending support by my silence. But what good, I told myself, was it to say anything, anything at all? My words would have no impact whatever on the master; he could ignore me with impunity. I was hardly a threat. And yet there was no way that I could turn back to Almighty God, no way He would accept me if I did because my rebellion was unforgiveable, and, therefore, I was without hope, hope reserved only for those human beings who accepted His Son into their lives as their Savior, their Lord.

So I would always be by Satan's side, giving him my allegiance, having to take down every word, every raving, every blasphemy, and constantly reaffirming my loyalty— for he is in need of that, craving those moments when I am at his feet, looking up into his eyes, telling him the sweetest words, the most beautiful compliments, pledging that I will follow him forever, even when he asks me every so often to put my book down and do a special favor for him, and I have to step out of the role of Observer, and become D'Evel. D'Evel convinces himself that if he didn't do it, someone else will, and D'Evel does what the master wants, deeds as sick as anything Mifult and others have ever dirtied themselves with, especially that time he demanded, "Words, words, only words, give me *deeds*!"

I am driven to perhaps the foulest moment of my existence, the slaughter of missionaries in a Central American country, and every member of their families. I plotted their ambush through my rebel surrogates, making the missionaries think they were on a mission of peace, whereas they were being led to their doom.

I stand in the midst of their dying, falling bodies, as they see me just before their souls ascend. There is this one lovely little girl, her blond hair stained red, looking at me not with hatred, not with fear, none of that as she has every right to do—for I have egged on her murderers, driving them to the monstrous carnage—yet she has nothing but pity on that sweet, sweet face. Oh, how can she feel that way about me, how can she ever, ever, ever be so forgiving, so very forgiving?

And I have to admit something quite ghastly to myself. I have to admit that I enjoyed that massacre, that the satisfaction it stirs within me was pervasive, that I wanted to go and find others, and have their lives, their earthly, mortal lives torn from them, and watch the pain they endured as this happened.

No, this cannot be! I am not like that. Throughout history that is what I have told myself.

But in that moment, the ground soaked in blood, cries filling the air, I realize the truth, yet this truth does not see me free; it entombs me with the suffocating realization that I am not so different, not so different from my demon brethren after all.

Then I return to Satan, and tell him what I have done, and as he congratulates me with fervor, I pick up my book and become obedient Observer, the stench of shed blood fading quickly enough.

Or has it, ever?

𝒟URING THE CIVIL War, I had a plantation owner as my host. He treated his slaves abominally. The men he beat, some of the pretty women he raped. Eventually he lost everything. Eventually the slaves were freed. Some of them wanted to kill their former owner. They went so far as to tie a rope around his neck, and were about to hang him from a large oak tree.

One of them spoke up.

"No!" he said. "It must not be."

"But why?" another asked. "He has been very cruel. He has violated our women folk. What mercy does he deserve?"

"He deserves none," a third added.

The rest shouted in agreement.

"*That* is why we have to show mercy," the one former slave continued. "None of *us* deserves even the slightest mercy."

His comrades did not understand.

He then grabbed an old banjo and started playing it as he sang:

'Twas I that shed the sacred blood;
I nailed Him to the tree;

I crucified the Christ of God;
I joined the mockery.

Of all that shouting multitude
I feel that I am one;
And in that din of voices rude
I recognize my own.

Around the cross the throng I see,
Mocking the Sufferer's groan;
Yet still my voice it seems to be,
As if I mocked alone.

The words came out a little differently than that; he pronounced them all with the thick accent of his people at that time. But that was the message that came through.

That hymn had the deepest impact. Several of the men broke out in tears, so moved were they.

Two immediately went and cut the rope, and took the owner and salved his cuts and bruises, and washed him down, and gave him food.

I could not stay, of course.

The Holy Spirit took up residence within that white man, and I was chased out, as always it is so.

I looked back at him, at the blacks who had been his slaves. I looked back further than that, to the Cross of Calvary.

Yet still my voice—

Someone else sang, but the words seemed mine alone.

ONE OF THE principle dilemmas I have had across time and space is finding a host whom I could occupy so that my journal can be continued. (After all, I am but spirit and cannot hold a pen or operate a computer or anything of the sort, so I must possess those whose physical presence enables me the means of transcribing all that my master wishes—as well as some thoughts that are mine alone.)

  . . . *that are mine alone.*

How often have I come face-to-face with that issue? When we are in league with Lucifer, is *anything* truly ours and ours alone? If we are so united with him that, in our devotion, we follow him after casting aside the wonders of Heaven, how separate can we be or, rather, are we one and the same?

  . . . *mine alone.*

The images that I take such great pains to have written down through my hapless hosts, are these so private, so personal that they *can* be called *mine?* Or are they merely *his* funneled through me, and then through the flesh-and-blood "house" that I inhabit, onto the papyrus and, yea, many, many centuries later, the computer disk?

It began with Cain after he had murdered Abel, and

was forced to run in shame for the rest of his life. (Cain could never be happy, could never know fulfillment, from the moment he shed his brother's blood, and, later, took the lives of others, always falling victim to anger mixed with guilt. Ultimately he gave my master yet another victory by going quite mad, screaming, screaming, screaming until he was cast out into the desert, because he was thought to be possessed by my kind, and died after stumbling into a bed of scorpions.)

There was also Nimrod. And King Saul. Many more after these . . . kings, harlots, centurions, even those among the priesthood of ancient Israel.

And later, Judas.

Yes, Judas.

(Satan and I indwelt him while DuRong controlled Caiphas, and other fallen brethren extended control throughout the groups of Sadducees and Pharisees, and then Mifult led a thrust into the house of Herod.)

Judas was, as could be imagined, someone in whom my master indeed took special pleasure. He put down everything I ever wanted in my book, with no protest whatever. He was the ideal servant, pursuing infamy while convincing himself of noble intent, trying to force the Messiah's hand, as it were, and get Him to start a war against the Romans, ultimately throwing off their onerous yoke.

Yet, after he hanged himself, Judas became only another link in an infernal chain, and we both left that limp flesh as I moved on to another, and another, my journal always being carried along also.

And with so many others through the centuries following, I labored so that the chain would not be broken, my journal *had* to be complete, and this drove me to the next body, and the one after that.

Generation succeeding generation, again and again,

taking over the very being of someone who could be my mouthpiece.

They would put down the words that I spoke to their minds. And they would hide the journal so that none would find it until that grand day of Lucifer's Revenge.

For thousands of years this went on; for thousands of years I abode in the shells of the worst criminals, the most despicable human beings of history. I saw through their eyes as they spilled the blood of those unfortunate enough to be in their way.

I remember Jack the Ripper.

I was there when he murdered his first victim. And the last. I was with him in that hidden place in one of the castles owned by the royal family, where he finally died from one of the sexually-transmitted diseases of that time that I cleverly led him to contract.

Evil people. People for whom it was normal to slice open another human being and, in some cases, take some of the organs—

They were my hosts. I could not touch Florence Nightingale . . . Martin Luther . . . Calvin. Those from whom I could have learned soaring truths, not abysmal lies cloaked in the most repellant corruption. Others had that privilege, the unfallen—not I, chronicler of venality.

On and on, virtually without relief.

Until one day in Auschwitz.

My host was a guard named Hans. He could be counted among the worst, showing actual *pleasure* in kicking prisoners, sending them into the lethal "showers," denying them water when they were thirsty, on and on.

And at night he wrote down these deeds, plus thoughts whose origin even he must have wondered about, thoughts beyond his experience but not mine, never beyond mine.

The latest of many over the centuries.

And not the best.

None of them was best. Was Jack the Ripper best, perhaps the lesser evil because his victims could be counted on the fingers of both hands and didn't require a computer printout? Was the cruel feudal lord in the nightmarish period of European plague best because he didn't *directly* plunge a dagger into an innocent heart but simply denied mercy? Was the modern robber baron who bilked a large savings and loan association out of tens of millions the best because no one *died* at his hand?

The lesser of evils?

Could *anything* or *anyone* be called that? *All* evil was part of the master's plan, all who practiced it manifested one aspect or another of his personality.

For Hans, the Auschwitz extermination camp was his private hell, over which he presided as a master.

Until one day. . . .

That moment, one so dreaded by Satan, one that would continue to aggrieve him mightily in the years to follow, that moment when he lost the body and soul of Hans forever. . . .

It came as Hans was dragging a nearly naked woman behind one of the barracks. His intention was to sexually abuse her. Other guards saw what was happening, and smiled, or laughed, as they walked by, one of them shouting, "Grab some for me, Hans!"

"I will!" Hans assured him as he slapped the Jewess across the cheek, and tore at what was left of her garment.

Suddenly she stopped struggling, *so* suddenly that he looked at her with some concern, thinking that she had died in that instant.

She was still alive under him, unmoving.

Her face!

The eyes seemed to be shining as though the sun were

reflecting off them. There was a faint smile curling up the sides of her lips.

"You *mock* me!" he growled.

She spoke then, words he would never forget.

"Mock you, sir? I do not mock you at all. I was praying to my dear Lord about you. And He answered me, in my spirit. That is what my countenance shows—joy over your coming salvation!"

He struck her again and again but still he could not wipe that expression from her face. Finally he stood, grabbed his rifle, and hit her in the chest with its butt, and she fell to the ground. He stood over her, intending to kick her several times with his hob-nailed boot.

"I forgive you, Hans," she whispered, pain apparent in her voice. "I forgive you and—"

His heavy boot smashed into her hip, once, twice, a third time as he kept saying, "Goddam Jew, goddam Jew, goddam Jew," over and over.

Her joy seemed stronger than ever!

"No, Hans, God does *not* damn me, my brother," she said. "Nor will He damn you. As one who has accepted His Son as my Savior and my Lord, I will stand at the very gates of Heaven someday as you enter, and, with my hand in yours, we will walk the golden streets together."

He was about to blow her head to pieces with his luger when another guard stopped him.

"Don't, Hans," he said. "Give her to Mengele. He could use her, I wager. Don't take individual responsibility. Let the butcher do it." (Even the SS thought of Josef Mengele in that manner, either with admiration or disgust!)

Hans nodded. The other guard picked her up and carried her in the direction of the labs.

That evening Hans went to a nearby beer parlor with several of the other guards and started to get drunk.

"Good for you, Hans," one of them said in congratulation. "One less Jew whore to have to watch over after

Mengele gets done with his scissors and his knives and whatever he'll do to her."

"She wasn't a whore," he said abruptly. "She was a virgin."

"You had her first then! Let's all drink to Hans' finest conquest, and may he have many more like her. Love them first, then leave them for the mad doctor! That's Hans for you."

Hans stood, and put all three hundred pounds of his weight into his fist as he smashed the other guard, who sailed clear across the smoke-filled parlor. Then he glowered at the others, and stalked outside.

. . . *we will walk the golden streets together.*

He spit on the dirt at his feet as he remembered those words.

"Jew lies!" he shouted. "There is no God! If there were a God, how could He allow scum like me to exist?"

Hans tried to forget the woman, her words, that look, the very idea that she could have genuinely forgiven him. But her image stayed with him, taunting him in the middle of the night, robbing him of sleep and, during the day, of appetite.

Days passed. His behavior, if anything, grew worse toward the other prisoners at Auschwitz. Even his fellow guards noticed this.

Finally, toward evening, nearly a week after his encounter with the Jewess, he was prepared to go off his shift when an odd thought seized him—indeed compulsion might be a better word—odd because of the man Hans was, a "pure" SS guard who had been taught to view Jews as vermin, and the collected masses of them at Auschwitz as diseased cattle.

He had to *know* what had happened to her!

No one had ever before forgiven him for anything. He had to know her fate. This need would not loosen its grip on him.

So he headed toward the labs, at an hour when he knew they would be closed down.

No! I screamed in his ear, afraid of what he would find. *You mustn't. Let her alone! Forget her—she's just one contemptible Jewess.*

But he ignored my inner voice, perceived more than heard, and managed to gain entrance through a rear window that was half-open.

He had a flashlight, its beam cast upon cages with human beings in them instead of animals, beds with chained men and women, jars filled with—

Hans came to a large tank in the middle of that particular room. It was quite tall, metallic, the top rim nearly two feet above his head. He pulled a nearby ladder over to it, and started to climb the rungs. As he neared the top, he placed two hands over the edge, and pulled back immediately.

So cold!

The chill rippled throughout his entire body.

Then he could see over the edge.

Several bodies were floating in the chill water, all naked. He examined them, not recognizing three, but the fourth, yea, her flesh nearly blue, he saw the Jewess; somehow she was not quite dead, her eyelids flickering briefly, her gaze meeting his own, and she smiled, smiled in recognition, her lips moving silently, but somehow it was as though he heard the words anyway.

I shall enter Heaven soon, past those gates. For you it will be a while but it will be. . . .

He fell off the ladder, then got to his feet, and hurried back to that window, and climbed through it, and then stopped, shaking, telling himself no one else must find out, no one must ever know.

He tried to pretend that all was normal with him, tried to put up a front of business-as-usual. But he couldn't. Nothing would ever be *normal* with him again.

The next day, during a break, he walked back toward the lab, saw bodies being dumped into a cart, and taken to the crematoriums. In a short while the ashes would be disposed of on the outskirts of the camp, a spot he knew only too well, having been assigned periodically to the burial detail.

He tried to pretend that he wouldn't be drawn to that place, tried, yes, mightily so, but failed, and found himself returning to the spot where the Jewess' ashes had been dumped, then covered over with dirt. He would stand there for a few minutes, then leave, and not come back for a day or two, then stay another hour, then leave; finally he would remain for a long time, sitting on the ground, and eventually talking not so much to himself but in a sense to her.

"How could you react as you did?" he would ask. "How could you treat me with such forgiveness?"

Finally, after repeating that question, in one form or another, he would start to weep, then stop abruptly, ashamed of the emotion that engulfed him, his Aryan conditioning kicking in to cut off the tears, the tears that should never be shed in the first place, but certainly not over a Jewess.

My master sent K'Rupt to harden the guard named Hans. Normally K'Rupt did his job quite well. But this time it was different. This time—

Hans changed.

Hans changed more dramatically the next time he went to that same spot, and unable to stand the guilt any longer, took a shovel and dug up the earth. He found more than just her ashes, of course, found deep, awful piles of it from countless other Jews and gypsies and other enemies of Aryan purity and opponents of their merciless domination, running his hands through the white and gray flakes, thin, sharp pieces of bone cutting his fingers and palms . . . then the tiny little testament, at first not sure of what it was, the print so small. He sat there in the midst of that mass grave, reading the words, sobbing, first enraged at his weakness, nearly throwing the little square booklet away but stopping himself and reading further, finally climbing out of the grave, and leaving that scene, not back to the camp, not there at all, but away, in the countryside, walking for miles. They hunted for him but he was gone, and no one had any idea what had happened.

I was in that body of his, for a brief while longer, and then I had to leave. The Holy Spirit entered, the Holy Spirit came in at Hans' invitation as the now former guard of Auschwitz knelt in a farmer's field many miles from the camp. For an instant we confronted one another, as a struggle swept on in Hans' soul.

"You must leave," He told me.

"Yes, I know, Stedfast, " I replied. "But I must be concerned about who will next take over the penning of my book. You know about my book, do you not?"

He looked sadly at me, nodding as He did.

"Is that all you think there is to it, Observer? You do not realize the truth, do you? The truth about your book?"

I was deeply puzzled by what He said but let those words pass by as though never spoken.

"It is all I have, my only purpose," I said, "transcribing what I must so that the master will have a record of everything."

"Then why do you leave, Observer?" the Holy Spirit asked. "Is not your work so innocent?"

"Because the Holy Spirit and the Devil cannot co-inhabit the same—" I replied from memory.

I cut myself off. Understanding invaded my mind.

"You and Satan are as one," the Holy Spirit said, not with triumph, rather the deepest regret to which I had witnessed. "You do what you do for him, in slavery to his

every whim, and yet count that as nothing. To be silent
in the face of evil is to be evil yourself, as you have been
since the beginning when you turned your back on all
that was holy. But you go beyond mere acquiescence, and
cooperate with evil, recording it for your master, and yet
you claim no choice in the matter. In one way you are
worse than he who is what he is and makes no pretense
about it. But to all his sins must be added your own, that
hypocrisy with which you try to cloak the willing syn-
ergy between the two of you over the ages in a façade of
innocence."

He spoke now with a touch of weariness.

"Past the lips of *any* being, human or demon, such
words as come through your protestations are like roses
that soldiers put in their muskets on holidays."

He looked at me with an intensity that I could not long
abide.

"That was written a hundred years ago," the Holy
Spirit added, "but it will remain true until the end of
time."

And there I stood, as Hans walked toward the farm-
house directly ahead, where he came upon a Christian
family that welcomed him, and to whom he poured out
his thoughts, his emotions, and found the kind husband
and wife accepting him as cleansed. (I knew it would be
quite wearisome for him in the weeks to come, as he
repeatedly confronted his guilt over the acts that had
been committed, but now that he had accepted Christ
into his life as Savior and Lord, he had the promise of
relief, freedom from the crushing burden that otherwise
would have been his until the day he died—though so
few of the SS admitted that they suffered from anything
of the sort, instead trying to wash the guilt away in an
alcoholic haze, or deaden it through ever more barbaric
actions.)

I saw myself in Hans as he poured out his inner self to

those strangers, feeling freer to do so with them than he had ever imagined possible because there was *so much* bottled up inside him, previously hidden behind that mask of Nazi hardness, Nazi training that attempted to squeeze out any vestiges of compassion for any other human being, enabling them to do what they were told was necessary for the glory of the fatherland. For me, it was not Hitler but Satan, and the fatherland was to be that over which his coming campaign would make him supreme ruler. But for me there was never to be purging as with Hans, for I had no one, stranger or friend, to whom I could turn in such moments of vulnerability.

I lingered as long as I could outside that modest little home, listening to the three of them. And then I returned to my book.

It was sprawled on the dirt of that field, a slight breeze ruffling the pages.

Who would be next? Who would go by that I might overtake them and enter uninvited?

A teenage boy on his bicycle, a scruffy-looking lad. Yes, yes! Satan would be pleased.

I approached him but stepped back. He was humming a hymn as he went on past. (I realize, of course, that this in itself was not a firm indication of his spiritual state, but it was unusual enough, in that war period, to give at least a hint. Young people then could hardly be expected to be humming such a tune alone, though they might have done so with others around in order to create some favorable impression in those who would be hearing them. Forty years later, if he was singing something from a heavy metal album, there would have been no doubt in my mind about the feasibility of gaining entrance to his soul.)

A short while later, a Gestapo agent stopped on the road for a moment. Then he got out of his car and ran into the field. With no emotion whatever, he removed his gun from its holster and shot himself in the temple. (That was probably the work of D'Guilt, though he had always had a hard time with *anyone* in the Gestapo.)

Next came two ministers, both on bicycles. They stopped for a bit, and sat down on the grass and talked, and talked.

The short one, younger, was talking about whether the Bible merely *contained* the Word of God or was, from cover to cover, His Word in every respect.

The older one, taller, a bit plump, took a stand in favor of the Bible *as* God's Word, whereas the other argued against this, citing all the potential for error of translation and transcription over the centuries.

After perhaps an hour they ended the discussion, and the older minister left. The younger one lingered a bit, inhaling the vegetation-scented air. As he was about to leave, he noticed that current portion of my journal lying there. With some curiosity, he walked over to it, picked it up, and idly leafed through the pages.

He took both of us home with him.

I THINK PERHAPS the very worst part of being what I am is that I can communicate best just with others of my kind, for they are my only true companions. *My companions. . . .*

I should think of them with affection, but how can I do that? Love is not really in our vocabulary, you know. Satan thinks hate, talks hate, practices hate. The only love he has is for himself.

How can you feel even a touch of love, a suggestion of it, ersatz love or otherwise—how can you say you love a creature that inhabits a human being who is sucking a baby out of its mother's womb, limb by limb, bits-and-pieces of fingers and toes, a tiny, tiny skull, fragments of skin, and blood, blood that flows in a *thing* that is supposed to be nothing more than mush, like cereal in a bowl in the morning?

The answer is that no real emotion exists between us, except what is born of the necessity of our circumstance. We tolerate one another. We come to one another with the burden of our multiplying iniquities, and sometimes there *is* temporary relief, a momentary cessation of pain continual—but then it is gone, and we are back where we

235

have always been, chained to a creature with whom we have felt less and less rapport.

There is Mifult, for example, the demon principally responsible for abortions as well as other forms of the abuse of the young. He certainly has been successful over the years, especially the past twenty or so, successful in corrupting the minds and the souls of those who favor this butchery.

"I have just seen Darien," Mifult says to me this very afternoon.

Darien on his journey down Angelwalk, the path he has been trodding as he searches for Satan, trying to piece together the puzzle of his own outlook, about the master, about the Casting Out, and so much more besides.

"And what happened?" I ask.

"He got to me, Observer."

We are standing near a man who is tossing fetuses, limp, bloody fetuses, into a plastic trash bag.

"I had to admit my dream to him," Mifult tells me.

Ah, yes, Mifult's dream. . . .

"*I am very much alone on a plain. It is totally barren—only sand as far as I can see. Suddenly I notice some specks at the horizon. They seem to be moving, though they are still too far away for me to be sure.*

"*I wait. Closer they come. I begin to see forms, of different sizes. Still closer. They are now near enough so that I can see what those forms are.*

"*Babies, and little children. Hordes of them. Almost like bees from a distant hive. There may be thousands, or more, forming a long line extending all the way from the horizon. They surround me.*

"*One of them approaches, holding out her hand. She says, 'Mister, why did you do those terrible things to me?' And I realize she has been the victim of a child molester.*

"*A boy comes up, his body covered with bruises.*

*Others as well. Suddenly the crowd parts and I see the
most devastating image of all: a tiny body, its arms and
legs missing, somehow rolling, rolling, rolling toward
me, crying, stopping at my feet. His head is turned
toward me, the eyes pleading, the skin wrinkled and
blotched and smelling, oh God, smelling of saline solution. The first attempt had failed, so he was pulled apart
limb by limb.*

*"I run. I run as fast as I can. Abruptly I fall and lose
consciousness. I think I come to again, but I am not sure.
Suddenly I feel someone tearing at me. There is intense
pain. Then more pain. I scream out. But there is no
response. I try desperately to fight against someone who
is pulling at me, but I realize, I realize, I realize that I
have no arms, no legs.*

*"The next instant I am at someone's feet. Looking up.
Pleading. I have become that baby—"*

It is always the final words that are the most compelling, perhaps the most shocking from Mifult's recollection of his nightmare.

"and—I—am—looking—up—at—myself!"

"You told Darien everything?" I ask.

"I did," Mifult replies.

"The master will be displeased."

Mifult nods.

Concede nothing to the enemy—a precept of warfare—
and no less so in the spiritual realm.

But Mifult did just that. He admitted the pain of what
he was doing, within himself and within his victim, but
even that was not the worst part of it. The worst was that
he admitted to a wandering unfallen angel that there
were victims at all. He swept away in an instant a major
tenet of a carefully orchestrated campaign to *encourage*
abortion by the attempted removal of guilt. How can
there *be* guilt over blobs of flesh, lumps of skin and bone,

and all the insignificant rest? No need to get all worked up over *that!*

Mifult is increasingly typical of the rest of us, those who can no longer bury their conscience in the adulation that brought about our state in the first place.

And yet, sadly, *some* are more than ever like the master, more than ever zealous in their pursuits, more than ever *eager* to wash their hands, as it were, in the flowing rivers of blood that have been spilled by my kind through the ages. They have stood in the very center of many battlefields, gaining *pleasure* as they walk over the spilled guts that come from victor and vanquished alike, grenades or lances or bullets or cannon balls tearing the wounded and the dying open to cries of agony.

"I'm afraid," the man will say. "I don't want to go to Hell."

"But *Hell* is where you are bound," the demons will respond, "where *we* will have you forever."

"Oh, *no!*"

"Yes, yes, *yes!*" a creature of stench and decay will shout back as that human soul leaves that now limp and superfluous body, reaching out for the latest victim— *only* the latest, for countless others are ready for the line, *their* turn decreed by *their* sin because there has been no forgiveness, no cleansing for the simple reason that there has been no acceptance of the One Who could change it all.

*T*HERE IS NO way I can enjoy any sustained contact with that which is noble and beauteous and uplifting, except through chance encounters perhaps, with Darien or Stedfast or another like them—at least contact in the sense of some form of symbiosis, as when a man sees a beautiful woman, and the two fall in love and there is a merging of mind and body and future in marriage. Any marriage of any kind is beyond my reach, merely something to look at when I am with human beings, if you can ever call what I do, what I am, if you can call any of it being *with* them. . . . I look at them as they touch one another, as they hold one another, as they share the feeling between themselves, as—

The unfallen angels have such a state with God their Creator. They and He are undivided. They are, in some indefinable way, extensions of His divinity, not as the members of the Trinity but as human lovers, separate but yet bound together by the way they think, feel or act with each other.

And to what or with whom are demons bound? To a God who inspires? That is not our destiny, perhaps it never was.

Did God know?

As the omniscient One, was it that He knew in advance of our coming rebellion? Was that why I have such a strong memory of Him watching us leave His Heaven by the thousands, and there being sorrow in His countenance—but not surprise, not puzzlement, not utter amazement that we would elect to follow a different master?

All of us left with anticipation, throwing off the shackles of what had come to be, for us in our delusion, oppressive goodness and purity, which carried with them the necessity of total obedience if we were to have continued in His presence.

Satan could no longer tolerate living in the presence of One greater than himself. That was the basis for his rebellion, and yet in time that very statement itself changed, *had* to change, because if Satan continued to acknowledge that God indeed was the master, not he, this would mean that Satan himself was the servant, and how could he have abided this demeaning estate for time and eternity?

So he nurtured the true conceit of his existence, a conceit which he was far less successful instilling in us, the conceit that made him think he was in fact *greater* than God, that the feeling of being less than Him was a trick, a trick perpetrated by God to ensure eternal subservience.

"I will not be fooled," Satan bellowed, and he repeated this a hundred times, a thousand times, countless, countless times until he came to believe the lie himself. It was a statement always there, reinforced by those fools among mankind who have convinced themselves that there is no God simply because they have convinced themselves that there is no God.

I speak, therefore I am.

I said it, therefore it is.

Many a deceived soul has stood outside and waved a

fist at the sky and said, "If You really are there, strike me dead, now, for daring to doubt first Your magnificence, then Your justice, and, yes, today, this very moment, the very fact that You *are!*"

And when they have been allowed to live, when God *seems* not to have responded, their defiance is justified in their own minds. And they go on to delude others, not realizing that perhaps they are, in the short term, free of God, as they would put it, but assuredly enslaved to *my* master who then has become *theirs* as well.

For some, wealth is a substitute, and along with it, the power that wealth invariably brings. For others, it is fame. For *all*, there *is* a substitute of *some* kind, taking the seat of the throne of their lives.

But God does intervene. God can take the wealth, the power, the fame of that celebrated New England family and show the actual poverty of their lives by the persistent interpolation of tragedy—the losses of loved ones, the scent of scandal drawing the rumor-mongers to them as ravenous vultures to a pile of dead meat, bleeding and bare and already in the process of decay.

Your idol is shattered in the dust to prove that God's dust is greater than your idol.

Words read and not forgotten, words heavy with true truth.

For such as this family, placing so much faith in its bank accounts and its political connections, the idols do fall, do break into irreparable pieces, do lie there in the dust, *as* the dust, mocking in their brokenness, as though crying out from the shards of what they once were, "Stupid one, stupid one that you are, see what it has gotten you!"

*I*T IS TRUE that I can go anywhere I want, in the twinkling of an eye, from the Amazon to the Indian Ocean; from the streets of London to the outback of Australia; from today to yesterday; from prehistoric caves to ultra-modern skyscrapers. I am not captive to time or place but still I am a prisoner, though there are no bars, no confining barbed wire. I am a prisoner of my insubstantial spiritual state.

Sometimes, as I have said before, I will see the Others, those once my comrades in Heaven but now my eternal enemies.

Enemies. . . .

I wonder periodically how that could be, how it could *ever* be. I tremble at what has changed, what has changed indeed, since I remember so very well what it was like in my former home. And, of course, so does Lucifer, once the finest, the most beautiful of all angels.

He remembers, as we all do, the absence of death, disease, pain, the *reality* of joy, peace, and that indescribable, sublime fulfilment of being in the presence of our Holy Creator.

Our Creator.

242

Not even Satan has forgotten that singular fact. Without Him, we would not exist.

God gave us life, blessed life. . . .

What have we done with this gift?

We have thrown it back in His face again and again. We have turned beauty into corrupted countenance after countenance.

And what *is* that countenance? If a mirror could offer our reflection, surely that sight alone would mean the end of any hold we have on sinners the world over. That is what I say now, but then I am probably wrong, for there are those still intent on worshiping evil whatever the face. Yet many, many indeed, seeing the reality of what we are, *would* shrink in fear and loathing, turning away forever.

We all have become images of Satan, just as we commenced life in the image of God. In Satan we see ourselves and we recoil—but it is the disgust of a drug addict as he jabs yet another needle into yet another vein, hating what he is doing but not able to mitigate the addiction—and after however long, he is frequently headed for Skid Row where many have been chained to drugs or alcohol or both for a very long time, their bodies battered and sick shells for souls that long for the relief they assume comes through death, not realizing that, without salvation through Christ, they yearn for something more awful than a lifetime of Skid Rows.

We are will-of-the-wisp vagrants, lost and lonely nonentities who wander from place to place, meeting often in cemeteries among the worm-infested remnants of our mad deeds—but just as frequently in great and grand buildings littered with the consequences of hypocrisy, men and women stumbling about month after month, year after year, leading others astray as our surrogates among the ripe fields ready for harvest.

$\mathcal{A}$ND WHAT IS the fruit of the Others as they approach the harvest of God?

It is St. Francis taking off the rich garments of his ancestry and putting on the rags of his obedience. It is a bowl of food to a starving child in a desert land. It is peace between enemies, a white hand joined with a black one raised before Him in a chorus of praise as *our* bigotry, as *our* violence, as *our* fruits are shed like the profane encumbrances they are. It is wounds healed, pain stopped. It is a baby being born, not a fetus terminated. It is all this and a vast tapestry of other people, acts, moments.

Though my kind is loathe to admit it, we do look at what we see in *their* wake and know that we have chosen wrongly. In comparison to ourselves and our malignant deeds, the Others truly are pure, clean, kind, and good, without the slightest taint of selfishness or despair.

But their kindness, their goodness, has been translated beyond thought and deposition into deeds; there is so much that is noble and decent for which they have been responsible, working under the direction of the Holy Spirit.

I think of Stedfast, who is the source of the legend about a guardian angel. He was with Darien every step of

my former comrade's odyssey along Angelwalk. Darien
was never aware; God kept Stedfast's presence a mystery.
Darien was never in any real danger; it was just that he
had to find out the reality of what my master was all
about, as humans often say about another.

Stedfast.

I have seen him usually from a distance since the
Casting Out. I have seen him by the side of Mother
Teresa, encouraging her, aiding the Holy Spirit.

Stedfast has been with redeemed men and women as
they walked up wooden steps to the guillotine.

He has held the hand of Joan of Arc amidst the flames.

He has been with the homeless.

He has turned away legions of demons as they tried to
wreck the lives of countless millions over the centuries.
He has been the Holy Spirit's dutiful, steadfast lieuten-
ant. He has done it all out of love for the Father.

To serve such a One who can inspire such devotion!

All that I am yearns for what they have, what they can
do, the joy they bring, the peace.

They can leave Heaven, they can return, they can—
See the smile of a Holy God.

God smiles, God cries, God gets angry.

He smiled often when we were there, my kind and I.
Back then there were no tears, no anger.

We—

I hold the words for a brief moment—and then they
gush out, through my host of the moment onto solid
paper through real ink, born from the invisible presence
of myself.

*We made God cry. We made God angry. We did this,
the master, all of us. . . .*

And that is why we suffer. As suffer we should.

Because of us, Hell is.

A ROUND TABLE.
Hands on top, palms down.
People with their eyes closed, heads tilted slightly backward.
A medium chanting.
Calling up the spirits.
—Shall I pose as the father this time?
—No, you should be the daughter. You were the father during the last seance.

It has been astonishing to me how *many* human beings are so eager to make contact with us, so willing to open themselves up to what they feel my master can offer.

I suspect that untold millions of people the world over who worship Satan in one form or another imagine they would be ecstatic if they could only *be* one of us, exercising the so-called powers they envision us to possess.

If they could only be one of us. . . .
And what would they become if that were the case?
The wielders of power?
Yea, they would have it, and a great deal else indeed. They would have the power to plunge kingdoms into

darkness and despair by corrupting the men who rule them.

They would have the power to cause voyeurs to ogle naked bodies in dark little rooms smelling of sweat, their eyes pressed against viewing machines with flickering images on their pupils, and a slot for the next quarter of a dollar.

They would be able to precipitate needless death after death, whether on the battlefield, or in dirty alleys, or in clinics founded for healing but turned over to slaughter riding on the twin backs of vanity and convenience.

And what more would there be for the ones running after us with slavering anticipation?

No sickness. No death.

Life eternal, life about which they need never fear that it was running out.

And they would have a leader, a *real* leader, one with single-mindedness of purpose, dedication.

They would never have to sleep. Or eat. And they would be witness to *all* the monumental events of all the years of history on this planet named Earth.

I have known archaeologists who would have given us their souls to be in the midst of Ancient Rome—not walking through its ruins, but through the thriving city itself.

Or with the Mayans or the Aztecs or the Incas when *their* civilizations were flourishing.

But not just archaeologists, of course. There were the historians who would have thought it truly Heaven to meet Caesar in the flesh, to be in Queen Victoria's court, to hear Lincoln give the Gettysburg Address.

Archaeologists and historians and others who would lust after the possibilities, the many enticing possibilities that could be realized by being eternal, by wandering the planet with us.

And artists who would have been delirious with joy to

watch Michelangelo actually painting the ceiling of the Sistine Chapel rather than just observe the faded centuries-old images to which they had to be resigned as mere mortals.

Or supposedly mad Van Gogh with his masterpieces. Or Raphael. Or—

I reconsider Van Gogh, knowing all too intimately that it was not madness at all with this man, it was me inside him, the artist acting as my host, my presence a deterrent, and how I wanted to leave, how I wanted to let genius flower fully without that deranged edge to it, and yet I could not, I could not leave because I was there at the assignment of my master, and I could not disobey him.

We have been with them all, the geniuses of mankind, the madmen. We have been witness to everything glorious of which they were capable as well as the debased side of their lives—Michelangelo's homosexual liasons and Van Gogh's promiscuous heterosexuality, about which my kind have mounted propaganda over the centuries since such artists have practiced their art, propaganda that uses these men to legitimatize that profligate nature they manifested resoundingly, saying in words so nice, so respectable, so logical, "How can you condemn men like these? Look at what they were capable of!"

Some fell for that—nay, *many* did—nay again, *most* of mankind, aware of the Michelangelos and the Van Goghs and others, assumed that genius, surpassing as it was with these men, the product of that genius inspiring people for centuries, that genius, whether they realized they were proclaiming this or not, evidenced a kind of de facto salvation for them, as they assumed that the divine images in the Vatican could only be of God, and that God alone was with Michelangelo when he did his work.

But then if images were tacit acknowledgment of the salvation of their artist-creator, surely all the statues in all the churches in all the countries on this troubled planet would lead onlookers to proclaim that there was no such thing as an artist or a sculptor of Christian scenes or figures who was *ever* anything but a saintly, utterly holy and saved individual.

And there is something else. As a consequence, couldn't it be said that church committees which did little more than authorize the keeping of such holy artwork on display, such holy statues, whatever might have been fashioned by the creativity of any man or woman, were suggesting that the outer appearance was *evidence* of inner spirituality, and worshippers needn't look any further to be assured that they were in the right place?

The specious nature of all this is apparent. To the question, "Should the Michelangelo who created some of the greatest artwork in the history of mankind be condemned because he *happened* to be homosexual?" Satan would have naive men and women answer with a resounding *no*.

But the truth is otherwise, and none know that better, none know that more intimately than those of us accustomed to feasting on the weaknesses in human character, exploiting these and, thereby, entrapping the unwary.

It is *so* clever!

By accepting the *artists*, whoever they are, as well as the art, the bridge is built, in decades or centuries to follow, for tacit acceptance of his sin, saying in effect if he can do such masterpieces that bring joy to millions, let's just overlook his one *little* problem.

The same holds true for great composers. Peter Ilich Tchaikovsky continues to thrill classical music aficionados. Ask the average ones about his homosexuality, and they would say, "How does that *matter?* It's his music that I adore."

But it does. It does. And it is a matter of which Satan has taken great advantage over the past decade or so, making people wonder if homosexuality can be so bad, so evil, so perverse if a Truman Capote was capable of turning out masterpieces of literature. And in any event, they argue, what he did behind his own bedroom door shouldn't matter to the rest of the populace.

And then came AIDS.

A major defeat for my master, a defeat that tore gaping holes into his very best seductive reasoning.

And yet he bounced back, getting people, lemming-like, to still accept the premise of civil rights for homosexuals rather than imprison them all and throw away the key, as God would do once each gay person died, and was turned over to my master.

A very large percentage of the gay population *enjoy* having pain inflicted upon them, whether by whips, whether by chains, whether by hot wax on their flesh. Immersed in his own perversity, Satan can guarantee that they will get pain beyond their wildest fantasies—but they will not *savor* a single second of it as they scream in agony for all of eternity.

Evil, sinful men redeemed by their special talents, by their refined tastes, by periodic acts of kindness unconnected with the crimes for which they are responsible?

Satan would fool people into saying yes, yes, *yes!*

But take another example:

Hermann Goering, one of the top three Nazis serving Adolf Hitler, enjoyed collecting fine art, antiques—a laudable hobby. Should he be less condemned because of this one aspect of his personality? Hitler himself loved animals, often treated women with great chivalry. Was he somehow less repugnant due to any of this? If Himmler showed kindness to a handful of Jews simply because he liked them, did that mitigate *in the slightest* the horrible treatment he sanctioned against millions of others?

If a fine artist, if an artist of noble output, if any such

artist is painting God, painting Jesus Christ, painting the most uplifting scenes from the Bible, and doing so out of divine impulse, gathering up the creativity required from the very center of his being, as a form of his own worship, and to the honor, the glory of the Subject, then that does say something, that does suggest my master has lost the battle with such a man.

But if this artist, Michelangelo or any of the others, were creating his masterpieces simply for the beauty of the art itself, simply to test his mastery of color and stroke and design, then where is the salvation in that, however impressed may be the admirers who stand and look in awed silence?

It is hard to think in such terms. It is hard to do so in the *real* world. Do human beings withhold their appreciation of a stirring ballad sung by a fine vocalist until they find out about every sin in his life, to see if that appreciation can be legitimatized? Do they refuse help from a doctor until they put him through some kind of quiz to make sure that he passes muster?

Of course not.

But—and this is the issue, is it not?—should they take the ballad, do they take the help from that doctor *as evidence or hint of sanctification?*

Again, of course not.

Yet that is the deception Satan will use to entrap the undiscerning. He will hide the bad with a mask of good. He will say, "What you see is the true self. There is no other. Don't believe the religious hypocrites."

I know.

All too well.

*D*ECEPTION.

And nowhere more emphatically than within the Body of Christ.

The little men on television speak of their corrupt doctrines. They rant on about Christians being every bit an incarnation of divinity as was Jesus Christ. They play with their heresies with the fervor of curious children masturbating for the first time, and yet these are old pros doing it in front of millions, an altogether different sort of indecent exposure.

Not only do they build a house on sand, but they build a house that has nothing in its materials to retard the flames that will ignite and consume its very structure.

Soon, I think, *soon that house will be brought down at your feet while you weep over the ashes that are the remnants of your pretensions.*

I know of a large-scale, awful plan of Satan's, a plan to attack the very nerve center of much of the modern Christian world. I can still recall his chuckles of anticipation.

Prime-time news coverage is guaranteed.

It is true, in the human world, as well as in the demonic, that people *do* get what they deserve.

And never more so than with the odious gang of my master's puppets who seem so righteous and caring as they reach out through the airways to take the faith of the elderly, the young, the gullible, and twist it all into a common dagger that my master throws back into the heart of all that is holy and good and decent and honest.

That moment, that moment of paroxysmal fury when the concrete-and-steel-and-crystal empires of the dishonorable majority of those electronic religion sellers, emitting the stench of their spiritual putrescence, become exposed for what they are, propped up movie sets, with no substance whatever, held together only by the dollars that are thrown at their dung-encrusted feet . . . that moment, yes, it is coming, it is roaring in from the north, it surely is, if demonic plans are not thwarted, timed to occur as a crippling blow just before that final, foretold apocalypse in which God will try—oh, how He will try—to scourge the earth of our influence.

For those caught up in the industry of Christianity hoopla, the publicity machinations, it will seem at the start a moment, a time, an event of rejoicing, steeped in self-congratulating speeches, as the powerful and the famous from Christendom gather, majoring as they do in the exteriors, parading their modern white sepulcres, and in this sham, seeming so dedicated, so righteous, while full of the picked-clean bones of those they continue to betray with promises of easy salvation, easy healing, easy money—the event of their assembling together all aglow with spotlights and neon signs and tinselly cheer.

Yet, in the end, the celebrating will not come from any within the Body of Christ—no, it is not this of which I speak but, instead, the collective infernal rejoicing by thousands upon thousands of hovering banshees, my comrades one and all, emerging from Hell to howl their delight at the stinking parade of blind shame that soon would be broadcast from the ashes of itself to the world around, even as that world begins the short ride to Armageddon.

*B*UT FOR THE *moment, there is a delay, a wait, which is almost unendurable for the impatient among us. . . .*

My master is not an environmentalist. Nor a sentimentalist.

He is uninterested in having a healthy world, a world of beauty.

Scarred landscapes are his children.

Toxic wastes excite him.

Air pollution is an elixir.

Oil spills are accolades.

Ozone depletion he celebrates.

Rivers clogged with fish dead of seeping chemicals fill his days with laughter.

Birds suffocating.

People dying from lungs of rampant cancer.

The eyes of others milky white, sightless because of addictives, whatever else.

Children, thin and pale, leukemia killing them.

Flies on dung and urine and phlegm from lack of sewerage.

Lifeless bodies, stomachs bloated, flesh decaying under the hot desert sun.

Always in the air an odor, the odor that only death brings.

And he stands there, this master of my kind and me, he stands there in the midst of his domain, gloating as ever, while we sing the *alleluias* that have been commanded from times of darkness immemorial, *alleluias* that are his and his alone.

"*I* AM VERY tired," says A'Ful.

"I can understand that," I respond.

"He has me doing the most terrible of deeds."

"And he has me recording them."

"In his eyes they are glorious; in mine they are filth." He launches into recollection then, moments of ignominy, though even that word seems insufficient to describe what my comrade has been forced to do.

AIDS.

He helped to cause the epidemic by planting the seeds of perverse behavior, behavior that obviously violated the laws of God and biology, which are, after all, one and the same.

"The very thought of what gays do among themselves sickens me," he says. "And the knowledge that I was an instigator, that I put before them what the master did with Adam and Eve—promises, Observer, promises of pleasure, promises that God was somehow impotent and, ultimately, the truth of the matter was that they didn't have to worry about Him at all, that they could go their own way without fear of retribution."

. . . the convertibles drive by, the flatbed trucks, the people walking in the middle of the street. Some seem,

257

on the surface, quite happy, their faces painted brightly.
Quite a number are lifting small bottles to their nostrils
and drawing in deep breaths. Others are smoking what
is obviously marijuana. A few are dressed in nothing but
essentially the lower part of their underwear. There is an
abandonment of inhibitions that they embellish with
their garish look. Several are kissing not so much out of
passion but as a pose for the TV cameras in evidence
and, frankly, to shock those not accustomed to things of
darkness being played out in the light.

A'Ful is trembling, his wings drooping behind him.

"The next step was to shift gays from the shame that originally accompanied their behavior to pride, to militant pride that would become, to them, a cause, with lawyers hired to protect their rights, with the media by-and-large geared to brainwash people into thinking that they had any right to have *any* rights at all, that they should be treated in any way like *normal* people."

He laughs cynically.

"Look at the Andy Rooney case," he points out. "All he did was state the truth about these degenerates. All he did was be honest. And he was punished for his words. As soon as he opened his mouth, they were on him."

"Yes," I agree. "You have convinced so many people that to speak out against them is to be guilty of bigotry."

"A master stroke!" A'Ful says with half-hearted jubilation. "Satan applauded me. I should be exaltant."

But it is obvious that he isn't.

The demon responsible is the demon burdened by the significance of what he has done.

"You know, I can hardly wait for Satan to win the war," he adds. "Then I won't have to tolerate these obscene monstrosities any longer."

With that, A'Ful has touched upon an aspect of our master's personality that no mortal journalist, no theologian, no one on the human side has ever stumbled upon, and it can only be that they simply don't know the truth.

Satan has no sense of loyalty, except to those of us who followed him from Heaven, and none can be completely certain about that, though we base our future upon it.

As far as the master is concerned, human beings are absurdly weak puppets whom he can manipulate at will. Once he has emerged victorious, once he has wrested Heaven away from God, he will then turn on everyone who has ever supported him over the many centuries of time. A being with no loyalty, no fidelity, has no compunctions about devastating the ones who helped him to victory—rather like the man who wants to be king and then once he is crowned, disposes of anyone who could be a threat to him, even those who helped him to sit on the throne.

I know. Because I have heard him tell us so.

"They think they do right by doing wrong," he once bellowed. "The pornographers, the drug dealers, the gay libbers—so smart are they? What they don't realize is that I am as appalled by their practices as God is. Nowhere is it written that I look at certain acts in any manner that is different from His own. I find these as repellant as He does."

The impact of that was heavy.

What we do, we do not because any of it is honest or moral or holy. Satan knows what is honest and moral and holy *better than any human being in all of history!* Of all the angels, he was the closest to God, the most magnificent of any of us. Could it *ever* be supposed that none of the divine truths would sink in? Nay, he absorbed into his very being all that God had told us while we yet remained. He saw the beauty of God's plans for the soon-to-be created Human Race. He saw the soaring majesty of what Planet Earth was to be like, free of disease, death, guilt, shame, indeed of anything which would hamper the potential that mankind would be capable of as time passed.

But Satan was willing—and is still willing—to throw all of this away and pervert the truth and deceive the unwary. If there were no knowledge of the truth, then there would be no conception of what he had to subvert in order to gain the victory he sought.

"I *know* that abortion is evil," he went on. "But I am willing to *use* it to tear at the fabric of a supposedly Christian nation—or any other, for that matter. I *know* that there is no such creature—and that is exactly what they are, dumb, brute beasts giving in to their brute passions—I know there is no such creature as an honest, decent, practicing homosexual who deserves even a modicum of respect, but I am willing to fill them up with ego, willing to get them to flaunt themselves in their annual parades *because they are a cancer, like abortion, that will drain away the decent moorings of any society, any civilization that tolerates, yea, that encourages them!*"

He went on and on telling us the sweeping story of what the future would be if we all did what we must to win the war against God.

And then the most stunning revelation of the lot, kept from us until then.

"The human beings we corrupt," he said, "those who pledge allegiance to *me* often do so because they have chosen *me* as the victor. The odds, they say, are in *my* favor. And they assume I will reward them for that choice."

Satan was overcome with laughter, and had to stop talking briefly in order to gain control of himself.

"Yes, I *will* reward them," he said. "I will give them exactly what they deserve."

He paused, surveying the group of demonkind. We all wondered what he would say next.

None of us was prepared.

"I will punish them for their deeds in *precisely* the same manner as promised by God Himself. They *will* roast forever in the lake of fire. The difference is that all of *us* will be watching from a safe distance!"

There it was, the ultimate treachery from the Arch Deceiver, the Prince of Lies!

Countless millions falling over themselves as the centuries passed, falling over themselves in blind obedience to their demonic king, and doing so with one transcendent motivation: that they could indulge their vile pursuits and escape punishment for these as Satan rendered God a foe made powerless by defeat in the eternal warfare between them.

And yet they would heap upon themselves the same eternal goals of fire that God had said *He* would mete out for their sin.

Satan clearly anticipated the moment of seeing so many who once had fallen before him in adulation now thrown into the lake of fire, screaming, "You betrayed us! You betrayed us!"—and the master yelling back at them, "Of course, my foolish ones! If I could betray *Jehovah*, the Creator of all of us, I should hesitate to do the same with *you!*"

But there was more, further indication of how much Satan was motivated by sheer revenge. He planned to take all surviving Christians and force them to engage in the very acts that had seemed so repugnant to them while there was still the expectation that God would win the war.

"How many will cling to their emasculated Creator when they have to have sex with animals?" he said, licking his lips. "They will *beg* me for mercy."

He paused, looking out over his audience, then: *"And I will give them not one drop of that mercy which they will be craving so desperately!"*

I S MY MASTER the instigator of *all* evil on the face of the planet? Or is he sometimes merely a bystander, gloating over certain events but not directly responsible for these?

He has sought to give the impression that the answer to the first question is yes, and to the second, *never!*

But, of course, he is a liar, and there is little truth in any of this.

Human nature, since the Fall, has been quite capable of mischief, and considerably more, all on its own. In some instances, Satan has had to do no more than provide a mere spark to the ammunition that would have exploded otherwise.

I never realized this more vividly than when I used a mass killer as one of my hosts. I was inside his mind, his soul. I witnessed many of the murders through the eyes of the man responsible, if he could be called a man by any stretch of the imagination—more like a demon wrapped in human flesh, only the thinnest of façades.

But there was one in particular, the grisliest of all. He raped a teenage girl, then cut her into little pieces, then mailed these parts to the editors of the biggest newspapers in the nation.

And sat back, in his then-anonymity, laughing.

Satan chortles at such things. But I don't. I don't at all. I never did. I tolerated my master's perversity as part of the package, so to speak.

. . . *laughing.*

Others died at this killer's hand, mostly teenage girls. In different sections of the country, north, south, east, and west.

He would use disguises, sometimes a moustache and horn-rimmed glasses, sometimes a blonde wig, sometimes shaving all the hair off his head, sometimes—

Always it was night-time when he hit the streets, looking for victims. The young girls responded to him because he was quite handsome. None ever escaped, except the very last. She was the one who helped the police track him down. He was in a warehouse when they trapped him. One of the officers had to be pulled off him as he exploded in anger at someone so evil that he could be responsible for the deaths of nearly forty innocent girls.

I left him long before his execution. Seldom was I more relieved. Countless times I have been *evicted* because of a host's conversion, and it has not especially bothered me, since that is one of the rules of the game, so to speak. And having played the game for a very long time, I have become accustomed to the rules. Usually I have left as a result of the death of my host, cold flesh not a hospitable place, nor helpful to the writing of my book—obviously.

And conversion to Christ was once again the cause. But this time it was not so much that I was kicked out but *liberated*, freed from the shell that had housed me through the most vile of acts, acts so debased that even I find it difficult to contemplate them, to see in memory what he did with the bodies of the innocent after he had committed their murder. I left this host gladly because I couldn't stand the thought that, now he was born again, as they say, he would avoid punishment, that he would be walking the streets of Heaven, while some of his victims who perhaps died without Christ in their lives would be consigned to Hell where my master could torment *them!*

Where was the justice in that? The love?

I remained there, in his death row prison cell as he said those words of acceptance, tears streaming down his face, tears of cleansing and release of all the sin, the anger, the pain that had been bottled up inside him. And in that instant as he died, I was forced to see the utter joy on his face. Yet turning slightly, I watched as the parents of some of the victims showed the anguish that they felt, anguish only partially relieved by the death of the man responsible.

"Can anyone suppose that *this* would do it for us?" a mother said afterwards. "That sending lethal charges of electricity through *his* body would somehow make the future any less empty?"

How *could* I bear the peace on his face after the Holy Spirit entered that despicable soul of his?

I forsook my journal, leaving where it had dropped in that scene of his capture and went off by myself, trying hard indeed to stay away but I could not. I had to return. Then the switch was thrown, and he died.

Outside, there was a celebration. Hot dogs were being sold. And hamburgers. Some folks were munching on heavily-buttered popcorn.

A banner waved in the breeze. "THIS IS FRY-DAY FOR YOU, KILLER!"

They were laughing. The media was there.

A man was playing a guitar.

A celebration I said. A celebration I mean. A grand and glorious event for them.

"This was too good for him," a man, holding a can of

beer, said between belches. "He should've been sliced and diced like he did to some of his victims."

He shook the can.

Empty.

" 'Vengeance is mine saith the Lord,' " he went on. "I don't buy that crap, you know. It's nothing but a pile of—"

A buddy came up to him, holding out the next can of beer.

"I'm gonna get sizzled tonight," he bragged. "They're gonna have to carry me out."

Beyond the barbed wire fence a hearse had pulled up to the back entrance of the prison.

They all turned and watched.

"Good riddance!"

"Hope you roast in Hell!"

"Hope? Whadda you mean? Where else would that monster be?"

"Thank God he's gone, wherever that is."

A single figure dressed in black stood near the prison as the hearse drove away. Her head was bowed, a veil over her face. Crying, she was.

"Look!" someone shouted. "Look at that broad!"

"Yeh. Acting like she's upset. Man, would I love to get my hands on her. Teach her what's what! Teach her good!"

Laughter, raucous, punctuated with blasphemies.

Hey, throw another shrimp on the barbie, will ya!

*I*T IS SAID that the most significant cause of killers such as that one is the kind of abuse-filled childhood from which so many evolve. Uncaring parents strip away their self-respect. And they lash out in anger.

But not all children who are subjected to monstrous suffering in their own homes become mass murderers. Some merely spent the rest of their lives paying another price for the sins of their so-called loved ones.

In this regard, then, some of the more recent cases of child abuse stand out in memory; others, while tragic, fade. (When you have been in on this sort of thing for centuries, a few are bound to rise to the top of your mind while the others are drawn down into the quicksand of your guilt, submerged perhaps permanently, perhaps not.)

But one in particular, indeed, yes. . . .

The burned child.

Not Rothenberg. Not him at all. He is not a candidate for damnation because he accepted Christ as Savior and Lord.

Another.

A child whose father poured gasoline over him and set him on fire.

A child who is scarred for the rest of his life, in mind as well as body.

A child who is, in the eyes of some, a freak.

It happened five years before.

But still the operations are necessary, still pockets of skin puff up, especially on humid days, as body fluids seep in, like air in a balloon. A scalpel must lance these areas so that the poisons can be dabbed out and then new skin taken from other, less-affected parts of the body, and—

In the course of his lifetime, this boy-later-adult-man will have nearly a hundred operations. The costs will reach into the hundreds of thousands of dollars.

He will never marry.

The father has been released from prison.

No community of moral, caring people wants him.

He must be forced down the throats of protesting citizens somewhere.

When he gets settled in, finally, he looks at himself in the mirror, runs fingers over his smooth face, and wonders if his son will ever forgive him.

The son must live not only with his ruined forehead, his cheeks, his chin, the rest of his upper torso, and fingers that will never be fully re-sensitized to touch—he must live not only with this, but with a lingering bitterness, a bitterness that twists his soul, affecting his every relationship.

"I can never be a father," he cries in moments of unquenchable despair, "because no one will ever want to hold me, no one will ever want to kiss me."

A quarter of a century after the burning, he dies, alone, in a room beside a round table with a phone on top and no calls to make.

The flames surround him, their heat licking at every inch of him. He can see a familiar form through the reddish glow, like a phantom.

"Why did you do this to me, father?" the no-longer-boy screams.

His father does not respond, lost in his own anguish.

"You made me so bitter, so filled with hatred that I turned away, from people, from God. I rejected them all, father."

The man does not answer. He cannot. There are no more words because he knows what he has done, and he knows what he must face, and he knows that it will never, never end.

"God damn you!" the no-longer-boy shouted. "God damn you to Hell!"

And then he stops. His pain is transcendent. He has only strength left to cry, as the other is crying, the torment they feel rising in their echoing sobs from that flaming pit throughout eternity.

Your actions damned you both, I add in this my book, recalling his profane words, words I myself hate even though I am still a demon.

You rejected the son, the Son.

I WROTE OF shed blood some while back, didn't I? Christ shed His blood for redemption; I have shed the blood of others for damnation. In that lies the difference between Him as the master of the saved and Satan as the master of the lost.

But, you know, the Arch Deceiver himself is often the victim of deception.

"*I* put Him there," he will say gloatingly. "I drove men to doubt, then anger, then murder. He died because of *me!*"

I think of that in idle moments when I am not occupying a host or when that host is asleep. I think of how true it must seem to Lucifer. He oppressed Pilate with cowardice; he instilled fear and envy into Caiphas and others, this made easier by their stultiloquent legalism; it was satanic oppression directed against Peter's sin nature that caused the fisherman to deny his Lord three times whereas, earlier, he protested that never would such a thing happen!

It was my master in Judas that—

No, I cannot pass the blame entirely to Lucifer.

Judas was also *my* host. I, too, was indwelling him.

And I, I alone, was the one using him to continue my journal.

How much of *me* did he manifest?

How much like bloated, festering, cankered Satan did Judas become?

If I were not the cause, then I had to be the conduit.

It is a truth that has occurred to me before, but each time I have been successful in pushing it aside, in burying it in some outer corner—

(And how like man I am in that regard, how like man indeed, dealing with the truth by frequently pretending that it doesn't exist, that I can escape its implications.)

. . . as I, too, looked up into that tormented face, seeing the trickles of blood from under the thorny crown, hearing the groans of pain as the body twitched and shook and wrenched in final agony, even so words of exquisite supplication escaping softly and with infinite tenderness past those pale and twisted lips, a supplication not rooted in condemnation, not seeking the damnation of those responsible but rather a supplication begging God to forgive the architects of this infamy, and then that final gasp, a small sound really, hardly audible, lasting only for an instant, that final acknowledgement signifying it was finished for Him, it was indeed over.

Truth nailed to bare wooden beams and raised up to be scorned by the multitudes.

And there I was, with the rest of them!

This moment came for me after Judas hanged himself, my journal at his feet, found by a passer-by and taken . . . and I go on, with the next one who will find it, a whore-demon attaching myself to any and all.

Do I have no shame?

Mister, want company for the evening, for the rest of your life?

*W*HAT WE DIGNIFY with the name of peace is merely a short truce, in accordance with which the weaker party renounces his claims, whether just or unjust, until such time as he can find an opportunity of asserting them with the sword.

That, really, is the state of affairs between governments on Planet Earth. Any recent naive talk of peace must be viewed in the light of my master's designs for this battered globe.

Satan is flexible, you see.

He can achieve a great deal in war as well as in peace. In war, the barbaric side of man's nature is ascendant. Atrocities are committed that would have been unthinkable otherwise. The slaughter of hundreds or thousands in a single battle is routine. But then there are the casualties of a score of children in a schoolyard when a nation is at so-called peace.

But peace can also provide a cornucopia of malevolence in other ways for the Prince of Darkness. It is in peace that governments grow lax. It is in peace that morality suffers the seductive doctrines disseminated by my kind through those men and women we succeed in dominating: materialism, dealt a crippling blow by the sacrifices mandated in wartime, rises from its dormant state to ravage the countryside, as it were, a malignant force interpolating itself into the lives of those who stand before its altars in dumb worship.

Peace can turn the minds of men from basic survival to reeking self-indulgence. They grow fat with excess, burdened by the lack of exterior menace; the longer there is peace, the more people are duped into thinking that that is how things always will be.

There is no better example of this than the aftermath of World War I, the "war to end all wars," as peace spread over the world, the possibility of hostilities on that scale just twenty odd years later viewed as only the delusion of irascible cynics or pessimists.

And there is the other consideration: What is peace to some is a slow and excruciating poison to others! Was the state of peace to the Germans peace at all? Or rather a two-decades-long humiliation that went beyond mere shattered nationalistic pride, until the survival of Germany itself seemed very much hanging by a few tattered economic and political threads?

It was at this point the Arch Deceiver introduced the human devil, Adolf Hitler. If King David was a man after God's own heart, then Hitler was a man after the awful depths of Lucifer's twisted and malignant self. My master was the *Fuehrer's* master perhaps more completely than with any of the demonkind, if that could be considered possible. Satan remade Hitler's personality into his own image.

When the extermination camps were built, Satan merely constructed his own version of Hell through his human puppets, telling millions of people that if they weren't

Aryans or they didn't give *him* complete obedience, they would be tormented unto death. When that death did overwhelm them, Satan was given yet another opportunity with the unredeemed ones to pile on more anguish, this time in the *real* Hell.

ONCE THERE WAS such a fear of communism.
Now the resurgence of National Socialism is cause for
increasing panic.

How Satan rubs his gnarled hands together at the
thought of *that*!

He has the elements in place, through various groups
such as the Ku Klux Klan, the Aryan Front movement
headed by a chap in southern California who is as scary
underneath as he seems nice on the surface.

"He's ripe for us," Satan only recently told us. "He
hates niggers, he hates kikes, spicks, he—"

On and on Satan ranted, enjoying the sounds of those
hateful labels, enjoying the prospect of fomenting a new
civil war within the United States, but on a much wider
scale than that of a century and a half ago.

"The harvest is at hand," he proclaimed.

An army of disaffected young people.

The runaways. The abused. Seething with anger, hungry for revenge.

"And I shall give them the guns to blow the brains out
of the generation that has been tormenting them," Satan
told us.

At the same time he has been pushing, pushing,

pushing the mothers and the fathers who are now the objects of their contempt, inculcating that generation with the doctrine of disposable parenthood: If you don't want a child, abort the thing; if you don't want the continued responsibility of the offspring that do survive this modern holocaust, then kick the creature out of the house, and get on with your own life.

By the thousands. Pouring out into the streets. By the hundreds of thousands. Clogging the arteries of this present society. Looking for a way to get even.

And so they band together in angry, seething groups to fuel each others' fire, groups which provide exactly what they are seeking.

Hate fears above all to be delivered of itself.

I cannot remember where I read those words or by whom they were written. But they are true, you know. For some, hatred is the alpha and the omega of all that they are. And it must continue, this corrosive venom that seems almost to replace blood and marrow. Once the original object is overwhelmed, defeated, cast aside as impotent, there must be another, and the process is endless, for were it not, were all the objects of all the prejudice, the bigotry, the lust for vengeance gone, sucked up and spit out, then that hatred would turn unimpeded upon itself and—

I have seen such as are possessed in this manner. I have seen them in every age of history. I have used many as my hosts.

And I serve one.

Yes, I do.

Oh, God, I do.

THERE ARE MANY plans in which my master is involved. Most are set to spring into action at the same time, each a piece in the puzzle of his design for the collapse of civilization, and his consequent takeover.

Especially interesting is the one he is working out with those the world no longer fears.

Especially indeed.

A dozen men sitting in chairs around a table in a room bare of any other furniture. Their expressions are intense. Faintly, in the background, there are the sounds of a military band.

"It is time that we . . . we . . . what is that American expression?" one of them, tall, thin, owlish-looking, says.

"Pull the plug?" another offers.

"Yes, pull the plug!" Owl says. "He has gone further than we thought. He has gotten carried away with his reforms."

"We are at a dangerous crossroads," a huge man responds, his frame that of a grizzly bear. "If he is allowed to go on, the survival of communism is at stake."

"He must be stopped, we all agree, is that not so?" Owl asks of the gathering.

They all answer in the affirmative.

"The day the Libyans posing as Iranians and armed by the Iraqis blow up that . . . that . . . ," Bear adds, not quite sure of the target, but sure that there is a target.

Someone reminds him.

"Yes! That is the one. As soon as that happens, there will be a worldwide reaction. Tell me, do they have everything they need?"

"They do," Owl replies. "Forged passports. A cache of explosives near a place in America called Colorado Springs."

"Gardens of the Gods," Bear adds.

"Quite safe?"

"Completely."

They adjourn in a few minutes, but Owl and Bear remain behind.

"It is an exquisite bit of planning," Owl acknowledges.

"Truly it is," Bear agrees. "In the midst of the chaos, with Reformer siding with the Americans and reacting in anger against the terrorists, we leak a story that there is an invasion of Iran being concocted, with Reformer pledging the resources of our vast spy network to help and, we intimate, perhaps much more than that."

Bear paused, sipping for a few seconds on a glass of vodka.

"We have an agent of ours from the PLO go in and assassinate him," he adds, "blaming it again on the Iranians."

"Suddenly the world turns against Iran more than ever before," Owl says, gleaming, "plunging it into its greatest isolation of the post-shah period."

"Then one of our own men takes over in the vacuum left by Reformer's death, and, posing as their true friends, we form a secret alliance with the Iranians, supplying them with arms."

"Will China go along?" Owl asks. "Can we be sure of that?"

"We can be sure," Bear says ominously. "The blueprint has already been drawn up. Beijing is satisfied."

Reformer had changed since 1985. Once a through-and-through communist, he seems to have very nearly abandoned the Party's decades-long goals.

"But the Party has abandoned the goals of Lenin and Marx," he remarked at one point.

What was the turning point for this man?

There were two.

One, the Leningrad earthquake.

Two, the Petrinsky nuclear disaster.

Reformer saw the depth of human suffering arising from both. His people, his fellow Russians had died by the tens of thousands.

He stood in the midst of the quake-shattered buildings, heard the cries of the dying, the injured.

And felt utterly helpless.

"We just do not have the capabilities enjoyed by the Americans," he whispered. "We learned little about disaster response, because we had had little experience in that regard. It was the western world that had their earthquakes, their tornadoes. We had been through our blizzards but little else."

"And nuclear plant safeguards, sir," the aide pointed.

"Yes," Reformer agreed. "Nothing tragic would happen to us, of course—only to the Americans, with or without our sabotage."

In the case of Petrinsky, he could look only from a distance, the region completely unsafe for any on-the-spot tour.

"The deaths, at this point, will go over a hundred thousand," an aide told him, "possibly much greater."

He gasped at the news.

"But there is more, sir," the aide added. "Many will

take years to die! For some, it will cause leukemia; for others, lymph cancer. Brain tumors will be another source of suffering and death. Also, leprosy may be involved, sir."

"Oh, God . . ." he said, his voice choking.

"God, sir?"

He waved his hand impatiently through the air.

"Go on," he said. "Are there more details?"

"The information I have given you concerns only the generations that have been born. There are pregnant women who will give birth to monstrosities, pathetic little human-creatures with misplaced eyes, with. . . ."

The aide stopped for a moment, his eyes moist, a sudden headache throbbing at his temple.

"Children who will face retardation," he went on with visible effort, "and unknowable numbers who may not have purely physical disabilities, at least like the others, but will experience emotional and related problems because their metabolism has been dealt a wrenching and devastating blow."

The aide could not go on, his mind filled with the details of a number of reports that he had compiled for presentation to the general secretary.

There was silence for a moment.

"We were so concerned about conquering country after country, about expanding the Soviet sphere of domination that we let our motherland go to hell," Reformer said.

"Do you mean that literally, sir?" the aide interjected.

Reformer only looked at him without answering.

THE BLUEPRINT. . . .

They think themselves so clever and to a degree, they are, in human terms, devilishly clever. They allowed Reformer to ascend to a position of power, offering only token resistance to his plans for reform. All the while, they sat back while he seemed to be amassing more and more power. He was *their* man; they *wanted* him to be in command.

Past tense.

He is not now the same man he was as at the beginning.

No, he is no longer one of *them!* Rather, he is their diametric opposite, with some streaks of good, some pockets of decency, though trapped by a lifetime of atheistic dogma. Perhaps Reformer would like it to be different, but that cannot be, at least not in any reasonable scenario that can be conjured up; yet unlike us demons, he is *capable* of making an attempt to change the scheme of things, of letting some acts of noble intent break through the nihilism. Accordingly, prepared for the worst conceivable eventuality, his opponents—termites in the house he is building, eating away at the structure—

are readying themselves for that moment when it will collapse and they will reassume command.

But in the meantime. . . .

Ah, yes, that is the brilliance of the scheme—they think it theirs but, of course, they are nothing more than the recepticles of it. In the meantime, NATO has been greatly altered; the two Germanies have been integrated, the communists able at last to gain positions in the new *Western* government, which was otherwise an impossibility, even though they may use the convenient label of socialists—indeed, how easily mere labels fool the gullible.

What a difference a year made back then!

You do not lock your doors to those who are no longer your enemies.

You open your house and welcome them.

The communists no longer need to use force to break in; they are being given the key.

All things work together for evil to those who are in slavery to Satan.

Sounds familiar, doesn't it?

$\mathcal{B}$UT THAT PLOT isn't the only one by unholy men in secrecy planning events of death and destruction. Another is being executed step-by-step from Germany. Though half a century has passed since the Holocaust, for some Germans, it seems like only yesterday.

The industrialists.

Behind reunification is a hidden agenda. The sons of the same men whose profits benefited from the use of cheap Jewish labor at concentration camps built near German factories—I know this was not at all a coincidence because one of my hosts was a vice-president of Siemans AG and I heard a great deal about men with big companies who helped the Nazis pay for the costs of erecting the camps with the condition that the locations be in close proximity to certain factories whenever possible or, when this couldn't be achieved, that trainloads of Jews be taken wherever the industrialists desired at any given moment—these sons still with billions of dollars at their disposal are supporting the neo-Nazi movement worldwide, but with particular emphasis in the United States.

Famous companies continue with remnants of the old mindset, directors and major stockholders and others who skim off part of their earnings to pay for the expansion of the Aryan skinhead movement, causing the deaths of Jews, blacks and Catholics, sending bombs to mayors, senators and anyone else who may be standing in their way.

I remember coming across a book by an author whose credits included a notable history of the Third Reich. A German himself, he lamented over his countrymen's historic tendency toward tyranny, toward violence, toward the destruction of any who disagree with them.

Adolf Hitler was one German who rose to the top of his garbage heap. But, even as I think the thought, I realize that there are a hundred like him yet entrenched in that land, a hundred or more who, given the opportunity, would create a thousand new Dauchaus, Auschwitzes, Treblinkas, Mauthausens and others.

A few years ago, one of my hosts stayed at a mountain-side motel in Colorado. Food eaten in the adjoining restaurant turned out to be quite bad. My host was afflicted with stomach cramps so severe that he thought he was going to die. He called the front desk for medicine, and was told that there was none, that he would have to drive to a community seven miles away at midnight, and hope that a store would still be open. My host begged for help but the assistant manager remained unsympathetic. My host then accused the man of acting like a Nazi. The reply was unforgettable: "I *am* a Nazi. Did you ever think that Hitler might have done the world a favor by getting rid of six million Jews?"

The Oregon courtroom that saw a judgment of millions of dollars against Tom Metzger, the force behind the growth of the American skinhead movement, also saw him declare that people like him were in government and industry all across the United States. "We are everywhere," he said proudly.

We are everywhere. . . .

America has those in secret places planning terror campaigns that have no connection with Middle Eastern terrorists but which will cause havoc all their own.

And the money, yes, the money for all of this, the money for the weapons and so much else, that money comes from wood-panelled offices in Hamburg and Frankfurt and all across Germany.

Some Germans haven't changed, you see. I know. I know all of it. I know the irony of what is happening— how money spent by Americans on German cars and cameras and many other products is being rerouted back into the land of the free from the land of the swastika.

Why does no one stop this insanity?

Simple. Money that buys weapons also buys people, also buys silence. And when the money fails, there are the sudden "heart attacks" from poisons undetectable by even the most advanced tests.

I know it all, as I have said. I was there at the beginning.

When my master rose up before us and spoke of the good old days of "burning Jews and hanging niggers."

I CANNOT SAY that I *like* being in cemeteries, and yet these places of bone and worms and crypts of the dead do seem like home more often than not; I am, after all, a creature of darkness, of death, of sheer and total damnation. I wear a tattered cloak of sorrow—I speak metaphorically since, as spirit, I wear nothing—a cloak of tears in an eternal night-time of torment, ravaged by fear of coming Armageddon.

Tears. . . .

Many are shed in the cemeteries of my life, yet there is an attempt to put everything in the best light. Look at the good deeds, it will be said. How many poor had the deceased kept from starvation? Surely that counts for something in the kingdom of the Almighty. How many missionaries had he supported? How much—?

Acts aimed at redemption but deprived of that goal in the divine scheme of all creation!

Nothing can be *done.* God did it all. There is but one requirement: simple faith.

But often the messengers get in the way of the message, because those who minister to the thirsty with apparent waters of redemption bring with them instead leather bags of contaminated filth.

I remember a funeral at Forest Lawn. . . .

Major Star had died. His agent was there. His manager. His fans. The media. A dozen limousines. Press vans.

The eulogy was given by pompous, egomaniacal Arch Strutter.

"This man's *deeds* speak for themselves," he said. "He lived his *seed faith* to the fullest. *And God will reward him accordingly!*"

How awful!

There I was, as a demonic intruder unknown to any of them, and I had a firmer grasp of theological reality than that overblown, opportunistic fool.

Yet I thought over Strutter's words, and realized how true they were, though not in the way he intended.

". . . God will reward him accordingly."

Indeed.

I stayed quite a length of time at that funeral. Others stood up, and spoke about Major Star, his decades in the movie business, all his fans world-wide, the total box-office draw he had exerted.

And then those present went on to the wake-like affair at the studio where Major Star had been under contract. Several individuals became drunk and there was a bit of a brawl.

In corners and at tables, huddled among themselves, they talked of Major Star's vanity, his appalling temper, his disdain for showing any degree of respect for his co-workers.

"What a bum!" declared a man who had earlier stood up and praised Major Star.

"You've really changed your tune," another at that table observed.

"That was good business, good PR. This is reality."

Days later, ads were run in *Daily Variety* and *Hollywood Reporter* heralding Major Star's impact upon the

entertainment industry, that there would never be anyone like him ever again.

Behind closed doors, there were sighs of relief all over
town.

NOT FAR FROM Forest Lawn was another cemetery, adjacent to a church dating back to the turn of the century. It hadn't reached landmark status as yet, and was rather run-down. An old woman had just been buried there that same day. Out front was a battered, rusty sedan.

There were only three mourners, not hundreds.

Her daughter, her son-in-law, her granddaughter.

". . . left behind no worldly goods," the minister was saying, "at least not the tangible kind, not limousines, not mansions, not hundreds of suits and pairs of shoes and millions of dollars in the bank. She left behind only one thing . . . a legacy of love."

His voice broke, for an instant; he coughed, then went on speaking.

"She had no one except her family. She outlived everyone else, all the old friends from decades before. When she died, she was with her family. She made one last comment to them."

. . . *the clouds be rolled back.*

"That's what she saw, Lord. Let me add one other line from a famous old hymn: 'I'd rather have Jesus than silver or gold; I'd rather be His than have riches untold; I'd rather have Jesus than houses or land.' "

It was soon over, this little ceremony. The daughter, the son-in-law, the granddaughter lingered, then left.

I turned to go.

But I was not alone.

Stedfast. . . .

Stedfast had come, for a moment, to pause at the grave.

"She was radiant, Observer," he said.

"I suppose she was, Stedfast," I replied.

"The lines disappeared, the gray along with it, the arthritis, the dulled mind—all that remained in her coffin, you know."

"You are always right, Stedfast."

This unfallen one turned to me, sorrow in his countenance.

"She went to glory," he said.

"But not me," I said in return.

Stedfast nodded.

"No, not you, my—" he started to say but stopped, doing the spirit-equivalent of biting his lip.

—*friend.*

That was what he meant. In Heaven we were close . . . we were created together, we worshipped at the Throne together.

Now there was no continuing bond—a broken thing perhaps, something shriveled up, mocking the former oneness, attendant with this the aging memories of salvation thwarted among the multitude of victims over which demons have been rampaging since the beginning of time, the ever-present residue of their torment haunting me in this my world of insubstantiality, ghostly echoes of remembered souls ripped from mortal shells and flung at the feet of my rapacious master, who would scoop them up as he wished when he was personally intent or hand them over to other demons awaiting such when he couldn't be bothered, preferring instead other prey, while they had their way with a new plaything.

"That old woman did but one thing, Observer," Stedfast said then, and nothing further.

Fairest Lord Jesus.

Stedfast did not have to fill in the blanks.

I knew. I had known for a very long time.

A truth encompassing this old woman's destiny, and mine as well. Her choice, the only redemptive one for eternity.

He will I cherish, He will I honor.

Which I never did, which I cannot, which mandated with harsh and compelling justice my entry not in the Book of Life—aglow with the sanctioning verdicts of presiding Divinity—but another . . . of judgment unmitigated, with names from every age, penned in blood spilt on ten thousand times ten thousand battlefields of one sort or another over the centuries of times past . . . not of life transcendent and joyous is it to be with those whose names denote their sad and condemned multitude—nothing, in fact, but the soul-encrusted corridors of Hell itself.

$\mathcal{D}$ESPICABLE PEOPLE DRESSED in expensive suits and backed by piles of money and not a few tactics of intimidation hold sway in the industry that Major Star left behind. Those who were glad that he was no longer on the scene will nevertheless latch onto another puppet put out there by the ever-powerful gangsters who wait in the shadows of the industry.

Many are Italian, or it might be said with greater accuracy—though being accurate never has been my master's strong suit—that they have been seduced away from the decency, the simple and pure human warmth typical of most Italians. The numbers of those thus born have shrunk, this loss of their exclusivity continuing to provoke much dissension within the Mafia, since there has been strong Sicilian pride evidenced in their earlier dominance of the makeup of the various mafioso families. Now, those from this particular region are joined by many awful human swine of the lowest possible sort from other nationalities, demons in fleshly garb, spawning all sorts of indecent things which cause so many innocent ones to be dragged down in the dirt along with them.

They profess to care about the racial bigotry they stir

up, hiding behind this ludicrous attempt to legitimatize themselves as they wrap a nation's flag around their behavior—but in fact they are interested only in power, in money, in sex-for-hire, and indeed, as such, they are tremendously effective allies of Satan's, doing his bidding in arcane ways that fatten their pocketbooks as well as their egos. . . .

That funeral for Major Star is only part of the story regarding untold numbers of people in the entertainment world. This industry is such a ripe field for demonic harvest that Satan has periodically toyed with the idea of designating a special session of Hell for agents, producers, movie studio presidents, actors, and so on.

"I shall call it Heartbreak Hotel," he says as he muses over the notion. "Yes! That is a good one."

He laughs at his own joke but he *has* hit the mark.

The top man at one of the major studios uses the power of his position to seduce any attractive young actor who catches his eye.

Never was this more flagrantly apparent than when his studio created a new series about young people, and a strong cast was hired. The lead actor was approached by the studio head and told that if the two did not become lovers, the actor would be dismissed within forty-eight hours. The young man refused. The next morning he received his walking papers, and another actor hired who was more "accommodating."

The original actor's scenes were cut and his replacement refilmed all of these. One problem: The actor who refused to go to bed with the studio head was still listed in *TV Guide* as starring in the series the week it debuted, and there was one quick night scene which somehow escaped being cut; the original actor was seen quite clearly. No explanation was ever offered publicly.

Since then, his replacement has done nicely, with

movie roles being offered, and the series itself enjoying a measure of popularity as a high profile draw for younger viewers.

Satan loves it when truths are twisted or lies simply substituted. A great deal of that goes on in Hollywood. It is not difficult to see this in so many of the films that are produced, when immorality is raised up as normal, even laudable—and when filthy personal lives are not only not condemned, but those living such lives become influential in any event.

I once had as a host a rotund actor, one of the perennially popular stars, who had a weakness for teen-age boys and young men. He would spend considerable time in a certain restaurant on Sunset Boulevard, eyeing the customers. The owner was paid off handsomely for allowing him to use the restaurant as a kind of jungle in which he stalked his prey.

Then there is that star of a medical series who has had the same male lover for more than twenty years.

The one-time television talk show host who is seldom without his latest male conquest when he goes to various show-business parties.

The supposedly rugged star of a once top-rated western series who is unable to get by without a new lover every few weeks, the AIDS crisis doing little to his sexual appetite.

Others have noted the reality I knew all along, that 60 percent or more of the casting directors are homosexuals or lesbians. Most are incapable of offering an honest evaluation about an actor's talent if they encounter someone whom they find sexually appealing. Step-by-step, an expanding number of young people are drawn into an addictive world of rampant perversion because it is either that they succumb to the "casting couch syndrome" or give up any hope of vibrant careers.

Yet little of this is ever chronicled by an industry that

supposedly relishes freedom of expression, and which is more than eager to "expose" the sins of Christians, conservatives, and others who have been criticized over the years. The reason is simple, Satan's success is virtually absolute: Scripts dealing with gay subject matter or using gay characters are regularly submitted to one or more gay and lesbian media groups for their approval, only approval is not the word used. The implications are camouflaged by words such as "consultation" or "out of a desire to fight bigotry." All very noble-sounding, though nearly every demon knows the truth and delights in it.

I am a demon, and yet there is no delight that I can feel, as hard as I try, when I find such a powerful industry as the television and movie interests controlled by gays or their sympathizers. Satan is delighted, of course. But I am not.

But such sin does not show the full extent of corruption in Hollywood—a significant part of it, yes, but by no means all.

Bribes are commonplace. Extortion is part of the fabric of the business, if not by the mobsters, then by the unions—even those not shackled to the mob, which is only a handful, to be sure. (It is interesting that organizations supposedly in business to protect the rights of masses of people end up being corrupted by handfuls of violent opportunists with ties to big crime bosses.)

Ah, the mob.

This kind of human garbage get their mansions through the profits made on the backs of the wrecked lives of their customers. They tool around town in their Mercedes and their Rolls and their Jaguars, driven by their hired help, smoking their imported cigars, and not looking beyond their bullet-proof glass at the devastation left behind.

It is not that being rich is sinful, obviously it isn't. But becoming rich off of the blood and innocence of others is. And how clever they are; when anyone calls them evil, calls them filth, they hide behind the accusation of bigotry—bigotry against their wealth, bigotry against their nationality, bigotry against their rough upbringing— waving it like a sword of offended righteousness.

That is their plan!

It is a way of diverting harsh scrutiny from their dirty businesses. They have *allowed* the stereotypes, the big- oted buzz words, to gain wide acceptance as a handy tool to make people feel ashamed of thinking *that* way.

In the meantime, they will continue providing the drugs that the Hollywood crowd craves. They will buy control of an ever-expanding number of businesses, from studios and production companies to catering services and a great many others.

The drugs, yes, but also the prostitution, the gambling, anything that is illicit and from which they can make a profit!

My master has always been convinced that drugs are among his most effective weapons. They are the means by which we can gain access to an individual, and then my kind take over completely.

Satan's pleasure in this regard seems almost orgasmic in its intensity. The pain of the drug addict is something he craves. The more people who become hooked, the happier he is.

"I can weaken any group, any company, any branch of government if I can just get them to try cocaine, to try crack or other drugs," he has said. "These eat away at their will, destroy their self-respect, and leave nothing in return, nothing except an open door for us!"

Satan has a very complete blueprint in terms of drugs. It began with the so-called Woodstock generation. It continues for decades afterward. By the year 2000, he wants drug use to be commonplace among elected officials, whether the mayor of a city, a senator, a cabinet member—one right after the other.

"The more frequent, the less shocked people will be," he tells us periodically. "The first case is scandalous. The second is alarming. But through sheer repetition, by the time it is announced that the hundredth official has been indicted, the public will yawn, the public will count it as yesterday's news."

"Or become so enraged that they mobilize and do something about it," I pointed out on one occasion.

"Perhaps," Satan replied. "But it's worth the gamble, don't you agree?"

I nodded in agreement, my thoughts turning to the addicts, the poor addicts, who had given over their souls so willingly.

As I myself have done.

But corruption in Hollywood cannot be laid wholly at the feet of the drug lords. Human greed isn't a trait peculiar to gangsters.

Much attention was paid to the case of a humorist in his suit against one of the major studios. They stole his script and made millions, yet feigned innocence. Yet this is but one of scores or more piled high like manure in Hollywood, and kept quiet by people not wanting to attack the sources of their livelihood.

I have been in a room with actors as they are being manipulated by mogul-types, lies streaming from the ugly little mouth of the producer or generic studio executive about misappropriated funds. Inevitably, I want to suddenly materialize, and shriek before this smooth-talking swine in my true disgusting form. "We are controlling you. We are in charge of your every thought, word, and deed. *Now get a good look at what your masters are really like!*"

I have watched the brilliant careers of decent men and women plummet because they had the courage to stand up to—even expose—the atrocities of major Hollywood executives.

I have seen these evil ones leave the life of the flesh and enter *our* world, shedding mortality and donning the cape of damnation. Many show remorse; many beg for a second chance. But in the game in which my kind and I are principal players, there is nothing of the sort. Once that old body is gone, there is no opportunity to do it all over again, to improve their chances in "the next life" despite what certain popular actresses keep trying to get those dumber than they are to believe.

Yes, Hollywood continues to be a place of dreams, as it has been for more than half a century.

Before the nightmares take over.

At Heartbreak Hotel.

*T*HERE IS HEARTBREAK at another place but it is not a hotel, though it has many people staying there.

It's called a rest home, but it is also, in a separate building on the same grounds, a sanitarium. For either the old or the mentally ill, and, often, the line is blurred between the two, it is a miserable life that they are called upon to lead.

It is not a place that demons frequent.

Is that surprising?

In earlier periods of history, when mental illness was more or less automatically equated with demonic possession, Satan had a field day, as the expression goes, playing upon the ignorance of the times, ignorance that gave him the credit in cases with which he had no connection or, as in some, no *continuing* connection.

"Those were the days of rich harvest," he would say as he reminisced. "While people became ill because of the pressures they faced, which had nothing to do with our kind, or because of chemical imbalance, or other insti- gating circumstances, all of *us* could ignore *them*, could rejoice that they descended to the misery we *would* have inflicted, but which didn't cost us a single precious moment. Human nature and human society did our job for us, so we could go on and *really* possess countless others."

"Pushovers, master?" I offered.

"Yes, that *is* the right word, Observer."

"Thank you, master."

But in the final stages of the twentieth century, with so much presumed enlightenment, it would seem that Satan had gone from feast to desperate famine.

Not so.

"There was never anything particularly appealing about possession," he added. "It was a great deal of work in many instances, and when we encountered exorcism, not at all pleasant in the final analysis."

He rubbed his talons together with delight.

"Now we get the same result, and all we have to do is sit back and watch the spectacle! It is even better than during the Dark Ages."

The "spectacle" was obvious in that place of confinement. For the elderly, the afflictions of Alzheimer's and other forms of senility were especially satisfying to Satan. He had never forgotten the cause of all the pain, all the suffering that was visited upon this planet where he has been running rampant for so long.

"If Adam and Eve had never given in," he said, "we would not have had a battle to fight, let alone win or lose. We would have been trapped, Observer, rendered impotent by righteousness all around us. Christ would never have had to die for the redemption of mankind."

He stopped ever so briefly, visions of might-have-been crossing his mind. I shared those with him in that moment, not by reading his thoughts—which I couldn't do—but because, with greater frequency, the truth of what we caused to be destroyed came through to me as well. Still, as with Satan, I rejoiced when I could squelch them, and not have to face the truth yet again, a world without sin, a world in which death never occurred, a world of joy and peace and perfect union with Almighty God.

Not the small parcel of the kind of world I see before me now. Aging men and women shunted aside by off-spring who cannot be bothered. Many unable to control their bodily processes, their actions, their hallucinations.

Some may be the way they are through a lifetime of abusing their bodies by pills, by alcohol, by other drugs— legally or otherwise—by promiscuous acts of intercourse with partner after partner. By thinking they have escaped punishment in this life only to discover that they have not, they have been reduced to shells of flesh housing souls of torment that do not have to wait until confine-ment in hell before they taste condemnation.

Others are quite ill, perhaps irreparably so, not particu-larly as a result of their own sin but in direct connection with the sins of their parents—abuse in childhood rob-bing them of any dignity, any fulfilment, any joy, any-thing at all but wallowing in a loathsome pit of sweat and tears and blood and—

How haughty some once had been. The proud and defiant prostitute servicing politicians and millionaires and other "society" clients, now a mumbling hag who shouts obscenities at colorless walls.

The Middle Eastern despot who exhorted millions to a bloody "holy war" and yet lived a life of such unholiness that he rivalled a demon in his behavior, now a pathetic figure indeed being abused by fellow patients.

The hotel magnate, the mayor, the Academy Award-winning actress, now confined, their former worlds shut out.

"The mind," I recall Satan having said, tapping his head as he did so. "If you gain control of even a single human mind, anything is possible."

He had that right, my master did.

If you gain control of even a single human mind. . . .

But little of this *had* to be to the extreme of driving people insane, though such cases did give Satan near-erotic joy. It could stop short, far short, and still be a victory, without the clinically-defined insanity *per se*.

"They're the invisible maniacs-waiting-to-be," he added, "in every village, in every town, in every city and every nation on this planet, Observer."

The streets are filled with ample evidence of the genius of Satan's plan. Only the diagnosed cases are confined to institutions or, rather, the *extreme* ones are. There are millions of men and women and not a few children who are like time bombs ready to explode, the maniacs to whom Satan referred.

"My warriors," Satan had remarked just a short while earlier, then corrected himself. "No, it is more accurate to say that they are my secret agents, the members of my demonic CIA."

There is a conventional wisdom that people who walk, who talk, who smile, who eat, drink, go to the bathroom, have sex, that these people are *functioning*, and, therefore, they are largely okay, and represent no danger to society.

One of Satan's most powerful delusions.

Because in so many instances he is gaining control of that which cannot be *seen* . . . he is gaining control of their minds.

The mass media are culpable, instilling in people desires that may never have existed before or, at least, lain dormant without ever being awakened.

How the master loves those who write their scripts to make adultery seem like *fun!*

"Fun," yes, one of the ugliest words in all of human language: fun to watch dirty movies, fun to get drunk, fun to go on a drug trip, fun to take to bed as many members of either sex as you can, fun to "do it" with children.

"We can destroy multitudes with that one word," Satan sneered more than once.

If it isn't fun, don't do it.

Letting the world have fun is devastating enough, but when fun is able to creep into the church, then Satan becomes personally involved instead of delegating so much to various demons.

Worshipping God is *fun*.

Satan hit hard with that.

Bring on the bands. The celebrity singers. The multi-media events. Complete with television.

Become a fun-filled show!

Advertise. Promote.

I remember one service I attended in a high-school auditorium one Sunday morning. A new ministry had begun there, and it would greatly expand in time, with satellite ministries in a dozen cities around the country.

I did not stay long. I saw that my master had done a brilliant job of infiltrating that group with the "fun" doctrine. No need for me to waste my time there.

The music was fun. The hand-waving, highly-charged emotional atmosphere felt *good*. Feeling good was a tributary of River Fun. Be happy. God wants you with a smile on your face. Give no time to pain, to sorrow. You're in the Lord's Good-Time Place.

In a short while I left the sanitarium. I saw a man slobbering food down his face. I turned away.

Have fun, you all.

*I*T IS CLOSER now, that event embodying our impatient fury.

It is but a little while, just a little while. . . .

My present host is an influential executive involved in the field of publishing—Christian publishing. Satan was very pleased that he could be taken over.

"This one is quite promising," he tells me. "We need all the Trojan horses we can get."

He is a Trojan horse because he is one of ours, yet they think he is one of theirs. He seems to bring so much that is needed to the Body of Christ: money, marketing experience, contacts.

"We're going to shake up the entire Christian publishing community," he tells his staff one day. "We're going to bring a backward industry right into the twentieth century and beyond."

"But, sir, do you think it's a good idea to be publishing these New Age books alongside our Christian books?" an editorial assistant tremulously asks.

"No problem!" he responds. "I plan to buy out an existing publishing firm, and put all the Christian stuff there. We'll keep the New Age garbage with the parent company."

"Is New Age philosophy garbage?" another staffer asks.

"New Age or Christian, doesn't matter," the publisher says. "The bottom line—that's what I worship. Anything else *is* you-know-what piled high."

"But everybody will see what is happening, sir," the assistant adds. "What if they figure it out?"

"Look, in time, it won't matter. That crowd gets used to just about anything. I'll give the guys at this Christian house the biggest budget they ever had. They can buy any author they want."

"But some authors aren't for sale," the assistant persists. "I can't picture that guy from Nebraska being up for grabs. Or a lot of others I can think of. That deceased one specializing in the cults certainly wouldn't have been. I can name quite a few authors who continue to stick to their convictions regardless of the money factor."

"However, the ones that *can* be bought lock-stock-and-barrel surely include some of the biggies," the publisher counters. "I remember that guy who had been with a family-owned firm for ten years, then an English publisher waved a lot of bucks in front of him, and his sense of loyalty went into deep freeze overnight."

The assistant lapses into silence.

And so it goes.

How smart, I think amidst the heat without end.

For a long time, the Christian publishing industry seemed almost impregnable. It began as a group of people dedicated to ministry, with books and magazines used as instruments to spread the Great Commission.

And then. . . .

It changed.

It changed so drastically—but not all at once: a questionable book here, a slick Madison Avenue-style marketing plan there, a little sacrifice of ethics from time to time, one Luciferian inroad after another, step-by-step until—

Ah, yes, the very last part of my book.

I think it was that Satan had a sense of the end approaching, of Armageddon around the corner, of the plan involving Soviet communists and militant Muslims coming to fruition. Yet even so, it was true that he had precious few opportunities left. There wasn't a lot more he could do with drugs. Political corruption had been milked for all it was worth. AIDS seemed to have put the homosexual thing on hold, at least for awhile, though there was still some manuevering room here.

"We have to hurry," he said at one point. "I suspect the Rapture will be soon. We have to do more to prepare the way for the Antichrist."

The End Times.

Was that period so close at last? Was it—?

*W*E MET OFTEN in the closing decade of the twentieth century, discussing that brilliant planned attack again and again, waiting for the right circumstances.

It would involve terrorists, yes, as I have said before, as Satan ultimately decided, and every detail would have to be coordinated flawlessly.

But the right target had to be picked. Blowing up just any church wouldn't do it, although we briefly considered that one with all the glass.

Finally, the ideal target was on the horizon, the attack constituting a blow against the entire Christian communications industry. It had to be one that would leave the most awful devastation in its wake.

And then our allies elsewhere would spring into action, men insatiably jealous over the accomplishments of their leader, men who were instead setting in place their own awfulness, a plan that would synchronize so well within the overall design being hatched by Lucifer the Magnificent.

In the end, my fellow demonkind were the losers, of

course, despite our anticipatory illusions of rejoicing. But meanwhile they gave in to the fantasy.

They, I say?

Nay. More than they. . . .

Even me.

Part II

A HUGE DOME.

I stand before its gleaming newness.

Like two very large saucers placed on top of one another, the exterior made entirely of crystal panes laid over large round girders. The afternoon sun reflects off its surface, blindingly at times.

I stand before the monument—and it is every bit that—built to last through more than one century. It has been crafted of the finest building materials: the crystal imported from Italy, the steel especially furnaced for maximum stress, the concrete, mixed by a special team hired to make sure there were no defects, the terra-cotta floors polished to a shine. There were miniature nuclear-powered generators, a state-of-the-art communications system that included ultra-stereo amplifiers-receivers-speakers throughout the main hall, and high-tech gadgets of every variety. A stunning architectural achievement by any yardstick.

Babel.

The building had its detractors from the very beginning, those who questioned the *need*, the *wisdom* of it, cautioning that God could never bless extravagance—whether ostensibly in His honor or not. The tens of millions of dollars it cost could have been halved, at the very least, and the difference used to fund missionaries overseas, erect a few more rescue missions to help the homeless, and still have enough left over to start scholarships for Christian students in virtually every state in the nation.

A squatty, modern Tower of Babel, reaching not to the sky in an attempt to touch the pillars of Heaven but to the limits of man's technological genius.

Pride goeth before a fall. . . .

How often I had witnessed that over the years, pride in one form or another, pride that began with—

I speak the name with trembling.

Lucifer.

My master.

Even before Eden, before mankind caught the disease.

I shiver at the thought of him, the intent of him, shiver at all that has gone before, and all that he hopes to accomplish now with this grand dome.

Can demons cry?

I do.

$\mathcal{W}$ORKERS ARE SCURRYING around inside, making last-minute preparations.

Two other men stand outside, looking at what they have wrought.

"We did it right," says the architect.

"My crew built what *you* designed," the contractor replies modestly.

"But *you* used quality materials," the architect adds. "Others might have cut corners."

"That's true," the contractor agrees. "But I guess it's because of this first convention. I wanted things to be just right."

"I know what you mean," the architect says. "To the honor and the glory of the Lord."

"We give them the showcase," the contractor muses briefly. "What they do with it is up to them."

They both fall silent for a moment, undoubtedly memories of the Evangelical Scandals of the 1980s still fresh in their minds.

"It's a really fine idea," the contractor acknowledged. "Build a convention hall, turn it over to Christian conventions of sufficient size, then rent it out for secular affairs the rest of the time."

"In the long run it will pay for itself," the architect said. "NRB wants to use it every January. NAE is just about committed. Even ABA is interested."

"That secular book convention?"

"Exactly. Real promising start."

"You bet!"

The two of them leave.

I think of what they said. It didn't *sound* so bad. The words seemed worthwhile. What could possibly be wrong with Christians supporting such an enterprise as this amazing building?

"Observer, come here!" that familiar demanding voice summons.

I turn.

DuRong is standing a few feet away.

I go to him.

"Record this," he tells me.

I acquiesce.

"This may be one of the greatest opportunities of all," he says. "Lucifer wants us to pull out the stops."

He makes a grand gesture toward the whole of the dome.

"They'll all be there, you know," he says. "Every major ministry, most of the minor ones—all the publishers, all the television and radio media. The first convention to be held there. How brilliant a stroke!"

I nod in agreement.

"The attention focused on them will be enormous," DuRong is jumping up and down with glee as he speaks. "We can peel up the layers that are so bright, so pretty, so holy, and show the world what is really underneath. Jim and Tammy will seem like St. Francis and Mother Theresa in comparison."

"Or Billy and Ruth," I venture halfheartedly.

"Yes, *yes!*" DuRong laughs. "That's a good one. Yes, like Billy and Ruth!"

He falls silent for a few moments.

"Why have we never been able to get to them?" he asks finally. "So many others, but not *them?*"

"Because—" I start to say.

"Go on, Observer. Because of what?"

I cut myself off.

"It is a very long story, DuRong."

"Tell me sometime."

"Yes . . . sometime."

CHRISTIAN MEDIA CONGRESS International.
The ultimate communications gathering in all of
Christendom—scores of countries involved; nearly two
thousand exhibits; an expected attendance of forty-
thousand people.

It was not a surprise when Lucifer decided to make
CMCI a special target!

We had a conference at a certain building that was a
special gathering place for us in the Southwest.

"Remind you of something?" Mifult remarked as we
entered.

"I have to admit that it does," I told him.

"Probably the same architect," he observed.

As soon as we all had gathered, Satan took the podium.

"I asked you to meet here because you are so familiar
with this place."

At that we all had to laugh uproariously. I checked my
notes from an earlier time, recalling the details of Arch
Strutter, the minister Satan had seduced early in his
seminary days.

All it took was three promises: 1) You will be paid a
great deal of money; 2) You will become famous through

your television ministry and your books; and 3) You will be able to build a monument to yourself.

Irresistible.

Arch Strutter fell for it and never recovered his previous evangelistic purity, which became ashes at his feet as he walked through them, led by the beacon of the seed faith which he now merchandised so expertly.

"What a warrior he has been for our cause!" Satan beamed, unconsciously strutting like pompous Arch Strutter himself. "That seed faith garbage has worked! But now we must expand our horizons, slow down with our attacks on individual ministries and plan something much bigger, where we can bring down *many* all at once."

"But I thought Swaggert and Bakker—" D'Seaver spoke up.

"We can do *better*," Satan cut in icily. "We can destroy a hundred *more* ministries, all at the same time."

And that was when he told us about CMCI.

The possibilities indeed were exciting to my fellow fallen.

The plan seemed devilish, in every sense of the word.

And here was how the master outlined it for us.

Representatives from the entire worldwide Christian community would be trapped inside the giant new convention hall.

"While that first *Christian* convention is in progress," he said, gleaming, "we will have had several bombs planted by an Islamic terrorist group. These will go off and cause further havoc."

As he pranced around and around on cloven feet, he added in other details, the structural weakness inherent in the hall from cut-rate materials, despite those earlier claims to the contrary.

"Even Christians can be bribed!" he shouted.

Yes, I thought, *money is a powerful tool for our cause.* I remembered the clergyman who decided that he would not eat a single morsel of food until his supporters sent in enough money to retire his ministry's debt.

I was there in the midst of his so-called strike. There was in fact no such denial of sustenance on his part; it was simply one of several promotional campaigns planned as part of an overall marketing effort.

"What's up for next time?" he asked at one of the staff meetings.

"We could rent you-know-whose prayer tower," someone offered, "but then he tried that gimmick once, stealing the thunder from you, I might add, and as we all know, it backfired on him."

Actually that evangelist had stolen nothing; it was the other way around. . . .

"I have an idea," said a young man who had only recently joined his organization.

"Let's hear it," the minister replied.

"We have you follow in Christ's footsteps and get a cross and strap you—"

"Wait, wait, wait," the minister interrupted. "We're not talking about anything real here, you know. I don't want to get too authentic. It's all a show. No place for—"

"The truth?" the young man interrupted this time. "Is that what you're saying?"

"Now, now," the minister said condescendingly, "you're new here, so I'll make allowances. But from now on, think Hollywood."

"In other words, what has truth got to do with it?"

"*Exactly!*"

The meeting in that very familiar building was nearly over. Everyone was excited.

"Do we need to vote?" the master asked.

"*Nay!*" we shouted as a group, as ever.

"Good," he said. "Now, go ahead and tear every damned one of them apart."

(Damned? Funny thing for him to say. . . .)

I was the last one to leave. The building was familiar indeed, for we knew every inch of it. There had been little to restrain us over the years. From the beginning, we were able to corrupt the very foundation of that ministry, as so many others, but this one was a particularly worthwhile success, costing as much as it did, money that could have been used to feed the poor, to pay for scholarships for Christian students, for a score of other purposes, all spent on monument to ego—a spectacular, wasteful display not of Christian humility, but of satanic excess.

I sighed as I went outside to join my demon brothers, turning for one last glance at the architectural and acoustical masterpiece (or oddity, another debate in itself), moonlight shimmering off the polished and shiny surface, off all that brushed aluminum supported on square steel girders, pane after pane shouting its silent blasphemy to the clear, cold night, and that huge stainless steel cross, weighing in at several tons, rather like the burden this earthly deceiver who founded that ministry will be shouldering when he finds his destiny is indeed not quite what he expected.

$\mathcal{A}$ GREAT DEAL of care is put into making sure each booth is meticulous: the right layout, the right materials, the right book titles prominently displayed. Before the Christian media companies ever attend the convention itself, they plan, and plan, and plan.

"The lighting must be improved," someone says in a special staff meeting at one publishing house. "Last year it was a little suspect."

"I agree," the president of that company replies. "We mustn't have any dark, obscure corners."

Color is a critical ingredient also.

"Leave the garish stuff to the pennant peddlers," the president tells the staff members. "We should have earth tones."

"I like that display from those guys in Nashville," his sales manager adds.

"The rich mahogany look?"

"Absolutely. As classy as you can get."

The president rubs his chin. "Why not alternating sections of cherrywood and that lattice-type wallcovering in very light beige?"

They all agree that this sounds quite good.

The meeting is ended with prayer.

My comrades *hate* this part. It chases away any success they may think they have had in focusing attention on booth decor, convention scheduling, publicity material, and all the rest.

"When we have their minds on the nitty-gritty details," DuRong points out, "especially sales projections, we're able to tune out what they *should* be thinking about—namely, winning souls."

"Yet not even the apostles," I speak up, "ever tried to pretend that it was possible to be thinking of Him *every* second of the day. Watering the lawn needn't be an act of worship as such. Going to the bathroom can hardly be approached in any evangelical fashion."

"Yes, yes, of course, but—" DuRong tries to say.

But I will not let him get off the hook so easily.

"You have learned so *little!*" I spit the words out. "You try to claim success where there is none. It isn't a *sin* to plan what an exhibit at a convention is going to look like. It isn't even a sin to spend a whole week on that consideration. Where is your victory, DuRong? Tell me! Show me!"

"I have only *the master* to report to," he retorts angrily. "You take your little book and go off with your unsuspecting host and engage in your literary pretensions."

DuRong is correct, of course: I am the journalist on the battlefield. By and large the soldier demons tolerate me, but that is the extent of it. I record the victories, the defeats. I experience little danger. I exist on the fringes, of the human world and the spiritual.

And I long for the heaven that will not be attainable for any of us except by force. We keep ourselves going by dwelling on that goal. Some *enjoy* their silent reverie, relishing the prospect of Satan's taking over the throne of God, and sitting upon it, and making saints from all of history do his bidding.

We keep ourselves going. . . .

M'Eo had the right view of all this not too long ago.

"It is nothing more than an obsession," he remarked. "Yes, I find it fairly easy to admit that. But then obsessions have propelled men to victory for thousands of years. Why should we be any different?"

*T*HE EVENING BEFORE the convention opens, everything is in place. Carpeting covers the concrete floor of the main hall. All the banners are in place. The cherrywood exhibit with the beige wallcoverings indeed seems tasteful. More so than those with multi-colored balloons and often cheaply printed bumper-stickers, one of the aspects of the modern Christian world with which Satan has had the greatest success.

Commercialization.

Some of it's unavoidable. But much is simply the money-changers-in-the-temple mentality that Christ temporarily exorcised some two thousand years before.

I remember the firm that one of my hosts worked for, its business simply generating new products. Not more *books*, because they weren't in the publishing end, but new *types* of product. And along with these came the need for names to give them, labels, product titles. I observed a planning meeting at one point:

Product manager: "What verses of Scripture haven't already been spoken for?"

Research director: "How about the one that talks about Jesus being a lamp unto our feet?"

Product manager: "Good! Now we have an idea."

323

Research director: "We do?"

Product manager: "Absolutely! We don't have any night lights in our line, do we?"

Research director: "I guess we don't."

Product manager: "Now we *will!* How's this for a slogan: *Let the Lord light your way at night.*"

Research director: "I really don't understand."

Product manager: "Picture it. A night-light in the form of a figure of Jesus. It'll sell like crazy!"

And it did.

There would be no such exploitation if there were no customers for it. Satan has always been masterful in taking sin and stretching it in one direction or another, often camouflaging it in a cloak of apparent holiness.

So many Christians are *things-oriented.* This achievement is one of my master's biggest successes, to be sure. In a society that is producing new cars, new electric shavers, new televisions, new computers at a rate that would have been unimaginable a few decades ago in a society whose advertising is the linchpin that holds all this consumerism together, it perhaps was inevitable that Christian industries would spring up that would endeavor to appropriate some of the "pie" for themselves, attempting to sanctify product-mania by a façade of reaching souls.

"The *world* has its stickers and gadgets and the rest," someone says. "What is so wrong with brothers and sisters in Christ grabbing a little of that? Every ministry needs revenue in order to survive. With products of whatever sort, we don't need to go begging for donations."

I think back to one of my hosts from nearly eight centuries ago, a contemporary of St. Francis. How strange that Francis of Assisi should be known as Saint. For *all* who accept Christ in their lives are saints. But the appellation nevertheless does seem quite appropriate for this man. After he gave up his life of wealth, he established absolute poverty as his ideal. Early on, during a pilgrimage to Rome, he dressed in rags and joined the beggars in front of St. Peter's Basilica, begging alms from passersby and the well-clothed priests going in and out.

He had no committees to help him. He needed no majority vote. There were no marketing meetings. As I looked at this man, I felt an overwhelming desire to go to Satan and shout my disappointment with all that he had become, to say, "Look at this man! Look at his humility! He had wealth; he wore the expensive cloth manufactured by his father; he had power. But he gave it all up. He coveted nothing other than his Lord's approval. But *you!* You had everything, you had Heaven, and yet it was not enough. You were admired but not worshiped, and it was *worship* that you craved. This man has had long and painful illnesses, yet not once has he cried, 'Lord, Lord, why is it like this for me, one who strives only to serve You, to honor You?' Rather he takes the sickness, the pain, and *thanks* God for it as though it were instead a blessing of bounteous proportions."

I looked at this man, and then around at my master, so very different from the One who was clearly that of Francis of Assisi. I saw Satan rejoicing in the poverty of those milling about St. Peter's Square. They were dirty, they were hungry, some were sick; a few would die in the shadow of the immense wealth of that Christian institution before them, death that came from malnutrition while priests, clothed in silk garments, and wearing diamonds and rubies and emeralds on their fingers, dined on pheasant (I almost said peasant, which may not have been so inaccurate as a figure of speech!) and vintage wine, belching from rich sauces while they palavered about the intrigues of the day. Satan was as active in "religion" then as he is now.

Seven hundred and seventy-odd years later, I stand not at the elaborate and beautiful Basilica but a new structure, and sense a similar dependence upon the material elements in life. This is not the Vatican of today, with vendors selling water blessed by the Pope at a premium over containers of "ordinary" water, but it is something else, a Protestant version—

I smile with irony.

Martin Luther detested the hypocrisy of the Roman Catholic Church of that era, one aspect of which was the emphasis upon wealth, upon trappings of gold and gems and all the rest.

But now—

A few years ago, at other Christian conventions, the trend was only barely noticeable. Now it has become a flood, each new "Jesus Love Me" ping-pong paddle and its perversion of true spirituality bringing forth cackles of delight from my master.

As it would have driven Luther and Francis and others of bygone times to their knees, tears of shame flooding from their eyes, and pleas of repentance from their lips.

I LEAVE MY host for a bit. I have that kind of freedom, you know. I can stay inside each one. I can leave.

But, as I have said, I do need a host to write down my words, the words Satan wants immortalized. It is a Bible of sorts, pieces of which have been picked up over the centuries and used by dictators, Marxist rebels, drug dealers, murderers, and muddled-headed proponents of New Age idiocy, the crusading feminist lawyers who claim dedication to protecting the rights of *everyone* and yet concentrate on the homosexuals, the pornographers, the radical-types who are my master's favorite—the meat and potatoes of his spiritual "diet."

My book, my book. . . .

One that will never be on sale through CMCI yet their kind can hardly be blamed for not being a ready market for it.

I have every reason to suspect that Mao used some of it to deceive hundreds of millions.

It would seem that Hitler based his ideas on thoughts gleaned from the pages of my journal.

Anton LaVey's writings were another example.

And Shirley MacLaine's grand illusions.

The list is huge.

I may have the most plagiarized book of all time!

But it is not only other books that have been derived from the pages of my own. It is the thoughts uttered by those duplicitous politicians who try to present themselves as strongly committed to wiping out the drug epidemic, yet are unable to control the use of certain "substances" within their own household.

It is the reasoning behind pro-abortion bias in the judicial system.

It is every cop on the take, every mayor ever bribed, every judge supporting the rights of lesbian couples to raise children. (How pathetic the very assumption that those so deeply in sin have any rights whatever.) It is every Jim and Tammy Bakker whose actions have shaken the foundation of the entire evangelical world in the United States and elsewhere, as they blindly wallow in a cesspool of millions of dollars and limousines, and that twenty thousand dollar diamond she bought because she simply *tired* of the old one. It is all that paint around her eyes and on her cheeks and lips and in her hair, paint as much of the soul as of the body, those faucet-face tears coming from some polluted inner stream of greed and hypocrisy.

I like to believe that my book has provided the catalyst, carried on the backs of countless hosts over the centuries, whispered into the ears of kings and janitors, of stockbrokers and welfare recipients, spread by them like a plague into the lives they lead and the society they bring to its knees because of institutions built on sand and not solid rock.

But it's also the minister who beguiles his congregation with sweet words of specious redemption, of that which is purely personality and nothing deeper than that, not of eternity, a redemption not of Calvary but of Madison Avenue, not at the plain, roughly hewn cross of anguish and blood but one of molded plastic adorned by painted gold and fake diamonds, and offered as a "gift" in exchange for a donation "to keep this ministry on the airwaves."

It's a—

I walk outside the dome.

—homeless old man begging for food and—

I witness a little moment out of a little corner of Hell.

—being brushed roughly aside by a minister in a five hundred dollar suit, a contemptuous expression on his face as he sniffs sweat and urine in the air—

Hell?

—and in less than a minute the old beggar turns into a nearby alley, drops to the cold, dirty asphalt, coughs up a gusher of blood, and then dies.

That's right, I say.

I AM SUSPENDED above the crowd, hovering unseen in the air, going from one end of the hall to the other, aisle to aisle, booth to booth. No one knows that I exist, no one but the dying before they ascend to Heaven or descend to join the other damned lost.

After a very long while, I encounter two who are genuinely dedicated to the cause of Christ, as they put it, relatively young men who have broken away from a larger book publishing firm to form their own.

Their words catch my attention, and I stop to listen.

"Our second year!" says the taller, heavier one, his dark hair a bit overlong for his age.

The shorter, slighter of the two, his blonde hair cut quite short, does not speak initially, apparently recalling the events of the past months, the struggle to get financing, the competition for distributors, finding the right printing firm and then yet more hard, hard work trying to persuade authors to give such a new publishing company at least a hearing, and on top of it all, the process of staffing up.

"Praise God that we were able to make it to this point," the silent one finally spoke.

. . . *praise God.*

I am not surprised to hear those words at a Christian convention, but I am surprised that I haven't heard them before now.

I have heard about package deals. I have heard about marketing plans. And profit margins. Plenty of that sort of thing.

But not God. Not saving souls.

Until now. . . .

"You know, when we decided that we had to get away," the shorter man says, "we knew the Lord was in it."

His partner looks at him, smiling.

"There was nothing else we could have done," he says, "nothing at all."

They do not say anything else then because they are in public, and neither wants to be overheard by anyone of flesh and blood. But that night, in their motel suite, a great deal is made apparent in an emotional outpouring.

Their former employer was a man who believed in a tense, back-biting atmosphere within the office while presenting to the public a variety of sanctified-sounding book titles, including more than one dealing with Christian ethics and related subjects. His purpose was not to inspire anyone, but to force them to compete with one another in a variety of ways, even if this meant instilling a spirit of suspicion and jealousy.

The two finally could not tolerate it any longer. Though earning exceptionally good money by the world's standards, they were sickened by the practices around them, sickened by a level of conduct that was not a single notch above anything they had experienced in the secular business arena.

"It should have been different," the dark-haired one is saying. "It should have been kinder, more loving, more—"

"Money," the other adds. "That's what was on the pedestal, my friend, nothing more."

I FIND MANY publishers guided by The Great Commission. For these, books aren't simply conduits to a money stream but, rather, the tools given to them by God to reach the unsaved as well as edify believers.

Is there some surprise that I know the words that suggest sanctification?

If Satan can send out false prophets and counterfeit saviors, arming them with ideas aimed as pistols at the heart of the Body of Christ, while soothing the members of that body with words of positive thinking and related heresies that anesthetize them against the pain of the cancer multiplying inside, then he would be guilty of nothing more than guns with empty chambers if he had nothing to say that *rang* true while *being* false.

My master has studied Scripture far longer and more deeply than a whole seminary of students, no matter how brilliant they happen to be. He has every word of the Bible memorized. He needs no dictionary, no concordance, no parallel versions, for he was there when the first word was being written on ancient papyrus and he knows the latest paraphrase or translation. Only God has more of a grasp of Holy Writ.

A celebrity is autographing copies of his book at a special booth. He is wearing a watch covered with diamonds, plus an emerald ring on each hand, and a hand-tailored silk suit. He has just paid eighty-five dollars to have his hair coiffured.

"God *is* wonderful," he says as a broad smile crosses his face. "You can't outgive Him no how no way, brother!"

"Praise Jesus," says the middle-aged man who has just handed him a book.

"You bet, brother, praise Him all the way to the bank," the celebrity adds in a smirking, unguarded moment.

"What was that?" the man asks as he turns up his hearing aid.

"Nothing, brother, just a private little moment between me and our dear Lord."

The middle-aged man smiles. The celebrity sighs with relief.

And so I go on from there.

There are other celebrities, a few sincere, a few having earnestly repented of sin-ridden lifestyles and gone on to give Jesus *true* honor and glory, not the tinselly kind that is little more than empty hype."

But the rest. . . .

Ah, yes, *the rest!*

There is a book about a transvestite entitled *God Never Wanted Me to Be a Man!*

It is selling briskly, and has opened up the possibility of other books containing similar material. Two executives from another company have also noticed the newest bestseller.

"If Liberace or Rock could only have been reached for Christ, what a bestseller *that* would have been!"

"I agree. The marketing department would have had a field day."

"Publishing another book by Billy is boring. We need some real juicy stuff."

"We'll just have to wait."

"Wait?"

"For the next train from Hollywood!"

They both laugh.

I SENSE THAT the impressions which are forming in my mind cannot be representative, but as I go about the giant hall, I do see an increasing amount of commercialism, an assimilation of the techniques of the world—but not only that, the mindset as well.

And some within are aware, are concerned.

"I remember what it was like twenty years ago," observes a silver-haired gentleman seated at the CMCI main booth.

"Big difference?" a younger man asks him.

"Oh, yes," Silver Hair says. "It reminds me of what's happened to Hawaii over the years, how billboards and tourist trinkets and too many cars and too much greed slopped over from the mainland and threatened to destroy what had always drawn people to the islands in the first place. They were unique, they were unspoiled, they were a place apart where one could go to refresh one's soul. You can still do that in Hawaii but it's getting harder and harder."

Silver Hair waves his arm around at the displays that are on all sides.

"We've grown mightily, my friend," he says with a

335

deep sigh. "But we've begun to lose something along the way. You have companies here that just don't belong."

"Like that New Age publisher?" the other says.

"That is *precisely* my point! They made it here by disguising their message with an evangelical *look*."

"What is worse is another firm, you know which one I mean, that takes over a respected Christian publisher, pledging autonomy while continuing to be the biggest of all publishers in that entire New Age arena. How long will that autonomy survive if Christian sales dip a bit, and books about mystic crystals and some over-the-hill actress' reincarnation experiences continue to set sales records."

Silver Hair is very pleased by the younger man's grasp of the situation.

"Have you noticed the higher percentage of Jesus junk this year?" he asks.

"I have," the other replies. "There's even a meter of some sort to measure one's tongue-speaking ability."

"What's the principle on which it works?"

"Sound waves, I believe."

"The louder you shout, the more sanctified you are—is that it?"

His friend nods sadly.

"You know what the worst of it is?" Silver Hair asks.

"What's that?"

"The secular media will do its job in here, and focus on the junk, focus on the hoopla, and leave an impression that that's all there is, that there is no real dedication to Christ."

"But that's not true!" the friend protests. "There are still plenty of people here who care about what's happening, who have their spiritual vision very much in focus."

An announcement over the dome's loudspeaker system temporarily drowns them out.

"Tickets for the Mick Jagger Christian Rock Concert

now on sale!" the voice booms. "Get yours at booth 107D."

Silver Hair and his friend look at one another.

"When was *he* converted?" the friend asks.

"In time for his appearance here," Silver Hair says sardonically. "Tina Turner's supposed to have led him to the Lord."

His friend's mouth drops open.

SATAN HAD A brilliant idea. But then he's sure that all his ideas are brilliant.

"I want to help a Christian journalist to do a book," he told us. "It will be an investigative look at what is wrong with the church today. It could sell hundreds of thousands of copies."

Oh! I thought. *What is the master up to now? Wouldn't such a subject be better handled by an enterprising young atheist on the staff of a major national magazine, someone with the instincts that would make him vicious enough?*

I found out my master's purpose soon enough, though at first blush it seemed that he had again succumbed to a certain madness that periodically roars about the lot of us all, threatening to swallow each and every one in its maw.

"We shall hunt for precisely the right one to research all the background and then to write it," he continued. "We shall open all the necessary doors, and he will be caught up in what he is doing."

"What are the qualities this writer must have?" V'Nity asked, logically enough.

"You will know him when you come upon him," Satan remarked.

Not terribly helpful, we agreed later as some of us gathered in the back room of a pornographic bookstore to discuss the matter.

"Where do we even start?" asked Mifult in a break from abortion duty.

"I guess a Christian college," I offered.

"*Indeed!*" my comrades shouted in unison.

And I was given the primary task of following that avenue, while others looked elsewhere.

So I tried college after college, "meeting" student after student, some of them quite bright, others rather dumb, none possessing the sort of impact that would make me realize *instantly* that he was *the* one.

Until I spent some time at a certain institution in the midwest.

A very angry young man was standing up before his class, expounding on a subject dear to his heart, but one that brings snickers from several of the other students.

"Christian psychology is a fraud," he tells them. "It is probably even a work of the devil."

How stupid! I told myself. *If it were that, a work of the devil, I would know far, far better than he!*

On and on he talked.

"It has its roots in secular humanism," he continued.

And some hymns have their roots in barroom melodies. Does that make them too profane for church use?

"It is being used to expound the most seductive doctrines ever to come from the master deceiver."

There you go again!

"Here's a quote from a leading Christian psychiatrist," Donald said as he picked up a book from the table next to him, and turned to a pre-marked page.

And what he read seemed devastating enough.

The students began to pay more attention to him.

"It really does say that?" a young man asked.

"I didn't make it up," Donald replied curtly.

He had them now. After class they gathered around, and talked, and he filled them with still more "information."

The book he quoted from was left open on the table. I looked over the same page from which he read. I repeated to myself the paragraph he used.

What? I said with a shout of surprise that no one could hear, of course. *How could he do that? How—?*

The paragraph was longer than the portion he quoted. And the second half put everything neatly into context, so it could be seen that the author was clearly severing all connection with humanistic psychiatry, *not* affirming its value for any *Christian* considerations.

In effect, he started out saying that the humanistic pioneers of psychiatry and psychology should be acknowledged for opening the door to a *way* of dealing with emotional and related problems of varying intensity— which is what the student read to others in the class— but that this was the sole value of what they contributed; virtually all the rest was the antithesis of Christian thinking, *the part that Donald conveniently omitted.*

Dishonest? Of course. That is what Satan loved about it. Such a tactic was old-hat with him, turning the truth into a lie.

$\mathcal{D}$ONALD DIDN'T GIVE up. Donald kept on bending the ears of any who would listen. But it wasn't just a college pastime to him. He graduated, and went on into the so-called adult world while proselytizing about his views.

And he began to attract attention, not from those in his immediate acquaintance who always tired of his rantings, but rather from the Christian media. All it took was the most absurd statement of that lamentable group he had been making.

"C. S. Lewis is a closet apostle of the New Age!" he declared at a conference.

When presented with the facts about the hugely favorable influence for Christ that Lewis had been over the decades, Donald merely looked contemptuous, unwilling to be swayed in his views by anything resembling the truth.

Presto, his statement about Lewis garnered him major attention!

(A long time ago, Satan came to understand that he could set the agenda for the media, secular and Christian, just by getting someone to say something outrageously stupid or scandalous.)

And he merchandized that attention into a contract for a book with a top Christian publisher.

The stage was set for a bestseller.

It had everything, this book, scandal galore. When honest reporting wasn't dramatic enough, Donald would go off the deep end in favor of utilizing the same tactics as when he stood before that college class, supporting his ideas by deliberate distortion.

Satan had won quite an ally, quite an ally indeed.

The trouble is that many people, reading that book, assumed that he had done his job as a journalist, and that what he had written was rock-solid in its facts and such.

They don't know the truth. The don't realize how badly researched it was. So they accepted the error as gospel, if you will.

And this is where my master goes to town, as the expression is. The book sold hundreds of thousands of copies, each one read by three, four, perhaps five people. More than a million are exposed to material as legitimate as Ivan Boesky talking about integrity in the securities business; or Donald Trump preaching the Sermon on the Mount, especially the part about the meek inheriting the earth; or John Fitzgerald Kennedy doing a seminar on fidelity to one's marital partner.

If just ten percent, think of it, in excess of one hundred thousand people in America alone, were *influenced* by this book, and they did something about it, Satan's gambit could be seen for the master stroke that it was.

And that is just about what happened.

Many honest ministries were seriously hurt, especially in the charismatic sector, since a majority of Donald's targets were clergymen advocating speaking in tongues along with the prosperity doctrine.

The latter was the *single* area where Donald's rage was on target. Satan had long ago discovered that money and sex were among the biggest lures he could wave in front of the unsuspecting. With television and its celebrity preachers, he had the means of communicating the motive of hard cash to countless millions, Christianity by way of the local bank or savings and loan association, the depth of one's relationship to Christ characterized by whether there was a Chevrolet or a Mercedes in the driveway.

There was little else of worth in Donald's book, yet so many were duped into thinking that *everything* in the book passed muster as well.

No one can ever assume that, in leaving Heaven, Lucifer somehow left behind the intelligence with which the Creator had blessed him!

It's the most dishonest book ever published in this market," commented a bookstore manager just before leaving to attend CMCI, where Donald is a guest speaker. "I only carry it because it sells, but I do keep it in the back of the store."

If it is so awful, then why not throw it out the back door? I shouted with words of piercing conscience un-heard, and glad that they were not because I, too, am unable to serve two masters, though long, long ago, in dark and terrible moments of clarity, I know I have chosen altogether the wrong one.

Does Donald realize now that he is a pawn for my master, just as a murderer, just as a child molester, a pornographer, a ruthless drug maestro, regardless of whether their address was Bogotá, Colombia, or Beverly Hills, California?

There is no rifle in Donald's hands to mow down children in a schoolyard. He holds no knife. He sells no drugs.

He lies.

So simple, isn't it?

Lies vomited up out of the reeking cesspool of his own embittered hypocrisy.

Standard operating procedure for my master, Donald's master, in the final analysis, for if God is truth, then this pitiable creature serves Him not at all. While engaged in the pretense of serving Him totally in his self-anointed crusade for integrity, he instead abets the purposes of Satan better, better than if he had declared openly what he was about, and then all could run from him, seeing him as he was to become, a foot soldier of the enemy of their souls; but not knowing, they wallow in their blindness at his feet, eating the spiritual junk food that he shoves down their throats, and begging him for more, more, more.

No one should be surprised, eh?

In the arsenal of the Prince of Darkness, such schemes are quite, quite effective; when purveying sin as he has done since the Casting Out, Satan always uses the most expedient of tools, deceit being the handle that fit them all.

I N THE END, Satan loved that one book but hated quite another. It had an ingredient the first did not.

Integrity.

Published by the book division of an old-line Bible college, it peeled up layers of evangelical hypocrisy and corruption as well as heresy, which should have been a source of demonic delight. But the result was an *honest* look at what was wrong within the Body of Christ, an impetus to do something about it, which Satan hated.

One of my master's most successful ploys has been for even well-meaning people, not to mention those who do not give a damn (a word for demons but not for the redeemed), to be seduced into misinterpreting and distorting Scripture, and for this to become a large part of the foundation for their ministries.

"I am a god," one of the deluded screams at his congregation. "I am as much an incarnation of deity as was Jesus Christ."

Angels weep, but demons gesticulate with satisfaction at stuff like that.

"You all are gods," he says as he waves his hand at the fools who sit in the pews of that so-called church, lapping up whatever he tells them because they trust him.

In a minute or two they all are on their feet, their hands held high, palms upward, as they shout, "Gods! Gods! Yes! We *are* gods!"

When the author of the second book tried to contact this wretch, he was rebuffed with a simple, "I stand on my record."

But it was that record that condemned him.

And yet he was not the only one.

There were others, some of which demanded an apology from the author.

The author refused.

"What am I to apologize for?" he said during an interview. "For testing the spirits? That is what our Lord admonishes us to do. For confronting the religious hypocrisy of our day? That is what He did—and remember, we are supposed to be as Christlike as we can manage to be. So what is it that I must reclaim in regret, as though never spoken, and indeed disowned in the process? What is it? Tell me."

No one did.

*L*EARNING TONGUES IN *Seven Easy Lessons!*
Don't Just Wait for the Greatest of the Gifts!

Inside the meeting room in the basement of the convention hall, a man dressed in a turtleneck sweater is standing before a group of several dozen individuals.

"Your life can be revolutionized in no time!" he exclaims. "Each day can be an adventure."

It is clear that those present are intrigued, all except one man in the audience. He seems impatient. As the minutes pass, he shifts around more and more frequently in his chair.

Finally he stands.

"Sir?" he interrupts the speaker, who looks at him rather sternly but, with some reluctance, gives him the floor, as they say.

"I have been listening very carefully to what you have been telling us," he says. "Your words are very appealing."

The speaker nods with obvious appreciation.

"But, sir, I have two questions to ask."

The speaker waits, thus giving his consent.

"They are interwoven," the man in the audience continues, "so I will ask them together: How can you

348 *Roger Elwood*

expect people to pay for your advice when the Bible says the gift of tongues is something God may or may not give to each individual? Does it not then cease to be free, something for anyone who completes your course, irrespective of what might be God's will in the matter?"

The crowd grumbles. The speaker begins to sweat profusely.

"Everybody's doing it," a woman shouts. "What's wrong with wanting the best?"

The man sighs.

"Have you taken any prophecy courses?" he asks.

"No, I haven't," she replies. "I'm not interested in what might happen in the future. I want what I want now!"

The others clap at that.

"Then surely you have studied the gift of teaching," the man persists.

"Not interested," she says as she folds her arms in a gesture of stubbornness.

"How about *any* of the other gifts, ma'am?" he asks with unfailing politeness.

Irritated, the woman stands and glares at the man.

"One other question," he says bravely. "How about love?"

"Love?" she repeats, momentarily puzzled. "What does love have to do with it?"

"If you were to speak with tongues, if you were to prophecy beyond compare, if you could teach everyone, and you did not learn how to love, it all would be for naught, dear lady."

"How *dare* you judge me!" she bellows. "How dare you try to impose your views on me! Where do you get off trying that stuff, *mister*?"

The man holds up his Bible.

"It's all in here," he says simply.

The speaker speaks.

"Leave this room!" he demands.

"Do you not want the truth?"

"Out! Out! *Out!*" they all shout.

He turns sadly, and exits to the corridor where I am standing, though he cannot see me.

"So sad," he says softly, "so sad."

The audience sits down, returning their attention to the speaker.

"And now here's the kind of profit you can make teaching others to—"

He brings out a chart littered with dollar signs.

I feel as sad as Darien must be when he sees this sort of thing.

Darien.

A kindred spirit in Heaven.

My enemy now.

We have met only twice since the Casting Out—when one of my hosts, a fellow playing a piccolo, had only minutes left to live; and in Hell, just before God accepted him back into Heaven.

How many of us wished we could have gone with him, could have forsaken that place of damnation and—

Not possible.

Never, never.

I remember a moment that was Darien's but which I desperately wished was my own, a moment unforgotten even for the length and the breadth and the depth of eternity. His words haunt me.

. . . the hard rock shelf on which rests Christ's body. He is passing from death to life. . . . Finally He sits up, then stands, smiles at me, and says just five words, "Now you know the truth. . . ."

"Yes, Lord, I know the truth," I manage to reply, barely able to say even that, aware of the moment to which I am witness.

A short while later, someone approaches from outside.
A woman."
Our eyes meet.
I find myself saying, "He is not here, the one you seek.
He has risen, as He promised."
It is as though the light of Heaven is on Mary's face,
her expression sublime.
I watch her go. My whole being weeps with the joy of
redemption profound, purchased in blood for all of
humanity and which included mercy for a foolishly
errant angel.
A voice, rich, kind, familiar. . . .
"Darien, are you truly ready now?"
"Yes, Lord, truly. . . ."

Darien, Darien, if I could have done so, I would have
stood by your side, and begged God, "Please, please, take
me as well! I want no more of this cesspool that has been
my existence for so very long, Oh, God, please!"

I should not have been called Observer. I should have
been dubbed Hesitation instead, or Some Other Time, or
whatever.

The moment passed.

As it always did.

Oh, how I hesitate before glancing in the next room.

"My dog, praise God, my dog was God's instrument of
revelation," a burly-looking man is saying as he works
himself into a frenzy before the crowd, and crowd it is,
this room a bigger one, every seat occupied.

"I just knew as surely as though sweet Jesus Himself
had spoken to me that when Sparkie barked, it was a sign
from Heaven!"

If I were human, with a stomach, I would be sick.

IN EACH ROOM in the basement of that building I encounter a different pitch, a term I had learned some time ago, and which seems altogether appropriate now. I next hear a man confessing his sins of adultery before a very large gathering.

"I was led by Satan's lust to sleep with my employer," he tells them. "I threw aside my wife, and she dumped her husband."

There wasn't a sound apart from his own words.

"Her body proved irresistible to me," he went on. "That first night we spent together—"

I look around the room. Several men have flushed faces. The women pretend absolute shock but hang on every word. Only one younger woman gets up and leaves, muttering, "Trash!" The others seem not to hear.

And then the speaker holds up the $17.95 hardcover book he has written and reads a lengthy passage from it.

I block out his words, since he cannot be counted on to tell anything but his own self-serving side of the story, and I read instead from my own book, because I was there, helping D'Seaver as this man sank deeper and deeper in his shame. . . .

*   *   *

There was power in the way he spoke to the multitude,
a thousand men, women and children gathered in the
auditorium, brought there by a testimony that had spread
throughout the Christian world.

"I obey Christ and Christ only!" he exclaimed. "He is
the center of my very being."

People got to their feet and shouted their approval.

"The Lord first and foremost, and all others next," he
went on, emphasizing yet again the central message of
his books and his personal appearances.

In the back of the huge hall, a man in his mid-forties
has entered but the crowd paid no attention to him. The
one on stage was the draw, not this rather mousey little
man who seemed terribly nervous.

He paused a moment, looking ahead, and saw the
author.

The author, the newcomer told himself, *yes, and
more . . . the author, the—*

On stage, the speaker was coming to the end of his
seminar. For an instant, he caught a glimpse of a familiar
face, and a chill grabbed his spine.

"And may—may—" he said stuttered, following that
face, seeing the man walk closer, very near the stage now.

"May God cleanse your minds, your hearts, your—" he
continued through sheer force of will.

The newcomer smiled at him, and turned away from
the stage itself, to the side, to where the dressing rooms
were.

"—souls and those homes of yours, keeping them free
from—"

*How could he? How could he stand there? How could
he say such things, knowing—?*

"—Satan's corruption, and always, always, I say, always strong and pure—"

Pure? Oh, Lord, I pray that you forgive him. I may never be able to do so. . . .

"—for Him!"

The crowd was on its feet, cheering again, as those listening had done several times that evening, their hearts open to the words of a man they had admired for many years.

Finally he walked backstage.

The newcomer stood there, in the corridor behind the curtains, saying nothing for the moment, but simply looking at him, smiling in a certain way.

"I don't know what to say," the author spoke. "I don't know what to tell you. I didn't mean for anything to—"

The newcomer said only one devastating word.

"*Adulterer!*"

Then he swung and connected with the author's jaw, spit at his fallen form, and walked away.

A man rushed up to the author and asked, "What was *that* all about?"

The author looked at him, then brushed past, and headed for his dressing room. After going inside, he sat down on a folding chair and started weeping. . . .

"*Wonderful,*" loathsome D'Seaver cackled.

"*I quite agree,*" another added. "*Are you writing all this down, Observer?*"

I was. I was.

It began with a million-copy seller.

And it ended in the bed of the owner of an important bookstore chain.

The book was entitled *Keeping Your Family Together through Crisis.*

This Mr. Robert Langworthy had been a top author for a very long time, his works selling into the hundreds of thousands of copies.

But he had not had that breakthrough sale until the

latest title. The subject matter combined with his straight-forward way of dealing with it had struck a nerve in the reading public, and they responded with their pocketbooks.

Twenty printings!

"What an opening," Satan had told us at the time. "He will soon develop some arrogant pride."

"And pride will go before his fall," responded a demon who seemed immensely proud of himself with that burst of insight.

"Observer," Satan said, "Observer, copy down every-thing."

I did. I did.

His lover was not a beautiful woman in the classical sense. But she had a charm that Robert Langworthy found irresistible, and she exuded a sense of power that he simply couldn't ignore.

He was married.

So was she.

But somehow that didn't matter . . . enough.

I sit alone, looking back at the wreckage of this man's life. I watch him one day as he faces a bookcase filled with his literary works. I grimace as he turns it over, flinging dozens of copies onto the floor. I—

He stands before the pile, his entire body shaking. . . .

Robert Langworthy attempted to go on, to put his life back together.

In Minnesota he signed the divorce papers.

In Florida, his lover put the final piece into place in the destruction of her own marriage.

A week later they tied the knot.

Six months passed.

The Christian world turned its collective back on him.

He consented to an interview for a secular newspaper's religion section.

"Why can't they try to understand?" he said plaintively.

They did. And can't.

Finally a publisher took one of his books. And promised an energetic campaign to re-establish his reputation. So he appeared at that first convention in the dome.

The book bombed.

The publisher did little to promote it. Of course, few writers can be satisfied in this regard, seldom ever thinking that their book has been "pushed" as much as they would like.

But it was different this time. The publisher just wanted a *name*, no matter how tarnished. With some luck that would be enough.

It wasn't.

Later, one of those who survived, at least physically, he found that his phone calls were never returned, everyone caught up with other matters of life and death, shorn of hypocrisy.

So he decided to start his own publishing firm, he and the woman he loved.

That is, the second woman. Not the first.

"People out there do want to hear why . . . they want to know that my attraction for this woman could not be tempered. It grew. It grew daily. What was I to do? Maybe the Lord was trying to tell me something. I had to listen."

Maybe. But he didn't.

It is soon all over now. Ashes to be trodden on and scattered.

Over, yes.
For Robert Langworthy. For his lover.
Not for me.
I observe. I report.

*F*AME HAD A great deal to do with it, you know. Fame twisted their world, and their minds along with it. But there are hundreds of thousands of *unknown* people, some of them wealthy, some of them "merely" well-off, people who have nothing more to cling to than the very bank accounts that they have been accumulating over the years. My kind have a field day with men and women such as this.

For them, it is dollars, not neon lights.

For them, it is trying to devise every tactic they can to keep *and* to increase the bottom line for themselves. And no matter how much they have, it is never enough.

But, going further down the scale, there are countless numbers who are not wealthy, who are not well-off, people who *yearn* to have a great deal of money someday, and who live beyond their means in lifestyles maintained by plastic credit cards and ever-expanding mountains of debt.

Hard times cause them to groan and wail and ask, "How could God do this to us? What is He punishing us for? What have we done wrong?"

Would you *listen* if He did answer? I ask of people who cannot hear me.

Would you give up your materialism and serve Him at any cost?

We followed Satan at the cost of Heaven.

Would you follow Him, whatever the price, *into* Heaven?

We gave up God.

What would *you* give up? A luxury car, perhaps? A diamond ring? An Oriental rug?

Odd, I tell myself.

What is odd? I ask myself.

I spoke that as though Christians would read it in my book, I answer. *But by the time they had done so, they would have been beyond choice, beyond redemption, those Christians who were Christians in denomination or church-affiliation only. The charade of their so-called Christianity would have been dust at their feet by then as they writhed in the grip of my kind, calling futilely for the intervention of a once-Almighty God rendered impotent by Satan's victory. Now why was that? Why to them? What good—?*

I pause, fluttering my wings momentarily, hoping fellow entities from Hell had not heard.

Truly strange. . . .

I COME ACROSS one of the saddest cases of all—a brilliant success for my master but sad otherwise.

Philosopher's son.

Oh, how the father inspired millions. I was in the same auditorium as he was the night he died. So was Darien. How it all stands out in my mind! The wisdom he showed about so many subjects presented to him by the students in the audience.

And then at the end—

It is obvious that Philosopher is very, very weak. He walks slowly back to his chair, and almost collapses into it. His family whispers to him that he must stop.

"I must go in a little while," he says with great tenderness to the audience, looking out over the thousands listening to him. "I am grateful that you have come here this night. May we make the next question the final one, please?"

Another student, a girl raises her hand, and Philosopher asks her to come forward.

"Sir, as you indicated earlier, you once could not bring yourself to believe in God. I cannot now, either. Help me, please."

Philosopher speaks, but his voice is barely above a

*whisper. He motions her to come up to him. She climbs
the steps to the stage and approaches him.*

*"I am dying, my young friend. Let me tell you that
there is a God, and even as I speak, He is welcoming me
into Heaven."*

*He looks at her, his eyes wide, a smile lighting up his
face. He reaches out his hand, and she takes it.*

*"Your father says to tell you that he loves you, and is
happy now."*

*Then Philosopher's head tilts to the left, the hand
drops, and he is dead.*

*The girl starts to sob as she turns around to face the
audience.*

*"My father," she tells them, "died a week ago. The last
thing he said—he—he said to me was that he prayed
I—I—I would accept the gift of faith and—and—peace
that he wanted to leave behind."*

That was Philosopher's legacy.

But what of his son?

His son is an angry little man, someone attacking the
very foundations of evangelical Christianity, often hitting the mark but just as often missing it.

He set himself up, set himself up as the conscience of
the Body of Christ, abhorring compromise—

Abhorring compromise.

Oh, yes.

And loudly so.

That was how it started with Philosopher's son, following very much in his father's footsteps but hating the
shadow in which he had to labor, hating the comparisons,
resenting it when he was deemed to be falling short.

And so he constructed an elaborate deceit, one he came
to accept quite totally, rationale that would have filled
Philosopher with disgust, but which seemed just right for
him.

I hear the son talking with someone at his publisher's

booth. He has just spoken at a rally the night before—and got a standing ovation—cleverly hiding some aspects of his outlook and giving the thousands in attendance only that which they wanted to hear.

"I live in the real world," he is saying. "When I hit my finger, I curse. When I see a beautiful woman, I lust after her."

Seeing that the man to whom he is speaking is rather surprised, Philosopher's son adds, "Do you think that *this* is the real world?"

As he says that, he waves his arm around to indicate the hoopla in the convention hall.

He is right, of course, and yet I know very well that he cannot use one circumstance as justification for the other. According to his viewpoint, then, all the rapes, all the murders, all the drug addiction, all the other social and moral crimes are part of the same *real* world, and somehow should be thought of within the same spirit of tolerance.

Years ago he raised money for a motion picture. And the whole Christian world stood up and cheered. The son of Philosopher would show what could be done when an evangelical Christian was in charge, the same Christian who did so well in exposing hypocrisy within the evangelical community.

The movie was *worse* than many of the non-Christian ones he had once protested against. It was riddled with four-letter profanity; it had gruesome scenes of revenge-oriented violence, revenge by the only Christians being portrayed; there was a gang rape sequence; and in the end, the moral of the story seemed to be that you have to kill your oppressor before he kills you.

The son of Philosopher had this defense: "I make movies in the real world."

(That phrase again. "Shame, son," your father would

say. "Shame upon you for what you have done to your heritage.")

Weeks before, a Hollywood studio boss, a man fanatically hostile to Christianity, remarked in similar defense about his sex-ridden bloodbath of a movie.

What is the difference between the two? it might be added.

The studio boss is an unregenerate atheist.

Philosopher's son is a Christian.

That makes it right . . . doesn't it?

(Scorcese, are you listening?)

I AM NOT alone most of the time at this convention, Mifult and DuRong and others are invariably there, in the aisles and at the booths and in the meeting rooms, taking advantage of any situation they can find. Often they come up against believers too solidly versed in Scripture and girded about with the Spirit of Truth for demonkind to make any headway, rebuffing inroads my kind attempt by instigating the spectre of greedy motivation—which has collapsed more than one Christian business, indeed, *any* clever deal-making strategy that borders on the unethical.

But still they try, my awful comrades. It is good that they, that I, cannot be seen. We are hideous, deformed. The smell of disease is about us, our visages making us phantom Medusas, dripping with the foulness that we have accumulated over the ages, damned even if there were never to be a promised Judgment Day. Often we will rummage through piles of bodies on some foreign battle-field, trying to find those with yet a fragile spark of life offering some hope that, at the very last instant, we can divert someone, anyone from Heaven to Hell.

We do this to the pleasure of the master whom we serve with all that we are and will ever be. Often we are successful, several of us drawn to the dying one like vultures fighting over a morsel of meat. Finally, when he dies, and his soul is ours, we rip and tear as though at flesh, driven on by his screams. I no longer stand aside, watching, but drawn by the "taste" of what could be called spiritual "blood," I dive in with ferocity that never ceases to startle me in the aftermath. Remember, I am Observer, the quiet one, the demon appalled by much that is indeed demonic, and yet there I am, so ravenous that it seems as though I can never be satiated, my very being *requiring* the pain of the victim writhing at our attack. But soon he is relegated to Hell for even worse miseries, and how jealous we are because we can no longer be those responsible.

I stand down the corridor from a large auditorium where the really important meetings, seminars, entertainment affairs are held. And I see an astonishing sight.

Mifult, DuRong, A'Ful, others are leaving in a mass exodus.

They look . . . frightened.

How can that be? What could make them react in such a manner?

I start to enter the auditorium. Mifult sees me.

"There was a reason why I wasn't allowed to abort *that* one!" he exclaimed, shaking nervously. "I didn't know what it was at first. All the normal excuses were present."

"I don't understand," I say quite dumbly.

"He would have been quite sickly. The parents could never have afforded the expense of caring for him. He would probably die before he was no more than two or three years old, *if* he lived *that* long. And so on. And so on."

Mifult seems to be going through convulsions but after a few seconds manages to steady himself.

"Don't go in there," he begs. "You mustn't—"

But I ignore him, and enter anyway.

Every seat is taken.

On stage at the front of the auditorium are only two individuals, a fragile-looking boy and his mother. Even though the loudspeaker volume is on full blast, the child's words sometimes are difficult to hear.

"I am very tired now," he says, and rests his head on his mother's shoulder, and dies.

She continues to stand there though obviously trying to fight back tears that are beginning to drip over her lower lids and down her cheeks.

Suddenly there is the sound of voices raised in prayer. The hundreds of men and women in that auditorium stand and—

I see Heaven opening up.

It is not often like that, my eyes beholding the majesty of my former home. But this time I do, I see angels descending. They stand around little Robbie as his soul leaves his body.

And something quite wonderful happens.

Peace like a river attendeth my way. . . .

That is the expression on Robbie's face. Peace envelopes him, as water surrounded the baptized Jesus in the River Jordan. All that is finite, all that is corruptible, passes away.

And the Holy Spirit descends not as a dove—no need of symbols or surrogates any longer. *The Holy Spirit* takes the child's hand.

Robbie casts a glance at the crowd in that auditorium. Their voices are raised in praise, many with their palms upheld. He reaches out toward them and in a beautiful way touches each one, some driven to tears as they fall to their knees.

He hesitates but an instant as he looks at his mother that final, final moment before, someday, they walk the golden streets together. Her tears are a river of their own.

I love you. . . .

Not words at all. A sensation. Something rippling in the air perhaps, gossamer-like.

She senses it instinctively, raising her head toward the ceiling—and at the same moment there is a touch of fear because she also senses me, her expression suddenly dark, a last fleeting reluctance to let go, to acknowledge her beloved's odyssey.

Fear.

Satan's greatest of all weapons.

But I will not be his instrument this one time. I will not allow it *this* time!

I start to leave the auditorium.

It is well with my soul, mother, I can hear him say clearly.

And then he is gone.

She smiles as she raises the fingers of her left hand to her lips, kisses these, and holds them out to the empty air.

He is not there, dear lady, I say, yes, I say that. *He is—*
Home.

I FIND OUT much about Robbie through the discussions I overhear later. He appeared to be in better shape, temporarily, than he really was. The leukemia seemed to be in remission.

His mother had written a book about her son, a book with an implicit message that if she had known in advance about what would happen with his life, she still would not have chosen abortion.

"How many people have been touched by his courage?" she said at one point. "How many lives have been enriched because of him, mothers and fathers and children who could face their own ordeals with just a bit less emotional anguish? How many souls are in heaven today because the Lord used my Robbie as an instrument?"

Linked.

Yes, they were.

The mother knew immediately when something was wrong, even before he himself was able to tell her.

Except that day.

They lived in the city where the dome had been built. They had taken Robbie to see it in various stages of completion. He was fascinated, thrilled. He enjoyed talking to several of the men at the construction site.

He begged her to take him with her when she was scheduled to speak.

"I want to be there with you," he pleaded.

And he seemed stronger just a few hours earlier.

She had no resentment—and that made Satan livid.

Something else did as well.

The reactions throughout the crowd within the convention hall and in the meeting rooms.

For a short while, they turned from their books and records and bumper stickers to thoughts of a dying boy who seemed only a bit tired and who put his head on his mother's shoulder for the last time.

None saw what I did.

For many it would have meant a total change of everything they were, of every aspect of their lives. How could they any longer *care* about trinkets and feel-good pep talks and other banalities? How could they not see beyond the cheap and easy answers to what mattered for *eternity*, instead of getting lost in the TV dinner mentality of today?

But for me, there was nothing of the kind, no redemption of outlook, nor any other aspect of my existence, for that matter.

A dog returns to its own vomit, you know.

$\mathcal{A}$S I GO up and down that huge convention area, I hear the whispers about little Robbie. His death there in the basement of the dome has had a striking impact that goes well beyond that one room.

I see a man crying.

"What's wrong, Alfred?" his wife asks.

He is sitting in the midst of their booth, which is filled with banner stickers, key chains, erasers with Bible verses printed on one side, notepads and other items. On an easel to one side is a sign about special CMCI discounts. Earlier Alfred had worked hard to close a deal with a major Christian bookstore chain, bargaining at the top of his form, and succeeding. He would make a huge profit from it since most of the merchandise was bought in the Orient at very low cost.

"All this," he tells her.

"I don't understand, Alfred."

"All this *junk!*"

"You've never called it that—" she started to protest, then stopped, realizing that they both knew what they were doing, what they had been doing for years, selling stuff that took the name of Christ and *used* it, not in any honest manner, not in any *real* attempt to evangelize, to spread the Good News of salvation through Christ and Christ only, but to make money, to see a bottom-line profit at the end of each fiscal year.

"That kid, Robbie," Alfred says, "I was *there*, Evelyn. I stopped in for just a moment but that was enough."

He wipes his eyes with a handkerchief.

"He had no regrets. He didn't curse the Lord. He showed only love and trust. And it was the same with his mother. They were so beautiful, Evelyn."

He looks with contempt about the booth.

"What does all this amount to? What does it contribute, Evelyn, except money in our pockets?"

He holds up his wrist.

"A gold Rolex. People are being killed for ones just like it these days. It's worth thousands of dollars. I pay a hundred dollars for a pair of shoes and don't think twice about it. But that woman, that boy, they had to struggle for the money to keep him going as long as he did. They had to beg for whatever they got. But I just bought a thousand-dollar suit because I'd always wanted one!"

He starts sobbing, loudly.

"Please!" Evelyn says. "People will see you!"

People do.

But they have other business. One little man in one little booth is really of no concern. They have their own problems, including finding the right titles for the Christmas selling season.

"What's wrong with that man?" a woman asks as she passes by.

"Who knows?" replies her female friend.

They both laugh at the poor fool.

And then they stop an aisle or two further down.

"We shouldn't have done that," one says. "Maybe he's going through some kind of tragedy."

Her friend nods in agreement.

"Let's go back. Let's see if we can help."

In the coming holocaust, those two will be among the injured. The poor fool will come upon them, and kneel beside them, and hold their hands as they cry out their pain.

Behind him, far down at the other end of the convention area, his booth will be in shambles, pencils and banners and everything else spread out in a hundred directions.

"Where is your wife?" one of the two women asks as the pain momentarily abates.

"I don't know," he mutters. "I don't know. She was heading for the rest room when—"

The woman reaches up, touches his cheek.

"We know what matters now, don't we?" she says. "There are no excuses anymore."

He nods.

$\mathcal{T}$HERE IS ANOTHER young Christian whom I encounter, much older than Robbie, whose story has an altogether different ending. . . .

He seemed happy, this babe in Christ, as he was called by those around him.

"We've lost another one," DuRong had said.

"Yes, as far as eternity goes," A'Ful replied, "but we can still do a lot with him here."

DuRong brightened up considerably.

"You're right!" he exclaimed. "Any plan?"

Indeed there was . . .

The young man, Erik, left the football stadium where the evangelistic meeting had been held, feeling light-headed.

"I'm clean," he said, "washed clean by the blood of Jesus."

He returned to his dorm at the college, ready to take on anyone he encountered.

His roommate was amused.

"You actually fell for that stuff," he said, smirking.

"It's not stuff," Erik protested, "it really isn't."

Arthur is sitting in a chair, looking up at his friend.

"I've never seen you this way before," his roommate admitted.

"I've never *been* this way before," Erik replied, "too many problems in my life, so much guilt, as you know all too well."

Arthur realizes how true that was. The two of them had spent long, long hours, days, weeks of conversation, revealing to one another their deepest possible thoughts, emotions.

Erik had gotten into drugs, and along with this, prostitution to finance his habit.

It went on for years. No one else realized what was going on—that is, the respectable people in his life, the ones who belonged to the normal part of his world—no one except the drug peddlers and his customers.

"I hated everything around me," he said. "I hated snorting white powder up my nose. I hated the depression that came each time after a 'good' session with the stuff."

He was shivering, sweat sticking his clothes to him.

"But . . . but I just couldn't stop," he continued. "I was hooked in every way imaginable."

Wanting to isolate himself from the possibility of guilt creeping in, he became more and more a part of the sub-culture that cocaine inevitably spawned where it took hold. If there was no one to tell him that his habit was wrong, that it was destroying him, he would never, he thought, have to face up to the reality of what was happening to himself.

And there was the sex.

He had flings with many women. With street hookers. With politicians. Even the wife of a minister.

"She never took off the cross she had hanging from a chain around her neck, not even when we were in bed together. I felt so dirty . . . so dirty."

But eventually the drugs and the danger of AIDS,

which he tried to ignore but couldn't drove him to seek help. With his family by his side, and Arthur as his friend, he was able to turn his life around and break away from the old habits. But he still suffered from the guilt these left behind.

"I actually liked what I did," Erik would say. "I *liked* the idea of sex without restraint. And I got *paid* for it all. I could live out my own fantasies through fulfilling those of my customers."

Fantasies.

What a helpful word, what a devastating set of circumstances used by Satan to entrap any who stand before the open door to Hell!

People have their twisted erotic fantasies because Satan has had his own!

Every sin known to man was first foreshadowed in Satan. Sin cannot come from God. God is total purity, total good, total justice.

Erotic sins are not exempted. Satan has known lust an inordinate number of times. He expresses it through surrogates.

But at least once he intervened directly. I remember it well. Even the Scriptures record it.

He had his own form of Immaculate Conception. He sent his followers, a horde of demons, to earth during the period just prior to the Flood, and had intercourse with loose women of that time. This was only part of the display of evil and sin in those days, but it was typical, and it was what drove God to judgment.

Have there been other times?

The answer to that question would require me to start another volume, which I cannot do, as it becomes increasingly difficult for me to continue with the present one!

*   *   *

"Then, with the money, I could buy more drugs which I imagined made me more sexually voracious. So I got further and further into sado-masochism and made more and more money that bought a bigger and bigger supply of—"

That stage passed, the confessional part of his rehabilitation. He never again went back to drugs, to paid sex. But he still could not salvage any degree of self-respect.

That was when he happened upon the evangelistic crusade, and attended the service that night in the stadium.

And then he could say, with utter certainty, "My sins were washed away! They really were. My guilt is still there but I feel better equipped to face it, deal with it, *conquer* it in time!"

His roommate listened carefully, and as his skepticism faded, he found what his friend shared with him to be more appealing than he might ever have imagined.

And soon he accepted Christ into his life as well. The two of them began attending a church that is located a couple of miles from the college.

Erik felt literally like a new man. And so did Arthur. They in turn witnessed to others. But, one Sunday, they decided to try a new church, because the one they had been attending began to feel a bit staid, a bit narrow in its outlook. The new church was a number of miles from the college, but the day was a pleasant one, the drive a welcome prospect.

They were ten minutes early for the morning service.

People gathered around.

"Where are you from?" a middle-aged man asked.

They told him.

"Good! Good! Praise God!" he said.

The man's wife remarked, "We're having a praise service today."

They smiled, though a bit uncertainly.

The man picked up on this.

"Anything wrong?" he asked. "You do speak in tongues, don't you?"

"No, I—" Erik replied.

"You *don't?*" the woman said. "What a shame! What a shame! Now we're going to have to do something about that, aren't we?"

Both young men were led away from the main auditorium, down a couple of corridors and into a "special" room.

"This is where God tells us it is to take place each time," a tall, thin man in his mid-forties told them.

"What is that, sir?" Erik's roommate asked.

"What is what, son?"

"About what you said, I mean, that something is going to happen here?"

"You will receive the baptism of the Holy Spirit."

"But I thought that that happened when we were saved."

The man and several others in that room broke out in laughter.

"You *do* have a lot to learn, don't you?" he said, chuckling.

And then it began. These people were more aggressive than many others in the charismatic movement, but the bottom line was the same. To be legitimate, to be accepted, these two young men *must* have the Gift.

That is one of Satan's most seductive heresies. It is also a direct copy of the tactics he used in the Garden of Eden. There was nothing illegitimate about the Tree of the Knowledge of Good and Evil; God put it there in the first place. But His clear admonition was that the fruit was off-limits. Adam and Eve were *not* to eat of it, period.

But Satan changed all that, planted doubt in their

minds, made them disregard God's unmistakable command.

And sin entered the world as a result.

"We can do it again and again, in one form or another," Satan has been telling us throughout the ages of history. "It worked once, it has worked other times, and it will continue to do so because of man's sin nature."

And now in the twentieth century he is finding continued success; this time it is not a legitimate tree as the tool but a legitimate gift that is at issue, that has been at issue ever since Paul wrote to the Corinthians.

"The difference," he says, "is that God is not telling Christians they *can't* have it. He is saying that He *wants* them to be blessed with it or—"

He raises himself up proudly.

"—perhaps prophecy, healing," Satan continues, "or one of the others."

We are back in that church in the Southwest; we feel comfortable there.

Our master is at the podium, gestulating.

"*But*," he says with special emphasis, "God adds one condition: that they wait on Him, that they do not covet after one particular gift but simply depend upon Him to bestow the one that *He* knows is right for them."

Satan starts to cackle, a cackle we are very familiar with, and which over many thousands of years has never ceased to fill even us with a certain dread.

"*But they don't!*" he exclaims. "That is the secret. Adam and Eve couldn't wait to do what God forbade. And today, all this time later, they fall for the same old trap. I almost feel that I should try something new, but then why? *This works so well, as you can see!*"

God tells Christians to wait. But they don't. They are lured by the promise of the Gift, brushing aside the other possibilities. They have services, they have classes, they publish books, they produce cassette tapes—all geared toward *getting* the Gift from Him.

Is a gift, any gift, in fact a gift in the truest sense when it is *demanded* by the recipient from the giver?

And yet countless thousands of Christians are increasingly beating on God's door, as it were, begging Him, pleading, insisting that the gift *they* want is the Gift they feel He *owes* them somehow.

"So foolish," Satan tells us. "They are so blind."

And we cheer. We must. Satan *needs* that. The vanity that forced him from Heaven *demands* our acclaim.

"As we all know," he continues, "tongues indeed is a perfectly acceptable gift that can bring about a changed life for those upon whom God chooses to bestow it."

He speaks from raw experience. There have been innumerable times when he was so close to claiming a soul forever, when he had that individual drowning in defeated living, and yet someone introduced the possibility that tongues might be the answer, and there was much prayer, much seeking after God's will, and finally the individual was given the Gift, and their life was revitalized as a result.

"For such people, tongues was the answer," Satan adds. "And for others it has been the answer as well, and the cause of our defeat."

He pauses, then says, slowly, *"But so can it be with any of the other gifts if the recipient is wise enough to give God the honor, the glory, the gratitude, and realize how miraculous all such intervention is from the Creator Himself!"*

Satan is proud that he can speak the language as persuasively as any clergyman from any denomination.

And with the gift of tongues, he is, in the current religious climate, having a field day on both sides of the fence, as the expression goes.

His plan is simple. There are many, many thousands of

Christians who, coveting no single gift, have been blessed by God with the ability to speak in tongues. And they have tried to understand this new dimension in their lives, to use it in a way completely in accord with Scripture.

Added to this group are the ones who seek only personal gratification, for whom tongues is nothing but a kind of pep pill to be used when they are feeling low and need an emotional lift. It is a mark of exclusivity, something that sets them apart, something that seems to make them *special*, even in comparison to other Christians.

And against these two distinct varieties of charismatics are set the fundamentalists, the conservative evangelicals who are repelled by the excesses epitomized by the second group. They understand the scriptural invalidity of the way a precious gift has been taken and distorted in its application to daily life. Some even say that such a gift was never meant to be continued beyond the era of the New Testament writers. And thus the stage is set for fireworks.

"Ideal circumstances!" Satan says in exultation.

Warfare of a sort ensues in the Body of Christ, a cancer that can spread throughout, dividing congregations, splitting denominations, tearing apart families!

Making it more insidious is a not-so-minor detail.

It may be that God, forgiving as always, will give the gift of tongues to some who are *demanding* it. It may be that the beauty of the gift, the joy of it, the edificational basis for the *true* gift as detailed in Scripture proves to be just what they need to cleanse lives that have been lurking in the spiritual shadows.

But there are many today from whom God has turned aside in refusal for His own good and holy reasons, who nevertheless *seem* to be speaking in tongues anyway. They continue to glory in their undecipherable utterances, boasting of this gift to anyone who will listen, tricking many in their ignorance and dragging down their lives into a cesspool of "I have it, and you don't, and that makes me a far better Christian" pride and judgmentalism littered with the landmines of doctrinal error, planted by my master, and ready to explode.

Satan has the ability to counterfeit virtually everything that is of God. He did it in the medieval period when the Roman Catholic Church became so bloated with the lard of its own power and importance, temporally and, Catholic theologians purported, eternally as well, blinding the various popes and priests and others to the multiplied error upon error that had risen up like stinking excrement around them.

He has done it other times over the hundreds of years since then, both within Catholicism and the Protestant denominations. Now, it is the Evangelical Scandals of the 1980s that have born fruit for his demonic designs.

"Think of it," he tells us all, "most of them are charismatics!"

He would wave that before the noses of those who are so obsessively anti-charismatic that they become jubilant when they hear of anything that causes skepticism about the *entire* movement, people who were not above using the charismatic thread that ran through the Scandals as a weapon—and with some success—never realizing that ministries having nothing to do with the movement also would be hurt.

"When one old woman who, too ill to go to church, spends her Sundays watching the heavy guns of the Four Square Church or Assemblies of God on television and suddenly sees those in whom she put her trust shown to be hypocrites or worse, it will be an H-bomb blast exploding in the very belly of Christianity," he adds, "because she is not going to be alone. There will be other old women as well as old men who will be so disturbed that they will turn away in disgust, unable to extricate themselves from the maze of betrayal in which they find themselves.

"But it's not just the elderly. Housewives in their twenties, thirties, and forties will find it almost impossible to watch a Christian program without some doubt, some question, some skepticism. I will play on this; it will be my foundation. And upon this foundation will I build the kind of apostasy that will precede the advent of the Antichrist!"

He is nearly beside himself.

"It is so *wonderful!* The carnal ministers, the ones mired in the filth of their private lives are the ones who will get the headlines. The other charismatics, the decent, honorable ones who try daily to live their lives by the guidance of Scripture, none of *them* will garner even a moment of media time!"

And he is correct. Satan is often correct. If that were not so, if his plans went awry most of the time, he would amount to a pathetic and emasculated foe. Whatever remarks can be said about my master, and hit a bullseye as far as truth is concerned, that is not one of them.

. . . *the ability to counterfeit virtually anything that is of God.*

There have been apparent healings that are not healings at all. What about the preacher who supposedly cured people of brain tumors, arthritis, bad hearts, and more by grasping their foreheads and throwing them backward? Whenever he wasn't doing that sort of thing, and anyone wanted to talk to him, all they had to do was go to the tomb of his dead wife where he prayed by the hour, and claimed to have gotten advice from her in the process!

Satan is very good at taking grief and making it something obsessive, driving people to mediums and weird cults. There has never been a medium, male or female, whom Satan has *not* controlled.

And then the cults, including the Church of Latter Day Saints, Jehovah Witnesses, Scientology—ah, yes, that group of spiritual perverts, people who base their worship upon the idiotic ravings of a man whose science-fiction career was on the skids and who was told by his agent at the time, "Hey, Ron, baby, why don't you start a new religion?"

Regardless of any pious pretensions or façades, they *all* are instruments of my master, through and through— part of the darkness of the End Times (and Satan knows this, though he disputes how it all will end up!)

There have been other miracles that Satan has duplicated. When Scripture says that the spirits are to be discerned, to see whether these are of God or the devil, God was speaking with compelling force. After all, a good counterfeit hundred-dollar bill can deceive many. If men are capable of such, then think of what my master can do.

Often, I have observed, charismatics are guilty of failing to heed what Scripture says about testing the spirits. As a result, Satan is pleased indeed with the victories he has had over the years due to a seemingly minor bit of manipulation that pays impressive dividends for him.

"Get them to feel disturbed or, as they say, uneasy in the spirit," he once remarked. "You do that to a charismatic and you can practically smell defeat in the air—for them, not us."

I asked him to explain in more detail what he meant.

"Many charismatics fall consistently into the trap of thinking that when they have this 'uneasiness in the spirit,' it is a bad thing. So they claim the—"

He stopped, trembling a bit, unable to say *those* words. But I knew what he meant. The blood . . . *His* blood.

" —and that is supposed to do it," he continued. "They

develop a ritualistic approach they think comes from spiritual courage and discernment, but it is instead a sign of outright cowardice, even spiritual blindness."

"How so, master?" I probed.

"If I suspect that they are on the verge of receiving some compelling divine truth, one that can give them new insight, and clear away the cobwebs of the old, I oppress them, I probe their sin nature. I—"

"*You*, master?"

"Well, you know what I mean—either me or one of your comrades. Now do not interrupt again. Understood?"

I agreed that it was.

"I bring about some kind of dark mood, some fleeting feeling of depression, and then I have them. They have been tricked into thinking that because they do not feel up, up, up, that because their mood is dark, sinister perhaps, that they have to reject whatever it is that God is trying to tell them, assuming, I suppose, that divine revelation flies into their lives only on wings of sunshine and light, without ever realizing that storm clouds can be of God also! What I have done, in these instances, is to short-circuit valuable truths."

Satan was quite satisfied with himself at that somewhat convoluted but unerringly accurate insight.

"It is a perfect situation, Observer," he added. "Make a special point of that in your book."

I assured him that I would.

$\mathcal{E}$RIK WAS IN his dorm room. Both he and Arthur had been traumatized by the events at that new church. I wanted to see if Satan's plan was working, so, true to my nature, I observed Erik every chance I got. After what seemed like a very long time, he convinced the men at that church that he could speak in tongues. They heard the sounds coming, and, on this basis alone, without any analysis beyond that, their reaction was immediate, and effusive.

"Praise Jesus, praise Jesus," said the man who had prayed with him, "praise His holy name!"

There was much back-patting, congratulating, and finally, the man added, "Please consider us willing to open our church to you *anytime*."

Arthur, however, had not spoken in tongues, and he was ignored, pointedly so.

"I felt like a leper that they had tried to cure," he said later, "but failing that, they were determined to pretend that I just didn't exist."

As it turned out, neither had Erik himself spoken in tongues, which he revealed to his roommate on the way back to the college that afternoon.

"But they were *sure* that you had. It *sounded* as though you were saying everything they had been—!"

Erik's roommate was surprised.

"You were just going along with them, weren't you?"

Erik nodded.

"I had no idea what to do," he admitted. "I just imitated that other guy."

"And he didn't know the difference," his friend muttered.

. . . *he didn't know the difference.*

That was the scariest part for Erik. If *he* could fool them, who else could do the same thing to those individuals at that -church, perhaps others far more evil than young Erik?

*U*LTIMATELY, ERIK BEGAN to doubt his salvation. He read a number of books about the subject of speaking in tongues, but became more and more confused. Going to several other charismatic churches didn't help.

Until he found one nearly a hundred miles away. Arthur didn't go with him this time, nor had he gone to most of the others. He was changing. He was drifting, disturbed by the incident in that church, the phoniness of it, phoniness raised to a level of sanctification in the deluded view of those who had tried to force him to speak in tongues.

After the service, which didn't include a demonstration of the Gift, as the others had, Erik walked up to the pastor, an elderly and sincere-looking gentleman named Harold Forrester.

"Sir," Erik said at the entrance as they shook hands, "I have a real problem. It's about this speaking in tongues stuff. Do you have any time?"

The old man looked at him kindly, nodded, and motioned for Erik to wait until he had finished shaking hands with the remaining members of the congregation. Then he took Erik outside. The day was a pleasant, sunny one.

The church was located in the middle of farming country, and there was plenty of open acreage all around them.

The scent of manure, pungent, filled the air.

"I love it here, Erik," the old pastor told him. "I wouldn't know how to live anywhere else."

He stopped at a tree trunk, an old one.

"It occurred for me right here," he said. "I was on my knees before the Lord, leaning my arms against the top, and suddenly I spoke in what we call heavenly language."

He turned and looked at Erik.

"But there was no joy!" he remarked, with a somewhat mischievous grin curling up the corners of his mouth.

Erik was stunned.

"But I thought there was *always* joy," he said.

"That was how I myself had approached the subject. I had been trying for years to get the Lord to give me the Gift because I *wanted* to *feel* that joy."

"But why then? When you were least expecting it?"

"That, too, was a question I wrestled with, Erik. I chewed on it for hours afterwards. Finally I called a friend of mine who had been speaking in tongues for some time, a fact that I frankly envied about him. So we got together at my apartment. And we were both on our knees, praying, when I spoke again in tongues!"

"But without any joy, I suppose," Erik says, sure that that was what had happened.

"Oh, *no!*" Forrester told him, his whole expression changing as the wrinkles of age seemed to recede a bit and there was something that could only be called a glow about him. "I've never experienced anything so intense— the greatest jubilation imaginable, Erik. It was the complete opposite of the first time earlier that same day."

He saw the frown on Erik's forehead.

"You see," the old man said, "my friend *understood* the words. It wasn't gibberish to him. He *interpreted* what I had been saying. And that triggered my joy, my profound joy.

"That was why the apostles proved to be so ecstatic on the Day of Pentecost. There they were, before thousands of people, from as many as a dozen countries, and speaking nearly as many languages. Peter, John, and the others saw before them the first mission field they had encountered since the death, burial, and resurrection of Christ, and yet at first it seemed impossible that they could ever communicate, simply because they didn't know Chinese or Greek or whatever other language the people spoke."

"But God gave them the gift of languages on the spot?" Erik asked.

"He did, he did indeed. And, later, when they talked about that moment among themselves, they were nearly overcome with the impact. In fact, those who heard them thought they were quite mad or quite drunk or both, because they acted with such abandon, and this was because never before in their lives had they felt so close to God, so touched by Him. It was a clear-cut moment they could point to that showed his intervention from the spiritual world into their world, the world of flesh and blood."

For a short while, Harold Forrester seemed not at all like an elderly preacher but a very young one indeed.

"Can you *imagine* how that must be, Erik? To sense God reaching *into* your very being, and taking charge of your vocal chords, and all of a sudden you open your mouth and you are speaking what *He* wants you to say!"

Abruptly his shoulders slumped. Erik was concerned.

"Sir, are you all right?" he asked.

The minister nodded slowly.

"From joy remembered in days of youth to the despair of this era," he remarked, "quite a journey, my young friend."

"I don't understand."

"Let's go to my study. I'll *show* you what I mean."

They walked back to the church, and Erik followed the

pastor to the little study, its shelves crammed full with books and magazines.

The elderly minister searched for several publications and spread these out on his desk with a grunt of disgust.

"Look!" he said. "Look at that stuff."

What Erik saw was an assortment of garish covers, with blaring headlines, often "colorful" stories, and a number of photos of familiar celebrities.

"They've Christianized sensationalism. Or maybe they've sensationalized Christianity. How offended the Lord must be! Publishers have turned a holy and wonderful thing, the bestowal of a gift from *God*, into just another circulation-boosting gimmick. But they couldn't do it without the cooperation of believers themselves, without the eagerness shown by certain groups or denominations."

He tapped the covers with contempt.

"I could open the pages of more than one publication and show you ads for mustard seeds from Israel, gram bottles of water from the River Jordan, Protestant prayer beads blessed by a bozo named Reverend John, or some other embarrassment to the Cause of Christ.

"As disgusting as that stuff is, the worst is the space given to pronouncements by famous figures and the utter garbage that is tolerated from their lips or their pen or their computer, as the case may be.

"Some of them can proclaim God's admonitions regularly, or so they say, and be guaranteed premium space anytime they want, even when what they offer is foolish and, yes, injurious to the cause of Christ, if not on doctrinal grounds, then because they make some other crazy claim that sets them up for yet another round of ridicule."

He turned around, and walked over to one of the bookcases.

"It's the same there," he said, spitting out the words,

"people blathering about what *they* think is the legitimate application of tongues and a hundred other subjects. Most don't know what they're talking about."

He sighed, deeply, something more than a sigh, actually.

"Everything has been cheapened these days," he said.
"Worship used to be done in a quiet little place with a
few people, the outside world sealed off, and not intruding. But mega-churches changed that, and television
provided the deathknell. Now you have some actor or
another getting up before that guy's congregation, you
know the one I mean, and giving his testimony!

"Oh, the speaker may very well be a very nice man,
maybe even a highly moral one up to a point. But I
question, I seriously question whether most of these
celebrities are people to be holding up as an example
before millions of viewers. No one should be an example
held up before others who is not a sincere, Bible-believing
Christian! Some of these guys may be okay in the board
room or on a music hall stage or a motion picture screen
perhaps—but they just don't have any business standing
up before a *Christian* audience. No one *else* belongs *but*
men, women, and children who have fallen on their
knees and sought redemption from the only One who can
ever bestow it!"

"Some would call that a judgmental, bigoted view, sir."

"Yes, *some* would. But Christianity is a very exclusive
religion. There is one basic requirement, the acceptance
of Christ as Savior and Lord. An actor can treat the family
dog as kindly as he wants, with an ocean of kindness, if
that were possible; someone else can give every cent he
has to charity—and *still*, despite everything else that
may be so wonderful, and fit the world's definition of
goodness, they *are* headed for Hell if they haven't taken
Jesus Christ into their lives. It's as simple, as profound, as
unequivocal as that!"

*W*HAT THE OLD preacher said was quite true.
. . . they are headed for Hell if they haven't taken Jesus Christ into their lives.

Who would know better than those demons whisking lost souls from their mortal trappings, and depositing them among the inhospitable coals?

My master is *always* looking for ways to thwart salvational truth from entering the lives of human beings everywhere.

With the prostituted use of tongues, or what he has tricked worshipers into *thinking* is that wondrous gift, he has surely found one of the most enticing, compelling traps so far.

Yet it is but one out of a common cesspool.

Healing is another entrapment for the unwary. Crusades organized around this theme are usually filled with people, many of them desperate, who try to circumvent the capabilities of modern science and medicine and invoke the miracle of healing directly from Almighty God.

God has not lost the power, of course; but I know very well that He will not be forced into healing as a public display, healing-on-demand.

. . . on demand.

How utterly presumptuous it is to *demand* anything of Him. Satan tried that while still in Heaven, and we all suffered as a result.

Healing is a gift, as is tongues, as is prophecy, and the others. When gifts are *demanded* of the Heavenly Father, He is likely to bestow nothing at all.

Sometimes, though, He will heal in the midst of the carnivalike atmosphere of such a service. He will intercede from the infinite to the finite and show that of which He is truly capable.

Sometimes, yes, but not often.

Still, an hour spent at one of the crusades would give the impression that more than 90 percent of those who *are* touched by this evangelist or that one are healed.

Untrue.

Most find their physical condition virtually the same after the adrenalin of the moment has passed.

What about the evangelist with the hidden microphone being given information on the sly that, to the congregation, seems as though it has been divinely implanted?

And the people planted in the congregation that have little or nothing wrong with them but put up a convincing act as they become "miraculously" healed?

A vast array of deceptions.

Sewn together with a common thread that draws the gullible to them.

Addiction.

It is a word much in circulation during these last decades. Cocaine, marijuana, heroin, the rest—all have been well-reported. Yuppies use them, so do street gangs, entertainers, high school students, others.

Yet I have found that *Christians* are as addiction-prone as the coke-head delinquent who sells drugs to support *his* habit!

Most don't snort white powder through their nostrils, but their addictive tendencies drive them onward ceaselessly as they scramble to get whatever they crave for their own particular situation. They gobble up the worst tripe imaginable so long as famous personages dish it out in sermon after sermon, in books and magazines, on cassette tapes and compact discs, a vast so-called information industry having sprung up to supply their habit, a habit that chains them to the heretical "feel good" doctrines that are proliferating—to Satan's delight and God's dismay.

Lambs to the slaughter.

And that they are, pushed by the obsession to be up, up, up all the time. Chemically-dependent people pursue "up, up, up" through drugs. Christians do so by submitting to the clutches of religious opportunists who understand that the same societal tendencies that have made the drug epidemic what it is also motivate those who would never buy so much as a single joint of maryjane.

"Forget all that bad stuff in the Bible," one or the other will say. "We're past that now. We've *matured!* Holiness is happiness, happiness is holiness. If you're not happy, you're not holy."

People listen.

People grasp and grope and grab to fill in the vacuums that exist in life. That is, after all, why the whole shepherding nightmare started, and, also, how so many have been able to garner so much success.

"Let me take your hand," the unwary are told. "Let me mold your new life in Christ. Listen to me, and only me. God has sent me to—"

And so on, and so on.

The problem is that Christians are among the most gullible of all people—and the most dependent. There is little difference in the gullibility factor of Germans being seduced *en masse* by Adolf Hitler because life has become tense and hungry and insecure—and those Christians who are roped in by any preacher with a message that sounds as though it will be satisfying, no matter how specious it might be from a scriptural standpoint.

Can tricky pastors be compared to the new Hitlers in the resurgent neo-Nazi movement?

Absolutely.

My master is involved with both!

Both deceive, both are deadly. If anything, the influence of the Bakker-types of the evangelical community is perhaps worse than the influence of the Metzgers of the white supremacy underground.

Since I am a demon, I know firsthand how many innocent lives are lost through the racial hatred espoused by the various Aryan-type organizations. But many of the victims are Christians, their redemption guaranteed— which does not mitigate in any respect the injustice, the torment in this life, but it does mean that they are now where no more hatred can touch them, where they will share without end in the love of God, basking in the radiance of His glory. Oh, how I envy them!

Yet the preachers with false words from their lips and extorted money in their wallets create an *atmosphere* of redemption—but that is all it is, as vacuous as the air they breath. People believing they will go to Heaven are instead greeted by my kind in Hell, no beautiful chorus awaiting them but the shrieking, discordant fury that is their eternity.

Woe to you, wolves who take on the garb of shepherds! Woe to you all when we get our talons into you with special delight!

To squash a human soul!

To brush aside the hand that reaches up toward God and direct it in worship toward yourselves!

Palms upward, oh, yes, that remains part of the illusion, but with piles of greenbacks and a plea from doomed lips, "Take it, take it! *All* of it!"

To make them happy in the midst of this blasphemy.

To wrap around them positively principles, principles from deceived minds who have pulled the wool over the eyes of countless thousands of Christians, with their recycled and thinly veiled humanism.

To brainwash them with the delusions of seed-faith principles.

To anesthetize them to what they really need to be doing, not grabbing at the manmade confections that look so sweet, but to get down on their knees, and let all the pus and gangrene and slop that has been building up inside them rush out in a confessional surge by admitting, finally, that there is *nothing* positive about their lives because they have been grasping at lies instead of deep-down-straight-from-He-Who-is-the-only-Source-of-it true truth!

And then when you get caught, as the expression goes, you weep and cry and say to the world, "The media are out to get us. Christians, unite against the devil's children."

But you are those children.

I F I WERE a born-again Christian, and not a condemned demon—and there is a wide, wide gulf between the two—if I were a Christian, especially one with influence, there is at least one television preacher I would concentrate on trying to throw off the air, and though there are others as well, somehow this one seems among the most targetable, because he is in such flagrant disregard of the norms of Christian worship and witness.

He is white-haired. And pot-bellied. He insists upon holding up before his followers the fact that he has the freedom to chomp continually on a cigar, if he wishes.

So I motivated my latest host to call his 800 phone number, and ask a single question: "Since unassailable evidence now exists that smoking causes cancer, lung disease, and other ailments, and since the Christian's body is the temple of the Holy Spirit, how can you justify your preacher's apparent addiction to cigar-smoking as a proper witness and not instead a stumbling-block to thousands of the brethren?"

At least that was what my host *intended* to say.

The flunkie at the other end hung up on him mid-way through.

Thinking that my host's true allegiance was the issue,

and that the person representing the preacher had somehow sensed this, I had my host persuade someone who
really was a born-again Christian to make the next call.

"I've been a believer for more than a quarter of a
century," the Christian said.

"Praise God!" the rep replied. "How can I help you?"

"I fail to understand how a constant montage of shots
showing your preacher's horses parading around to the
accompaniment of rather raucous bar-room music is
anything that could be considered edifying to the Body of
Christ."

Again the Great Disconnect. (Not the Great Commission, of course.)

This Christian was irate. So he called a second time.

"Doesn't it bother your arrogant pastor that worldly
music of the most unseemly sort is inappropriate for a
Christian program?"

"He doesn't see it that way."

"He's not bothered by the offensive nature of that
stuff?"

"Are you one of those offended?"

"Yes, I am."

"He cares not one whit about your kind."

"What *does* he care about?"

"Only what *he* thinks is right. Anything else is unim-
portant."

"Even if it contradicts Scripture, even if—"

Yes, another disconnect.

How anxiously my master awaits an opportunity to
seize upon the moral and theological weaknesses in *that*
ministry and exploit them just for the hell of it. But then
he may not have to do anything else. People of that bent
are pretty good at ultimately discrediting themselves and
the Lord they supposedly are serving.

*H*OW MANY OF the flock whose sins have entered the province of what is called "public knowledge" and supposedly repented of those sins have been able to rebuild their ministries and go on, as though nothing ever happened?

From the standpoint of divinity, shall we say, it is the very core of why Christ died for the sins of mankind. Those sins are actually forgiven before they are ever committed. They are *forgotten* by God, and the repentant sinner stands before Him cleansed.

Demonkind are continually tempted by this forgiveness, just as human beings are tempted to commit the very sins that then must be put under the crimson flow at Calvary.

If any of my fellows were, themselves, to accept this forgiveness, then Satan's empire would collapse overnight. It is the same with humans; that forgiveness breaks Satan's power over them. Humans have done so throughout the past two thousand years, while demons never have.

How ironic that the creatures feared by countless millions of men, women, and children are, in this regard, far, far weaker than the ones they would seek to torment and subjugate! It seems we are *bound* to Satan, too cowardly to risk his wrath, and yet lowly man has again and again proven courageous enough, faithful enough, to break those chains of domination and become free, free forever.

But that very forgiveness, in the case of straying televangelists and other Christians of significant public recognition, represents a big opportunity for Satan in such matters, upon which he can easily capitalize.

How does the flock *know* that the confession of sin is *genuine*? How do they know that it isn't merely for public consumption while the heart, the soul, of the individual is anything but repentant?

There is a booth on the convention floor with magazines and books being presented by one such ministry. The evangelist in question was involved in the sin of adultery with prostitutes; he had slept with not just one woman of the night but many of them, even though the public became aware of only the one, and it was only *that* one to which he confessed. He said nothing about the others. Was his broadcasted confession intended as an oblique umbrella for *all* the moments of sin, of consorting with whores in a dozen cities while he was on his crusade tours? Or was he clever enough to admit to *just* that one, knowing that attention would be deflected from the others and, with any luck, those would never be found out?

The question remains: If he did not publicly *acknowledge* the rest, did he privately come to the Lord and, on his knees, ask for forgiveness? If not, was his public admission of lust only a public relations ploy to save some scraps of his ministry so that these could be pieced together and he could continue, after a seclusionary period of time, right along as before, filling to overflowing the luxurious building bearing his name?

The doctrine of forgiveness is at the same time God's

greatest blessing and an opportunity for Satan the Deceiver. That doctrine is pervasive, so central to the faith
of Christians everywhere that when someone confesses
sin, when someone claims forgiveness, when someone
jumps up and down and proclaims cleansing as a result,
then his brothers and sisters in Christ tend to *believe*
him, taking comfort in such phrases as "Well, after all,
that's why Christ died at Calvary, isn't it?" or "We can't
judge because only the Lord knows for sure, and we have
to accept such matters at face value, don't we?"

But it has happened before, of course; it has happened
in the case of a well-known writer of prophetic books
who got involved in an extramarital affair many years
earlier, and he had to go into hiding for awhile. But,
today, he is back as strong as ever, and more than one
publisher is offering a book by him at this convention.

If his repentance was genuine, then his new legitimacy
within the Christian community is something that shows
the strength and beauty of the Christian approach to life. If
that repentance is not altogether honest and true, then it
can be viewed only in one light: a device to get back into
favor so that he can continue to earn a living.

But how does anyone know for sure?

If only God Himself has the answer, then no finite man
or woman can possibly be certain.

But it is not just God.

My master, this chief of all demons, this Lucifer the
Fallen, also knows. He also is alone with such a man,
evangelist or writer or whomever, either through his
appointed demons or, if he takes a special interest,
directly himself—alone in moments when the public is a
long way away, and there is no one else but himself and
his conscience and all the truths that either have been
played out before the crowd or kept in a private little
corner of his mind, his soul.

It is then that God knows. It is then that Satan knows. It is then that the truth is apparent.

And in the case of the evangelist, in the case of the writer, in the case of so many others who have *seemed* to be different, to have turned their lives around, in these cases, cleansed as they supposedly were and so fine in the minds of their adoring Christian public, Satan stands rejoicing at the deception, counting the dirty secrets yet remaining, counting each one, and looking at those who gather before their celebrity leaders in trust and listen to what they have to say, read what they have to say, and proclaim, "We welcome you back with open arms, we have faith anew in you."

If they only knew.

*E*RIK HAS PAID for a one-day pass.

I watch him as he stands at the entrance, looking at the huge hall, with its three-score rows of exhibits, banners hanging from poles, the sounds of thousands in attendance, just like himself, music blaring from several directions.

"On Christ the Solid Rock I stand. . . ."

He catches those few words, but the beat isn't the same as with the old hymn that he had heard years before as his grandmother hummed it to him. The arranger had added an electric guitar, and the vocalist sounded like a cross between Elton John and Billy Idol.

Erik walks about, picks up an occasional book, leafs through the pages, then puts it down.

Someone taps him on the shoulder.

He turns.

"Can I help you?" the short, heavyset man asks.

"I was just looking," Erik replies.

"Could you use some pencils?"

"I—I don't think so."

"They're engraved with Bible verses."

"Does that make them holy?"

"No, it doesn't but—"

"But what?"

"It's a great fund-raiser."

"Why?"

"Isn't that obvious, young man? Because people will *read* the verses. These are *Christian* pencils, after all."

"Will they?"

"Will they what?"

"Read the verses?"

"Oh, yes!" he replies, anxious to get beyond that point. "My pencils are a bargain. And we're offering a convention special. An extra 12 percent off the retail price."

"A cheap way to witness, is that it?"

"If you say so, buddy. The cost per—"

"Are you making a profit?"

"Sure I am. Anything wrong with that?"

"Are you a Christian?"

"What does that have to do with anything?"

Erik is silent, just looks at the little man.

"This is a great market, you know. Just a few thousand stores grossed more than two billion dollars last year."

"What about soul-winning?"

"Soul-winning?"

"Yes."

"Whadda I know about that stuff? I'm Jewish. For Christ's sake, I gotta wear a cross to sell in here?"

Erik walks away.

He is tired. He feels a little sick. He hasn't been feeling too good for a while, now. Not since—

$\mathcal{E}$RIK IS CONVINCED he has no choice.

The joy he knew so briefly is fading fast. He felt uplifted somehow when he had talked to that old preacher in the country. But here, with all these Christians who hardly seemed inspired at all, except about money, he felt confused and angry. *Is this what Christianity is really all about!* he asks himself. *Is this all there is!*

Even here he has heard again and again the argument about the Gift. Some of the new books he has leafed through have said that he can't really be saved if he doesn't speak in tongues. He wonders if he is a Christian at all, because he knows he doesn't have the Gift.

He looks within his mind at the old images, that lifestyle of sex and drugs that had once grabbed hold of him until he no longer wanted to live if he had to spend one more day in one more strange bed, snorting from one more plastic pouch.

"I can't go back to that," he whispers, not caring whether anyone hears. "I can't go back to that cesspool. And yet the old minister seems to think—"

(D'Seaver is by his side. I hear him whispering the lies

in a rancid stream, all the reasons why Erik should do what he had decided earlier to do.)

Don't listen to the old fool. He is just another phony, another hypocrite. As soon as you left, he was probably chuckling. They always do, you know.

"But he seemed so genuine. He seemed to know—"

He doesn't know a thing. His mind has turned senile.

"But he used Scripture. He tried to show me that tongues were a wonderful gift but I—I didn't need it to be—"

You do. You do! Don't be deceived. If you don't speak the heavenly language, you cannot be sure of your salvation!

"But I—"

Listen to that inner voice. There is no hope for you. You are doomed to wander on the fringes of lives more happy than your own. They won't accept you unless you have the Gift. You don't have it so what is there left for you?

"But Jesus will forgive me."

How can you be sure?

The elevator is packed.

He takes the stairs from the ground floor, to the second, to the third. Someone bumps into him, a middle-aged woman.

"Are you all right?" she asks, greatly concerned.

He tries to get away from her but she persists.

"You don't look well, son," she says.

"I'm damned," he tells her.

$\mathcal{E}$RIK STANDS AT the railing on the third floor. The vast hall spreads out below him.

It's all right, Erik. You've done your best. Look at the light, Erik. The light beckons. It's a soft light. It's warm, Erik. Reach for the light and it will surround you. It will comfort you. The light is everything. Believe in it, Erik. Let the joy overwhelm you.

He reaches out, freon-chilled air against his cheeks, sanctified rock music staccato in the background, banners flying, faces turned upward, pain as flesh meets wood and plaster and cardboard and then concrete, people rushing forward, a montage of their shocked expressions, someone's bad breath, laced with a hint of tobacco.

"I'm damned to hell. . . ." he whispers as his mouth fills with blood.

How sad, they say. Troubled young man, they say. If only someone had reached him for the Lord in time, they say.

No more light.

D'Seaver cackles.

$\mathcal{T}$HE REACTIONS HAVE been immediate, of course. The booth wrecked by Erik is an expensive one, and elaborate. It cannot be reconstructed for the remainder of the convention. The publisher is trying to be sympathetic, but he is also extremely upset. Crucial sales may be lost in the interim.

Massive confusion dominates. Even so, despite worries, order forms are being whipped out, and quantities of product are being sold. Even in the midst of tragedy, the show must go on.

But that is as it should be. Satan will not admit this. He would like it to be viewed as callous, insensitive, a clear indication of the paucity of true spirituality that has come to characterize such trade shows, as they are called.

Wrong.

He is very wrong.

As important as the life of one young man named Erik happened to be, no ministry, no publishing firm, no Christian educational institution, no convention should be allowed to grind to a halt, as the expression goes. If that were the case, then my master would have an easy way of it. All he would have to do is engineer a few dozen tragedies at the most influential Christian organizations, and the entire Christian community in the United States would be so traumatized that he would have golden opportunities for making headway, driven onward by the scent of victory.

So *this* show *does* continue to function, in fits and spurts, taking a little while to regain its momentum. And always there is discussion, sanctified gossip about Erik, with some of the details of why he did what he did gleaned from television interviews with a number of fellow students.

Two men are having a heated exchange in the cafeteria section of the hall.

"It's the way tongues as a gift is twisted these days by you crazy charismatics!" one is saying.

"That had nothing to do with him taking his life!" the other retorts. "He was a troubled young man."

"And this heresy put forth by the emotional screwballs abounding in the charasmatic movement was the gun that they put to his head. All he had to do was pull the trigger."

"The *trouble* is that none of your Baptist churches gave him what he needed. They painted a picture of tongues that made this gift from God seem like a work of Satan's."

"The counterfeit is precisely that. It reduces the concrete reality, the truths of Scripture to a level of ecstatic gibberish, and what is left is utter theological nonsense— just the sort of vacuum that Satan favors!"

"*Your* problem is that you have become a dried-up shell," one of the men shouts. "God gave us emotions. God doesn't expect us to keep them bottled up, as though we are to be ashamed of having them in the first place."

"That's *not* what I'm saying, my brother. I *am* suggesting that emotions can be manipulated by the Arch Deceiver. I don't propose that the gift of tongues is invalidated today. I just offer the possibility that it is misunderstood and misused much of the time."

"Your attitude is the same as the Lord experienced two thousand years ago. You and all the others who look with such disdain on charismatics are guilty of a modern pharisaicalism that is closing the door to salvation for countless numbers of people."

The first man leans across the small square table until his nose nearly touches the other man's.

"And that is the greatest fallacy of all: the way you and the other loonies have gotten hold of isolated portions of scripture and twisted these to satisfy your own limited view. Speaking in tongues has *nothing* to do with closing the door to salvation *or* keeping it open for that matter. You all have meant needless guilt for thousands, perhaps hundreds of thousands of born-again people who keep striving for the gift, and when they don't get it, they begin to doubt themselves."

And so it goes. They don't end up physically assaulting one another, but there are moments when they seem not far from this extreme.

Finally, though, one apologizes for the insults, and the other apologizes for his anger. They stand, embrace one another, then go their separate ways.

Satan lost that one.

Satan loses many such moments during the convention. He tries so hard to get men and women to have their theological arguments or debates, and then attempts to build up a permanent barrier between them, a wall of festering feelings that is, in a way, as solid, as impenetrable, as anything physical.

And while there are successes, while he does cause pain in the Body of Christ, while the carnival-like hawkers of cheap trinkets and other such merchandise seem to be proliferating, there are the firm, the steady, the properly-motivated pockets of genuine ministry. These

are people whose primary purpose is to reach souls for
Christ, and books and magazines and plaques and posters
are the means they have chosen, people who lament the
intrusion of hoopla at the altar of sales, sales purely for
profit, with souls saved as a byproduct rather than the
reverse being true. These dedicated servants, appalled by
what they see, become ever more determined not to
succumb. And so, ultimately, Satan has lost another
round.

And he cannot abide this. He simply cannot.

So he calls in the artillery.

Literally.

SATAN GOT THEM to do what they did through hatred, their Muslim fanaticism already incorporating the "Americans are devils" mentality that led to the capture of the American embassy in Teheran, and so he had had to exert little persuasion for them to make the leap into something on the scale that he had in mind.

It has been fashionable in some circles, particularly those with a humanistic bent, to label as prejudice any attempt to call the Muslims or the Buddhists or the Hindus "heathens." But that certainly is what they are. Their religion rips from the Iraqis and the Libyans and the Iranians and others any façade of civilized behavior, any semblance of humanity, and makes them instead barbarians of the worst sort, ruled by men for whom no atrocity is too repugnant so long as it serves their delusion of a worldwide Islamic kingdom—which, I must add, would be nothing more than another version of Hell.

No one realizes this more than Satan and the rest of us. In fact, we are *more* aware of the evil dimension of fake religions, the counterfeit cults, the mystical Eastern heretical sects than *any* evangelical Christian, because demons are responsible for their existence in the first place, by which we have deceived untold millions.

But it is more than that. No Christian who has ever lived and died in Christ has even a small fraction of the knowledge about Satan that *we* do, simply because we have gotten it from the source, Satan himself. That needs to be said. And I can see with clarity that is profound, truly, truly profound how corrupt the Muslims are by the very nature of their beliefs, beliefs aided by demons for the sole purpose of increasing the harvest of souls for Lucifer the Fallen.

Any religion without Christ is spiritually bankrupt. But it is the Muslims who seem to be the most twisted, the most maniacal, the most evil, paying homage to a leader who was the worst kind of Satanic puppet because he seemed so good, so righteous—but of whom we all had total and absolute control. It is ironic that they hang a death sentence on Salman Rushdie, the commendable author of *The Satanic Verses* when they are the ones, as far as eternity is concerned, who are condemned, and just not condemned, I say, but condemned to Hell. They are the vipers of the world of flesh and blood, and I, for one, rejoice when they find themselves in damnation forever, crying out for the forgiveness that they so vehemently deny so many others.

That we must depend on these scum is appalling—but then we use whomever we have to, murderers and rapists and homosexuals and pornographers and feminists and hordes of others, so it shouldn't distress me that Muslims are part of this squalid list—yet it does, it always has when such as the Muslims and the Scientologists and the Mormons and others of their ilk rope in the innocent and never let go until the flames of the pit of eternal darkness entrap seducers and seduced alike. (Christ would not have used the word *scum* but then I am afraid that I have absorbed more of my master's mindset, his very words, than I have been willing to admit through the centuries.)

There had been plans for more than one terrorist strike within the United States for some time. The first had occurred months earlier when an American president had died of natural causes while still in office. Just as the British prime minister was entering the main air terminal outside Washington, D.C., a little girl approached.

She is standing alone near the front entrance to the airline building where a delegation from England is scheduled to arrive.

Dressed in clothes that make her seem a harmless doll, she is holding a rather large handbag. Every so often she looks up at a passerby and smiles.

At the opposite end of the building, a British Airways plane lands. A total of twenty members of Parliament disembark. The Prime Minister and her husband are also on board, but she has had a slight case of airsickness. The others wait at the gate.

"She is supposed to be made of iron," whispers one of them.

"Please, Harold, do not be sarcastic," an associate responds. "You try to hide how much you really do admire the lady, but despite yourself, you cannot."

The other man is silent.

In a few minutes the couple joins them, and surrounded by security guards they head toward the entrance. The Prime Minister seems quite recovered, walking with a sure step.

As the party approaches, the little girl runs up to the first member of the delegation, and gives him the handbag. She is smiling with the sweetness, the innocence of the very young.

"Please, mister, my mommy—"

She is unable to finish.

An explosion demolishes a large portion of the building, pieces of it scattering for nearly a mile. Most of those

Roger Elwood

directly inside are killed—as well as many more on the outside, bodies flung in a dozen directions.

Several times the number of those dead are injured, blinded by shards of glass, flesh torn by metal, limbs severed, bones broken.

"A war zone!" says the U. S. Government official observing the scene.

And that it appears to be. The terminal in ruins, girders twisted like a toy erector set abused by a very angry child. . . .

*M*Y MASTER COULDN'T have been happier about the chaos at the air terminal. He stood amidst the wreckage, saw the broken and twisted bodies sprawled in a dozen different directions, saw the prime minister on her knees beside the man she loved, and laughed.

"Glorious—" he started to say until I interrupted him.

"Why was this necessary?" I asked him.

"You tolerate the murder of six million Jews but the deaths of a dozen or so makes you question the wisdom of my actions?" he said angrily. "I fail to understand the significance, Observer."

"Is it possible that you go too far from time to time?" I asked, a little of my insolence already dissipating against his intimidation.

"If there is pain, if there are questions such as 'Where is God in situations such as this?' how *can* there be even the remotest chance of going too far?"

Satan was licking fluids from the festering sores on his lips.

"I used to hate the taste," he said, distracted for a moment, "but now I rather like the bitterness. Would you care to sample some, Observer?"

I backed away, repulsed.

"Better yet, since you are my servant, I command you to kiss me on the lips, taste the pus, tell me what you think of gangrene, Observer!"

As far as humankind is concerned, we are beings without substance; some go even further and call us nothing but the insane fantasies of the religious right perhaps. (How successful we've been with *them*!) But when you are a demon, well, it is altogether different. Just as dogs can hear sound that humans cannot, so can we see what man does not until the moment of death. We can do all manner of abominable acts among ourselves.

I wanted to pull away. I wanted desperately to rebel. I wanted to throw him aside, and go begging to the gates of Heaven, not just because of what he had asked me to do, the humiliation of it, the disgusting filth of which I was being called upon to partake, but also, and mostly, because of the crumpled and battered bodies sprawled all around us, because of a little girl's skirt stained with red, her flesh shredded by the force of the blast and a multitude of glass shards, because of the most powerful woman in the world, not caring who saw her in the sudden surge of grief that bespoke her utter helplessness, she who had the power to start a great war virtually anywhere on the planet, was now reduced to a near-hysterical level of wrenching grief, her power meaningless in the one way she would have chosen to use it just then if she could, if she could.

None of this shamefulness *had* to happen.

None of it would mean the difference between success and failure in any of the planning hatched in the mind of Satan.

There was simply no *justification* for this latest monstrous deed, though I wondered why this one had affected me so, for it really was just part of a perverse tapestry woven out of the bones and veins and other innards of the countless victims of his rage.

Yet undeniably I *was* overwhelmed, as though I stood before the battlefield of Armageddon, witnessing hundreds of thousands of bodies, some not quite dead, their hands raised toward a stormy sky like stalks of marsh grass in a bloody inlet—a moment we all knew was yet to come, and about which we often thought, surrendering to the delusion that the dead were Satan's and by no means God's. And so the sight of spilled guts, the more the better, should in fact precipitate our rejoicing, and against such a panorama, stretching on, it seemed, to the very horizon, the sight of a few limp forms and some twisted metal and a child's dismembered doll, none of it should begin to compare, none of it should have the impact of Armageddon.

But it did, as I've said, it did. In a sudden and special clarity, I realized why, because, oh, God, oh, God, if there were only the small horrors of the past—the bombing of an embassy, the crash of an airliner, the sinking of a ship, all small indeed if numbers were the only guide, not conscience, not morality, not any sense of humanity but cold numbers devoid of anything but mathematical precision and impersonality—then Satan's blood lust would have gone unquenched. For him, these "minor" atrocities were simply appetizers before the main feast.

I speak of that Final Battle described in the sacred pages of Scripture, that climactic clash at the end of history. For if God never truly fought back, then how weak He would seem, how empty His admonitions, how absurd those many proclamations of omnipotence and omniscience and all the rest in the face of what would be thus an inevitable victory for Lucifer, then-conqueror of Heaven, once-slum lord of Hell, the sum total of everything we had been through since leaving Heaven—only to win it all back.

How strange then, lost in such contemplation, there in the midst of that shattered terminal, cries piercing the air, people screaming for help, please, please help, how strange that the thought of my master having his way with the universe, the *opportunity* to recreate everything in *his* image, how melancholy it made me. I experienced not a fleeting moment of celebration, which I should have felt as one of his followers, as Mifult and DuRong and so on and so on and so on would undoubtedly feel, for they were more *into it*, as the expression goes, more attuned to the mission from the very start.

But for me, the journalist from Hell, not a single instant of pride was left, nothing of the kind but rather the terrifying sight of the aftermath of apocalypse. I had a vision of land after land piled high with his victims, from Rome to London to New York to Los Angeles, the Holy Ghost in chains of darkness forever, no longer a restraining influence, indeed only a defeated foe, the once transcendent might reduced to simpering impotence, mocked by creatures liberated from the dark alleys of their existence, and now parading before Him, venting their blasphemies . . . and next the Father and Son, my master reserving for his most profound enemies an unspeakable—

"Observer!"

That familiar intruding voice.

"Come! Do as your lord commands."

I looked at the dreaded one.

"Taste what I offer you from these diseased lips! Drink from the pool of death and decay!"

I did.

And it was good.

IT IS SOON. The hard-line Soviets are poised. Reformer has only days of life left. . . .

They are dressed as repair men, these Muslim filth, filth because of what they are, because of their very worship, because of what they are doing. They enter the basement of the hall, near the power generators.

"Allah will honor this," one of them whispers.

(Not Allah, fellow traveler. Nor Muhammed, that possessed charlatan.)

His comrade smiles, nods.

These two will do their work with a tiny fraction of the huge shipment of plastic-type explosives sent to a certain Middle Eastern country by a West German firm, enough to supply the needs of terrorism for more than a century, yet another indication that the scruples of German industrialists have not changed much since they cooperated with the Nazis for the slave labor from Auschwitz-Birkenau and other extermination camps.

Both men—are they to be called that, really? I know demons I like better than this sort of slime—have been close to the region's most reprehensible despot, a maniacal beast more like my kind than any human being, a

419

latter-day Hitler bent only on the satisfaction of his
warped territorial desires and hunger for power.

Some time before, the world community found Sad-
dam Hussein to be a monster, along with Muammar
Muhamad a-Qadhafi, and such an opinion was correct,
these scum unworthy of the leadership of any country.
But the Middle East is prone toward the setting up of
such individuals. One is almost guaranteed to emerge on
the scene every few years. They all serve a bankrupt and
satanic religion that will corrupt *any* who join it. And
once my master has control, he will fling them out on
some kind of battlefield, to do what he demands of them
even as they carry the supposedly holy *Koran* by their
side, and do their absurd, sometimes childish rites,
claiming Allah's wrath on America and any other nation
that gets in their way.

The two terrorists at the dome once were part of an
elite Muslim guard until they disappeared from view two
years earlier. It was assumed by the CIA that they had
been executed for some infraction or other. But they had
simply gone underground, to be trained for the Ultimate
Mission, a code name for an act of such destructiveness
that the leader they think they are serving now, known
among us demons as Idiot-Muslim, will earn a place in
the history books.

I look at Idiot-Muslim—this is only an arbitrary designation, at least as applied to him because, as we know,
all Muslims are idiots of the most pathetic sort, for how
can they be described otherwise when they allow themselves to be chained to obeying a book as wretched as the
Koran, a book whose pages are put to better use as toilet
paper for human excrement than the source of any
specious inspiration—yea, I look at Idiot-Muslim and I
see a prototype of satanic perfection, a mindless automa-
ton controlled in every respect by the Prince of Darkness.
Even I, who sided with Satan from the start, would

rejoice if someone cut out his throat and threw his body in the Sahara so that deserving buzzards could feast, and as many as possible from his heathen kind became additions to the carnage so that the world would be a bit less polluted, polluted as it is by their presence.

I am not surprised that Lucifer feels at home in the presence of Idiot-Muslim, for they are of a kindred bond. My master rejoices when a devil such as this one uses nerve gas to destroy his own countrymen because they dared to oppose him. It is said that he is not mad. It is said that he is quite a brilliant tactician. But, I ask, where did he obtain that brilliance, that complete and total amorality that is the foundation of everything he has done over the years?

I know the answer all too well.

*T*HAT I AM more enraged by such vipers than are millions of Christians is commentary richly evocative. It is not that Christians fail to become upset, of course; they do—and yet there is perhaps what might be called a "comfortable" edge to their anger. By and large they seem content to sit in their pews, and listen to their pastors, and return to their homes, and stuff themselves with food, and *tsk-tsk* at what is going on in the world.

Moral degenerates such as these—in Libya as well as Iraq and elsewhere—could slaughter an entire village, and decapitate every man, woman, and child, and *tsk-tsk* indeed the response would be. They could kidnap a diplomat, a clergyman, a school teacher, a crippled widow, they could kidnap anyone who catches their eye in the madness of the moment, and far too many Christians would shrug and shake their heads, and forget in a week or a month. When they are reminded, when they are confronted with the echo of that awfulness, they respond, oh, yes, they respond, *tsk-tsking* at the very mention of it, perhaps with a special collection or two for the bereaved families.

What drives countless numbers of Christians to greater uproar is not so much the moral aspects of those atrocities, or anything to do with the atrocities at all. If this kind of news were all that reached Western shores from the Middle East via the nightly television broadcasts, the newspapers, and the magazines, there would be concern, yes, and a few sermons might be preached about the barbaric Muslims, and then it all would die down.

But let *any* development in the Middle East affect their lifestyles, their wallets, and the decibel level goes up dramatically. A slaughter in Iraq or Kuwait is devastating, but let that slaughter be connected with *money*, let it affect the grocery bill or the gasoline bill or whatever in Oshkosh, Wisconsin, and *then* the hue and cry will become deafening.

These are the Christians who are comfortable in their faith, who find it reassuring, Christians who often do business with other Christians, who go to church with other Christians, play golf with them, and so on, and so on. It is a peaceful existence. Atrocities elsewhere in the world shake it but briefly, and then normalcy returns— but, ah, monetary influences rip it asunder, and repair is not so easy, not so quick.

If I were God, I would be weeping.

Other explosives are placed elsewhere. Like putting chewing gum under a theater seat.

Simple as that.

"Allah will bless us, Abdul," one of them says.

"Greatly," his companion agrees.

Allah will rejoice over crushed skulls, caved in chests. He will stand in the middle of this new battlefield, and proclaim glorious victory!

In fact, that is what he does. He stands there, laughing harshly, this Allah of their worship.

A familiar sound to my kind.

We have heard it often.

THOSE AT THE CMCI convention have less than an hour. It is midday. The noise of voices blending together is loud. Deals are being made. Deals everywhere. Free freight. Full return privileges. . . . I overhear Bookstore Manager talking with his wife, who co-owns Heavenly Choices Family Store. They are walking away from a booth where the publisher was eager to get their order.

"That was robbery," he tells her.

"I know," she agrees happily. "Great price."

"And sixty days billing!"

"Then add another sixty days for late payment."

"Four months to pay!"

"Won't they be reluctant to take our next order?"

"Publishers will do *anything* for a sale. Besides, we can dump them if necessary. There are *plenty* of others. Just *look* at them all!"

"It's true. We have to wait on the Lord for *our* money, you know."

They both break out laughing.

"It's a dog," the executive vice president chortles.

"I know, I *know!*" his assistant says, enjoying the moment as well.

"They thought they had us," the V.P. adds.

"Everybody knows they take forever to pay their bills," the assistant says. "Why would we give them anything good? They're too dumb to know the difference."

"We made them think that title was going to be a bestseller."

"Yet they were convinced they had *us* over a barrel."

Both men are licking their lips, and eagerly rubbing their hands together, as they await the next chance to witness for Jesus Christ, and to give Him the honor and the glory.

Big-Time Agent has his client, Name Author, at his side. They are having a meeting with the chairman of the board of Great Commission Books, one of the larger publishers, in a room in the basement of the great dome.

"His price doubles in six months if you don't renew the contract now," Big-Time Agent says softly, but with a steel core in his words.

"We just don't know," President replies. "Sales are good, but that *is* a great deal of money for a *ministry* to have to pay."

"Cut the crap," Big-Time Agent retorts.

"Crap?" President says, his eyes raised.

Big-Time Agent blushes.

"Sorry."

"You should be. This is God's business, you know."

"And I want to see God's author being treated as he should be. Are you going to agree or not? If I go out that door, you won't touch us again for less than a hundred twenty-five thou!"

Publisher leans forward.

"One hundred thousand, period."

Big-Time Agent starts to stand, as does Name Author.

"All right, all right," President says. "One hundred seventeen five!"

Big-Time Agent smiles.

"It's a deal," he says.

They talk over a few more details, shake hands, then Big-Time Agent and Name Author leave.

President turns to an assistant.

"What crapola!" President exclaims.

"We get it back in royalties, as usual?" the assistant ventures.

"Absolutely! These guys bluster around a lot but they practically never ask for an audit."

"As a fail-safe, sir, should we play with the discount structure so that half-royalties kick in?"

"You're learning," President says. "You're learning real good."

Only half an hour now. Hidden clocks are ticking, ticking, ticking everywhere. . . .

Within minutes, Big-Time Agent and Name Author are with another publisher.

"We just negotiated a deal with Great Commission Books," he tells this CEO.

CEO is English, his mind bestirred with some reminders of the old days when publishing was still a gentleman's game.

"How much?" he asks simply.

"Hundred fifty thou," Big-Time Agent says without a flicker of his eyelids.

"That is quite a sum of money."

"My guy's worth it.

"He may be but—"

"If we walk out of here now, the price will be two hundred thou the next time. You save big bucks *this* time!"

CEO nodded.

"We'll talk," he says, thinking about that contractual clause dealing with a reserve held against returns.

At one end of the dome, near a side exit, an elderly woman is walking with her husband. They had had to sell their store after years of trying to make a go of it.

This is their last CMCI convention; they attended purely to be able to say goodbye to some old friends.

Hours had passed. They are leaving now, tired, sad, casting one more glance back at the carnival, and whispering, "May God forgive them," just as they emerge out-of-doors, and the ground rumbles under their feet.

That couple is not alone. I see plenty of other men and women who, as they walk about the giant hall, shake their heads with embarrassment, and whisper among themselves about what is going on, the usurpation of the name of Christ for any commercial purpose.

May God forgive them, other servants of Christ echo those words about the bottomliners, the hucksters.

He will. If they ask.

But how many even *realize* the depths to which they are sinking? How many *understand* the blasphemy behind the merchandising of images and trinkets and the rest for profit? How many have rationalized themselves into a corner, and continue on as spiritually suicidal lemmings over a cliff, taking others with them, those who buy this stuff and put it in their homes, their offices, their cars as though they are paying homage to the Lord whereas they are only contributing to the cancer spreading throughout the land?

Oh, the carnival barkers of Christendom will protest if confronted, and issue forth with words about judgmentalism and the like, and they will flash sweet smiles of innocence, and then go on with their tacky spiels.

I remember Coney Island in the old days, you know. . . .

Where's the cotton candy, folks? The butter-dipped popcorn? The buy-a-kiss booth? (Everything else is for sale, why not that? Just say it's for a scholarship to send worthy kids to college, yeah, that usually guarantees some kind of support.)

Something else, come to think of it, I say to myself.

Where's the funhouse?

Suddenly I smile a demon-smile, a thin tongue darting out from between my blood-red lips as I walk those aisles of greed.

You're in it, people. You're in it.

*I*T WAS NOT always the way it has become. Many years before, the mission of CMCI was quite simple: gather together the ministries and other organizations dedicated to the Great Commission through the use of all available media.

I remember attending the very first CMCI convention. Mifult accompanied me.

The speaker was Silver Hair.

"We have begun a mighty new thrust," he addressed the several hundred individuals in attendance at the small midwestern convention center. "There are exciting times ahead. But never let us forget the central purpose: the edification of believers, and the winning of new souls to Christ."

Mifult turned and looked at me, as I did with him.

"We have a tough battle ahead of us," he remarked. "They are very dedicated."

We saw examples of that dedication shortly thereafter. A publisher was exhibiting a book with a highly questionable theme. Silver Hair noticed it, and personally demanded that the publisher withdraw it. The publisher refused, and was then escorted from the hall, his booth closed down in the process.

That happened often over the intervening half-dozen years.

But then CMCI grew at an ever-increasing rate. More publishers opened up shop, more record companies, more ministries—all found the CMCI convention a magnet, the one arena in which they could individually and collectively offer themselves to the largest possible group of people.

T-shirts were introduced. Bumper stickers.

"The advent," Mifult would say later.

"Success for us," I told him sardonically.

The advent.

Indeed.

The advent of the junksters.

And also the beginning of the decline of CMCI.

"It is so much like its secular counterpart now," Mifult said a few years ago.

"Worse," I remarked. "With the others, there is no pretense."

Pretense. . . .

The plaything of satanic puppets seeking to justify what they do.

Today, in the midst of that sparkling new hall, I see a plain booth, a booth with a few tracks and some Bibles, and a dignified gentleman standing, looking at the passersby. Further down that particular row is a garishly-colored display on both sides of the aisle with scores of different books being offered. The publisher is greeting buyer after buyer, a broad smile on his face and a cash register for a brain—the smile quickly fades as soon as someone mentions the book he published a couple of years ago, supposedly the intimate revelations of a former bordello madam that was found out to be nothing but the sexual fantasies of a schizophrenic housewife in the Pacific Northwest, and he is suddenly called upon to apologize. While he is doing so, the buyer for an important chain of stores becomes irritated at being kept waiting, and starts to leave, and the publisher turns around and rushes after the buyer.

"Losing that fish would ruin his day," Mifult remarks.

"Indeed," I say.

At the end of the day, that dignified gentleman, smiling warmly, leaves the hall, grateful for the one individual who stopped at his booth, and to whom he could minister in faith, believing.

I RE-ENTER THE huge hall.

I look at the bright colors.

I listen to the din of collective voices.

I stand for only a moment before the miseries are unleashed, engulfing those who are redeemed and dedicated to the saving of souls, together with those present only because there is money to be made, power to be gathered upon themselves and welded in defense not of the Kingdom of God but their own turf.

I see a man, obviously quite old, sitting on a metal folding chair. He is looking around him.

There are tears streaming down his blotched cheeks.

I hear him whisper.

I do hear him whisper.

"Father, forgive them. . . ."

He grows faint. His body tilts to one side.

He sees me.

"Are you—?" he asks in a raspy voice.

"No," I tell him, with a kind tone that is in opposition to my loathsome appearance.

I step aside then.

His concern evaporates. The tears are gone. There is now only joy.

"Are you the one to take me through the gates?" he asks as his soul takes leave of mortality.

The angel of light answers radiantly.

They go together past me, way, way past on a journey I can never take.

The old one's body slumps. This is noticed, but not immediately.

Some hot deals are being made, you know.

I can imagine hidden devices giving up their last few seconds.

Ticking-ticking-ticking. . . .

*T*HE EXPLOSIVES GO off.

That grand dome shakes like a giant beast, its concrete-and-steel-and-glass roar deafening. All communications with the outside world are instantly cut. No one can enter. No one can leave, all entrances and exits electrically controlled. The glass windows are unbreakable.

People are trapped.

The explosions have been timed. Periodically another set will go off. There is psychological warfare in this, apart from the very physical manifestations.

Idiot-Muslim knows all about madness, you see.

I WALK AMONG them. I have no host just now. Hosts can be cumbersome. Spirits have no limitations. I can flit from one end of the hall to the other. I do.

I and others of my kind. Buzzing about. Prodding. Possessing. Doing what we do, at our master's command.

And we do very well. . . .

Arch Strutter is cowering in a corner, terrified. He is not thinking positively. He is not thinking at all, it seems. He is babbling nonsensical stuff while holding a paperweight that was to be his latest "gift" to those who supported his ministry; shaped like an abstract cross, it was covered by gold paint already turning green from the sweat of his palm.

A man running past sees Arch Strutter, spits at him, and rushes on.

But then I see the two young publishers who have rolled up their sleeves and are helping the seriously injured. The dark-haired one catches my attention—the front of his white shirt is stained red. Every so often he grimaces.

Demons pass *them* by.

But not Donald.

He is standing in the midst of what remains of the booth erected by his publisher. Earlier in the day there had been an announcement that a book by another author was withdrawn from publication because of a multitude of falsehoods in it, that particular author indulging a penchant for personal fantasy and dressing it up as non-fiction. The publisher is standing next to Donald, wondering why God has chosen to rebuke him so harshly, and all within such a short while. (That he would think God had destroyed an entire new building, affecting the futures of hundreds of firms, just to get back at *him* isn't reassuring about how he will come out of all this.)

Donald is rubbing his hands together, wishing that he had a Christian psychiatrist nearby, but not daring to admit it out loud.

The publisher, his five-hundred-dollar suit torn and dirty, is looking around at the devastation, and wondering if his firm can survive the shock of loosing a large chunk of the convention revenue that was to have been earned.

WRECKAGE IS EVERYWHERE.

People are crying. People are praying. People are dying by the dozen.

The man with the Scripture pencils is standing in the debris of his booth, thousands of them scattered all around him. He is holding a tattered sign boasting a 12 percent discount.

Silver Hair is cradling an old woman, her right arm hanging limply by her side.

"Grab hold of Jesus," he tells her.

She is crying.

"My chest!" she says so softly he can hardly hear her above the din. "I have a terrible pain in my—"

Silver Hair can do nothing but pat her gently and whisper Bible verses, but that is the best he knows, and he does it; he is not a doctor; there are no doctors around; there is only chaos,

He continues holding her lifeless body until someone tells him.

$\mathcal{R}$OBBIE'S MOTHER NEVER made it from that room. She regains consciousness. The tattered, bloody cloak that enfolded his soul is lying a few feet away. She crawls over to it, kisses his cheek one last time, wants to stay where she is, praying that she will join him in glory then and there. But people are crying, people are in pain, people need her as he did—and now that he is gone, that part of her yet remains. It cannot be ignored, buried under her grief, for she must continue honoring her Lord. She has little choice but to get to her feet, get to her feet, get to her feet, and help, if God will supply the strength.

He does.

*I*N THE CORRIDORS outside the main hall there are more bodies, people who had been heading toward the exhibits or, having finished their business, were about to leave.

Now piled high.

Elderly ones. Children. The middle-aged.

The holocaust has entrapped them all.

I see banners.

"Save a whale—be a hero. Save a baby—be a jail-bird."

I see Bibles clutched in death-frozen hands.

I see trinkets.

I see a terrorist stumbling toward me. He has just emerged from a doorway leading to the basement. He is mumbling something about Muhammed.

"I must be protected!" this craven one screams. "I must be protected from—from—"

In a split second I see the demon pursuing him.

No Name.

This one is so loathsome that no name can be found to describe him. He is worse in appearance, if that could be possible, than Satan. He has promulgated acts of atrocity that make many of the rest of us recoil.

439

And now No Name is on this man, this fool.

"Stand against the creature," I say mischievously, aware that No Name's greater malevolence makes my own seem less terrifying to him. "Proclaim Allah. Hold up Muhammed as your protector."

"Oh, yes, may my lack of faith be forgiven in this my moment of danger!"

He turns, faces No Name.

"I seek the protection of Allah," the terrorist says. "I seek the sheltering arms of Muhammed, the Lord's prophet and defender, *my* defender as well. You cannot stand against him!"

The demon roars with laughter.

"You do, huh?" he screams with sarcasm that erupts from him with festering disease from every sore.

The terrorist now stands proudly, with utter faith the spine of his defiance.

"I can sense the prophet reaching out toward me now."

"Good!" No Name says quietly now, his red-rimmed lips pressed closely together.

He reaches out those taloned hands toward the dying mortal in front of him.

"You see, blind one that you are, I *am* the prophet you claim, I am he whom you love. I, Muhammed, welcome you. . . . *for eternity!*"

The terrorist's heart abruptly stops beating. The breath of life passes from him, and that body of flesh and blood drops to the floor.

His spirit is seized by No Name's, and they stumble along the path to Hell together. . . .

How safe the architects of this infamy seem, at least those on the human side, of course, I tell myself, planning as they did all this from their haven just outside Moscow, an estate far beyond the livelihood of 99 percent of the citizens over whom they hold sway. Such hypocrites—*talking of the good of the motherland when what they are really trying to save are the tottering remains of the Communist Party*—will gather soon around that same table as before, and they will be chuckling with delight. It has worked! It has worked! Soon their hired assassin will strike down Reformer. Soon—

A TRIO HAS gotten together in the middle of the hall, trying to calm the hysterical masses with soft hymns. They have just finished *Nearer My God to Thee.* They are starting another: *"All hail the power of Jesus' name, Let angels prostrate fall. . . ."*

"Not that one!" Satan is screaming. "Stop them! Do something! I will never fall prostrate before anything but a statue of myself proclaiming my greatness."

Another explosion. More girders fall. More debris flies through the air. But that trio survives.

And they have started another hymn.

"Blessed assurance, Jesus is mine! O what a foretaste of glory divine!"

Satan stomps his cloven feet in front of them, shouting obscenities that they cannot hear, blasphemies only for the rest of us.

And there is a reason beyond simply the hymns.

Arch Strutter . . . one member of the trio.

"Are you washed in the blood, in the soul-cleansing blood of the Lamb?"

"DuRong!" Satan shrieks. "Come here *now!*"

DuRong obeys.

"I thought you would see to it that those words would *never* come from the lips of *that* man!" Satan demands.

"We lost him, master," my comrade replies simply.

"How?"

"A little child, looking for her mother in the wreckage, saw him, and came up to him, and said, 'Sir, my daddy is out of town and my mother is here but I can't find her. I can't find her. Would you help Jesus and me find her, please?'"

"And that was it? He caved in just like that?"

"He did, master. He did. He looked at her sweet face, her sweet, trusting face, and then at the cheap little trinket he had been holding. Then he got to his feet, threw that cross to one side, and walked with her, hand in hand!"

DuRong is acting strangely.

"Yes, yes, go on!" Satan blusters.

"I cannot tell you the rest."

"I order it."

DuRong hangs his head.

He does what the master expects of him.

"There is nothing. Childlike faith collapsed our years of deception. There is nothing more than that."

"Is she the one clinging to him now?" he sneers.

"Oh, yes. . . ."

Satan, disgusted, goes off to help in another part of the hall, not noticing DuRong's sardonic smile.

Arch Strutter and the little girl find her mother half-buried under debris.

He ministers to the two of them with great power and wisdom.

"Bless you," the woman says at the end of her life in the flesh. "Take care of my little girl."

"Mommy!" the little one cries.

The broken body is now lifeless.

"I want my Mommy back! Tell Jesus to bring her back!"

He is at a loss for what to say. Positivity wouldn't cut it. He cannot tell her the same old words. This is not the time, the place.

He bows his head momentarily.

A hand touches his shoulder.

He looks up.

The little girl is smiling through her tears.

"Jesus spoke to me," she tells him, her voice breaking. "He said He would take care of Mommy until we are together again."

Another explosion.

Part of the ceiling plummets.

Arch Strutter sees it. He pushes the little girl to one side. She escapes untouched. Arch Strutter does not. A chunk of concrete hits his temple. He falls inches from the child.

She runs over to him, plops down by his side, starts humming the only hymn she knows in its entirety, her mother's favorite: *"What a friend we have in Jesus, all our sins and griefs to bear. . . ."*

He closes his eyes.

"Your little one will be fine," he tells the mother.

"I know," she says as she takes his hand.

*T*HE DEVASTATION DRAWS fire departments from a hundred miles in every direction. FBI investigators are flown in directly from Washington, D.C. Local as well as national news media descend on the scene. Frantic efforts are extended to save as many lives as possible, but one lingering problem is that the terrorists had planted *many* bombs to explode at various intervals—there is no way to know how many if any remain undetonated.

Firemen and other rescuers are added to the growing list of fatalities.

Finally—

"We can't send any more men in there for at least the next twenty-four hours," one of the fire chiefs tells an associate. "We've got to wait, to be sure that there won't be any more explosions."

"But some people must still be alive in there, sir," that associate reminds him.

"I know, I know, we've got a nightmare here. I pray to God that it's not too late for any of them."

It isn't.

The next day dozens are pulled from the wreckage.

And in the basement. . . .

I would never forget that group even as I stand in the

lake of fire, surrounded by the punishment I so well deserve. Nothing could take them from my thoughts.

Ten human beings. Four elderly men and women, and six children under the age of ten, two just three years old.

They were in a small room that somehow had been left relatively untouched by the collapse of the dome. All around them were broken steel girders, and shattered glass, and great chunks of concrete—but that room was whole.

They were there because of a social program that provided for orphaned children to spend time with foster grandparents. None of the young ones had flesh-and-blood parents left. The CMCI executive board had flown them all in as a special ministry.

I stood to one side, watching little children sitting on the knees of old men and women, listening to prayers or hymns or other simple, kind words of attempted comfort, and little fear—what otherwise would have been massive waves of it largely swept aside as their faith took over, faith that was vibrant, that stayed firm and strong. Even as another blast shook what was left of the dome— and, yes, the children would cry a bit, would cling to their temporary guardians, depending on them for the kind of resolve that, in a large and frightening world, the little ones could not quite muster on their own—those elderly folks, accustomed to thinking about death, finding the moment joyful when they are able to dry tears other than their own, which took their own minds away from what had happened all around them.

K'Rupt came in as I stood there.

"Go after them," he said. "Destroy each and every one."

"No," I said.

"What was that?"

"No," I repeated.

"It is what Satan would want if he knew, if he were here as you and I are."

"No," I said a third time.

K'Rupt was livid, the rage coming out of every pore of him.

"Then I will do it myself!" he screamed.

"You can take their bodies, yes, but that is all you will be able to touch," I told him.

He looked at me.

"They all are redeemed?" he asked.

"Every single one."

He hurried to an old, old woman who was holding a three-year-old girl on her lap as the child slept with remarkable soundness. He was about to touch that wrinkled face, that ancient flesh when, suddenly, he was thrown back with such force that if he had been a physical being, and not one of spirit only, every bone in his body would have been smashed to powder.

Again and again he tried to enter the body of an old one or a child, and was tossed to one side.

"Damn them to hell!" he screamed.

"No, you are very wrong," I told him. "*They* are not the damned."

He had been stamping the floor with his twisted cloven feet.

. . . *they are not the damned.*

Those words struck him as though I had taken a fist and hit him squarely across the jaw.

He started weeping then.

"Oh, Observer, it is always thus with us," he said through the sobbing. "We cannot endure the cleansing that has purified their souls, and so we try to destroy them any way we can. We make the old bitter, and get them to commit suicide. We have the young born as drug addicts because of the sin of their mothers. And if we don't succeed with the old themselves, with the damnation of their souls, then we have our sport with their physical selves by motivating their so-called loved ones to fling them aside as forgotten human wrecks in some cold, hard institution where they no longer will be a bother."

A six-year-old boy was standing, singing a hymn, his eyes bright, his expression untroubled.

K'Rupt was only inches from him.

"If I could, Observer, I would rip him open right now and feast on his innards. But I cannot. So I will wait, and I will seek out an opportunity, later, instead to foster those circumstances that will rape his innocence and send him into the world on feet of revenge. Since he is redeemed, I cannot touch the soul of this child. But I can do a great deal to torment his mind, his emotions."

"Oh, yes, you can," I agreed, and added sardonically, "That is truly something to which you can look forward."

"But—" he started to say.

The hymn-singer finished. An elderly man with him had a sudden chest pain and fell back against the ground.

"Don't die," the little boy begged.

"You are safe," the man told him. "An army of angels is arriving to protect us."

"Are you sure?"

"Oh, yes, I see them now."

The old man was right.

For a moment Heaven had opened up, releasing a stream of angels directly into that room.

"They are so beautiful," he said, his voice fading fast.

He saw me then. He saw K'Rupt.

"How long have you been here?" he asked.

"For only a short while," I told him.

"You cannot harm any of them. You cannot touch a hair on the head of even this little one."

"Yes, I know."

He was gone, an angel taking him, and the two of them

entering Heaven. In that instant, catching a glimpse, I saw the Son, the Blessed Son, and He saw me, and this divine one, this *Jesus Christus Theou Huios Soter* reached out to me, as He had done once before in the wilderness, and in that moment I could have broken away, one more chance to turn my back on the evil of many ages of time.

"*No!*" K'Rupt bellowed. "No, it cannot be."

"Oh, yes!" I shouted in anticipation. "Yes, it can. And if it can be me, it can be *both* of us, K'Rupt. *Now* we can leave the filth, the pain, the future we know to be ours otherwise. Now we can change all of that."

He hesitated, K'rupt hesitated.

I stepped forward. An angel came to me, smiling.

"Welcome, Observer," this one called Blessed Assurance said.

K'Rupt was smiling.

"It is true, isn't it," he said.

"Yes indeed," another angel called Calvary's Mount replied with utter tenderness.

As the ascended Savior stood before the gates of Heaven, the two angels were ready to take us back with them. In an instant Heaven would be closed again.

A voice.

In the background, a voice.

Satan was calling.

"The master!" K'Rupt said. "We must not desert him. He needs us."

He pulled back.

"Break away," Calvary's Mount urged. "Just take my hand."

K'rupt placed his talon in that angel-hand but as he did so, the talon was gone, and he had a hand like Calvary's Mount.

"Observer!" he said with astonishment. "Look!"

"Yes, I see," I told him. "Oh, God, loving, loving God, I *do*!"

My talon! Gone as well! We were doing it, praise God, yes!

And I could feel the accumulated miseries of long centuries being purged from my very being, a glow beyond description spreading—

That voice was stronger. Closer.

The master *wanted* us. The master demanded us.

And I had to admit something quite ghastly to myself, I had to admit that I enjoyed these massacres, that the satisfaction they stirred within me was pervasive, that I wanted to go and find others, and have their lives, their earthly, mortal lives torn from them, and watch the pain they endured as this happened.

It returned, that one vision of Armageddon, but it was not alone, a panorama of others, blood the uniting thread of all, blood everywhere, the blood of soldiers, of peasants, of assassinated presidents and murdered priests, graveyards all over the world filled with the residue of pleasurable acts.

. . . *pleasurable acts.*

It went beyond that one massacre, beyond garbage bags of babies, beyond the wasting away of AIDS patients as my kind and I tormented them unto death, and further on, all of this and deeper still, a pit so rancid, so—

I *wanted* it. I *wanted* every pint of blood. I *wanted* to wash my hands in the fluids that seep from crushed and torn bodies. I *wanted* anything that caused their screams to reach my ears so that I can thrill to—

No, I screamed. *No—! I have denied this before. It was only that one time, only with those missionaries. It could never be that way again. Never!*

But yes. But yes. But yes.

I heard Satan laughing in the background, laughing in ignoble victory over his duped slave, the master of deception finding me easy prey. As was K'Rupt, and all the rest of us.

K'Rupt pulled away from Calvary's Mount. I pulled away from Blessed Assurance.

In one ghastly surge, everything poured back in on us, my comrade and I, the filth just banished moments earlier now returned stronger than before, more damning than ever, because having known it all and then bid it goodbye, we had to succumb once again. And suffocated by that awful reality, we fled that room, leaving its aborted promise in our infernal wake.

$\mathcal{T}$HE FLAMES IN the giant hall have died down. I stand in front of the wreckage. Crosses lay on their sides, blackened. Scattered everywhere are signs of hoopla now fallen in mockery, banners proclaiming the triumph of Christian love alongside special quantity discounts.

We've won, I think with sorrow. *We've crushed—*

No!

I won't let myself succumb to such deception, though I belong to the deceivers, if unwillingly, if wishing it could be different while knowing it never will.

Not crushed! my mind shouts. *It only seems that way. You look merely at the residue of one battle, foolishly presuming it to signal the direction of the war.*

Lucifer stands next to me.

"Wonderful sight," he says. "All their hypocrisies lying in waste!"

He is trembling with delight.

"The media will be our greatest servants," he adds. "They will spread the news throughout the civilized world."

Lucifer knows the routine well. He had used the media often in his pursuit of domination—newspapers, magazines, books, television, and radio becoming puppet outlets for seductive heresies and whatever else he cared to disseminate.

"I can imagine what those news shows will do with this!" he adds. "Perhaps it will consume their entire broadcast time. They are never less than hungry for anything that will promote their hidden agenda. And I know better than anyone that they *do* have one! Something wonderful to anticipate, don't you agree, Observer?"

I nod like the robot I have become, programmed to obey, and only that.

"Write it all in your book," he tells me, his hideous frame spewing forth the filth and disease of centuries, geysers of yellow-green fluids from continually bursting sores. "Those glorious moments must be immortalized."

He moves with effort, a weariness belying the aura of triumph he is trying so hard to project.

"I want every detail described perfectly," he rambles on, his lips curled into a curious smile that I have not seen before, and I am tempted to ask him what has amused him at that very moment. But I do not, remaining silent in my puzzlement. "Some of those ministries will never recover, especially the ones built on the vision of a single man. Take away the man, and there is no other foundation, so it becomes like dust."

He turns to me, puts one hand on my shoulder.

"Miss nothing, Observer. That is your assignment, and so it has always been. Capture it all, for you have never had any other purpose. Remember, I trust you to write the truth, Observer."

I smile though he knows not why.

. . . *I trust you to write the truth.*

How easily those words come, Lucifer, master, devil! How you brandish about that which you have tried to corrode in humankind, and now you expect *us* to be worthy somehow.

My book, precious journal, eons of thought and deed, this is all that will be left in my wake at the end.

A Book of the Days of Observer, Once an Angel of Light.

"I hear what you say," I assure the devil.

"Good! Good! As your reward, I will see that it is required reading past the Gates of Heaven."

"As it is in Hell?" I ask, shivering though unnoticed.

"How right you are," he replies. "How right you are."

Satan laughs then, loudly, coarsely, as is his way—but this time for a reason unknown.

I think of my book of the ages, its chapters of blood and sin and—

Yea, I do as my master asks, as I have always done.

I capture the moments. I capture the moments.

Every last one.

There was an instant, after Darien had been rescued from Hell by ever-present Stedfast, that my master's resolve cracked and bent, though he snapped back in defiance quickly enough.

He had tried hard to seduce the purity that Darien represented, rebellious purity perhaps, but purity nevertheless. Satan used every weapon, every trick, every sinful overture at his disposal.

None worked in the end.

I remember Darien begging me to break away from Satan. I wavered, as always, and as I have said before, and often in this journal of mine, I could have joined him, could have been also pulled from that sulfurous place—but as the master approached, as he called to me yet again, yet again, yet again, any flash of courage, any residue of willpower dissolved and I went to Satan, managing nothing more than a whimper of shame.

Gone.

Darien was gone then, Stedfast's intercession quite

sufficient to take him from ten thousand upon ten thousand monstrosities hovering, and I one.

I could see Stedfast looking at me, not in hatred nor shame but love, love sublime, love that did not pity, love that was unimpeded because it was only itself, nothing to dilute it in any way, love flowing out to touch me, and I knew that it was his own, indeed it was, but mixed with love from Someone else. I said goodbye to Stedfast, I said it in my mind and my heart, and he turned away, and that was it, no more moments ever again like that one.

Satan had walked ahead of the rest of us, and stood there, looking upward, looking upward as, for an instant, we all shared the same recollection of that place to which Darien and Stedfast ultimately would be traveling, that blessed place, the one we gave up, the one—

Through the volcanic-like geysers, there was for an instant, barely visible, the bent-over shape of a wretched creature falling to his knees, weeping.

And in the background, we hear, faintly at first, then the sounds coming ever louder, the early hints of portended battle starting on war's prophetic field.

*R*EFORMER DEAD . . . HOURS after he pledged support for the Americans against the nation responsible! That faithful aide is wounded, too, but not fatally; he quickly hides a small leather-bound book that the general secretary had been carrying at that precise moment, hides the volume because no one else would understand the *why* of it.

The world is stunned at these atrocities.

In the United States, millions rise up in anger and demand swift revenge, revenge for those who had been murdered, and for Reformer as well.

The President is asked to retaliate. He wavers. With Reformer's support, there was a chance that the two countries could act together, that they could stun the critics into silence by this very cooperation.

But someone new is in charge of the U.S.S.R.

A leader from the old guard. Everyone else thought the old guard was dead, crumbling like the walls that once secluded it from the world.

But things are different now.

Very.

And from somewhere in the Middle East, a man rises up, talking peace. . . .

456

Epilogue

I LOOK ABOUT me. I see demonkind and human-kind together, writhing in agony, as I have been doing.

I see Hitler.

I see mass killers Manson . . . Gacy.

But not Bundy, no, not Bundy.

I see a preacher who claimed in his mortality to have been the Lord's instrument for life immortal, just send in the green-backs to keep him going.

I see that actress, the one whose exercise routines mean little now.

I see many presidents, many senators, many mayors and governors and police chiefs, side-by-side with drug dealers and x-rated movie producers, and countless others.

I see nuns and rabbis. I see Muslims, Buddhists, Mormons, others. I see Baptists, Presbyterians, Pentecostals, Lutherans, Episcopalians, Seventh Day Adventists, Nazarenes, Quakers—each and every denomination, group, sect represented here in the midst of damnation.

They never realized that the label itself, the form, the ceremony were not enough.

I see millionaires. The very poor. White. Black. Yellow. Sane. Mad.

457

The lake of fire gives no place to bigotry, to status.

I see painters, poets, so-called Christian rock singers.

Some of you were right on, and went the way of the redeemed. But some of you ended up here, the flames searing your pretense.

I see those gay, those straight.

I see the radiant Son of God!

He is walking among us. Souls are reaching out for Him, but He must tell one what He must tell all: "It is too late, my lost sheep."

He stops before me.

His gaze reaches into the very center of my being.

Something is in His hands, hands free of Calvary's scars.

"These are some of the bits and pieces of your book, Observer."

I see His arms holding a large pile of scrolls, of diaries, of random sheets of paper that somehow do not burn up right away, that do not burn because they are protected as long as they are in His arms, as long as they are sheltered by Him.

"Look at them, Observer," Lord Jesus the Christ says.

I obey the Son, I obey Him at least this once, this final time. I can scarcely believe what I see or, rather, do not see, as He hands me scroll after scroll, sheet after sheet, each burning to ashes even as my eyes scan them, even as my eyes see the monstrous, the oppressive, the maddening truth.

I look into that face again, those eyes, hear that voice telling me what my mind cannot wholly grasp in that moment.

"Your hosts, Observer . . . they were just another excuse wrapped in the dementia of your kind," He says with no satisfaction. "You were not as committed to Satan's cause, so he used this book. It was a trick,

Observer, a trick to get you to lead them into damnation."

All that time! Centuries piled high upon one another. Entering host after host.

And for no reason except to camouflage the damned truth about my weak and pitiable self.

He drops the other pages at His feet. They are gone in an instant, they are gone as is the whole reason for being to which I had clung, with which I was deluded for so very long.

"Lord Jesus?" I ask, sobbing.

He hesitates, turns, waits for the question that He knows already.

"A *real* entry, please?" I beg. "No more lies. . . ."

He nods.

"Have you no pitiable scrap upon which I can write?" I ask, trembling.

I reach out the talon that is my hand, in anticipation, thinking that He will do this for me, thinking that there is something I have to say that can survive the thirsty flames.

He seems quite sad, and I imagine—or is it real?—a single tear rolling down one cheek.

"It is no use, is that not so, *Jesus Christus!*" I say with certainty that astonishes me.

His very manner seems answer enough.

. . . *the truth.*

Oh, dearest Lord! Can it be so, that when You pass by, as You must, on your way to the new Heaven, the new Earth, can it be so that I *am* to remain behind?

Yes, it can, Observer, it surely can, it surely is, He says, though only with His expression, the whole of His countenance, words unnecessary just now.

Now the Son of God leaves the flames. Now the saints await.

There has been spread out before me, and perhaps for

all of eternity, a revelation as tormenting, it may seem later, as the flames themselves, it and they as one.

My hosts. . . .

Needless players in a farce.

I wanted only their anguish, feasting upon every inevitable moment of it, cloaked as it was in my dreary conceit, that pathetic and doomed scenario of self-justification that had kept me going, kept me going, kept me—

A Book of the Days of Observer, Once an Angel of Light.

Never would it be compiled from fragments written across the centuries, a kind of Satanic bible demanded by my master.

A Book of the Days of Observer—

The flames were not to blame, you know. They could not consume what never was, what never could be.

Mine.

And mine alone.

Wrenched from the possessed and accumulated miseries of unwary human slaves as they went through the pointless motions of my deceit.

I turn to Satan, I turn to Lucifer the Magnificent, and see his expression, see the lingering shards of his cruel hoax written on that awful face, see that he knew, that he had known from the beginning, that this was just his way of getting me to—

I might as well not have existed, for even an instant. What was the reason of it, what was the purpose, what was there to drive me on in continued rebellion against the only One who could have given me hope, real hope, not the doomed ravings to which I succumbed . . . ?

I look around me again, from Satan to Mifult to Muhammed, who was supposedly so good, so noble, yet in reality nothing more than another deluded figure manipulated by my master—all caught up in the destiny wrought by what they became—and the millions, the countless doomed they dragged into the flames along with them.

A Book of the Days—

My book . . . my book.

So easily reduced to nothingness.

Every last blank page.

Oh, my Lord, my Lord!

There is then from one end of that lake of unalterable judgment to the other the awful echoes of shrieking madness torn from these my phantom lips forever and ever . . . *and ever.*

A Bo.k of the Da.s of Obs..ver, Once an Ang—

It was to have been the master volume, the one into which all the scraps from centuries past were to be compiled, now gone in dust, trod underfoot by lions and lambs and bright-faced redeemed led by joyous cherubim traveling Angelwalk toward a golden temple rising out of the mists atop a majestic mount called Sinai.

Somewhere in the air perhaps are cries of pain, cries from ten thousand upon ten thousand throats, and a single sad and soon lost voice, "It is gone, it is gone and none, none at all have ever, ever read it, because there is nothing in its pages, and there never has been."

Finally, in all the ways that matter, truly, truly matter, through time and space and eternity, Observer is no more.

And no one knows. No one knows.

The deeds we do, the words we say,
Into still air they seem to fleet,
We count them ever past;
But they shall last—
In the dread judgment they
And we shall meet.
                    John Keble

Finis

III

Stedfast

Guardian Angel

To Gigi and Boy-Boy
who could teach
the hardest of hearts
what love and devotion
are all about

Human beings are promised a Heaven without tears, without pain . . . but that is not the case for angels. It is something that we have become accustomed to waiting for, an anticipated blessing that will be ours when we all experience the new Heaven and the new earth.

We regularly journey to the present earth, the earth so pitiably torn by Satan's ravaging presence, and spend a brief time there—or longer, if we are particularly brave—and then we must return to Heaven with the bleak and tragic baggage from that sojourn weighing us down, for we cannot tolerate what Satan has done with the planet. We feel a desperate need to engage in the spiritual equivalent of taking a bath. And that is what we do, as we stand before the Father and let His purity cleanse us . . . until the next time.

Holy, Holy, Holy, that day when there is no more next time, when we do not have to brace ourselves for the battles that now take place on Planet Earth and in the heavenlies. Wonderful it shall be, and ready my kind and I are.

—*Stedfast*

Acknowledgments

*T*HE YEAR WAS 1988.

I had decided to leave all secular career pursuits, and turn my time totally over to Jesus Christ. For one thing, I would no longer edit any non-Christian science fiction, since the whole direction of that genre had become increasingly nihilistic or pantheistic or atheistic or any number of other -istics that happened to be popular at the time. I would interview no more celebrities, except for the Christian media, I would focus no more attention upon the wrong role models for young people, to name one age group. Thus, I would cease involvement with any pursuit not anchored in a Christ-centered perspective.

Today. . . .

Now a number of years later.

The book that was used so dramatically by the Lord, in 1988, to solidify the change in my direction led to a successful sequel, a number of other books, some awards, and a great deal of media exposure.

Judging by the sales figures and the majority of the reviews, the Christian reading public is more than a little receptive to fiction that tackles subjects more serious than fluffy romances.

I even received a letter from an officer who was involved in Operation Desert Storm; he had read most of my books, and was pleased that someone had encouraged him, through fiction, to *think*. He shared each one with his buddies, and found the novels to be an effective witnessing tool.

I owe an enormous debt to Joey Paul at Word, perhaps more than to any other individual. He enabled me to write *Fallen Angel* and *Stedfast* as I really wanted to do, in a way that would maximize Christ-centered truths and address issues that other publishers might not have allowed. He is the best possible kind of editor, the greatest with whom I have been privileged to work over a twenty-seven-year career, for Joey allows a writer to do what that writer hopefully does best—*write*. I feel as though Joey and I are brothers as well as editor-writer, and I would be happy indeed if we continued our association for a lifetime.

There are many others—Warren Wiersbe, Harold Lindsell, Jess Moody—who have been so very helpful over the years.

God bless them all.

Roger Elwood

Introduction

STEDFAST IS THE third *Angelwalk* book, the second sequel.

It is different in many ways from *Angelwalk* and *Fallen Angel*, though Stedfast was a character in both of the previous books.

But then Stedfast is different, as well. Whereas Darien of *Angelwalk* was a questioning, somewhat rebellious angel while remaining essentially unfallen, and Observer of *Fallen Angel* was an altogether demonic angel, yet a quite reluctant one in the long run, Stedfast is neither questioning nor fallen. He is one of the elite corps of angels, if I may put it that way, always steady, always serving the Trinity, always perfectly obedient and faithful with not even a thought out of place.

Legends are often born from nuggets of truth during the course of earthly history. And Stedfast, according to the *mythos* of this series, was the origin of the legend of the Guardian Angel.

He is wiser than Darien. Ah, he is certainly that! He knows the answers to the questions for which Darien was searching in *Angelwalk*.

Steady as a rock. . . .

That's Stedfast, for sure.

But this angel is also one with an enormous capacity to assimilate the feelings of every creature with which he comes in contact, their emotions his own, to a real and vivid extent.

He is a sponge, this Stedfast.

And he yearns for the day when, like redeemed humans, he will know only the joy, the peace of Heaven.

Without the tears that only the angels, only the Trinity will continue to shed until then. . . .

This indeed is a striking truth. The Creator weeps in Heaven; His human creations do not. For divinity, there is sorrow, there is anguish. But flesh-and-blood beings who have accepted Jesus Christ as Savior and Lord have been promised freedom, forever, from such as this.

We have to wait for our full participation in that same promise, unfallen angelkind and I among them.

Until the new Heaven, the new earth, that wondrous transformation toward which all of history is heading.

That is when we shed our own veil of tears, and walk together in the special sunlight of that special day, never again looking back, the past washed away in a flood of eternal joy . . .

Stedfast's Prologue

IT IS GOING to be soon. The ethereal fabric of Heaven itself hums and buzzes and flashes with anticipation.

That Moment. . . .

Oh my, what can I do? How can I face it without embarrassing myself and the rest of my kind by emotion unstoppable?

That Moment for which we all have been waiting— how indeed we have been waiting for it to arrive! Countless have been our entreaties before the Trinity as we bow in humble adoration, but also with our incessant petitions, again and again—and been told over and over, "Not as yet, dear ones. Not as yet."

So we turn away, perhaps to welcome another soul past the Gates, perhaps to leave that place of wonder and joy altogether on a mission of one sort or another, or simply to sit beside a crystal lake and think back over what has been, the sum total of our existence until—

That Moment.

Oh, blessed Jesus, it is soon. It is going to happen soon. We will no longer be leaving Heaven to stride in our obedience across continents of bloodshed and fear, of crime and disease, of sin in every form devised by the fleshly nature of Humankind.

Soon it will be that we will visit instead the new earth, cleansed and reborn, just as the faithful have been, and we will walk hand in hand back to Eden.

Oh my. . . .

But then, in the interlude before that odyssey begins, as I sit here beside the crystal lake, preparing myself for what I will say to the gathered multitudes, human and angelic alike, awaiting that which has been prophesied, I think back, so far back, so long ago, and I shiver, yes, I shiver as bits and pieces present themselves to me. . . .

Their souls cry out, you know.

The damned always do that as they are taken to Hell. They could have been in the company of angels, but they chose other companions instead.

They cry a great deal.

That is what I hear most of all. More than the gnashing of teeth.

The sound of their weeping, their tears.

Tears do speak in a certain way, if you listen carefully— not with words, certainly not that, but in other respects.

Forgive me, please, for being vague with this. I am so because the *sensation* of which I speak is not altogether definable, nor easily so.

It is a feeling, I suppose. . . .

Yes, that may be the best answer, if not a satisfactory one.

My comrades and I were not created bereft of feelings, you know. We have them, my fellow angels and I. We have our own, and we also experience the feelings of every being with which we come in contact.

When they, the mortal ones, the ones of flesh and blood and bone and marrow, are evil, when they are held often inextricably in the sway of sin, the feelings born from them tend to be repugnant. In this we get a hint of what Hell is like, a hint that is, by itself, enough to make us so very glad that we chose Jehovah the Almighty instead of Lucifer the Magnificent.

And yet any allegiance won purely by fear is tenuous at best, for the one feared the most can always be replaced by another of more fearsome intent. But it was not so with us, the unfallen. We have loved our Lord and Him only. We would *gladly* go into Hell itself if He only asked.

Did Lucifer?

Love Him, ever?

It cannot be said that Lucifer did, *truly*—oh, perhaps, after his own fashion, for the first few thousand years or so, or their equivalent, before the Casting-Out. But after that, which is but a small portion of eternity, his *desires* overtook him, desires that made him jealous of everything that God could do, everything He was, everything indeed.

. . . *everything He was*

But Lucifer forgot the love part, forgot the kindness, forgot all but the *power* of God.

"I want what He has," I overheard the loveliest of all of us saying. "I want His throne! I want to *rule!*"

He approached me as I stood in a quiet place.

"Stedfast, I *need* you," Lucifer purred, exuding all the charm of which he was capable, for his countenance had not as yet suffered the devastating corruption of his deeds.

How glorious this angel was, a face of great magnificence, like the finest sculpture ever done by man during the height of the Renaissance.

"I will not," I replied.

"But you will be always in subservience to *Him*," Lucifer continued, astonished that I could resist what a third of the other angels had committed to in His presence.

"And not to *you*?" I scoffed. "You ask me not to choose freedom, which you pretend to offer, but, rather, between two masters. If it is a slave that I am destined to be, then I must follow in the steps of the greater of the two."

He waited, thinking that, surely, this meant him.

"Oh, my friend, my friend," I said to Lucifer upon realizing this. "Can you not now see . . . ?"

He could not. He was lost by then. He had become the captive of his own passions.

I looked at Lucifer with great pity.

"Goodbye . . ." I said.

"You will miss me, Stedfast," he replied. "You know that. You will wish you had gone on with me to victory."

This magnificent being raised a glowing hand, not yet devoid of its glory, now doubled into a fist.

"There will be a point," Lucifer said, smiling, "at which you—"

He lowered that hand, his body shivering ever so slightly.

"Why am I so cold?" he said out loud, undoubtedly regretting the momentary vulnerability this lent him.

"Judgment," I told him. "You have felt a taste of it already."

"*Nonsense!*" he screamed.

Our Father which art in Heaven.

We both heard that chorus.

"Why are they *doing* that?"

"They are singing a song of triumph."

"But I recognize it not."

"It has not been written as yet. It has not been spoken as yet. It resides only in the mind of the King of kings and Lord of lords."

Lucifer clutched his temple.

"You have not yet broken the bond," I told him. "It is still there, your mind and God's connected."

"*No! I will not be a mere extension of Him any longer!*"

The rage of that cry echoed throughout the Heavenly Kingdom.

And lead us not into temptation but deliver us from evil. For thine is the kingdom, and the power, and the glory forever. . . .

Lucifer was granted that which he wished. The bond between him and Almighty God was broken.

We all felt it. For a moment there was a hint of darkness in Heaven, transitory but chilling, though we and the Trinity alone felt it, human souls to be insulated from such for eternity.

Lucifer started to change in appearance even then, the glory that once had been his and his alone amongst us suddenly dimming and something else taking its place, something foul and perverse.

Sin.

Sin was separation from God, a death of communion with Him.

Lucifer had sinned. Along with ten thousand upon ten thousand of my once fellow angels.

They were finally leaving.

"I will be back," he shouted, "to storm the gates!"

Lucifer turned for the last time and saw us there, saw our sorrow, saw the tears.

"Weep not for us," he roared with defiance. "Rather, weep for *yourselves*. Realize what lies in store as I gain control over that planet which Jehovah created with such hope, and along with it, the rest of the universe. I will take that hope and destroy it forever!"

The horde of them, now screeching, loathsome *things* consumed by their own vile natures, that horde fell to the world below, and beyond, to the pit of another place, a new place, a place created for the damned and by the damned . . . like themselves.

And that is their story.

Feelings. . . .

We are the only creations of God to experience such feelings of darkness in the midst of His holy Heaven, you know.

We do that because we regularly journey between Heaven and earth. Those human beings who have accepted Christ as Savior and Lord and who have been allowed into Heaven as a result are shielded from the pain of earth, the dying of earth—yes, even the tears.

My angel-kin and I all await the moment when we will experience the same kind of peace. But we do not know it just now. For us, there is little solace so long as we trod the path called Angelwalk. For each of us has his own Angelwalk, which is as much a name for the very journey itself.

Angelwalk. . . .

It is a path of pain, a path of joy—it is both of these and more.

It is the story of Darien, my fellow angel, with all his uncertainties, with his quest to piece together the reality of Satan for himself.

Another story is mine. I had no doubts, you see no uncertainties. Nor did Michael, or Gabriel.

Another story indeed. . . .

We take our feelings with us when we journey to earth, and we take them back with us when we report to the Trinity.

We stand before the Throne, and we weep. We weep for the lost. We know what God intended for the planet, and we weep over what it has become. We beg Him not to send us back—surely, we will not have to return, surely we can instead continue to stand amidst the cleansing atmosphere of Heaven itself and be washed pure again, without going back to the dirt below.

Surely. . . .

God cries, too.

Oh, He does. Jesus truly wept in human form. That did not end the moment the Son of God ascended. This capability was with Him before the Incarnation. It remains today.

We often serve to help the blessed Comforter, and we do our best, mostly when humans are in pain, when we can step into their lives and stay by their sides. We cannot hold their hands, of course. We cannot rub their foreheads. We cannot put our arms around their frail bodies and sing to them. But we do more, much more, you see.

This, then, is my story, which I recount now as I stand in front of Father, Son, and Holy Spirit, and before all those created beings, human and angelic alike, who have remained loyal, loving followers of the Most High. It would not surprise me if some scribe is quietly marking down what I say, to be put in some form on the shelf of a majestic new library somewhere.

I know I cannot delay any longer, for as soon as I finish, I shall join these the residents of the Kingdom as we all begin the long anticipated journey triumphant from the new Heaven to the new earth, all things new, forever and ever. . . .

The
Odyssey

*E*VERY SEAT IS taken.

On stage at the front of the auditorium are only two individuals, a fragile-looking boy and his mother. Even though the loudspeaker is on full blast, the child's words sometimes are difficult to hear.

"I am very tired now," he says, and rests his head on his mother's shoulder, and dies.

She continues to stand there, though she is obviously trying to fight back tears that are beginning to drip over her lower lids and down her cheeks.

Suddenly there is the sound of voices raised in prayer. The hundreds of men and women in that auditorium stand and—

I see Heaven opening up.

I see angels descending. They stand around little Robbie as his soul begins to leave his body.

They are waiting, I know, waiting for me, waiting for me to do that which has been ordained. And I know, how blessed it is, I know what I must do. I must take that soul, pure and healthy from that diseased and now dead flesh, I must lift it from corruption and give it to incorruption.

Something quite wonderful happens. Words come from

481

the soul of a child, words without pain, words of sublime joy.

"Peace like a river attendeth my way. . . ."

Robbie starts to sing that remembered hymn, and the gathered angels join him, sharing its wonderful lyrics as none who were still trapped in their fleshly bodies could ever do, could ever do with the same meaning.

And that expression on Robbie's face! Peace envelopes him, as water surrounded the baptized Jesus in the River Jordan. All that is finite, all that was born to perish, has passed away.

In an instant, the Holy Spirit descends not as a dove—no need of symbols or surrogates any longer.

I hand Robbie to Him—a brave and beautiful child, now glistening, now cleansed—I hand this precious one to this Member of the Trinity. The Holy Spirit looks at me for a moment, smiles, and I feel His radiance throughout my very being. He smiles, yes, and He says, "You will miss him while you are here, will you not?"

"Oh, I will, I will," I admit, incapable as I am of lies, deception.

"You were with him for so long, and now you will wait expectantly for the reunion, is that not so, Stedfast?"

"Yes," I agree. "He was so fine, this child. He smiled in the midst of pain. He never became angry. He stayed faithful even as the disease ravaged him more and more severely. If I were of flesh and blood, he is the son I would want, I would pray for."

The Holy Spirit, touched by my words, says, "The Father knows. He knows, and He rejoices because of you."

I have brought joy to my Creator! I have pleased Almighty God!

"It is time now," the Holy Spirit says as He turns to the child. "Robbie, are you ready?"

Robbie nods eagerly and reaches out toward me.

"Thank you, Stedfast," he tells me. "I prayed to Jesus about you every night. I thanked Him for sending such a beautiful angel to be with me. The pain didn't hurt as much because I could feel your presence, and nothing else mattered, Stedfast. God bless you, God bless you, dear, dear angel, angel of mercy, angel of joy."

I try to control myself though barely managing to do so.

Robbie casts a glance at the crowd in that auditorium. They had come to the Christian media convention to buy and sell. They had come to hear speeches. And none would ever be the same again after listening to what his mother had to say of her struggle to save the life of this her beloved son.

Voices are now raised in praise, many present with their palms upheld. Though none can actually see what is happening, they can somehow sense the presence of divinity. This child, now free, now whole, reaches out toward them and in a beautiful way touches each one with his gentle and good spirit, some driven to tears as they fall to their knees.

Robbie hesitates but an instant as he looks at his mother that final, final moment before, someday, they walk the golden streets together. Her tears have formed a river of their own.

"I love you," he whispers. "I love you so much, dearest Mother."

Not words at all, at least as far as she or any of them can perceive.

A sensation.

Something rippling in the air, perhaps, gossamerlike.

She senses it instinctively, raising her head toward the ceiling—and at the same moment there is a touch of concern, a last fleeting reluctance to let go, to acknowledge her beloved's odyssey.

"It is well with my soul, Mother," I can hear Robbie

say clearly. "I see Jesus waiting, you know. He says He will take your hand, too, Mother, and very soon. Don't be afraid. My Lord, your Lord loves you as much as I do."

And then Robbie is gone.

His mother smiles as she raises the fingers of her left hand to her lips, kisses these, and holds them out to the empty air.

"He is not there, sweet lady," I say. "He is beyond the Gates now. His feet touch streets of gold. His ears listen to the songs of angels. There are so many gathering around him. He is at peace, this child of yours. He is—"

Home.

Observer also was there at the time, Satan's demonic journalist, so chained to his master, yet so reluctant. Other fallen ones had urged him not to enter, for they all were leaving in a panic. There was too much faith, too much sweetness, too much love in that room, and they could not endure it.

But he stayed. And I did.

We saw the same beautiful moments. And we left that place touched by what had happened, me to the rededication of myself to the Cause of Christ, Observer back to his puppet master.

"I could do nothing to stop it," Observer told me.

"Did you want to stop it?" I asked incredulously.

"No," he admitted. "I pray that Satan will never find out."

"Would he punish you?"

"Yes. Horribly."

And I watched him go, my former comrade. I watched him go, and I remembered how it once was, before evil began.

Those first wonderful days!

True and I were selected by the Trinity to help Them in

the process of creation. Yes, it may seem strange to say that, for surely They need no help with such matters. But it was done not for the sake of Father, Son, and Holy Spirit. Rather, it was for True, for me. Even then we were being groomed, I realize now, groomed for special tasks and special destinies.

And there he and I were as Adam and Eve came to life, Adam from the soil, Eve from his side.

They saw us, and they smiled without fear.

Without fear!

Think of the wonder of that. It is the same awe many feel when a baby killer whale is born at one of those modern sea-life-type parks, born and swimming in an instant, as though it had been doing so forever.

Thus it was with the first humans, born out of noth-ingness, yet accepting us with no reluctance, no doubt over whether or not they were hallucinating, just simple faith, faith together with trust.

The destruction of this is a very large part of the foundation of my hatred for Satan.

The death of pure trust.

I find that as tragic as the death of faith, for once faith is present, trust should be, *yes, easier!* Yet without faith, trustlessness is understandable. It cannot be transformed into what is nobler, grander. It hangs like a dark cloud, submerging all who choose to allow it to dominate every second of life.

Those who have faith and do not couple it with trust are bastard creatures, born indeed, alive and walking and *doing*—but with victory robbed from their lives, exalta-tion drained from the days accorded them.

Adam and Eve had it.

Adam and Eve lived it.

And we, True and I, saw it in their eyes, in their words, in the very walk of those two.

That was why they did not fear the serpent.

Later, other angels, including Darien, joined us. Later, the Garden was alive with them. And because of this, because of our radiance, there was no night. Oh, technically there was night, but we banished it by our presence. We set the Garden aglow with color, sparkling with some of the light of Heaven itself—for that was what we were made of, you know, the glow of the Creator transfused throughout His Kingdom, from which we were created by His loving Hand, as though, playfully, He would grab some of it, hold it, and then let it go as another angel beamed to life, countless thousands of us, thousands times thousands, God remarkably like an innocent child in a long-ago time on earth, a child grabbing at sparkling soap bubbles he has created—and there the comparison ends, for when a child opens his hand, he finds nothing, but when God did, He found us.

LIKE A RIVER glorious. . . .

There was indeed a river named Glorious in Eden, the water like molten crystal, sparkling under an overhead sun whose pure rays were not filtered through layers of pollution spewed up into the atmosphere.

There was no industry in those days.

There was no death.

There was no sin.

Like a world glorious.

That was how it used to be, you know. Adam and Eve began in Eden, but this was intended as only the start. God was prepared to take them on a wondrous journey around the world, their Guide through the wonders of a planet that was, in so many ways, a mirror image of Heaven itself, an extension of its glories. Eden was the nucleus, with everything else spreading out from it. Eden offered to this first couple a taste of what the world was like. God planned to show them the rest.

I saw what the two humans had not as yet.

I saw a world of waterfalls of liquid gold.

I saw a world of colonies of unfallen angels clustered together, chattering about what they saw around them, comparing it to their previous heavenly home, and excited about the future, for they were to be caretakers of this new place, sprung as it was from the mind of God, as they themselves had been.

There were no battles for us in Eden nor anywhere else on earth at that time, it seemed. Satan had been vanquished. We all assumed, so foolishly, our former comrade would never again reappear.

I saw a world where no living thing died in the mouth of another.

I saw a world in which a lion sat contentedly simply looking at a color-drenched butterfly going from flower to flower in a field of orchids.

I saw a world that—

—was so much like Heaven itself!

I said that before, I know, but it is so blessed a fact that I cannot but repeat it.

That had been the purpose, of course. God wanted His newest creations—Adam and Eve—to exist in a world of the finest elements that He could provide.

And Planet Earth was that, the very finest.

The Father intended this to be forever. If there were no death, then mankind would never die. If there were no death, then mankind never needed to eat meat. Eating involved decay of one sort or another, animal or vegetable. But with eternal life, there would have been no hunger, no thirst, cattle and geese and lobsters spared.

Funny, isn't it, how I always took pity, somehow, on the lobsters, crammed into their glass tanks as they were, then taken out and shown to the one into whose stomach bits and pieces of them would soon drop, before which the eater would examine the eatee and say, "Yes, that's a good specimen," and into the broiler it would go.

None of that in the original Eden.

I saw lobsters, yes, I saw a whole inlet of them; they were moving about rather briskly for their kind, not shackled by the need to hunt prey, and so they had no cares at all, and could live as they were meant to live, without stress, without fear.

Perhaps talking about lobsters seems inappropriate, but it is not that at all. They are hardly of a shape and a look that engenders any degree of affection. Yet in the world of that Edenic period, they were as well cared for as any creature on the planet. It was not by appearance that they were accorded what they enjoyed but the very fact that they *were*, period, that they *existed*, and the least in God's Kingdom had all the respect of the greatest—except for man.

I saw this world in all its wonders. And I craved the day, still hence, when I could join the Father, and assist Him as we walked with Adam and Eve, sharing it with them, their guides through the most miraculous journey either of them would ever have.

For since death had not as yet entered the world, so it was that they were aware of the angels around about them. So it was that I, Stedfast, joined with them to be one of their guardians—the other a dear comrade named True.

And so it was that they were aware of us. Sin would change that. Sin would establish a barrier between us, between all humans and all angels. Future humans would talk about us, would write poems and songs about us, would speculate about us in books—but with no memory of what it once was like.

We were torn from Adam and Eve, and they from us.

That day came as a chill breeze through a graveyard, unexpected, making us shiver at the consequences.

A bright world, a world of seamless purity torn from eternal light into abysmal darkness.

Darien had left to do the Creator's bidding elsewhere, but I remained, along with True. We tried to dissuade Adam and Eve, to whisper into their ears, to stop them in some way or another.

We could not *physically* do anything. Even then we were spirits only, a breeze against the cheek, an insubstantial sensation, but not more than that.

We lost.

We lost that first battle, and, thus, began the war.

That has stayed with me through the centuries since, the thousands of years of separation from God that have dominated history's walk.

We lost that first battle. . . .

All of mankind has suffered because we weren't strong enough, our words like puffs of cotton, easily waved aside, when they should have been heavy weights pressing down Adam and Even in constraint.

Those first moments after Adam and Eve were cast from Eden are not chronicled in Scripture. Nor have I found them so anywhere in all the literature of man.

But I know them. I knew them then. I know them now. They are fresh in my thoughts, and will not be exorcised until the new Heaven, the new earth.

To have that awful time wiped from memory will be one of the Father's greatest blessings.

To no longer witness in recollection—oh, please, let it be soon, dear Father—death rushing in, animals not accustomed to pain suddenly consumed with it, many dying in their tracks, creatures large and small, creatures of the air and the sea and the land, all gasping or groaning or shaking their lives away.

And we, my friend True and I, could do nothing.

Oh, how worthless I felt at such times of remembering how we failed, trying to reconstruct in my mind what it had been like in Eden back then, those moments of communion, flesh aware of spirit, spirit understood by flesh—communion, yes, but also connection, *angels and humans as almost a single entity, an interweaving of one with the other.*

Joined.

Oh, yes, we were, Stedfast with Adam and True with Eve.

Stedfast and True—we were the angels with the most precious assignment of all, to be with the first human beings. We were their companions, their friends. How cherished those moments were, blessed and—

Missed.

Having tasted all that was fulfilling to us and pleasing to the Father, we could not have been less prepared for the expulsion of Adam and Eve.

To be joined together in holy matrimony.

What it was like for a man and a woman in the most ecstatic moments of their passion was very close to what True and I felt. We were "married," in a sense, to Adam and Eve. Indeed, we had the greatest possible intimacy.

Marriage, then, is yet another hint of Eden, not a relationship to be mocked by an endless repetition of marriage-divorce, marriage-divorce, marriage-divorce, a marriage license no better in such instances than the key to a cheap motel room for a night of illicit passion.

How do I describe that moment, that moment when Adam and Eve were ripped from True and myself?

True did not want to release Eve. He cried out to her, "Recant! Recant! God forgives. Please, please—!"

She did not. Nor did Adam.

They saw only their nakedness and they were ashamed.

There was something worse. While they lost Eden, they did not lose their memories of it. They would be tormented by this until the day they died, remembering the beauty, the peace, the joy of Eden, and doing this in the midst of the new world in which they found themselves, a world filled with death.

From never-ending life to always-present death.

In Eden, Adam and Eve could stand before a beautiful flower, and admire it again and again, week after week,

month after month, for years at a time, knowing that
nothing would ever affect that flower, its colors unceas-
ingly vibrant, its shape always delicate, its scent forever,
no disease to kill it, no hungry insects to drain away its
life, no change of seasons to make it turn brittle, then fall
to the ground. It was a flower made by God simply as a
way of pleasing them.

It was all for them, these first two humans, a world
into which the Father had placed them for their enjoy-
ment, for their exaltation—but also for their stewardship, a stewardship that was to have been of great
sensitivity and care, for this was one way they both had
of returning to Him the supreme love that gave them life
in the first place—that flower and many others even
more masterfully-made, that lake and its pure water, the
air which they took into their lungs a gift directly from
God, their only obligation so simple, an obligation to
appreciate His grace and goodness and generosity, to
show this appreciation merely by obeying His one outright command—not a cruel one, not a command that
would limit their world to any measurable degree—and
yet they turned their backs on the Father, resenting the
one part of the garden that was off-limits to them, where
stood that one tree out of countless numbers actually
more attractive than it, its fruit eclipsed in appearance by
any number of others hanging from trees to either side of
it—but it was the only small requirement that God had,
the one simple test to which He put them. And thus
went their loyalty, loyalty as filthy rags in the midst of
paradise.

They were gone.

True and I stood there, side by side, watching the man
and the woman as they ran into a world that showed the
first encroaching signs of their foul transgression, a tiny
bird having dropped from the course of its flight and
landed in front of the two of them. They paused for a

moment in their sudden exodus, Eve bending down, picking up the gray and white creature, not quite dead, its head turning, looking at her, then at Adam, and saying by this, *What have you done? What have you done to me, to the rest of creation?*

And then it was gone, its body cold in an instant.

Adam and Eve dug the first grave. . . .

"Goodbye, True," I told my friend.

"Goodbye, Stedfast," he replied, his brilliance dimming in his sorrow.

He turned, briefly, and looked back, and I with him, the Garden the same as at its moment of creation, as colorful and alive as ever, within its boundaries the cold, awful grip of death still vanquished . . . for the moment but not for all time.

"No one can enter," he told me. "No one can enter until the new Heaven, the new earth."

"You are to guard it until the end of time," I said.

"I shall face hordes of demons, Stedfast," he said, stating something that would have seemed incomprehensible just a short while earlier, but now had become, in human terms, a fact of life.

He was only momentarily tremulous at that thought.

"Lucifer himself shall stand before me."

"But you will remain . . . steadfast."

"Yes, oh, yes, steadfast and true," he said, smiling, reaching out to me, our spirits blending briefly, "our valor our gift back to the Father who made us all."

And then my fellow unfallen and I parted, doing so for unknowable centuries ahead of us . . . my good, good friend remaining there, alone, somehow succeeding in preventing entry, until One and only One would tell him that the time had come to stand aside, stand aside indeed, and rejoin his comrades . . . and I, Stedfast, wanting to stay, to be with him, to help in whatever fashion I could, but called by the Master of us all to minister instead to

Humankind, not other angels so self-sufficient, as they were, of course, so able to stand and fight the enemy . . . but always my thoughts, though not my presence, were with this one angel, knowing all too well the multitude of loathsome monsters which were certain to confront him throughout the jumbled history of mankind, to offer him, as enticingly as possible, their own version of the forbidden fruit of Eden, in return for his doing something quite simple, that is, merely standing aside and allowing simple entry, but always this angel would be resisting, never giving in, a gentle angel, yet with the unflinching valor of a warrior and the spirit of a poet, turning back tides of evil for all of history, remaining, as ever he would, strong and brave and . . . yes, blessed friend . . . True.

I WALK THE centuries. I see the effects of sin more than any historian because I see them as they occur, not simply as I plow through manuscripts that turn to dust at the slightest touch.

I see it all.

Until the new Heaven and the new earth, as promised by God to human and angel alike.

But in the meantime. . . .

So much of what I have witnessed has been due to the inability of one individual to communicate fully with another. It was not that way in Eden. Adam and Eve did not need physical intimacy to become as one. They were already in total union with one another, with the Father, and with all of creation.

But they sinned, and the links were broken all around. God no longer spoke to them audibly. He did so to others in the centuries to follow, but such times were miraculous interventions rather than normal occurrences.

That first creature fell from the sky.

Cain took the life of his brother.

From that awful moment to the infamy of the Holocaust to the mass destruction of Hiroshima and Nagasaki to the Vietnam War to poison gas on the battlefields of

Iran and Iraq was not much of a leap, in the final analysis, because it all sprang from the same awful abyss of mankind's rebellion against God—that and a global allegiance to Satan, sometimes knowingly, sometimes otherwise.

Families have been splitting apart since the earliest Old Testament days because they did not communicate. Governments have been at war because they did not communicate. In the latter part of the twentieth century, there seemed to be a multitude of greater than ever *means* to effect communication, but less and less communication itself.

All of creation has suffered.

Communication is not simply *talking*. It involves understanding. There was plenty of talk before and during the American Civil War, but nothing was accomplished until too much blood was shed, until the South found itself losing far too many of its men—*and then the war ended.*

There was not enough understanding that slavery was an abomination in the sight of God. There was not enough understanding that those who claimed the name of Christ and supported slavery were skirting blasphemy.

Once again, blood covered talk, silencing it, because understanding was the greatest casualty.

I was active during this period. I was with the North as well as the South. I took dying Rebels and Yankees to the gates of Heaven. I took slaves and free men.

And I watched many snatched by taloned creatures of loathsome countenance and dragged beyond the mouth of Hell.

It mattered not which side the dying were on. Any soldier fighting in defense of slavery was not guaranteed damnation because of this; any soldier fighting in opposition to slavery was not guaranteed salvation as a result.

General Lee went to Heaven.

That may be surprising to some . . . *Robert E. Lee in Heaven!*

I have not seen some quite prominent Northern generals there, men whose pulpit was a liquor bottle, the only source from which they drank, feeling no need for spiritual refreshment.

Robert E. Lee was simply obeying *his* commander. What Lee did, he felt was the honorable course even though, in the end, he acknowledged that he had spent many, many nights dealing with emotions that were on the other side.

Some plantation owners are in Heaven. Slaves were, to them, well-nigh members of their family, given similar privileges. Their slaves got such food, good clothes, and medical attention that were equal to that of any white person on the plantation.

I remember one group of slaves that had fought to defend their owner's property *against* invading Northern soldiers, not because they had been ordered to do so, but out of a sense of personal loyalty, given freely, and reacting against strangers coming in and taking over.

"What could we do?" the survivors cried. "They were bent on destroying the only way of life we have ever known. For us, there had never been hunger. Our sicknesses were healed. We had clothes to wear, quarters in which to sleep. Only our freedom was missing. And yet there were those Negroes in the North who were not slaves to any man but to a poverty more demeaning than anything we had ever known in the midst of our so-called slavery. What were we being freed from?"

Most died.

Every white man, every black man on that plantation, except some women and children.

Those men empowered to liberate the slaves were responsible for killing them instead.

Among them, I remember Jonah.

This Jonah was not swallowed up by a giant fish but by war.

He was a slave who died in the arms of the woman who had been the wife of his "master."

"I tried so hard," he told her. "I tried to do what I could to . . . to . . . Oh! I see Heaven! They're calling me to come. . . ."

"Tell me, Jonah," she pleaded, "is my husband there?"

He had been shot just seconds before Jonah was; seeing this, the black man had started firing back at the men responsible.

Jonah was slipping away, but he managed, barely, to tell her, "He is. I see him! He's smiling . . . beside him are my mamma and my papa. They've been waiting for me all these years, all these—"

Jonah let out one last gasp of pain, and then he became limp, lifeless in the woman's arms.

Soldiers were gathered around her.

She stood, yelling at them, "Is this anything to be proud of? Is this what you call liberating an oppressed Negro?"

I encouraged many scenes like that during the course of the Civil War. I saw many that spoke of the hypocrisy of using a biblical justification for slavery. I saw black people beaten to death, black women used as sexual slaves to their white masters. I saw hangings of blacks caught for the simplest of crimes. I saw the foul, stinking domination of one man over another, the weaker subjected to the worst indignities, the baser inclinations of human nature.

But not Jonah.

Jonah's story was different.

Jonah's soul left his body as I stood before him.

"My master is waiting," he said anxiously. "I can see him just beyond."

"He is no longer your master."

"He isn't?"

Jonah seemed puzzled for an instant, then began to grin from ear to ear.

"Jesus! Jesus is my Master!"

"The moment you accepted Him as your Savior, your Lord," I told him.

"Praise God Almighty!" Jonah laughed joyously.

The plantation owner approached us as we entered Heaven.

"Dear Jonah," he said. "Dear, good friend."

And it will be that way for these two throughout eternity.

Since the beginning, societies have been groaning in near-continual pain. There has been little relief. War after war after war . . . they have caused a kind of preview of hell, with millions bombed or shot or bayo- neted or gassed to death, millions more maimed in their bodies or their minds—or both, perhaps.

But there have been other kinds of wars: The drug war, the war against corruption in government, the war against allowing millions of babies to be murdered legally and in a socially "acceptable" manner.

Sometimes, though, wars are not on a grand scale, or even between countries. There is another kind that goes on within the human mind, heart, and soul. . . .

Some
of the People
and Others

~

O*NLY THE LONELY. . . .*

I remember hearing a song with that title during my travels in the midst of the twentieth century. I remember the lonely I have tried to console in the final moments before they slipped off the confines of that body of flesh in which they had been trapped.

Trapped?

Oh, yes, it was like that for many of these individuals, their bones and muscles and veins a prison as confining as any with bars and concrete. Some looked at themselves in innumerable mirrors wishing they were handsome or pretty, thinking that if this were the case, they would have friends, they would have fun, they would have a vibrant *life*. Instead they were confined to the wings while the stage belonged to the charming, the attractive, the "worthwhile" human beings who had so much going for them.

Self-worth. . . .

They measured the sum total of their existence by what they could accomplish in their careers. Each award brought a fresh surge of vigor, as though they had at last earned the right to be respectable, to be accepted, even to function in the same universe as those they had secretly envied for so long. Each new recognition gave them some hope of getting a single moment of time from others because, look, they were saying, we *are* worthy.

I remember one such sufferer in particular. And sufferer *is* the correct designation. William *suffered*, his very soul knotted up continually, dragging him downward to an awaiting abyss of sorts, dark and lonely and filled with the reverberating cries of his often self-inflicted personal anguish.

William was a Christian, indeed he was, but perhaps the most tragic sort of all. Indwelt by the Holy Spirit, with an angel at his side from the moment of his birth until his death, he also had been picked by God as someone with a special mission, a very special mission indeed.

He had a gift.

Music.

William wrote songs—ballads, hymns. He started out in the secular world, and did quite well. But then came a point at which he decided to dedicate his talent to Christ and Christ only.

Even greater success emerged for William.

His songs were hit-parade regulars, sung in churches across the nation. He had every material thing that he could want.

Yet what William wanted was to die.

"I yearn for death, Lord," he would pray. "I eagerly anticipate the joy of walking with the angels along the golden streets of glory."

Heaven played a part in so many of the songs. People were comforted by William's words, by his melodies. But for him, those words were cries from a heart long ago wounded, and the melodies merged into one long mournful cry of despair.

William had no one.

He was known by millions of fellow Christians. His personal appearances were in demand at Bible colleges and conventions from coast to coast. He—

No one.

And no matter how he analyzed it, that was the conclusion he invariably had to confront.

For William, there was no question of acceptance by others for the work he did.

"They listen to my songs, and they hum the melodies," he said during the last hour of his life. "Young people who devoured heavy metal now tune into my stuff. I can pick up the phone right now and talk to heads of record companies, world-famous evangelists and family counselors, even renowned Christian actors, actresses, and politicians."

He stifled a sob.

"Yet I am *alone* here in this condo. Oh, yes, 'beautiful Hawaii' is beautiful enough. This is where I always dreamed of living. I can stand on the back balcony and see some of the most beautiful sunsets anywhere in this jewel of God's universe, this world so beautiful—yet so ravaged, like my life itself."

He threw his head back, his eyes glistening with tears.

"Where are the people? Where is a wife to kiss me, a child to touch my hand, a word of love?"

"I love you," I told him. "Jesus loves you."

He broke out laughing.

"Jesus loves me, this I know . . ." he mused.

Anger flashed across his face.

"Where have you been all the years of my life?"

"By your side."

He looked at me.

"I never saw you before."

"But you felt my presence, William."

He was about to shout his denial, about to scream the

pain that had isolated him so long from sharing his feelings with others, for surely if they knew the depth of it, that pain of his, surely they would fling platitudes at him and, in the end, turn away.

But he did nothing of the sort, instead falling silent in thought.

When my parents died, I thought I could not go on, no way was there that I could do this. When you have an inner world of three, yourself and two others and that is that—and that is all there ever has been—and two are subtracted, two are ripped from the tapestry of what passes for your life, if life is not a misnomer in your pitiable case, leaving a gaping hole where the only love of your life had been, when you stand by two open coffins, and kiss the cold foreheads of the only two persons with whom you have ever known intimacy, and then you return to a motel room, and realize that there can never again be anyone to call, to really, really call, when—

"The reviews mean nothing after that," he told me.

"There is something else, isn't there, William?"

He bowed his head.

"You know?"

"I do."

"How much I hated them at the same time I couldn't live without them, at the same time I loved them with mind, body, and soul? Is that what you mean?"

"Yes. Tell me, William. Tell me it all."

"It is so shameful."

"Be honest."

"Before I die? Isn't it a moot point now?"

"William?"

"Yes?"

"Feel cleansed, feel whole for a few fleeting moments in *this* life. Wouldn't you like that, William?"

"Yes, I would, I truly would."

"The guilt. You would like to be free of the guilt, even for a single moment."

William knew I was right. He felt so very guilty about his parents. He hated them, he loved them, he hated them, he loved them, over and over, in endless cycles, until they were no longer around, until he could no longer shout his feelings at them.

"We never talked," he said. "We fought."

"Why, William?"

"Because—"

The words were loathe to come, his tongue reluctant to speak them, his brain rebelling at the thought of—

What they had done to him!

"Done, William? What *had* they done?"

"Kept me."

"Kept you?"

"To themselves. Chained. Imprisoned."

"Surrounded by love . . . is that so bad, William?"

"The imprisonment of their love . . . that's what it was. The thing cherished became the thing that stifled."

He strode over to a television set in the room, a large one with an immense screen, and turned it on. He flicked through several channels.

He looked with encompassing longing at the fleeting seconds of people together, talking, kissing, laughing, connecting in wonderful ways with one another.

"Communication," he said.

"With others?"

"Yes. Isn't that the natural scheme of things?"

"Agreed. . . ."

"A man shall leave his parents at some point and cleave unto his wife. A new family is begun. When the original parents die, it is traumatic, it is all kinds of pain, but then they are buried, and the man returns to his own family. His wife and he grow old together, and *their* children get married, and begin their—"

He started crying.

"I wish I could touch you now, William," I told him. "I wish I could rest a hand on your shoulder, and give you what you have always lacked."

"A hand, a single hand," he sobbed. "Not out of duty, not even out of a sense of *ministry!*"

Not now, William, not in the flesh. But you shall truly have it . . . beyond what you could have imagined.

"Are you still here?"

"I am."

"Soon?"

"Quite soon, William."

"My parents? They'll be waiting."

"Truly so."

He stood, looking around the room, at the walls covered with commendations, with photographs of him posing with the famous of the world, the church, shelves lined with awards and statues.

"My life . . ." he whispered ruefully.

"The letters," I said, knowing what his answer would be. "Take out the letters, William. Read through a few of them."

"I have no letters. I threw them all out. I gave to the ones who wrote those letters what I could not obtain for myself. Reading what they were thanking *me* for only reminded me of what *I* was missing."

"A reason to go on living, in some cases?"

"In some, yes."

"What about the others?"

"Renewed faith. My words were instruments that the Lord used to—"

"It wasn't a charade, William, if that is what you are thinking."

"What other word is there? 'Hypocrisy' perhaps. If not

a charade, then surely hypocrisy. Tell me, how could I have taught them anything? How can a blind man lead others who are blind to the light?"

"That was your mission, William. You wrote of pain. You sang of love and rejection and redemption. You took each song as a cup from the living spring of yourself and you gave it to the thirsty."

"While remaining famished myself!"

"No longer, William."

He had bowed his head, as so often before, half in prayer, half in the burden of what he felt in those sad, wrenched emotions of his, emotions that he fought with continually, trying so hard to *force* himself into some semblance of joy.

Now he looked up.

"Light?" he said, puzzled, feeling it at first rather than seeing it.

"Yes, William, not a nebulous light, disguised darkness from the pit of hell, not a light as that simple-minded actress would describe, but the light of Heaven, William, the light of Heaven coming from Almighty God Himself."

"This is God?"

"As much as your laughter, your tears are you, yes."

"I—"

He felt it first, then he saw it as he dropped to his knees, looking around fearfully at the emptiness of that condo.

"I die alone," he said, "as always I thought it would be."

"No," I said, "no, you do not, William. For now—"

He thought he saw me then, appearing before his eyes from nothingness.

"You are so beautiful," he said.

"But, William, you are not looking at *me*."

"Then what exactly do I see?"

"Yourself, William. You are looking at your own spirit now, without the burden of flesh."

"How can something so radiant be—"

He turned and looked down as the ascent began, saw the old body, now limp, alone as always.

"—me?"

I was by his side, and he saw me at last.

"Take my hand, William," I asked of him.

He reached out.

"We are so much alike," he said.

"God created us both, but it is you, as His finest, who are His greatest source of joy."

"Me? God's joy?"

"Oh, yes, dear, dear William."

A tune.

"I hear—"

A tune sung.

"Oh, my, I hear—"

By angels.

"One of mine! They're singing—"

At first he heard the angel chorus with that familiar melody, but now they were joined by a vast multitude, each voice raised high.

"Their arms, their arms are outstretched," William said incredulously.

"They've been waiting, you know," I told him. "Ten thousand souls singing the melodies of your heart."

I took him forward and they surrounded us, mother and father and all.

"What were you saying about loneliness, William?" I asked.

He had forgotten.

Such a beautiful conclusion, is it not? A man taken from despair and loneliness into the greatest companionship he could ever have known.

There is another man of whom I am not fond at all, unlike William, whom I have grown to love. I doubt that this other will ever love anyone except himself, and the warped ideals he holds dear. . . .

*H*E IS A doctor without conscience, as are all such individuals who rationalize the performance of abortions, that bland, nondescript term for murder. A doctor professing any dedication toward extending life cannot then take it away so "conveniently" without justifying the accusation of "Hypocrite!"

I can say this because I am unfallen. I can say this because, in the foreknowledge of the Trinity, I was created with the sole purpose of ministering to the whole of mankind, saved and unsaved. Is that a striking thought perhaps? That God allows the unsaved to be touched by one of His created angels? Is that not heresy?

It shouldn't be. It cannot be. The God of love and mercy and grace and goodness never stops possessing those qualities if the intended object of them happens to reject His existence.

He is the subject of His own parable at times, the constant knocker at the door of a cold and unreceiving heart.

He is, yes, through me as His emissary.

But there *are* some who are successful in never coming to the door, never opening it, always keeping us out in the cold.

Delusion is one reason. And this doctor is one example, a man whose surgeon's hands have saved many lives and destroyed countless others.

So easily.

Without compassion, if compassion is a word ever considered in the midst of such circumstances.

For this man, it goes beyond lack of compassion, since he has done so many abortions during his "career" that it is just a clinical routine with him. He has wrung the necks of so many breathing, kicking babies that the motion becomes meaningless, one swift movement of his strong hands, the same motion that twists off the tops of bottles, shucks ears of corn—the same movement comes from a man who attributes no less importance to the bottle-top, the ear of corn, and no more importance to that little, perfectly-formed *human being*, all these the same with him, all ending up in trash bags, disposable and forgotten, on to the next, and the one after that.

He is called a "great" man. He is compared to Salk, Schweitzer, and others.

No.

He is a Mengele instead, someone who uses noble or innocent words to gloss over barbarity.

Thinking of his kind, I am driven by strong emotions. Oh, yes, I do have emotions, deep and strong. And yet I cannot cry. Those of unfallen spirit cannot shed physical tears. Our "crying" is different. When one of us feels sad, we all do. We are connected through the sublime oneness that we have had with the Creator.

It is quite similar between us and the innocent unborn. *We are connected.*

They are surrounded with warmth. They feel secure. They receive only sporadic hints that something is going on beyond the limits of their tiny, tiny universe.

We, my kind and I, are in the womb with them.

It is the mother's body that protects them physically. It

is an angel assigned to each child who protects it spiritually.

We are there for nine months . . . *if allowed.*

But so often the peace they know, the special joy between us is shredded, pulled apart limb by limb.

And that is when their minds send a message, a message of unknowing terror, a message that questions the pain.

No words.

They have no vocabulary. But that scarcely justifies their description as formless blobs, mere pieces of tissue in the mother's womb.

They have no comprehension except the warm fluids and flesh around them. But that doesn't make them without humanity.

They are not sure what pain is except that it hurts, it hurts desperately, and they would like to have it stop. But that doesn't make the killing of them simply an act of "choice," babies as disposable as diapers.

So beautiful—I think each time I join one before forceps intrude, ripping limbs asunder—*so beautiful in your purity, born with a sin nature but not yet guilty of sin, like an angel, an unfallen angel.*

That thought drives me to my kind's kind of tears.

You are like we are, like we will always be, now you are—*but the moment you enter the world, the process begins, the people, the environment, the devil.*

I reach out, touch for an instant the tiny head, the fingers, the feet.

We once existed in the mind of God as you exist in the womb of a woman as He existed, incarnate, in Mary. How could anyone outside that wall of flesh surrounding you ever think to do you harm!

It happens.

The moment of saline, or forceps or whatever procedure the kind doctor chooses to relieve his patient of an unwanted burden.

The living child twists and turns but there are no screams. This cannot occur. The vocal chords are not as yet able to function. The mouth opens, closes, *snapping open, snapping closed.* The eyes remain shut.

It lasts sometimes for minutes, this process of destruction. It is not a quick death at all, despite the industry's claim to the contrary.

I remember executions I have attended.

Why is it that condemned murderers are accorded deaths proven to be *less* traumatic than innocent babies condemned only by the callousness of their mothers who sometimes selfishly cry about *their* emotional anguish — but that is as far as it goes, no compassion for the human being they have caused to be slaughtered.

Too harsh to say it that way?

I have seen the buckets. I have seen the trash cans. I remember some doctors at a large clinic getting together and talking about how to save money. One of them pointed to the disposal containers — notice how inoffensive that is — that were being bought from a local medical supply outlet.

"Plastic trash cans at a local discount chain are on sale this week," he said. "We could buy a truckload, and cut costs right there."

The others applauded his ingenuity.

And so that is where the body parts are thrown, not gently wrapped in cloth and then carefully placed, but shucked like chicken bones.

I witnessed a similar meeting at another clinic; the purpose was the same, the method different.

Ovens.

They were trying to cut costs in that area.

Another discount chain was mentioned.

Something else has happened before the bits and pieces of another helpless one have been dust-pailed together and dumped. . . .

Only an instant after his eternal transformation, I hold what had been a dying child in my arms as I stand before the Holy Throne.

I hand this perfect human over, full of life as he is, free of pain, to the Father of Mankind.

"Thank you, Stedfast," that wonderful voice fills the whole of Heaven.

The Creator thanking *me!*

How can that be! I ask myself. *Is it something that is so glorious that I wish it into being! My own fantasy, as it were!*

And then I know, I know, I truly know that there are no delusions in Heaven. It is what I could call the Place of Ultimate Reality Eternally.

I wonder if the wonder of that will ever lose its impact upon me. I doubt that it will. I pray that it does not. I find myself wanting to please Him more and more as my odyssey through the years continues.

I leave, then, turning but so briefly to look at what is no longer a child as angels gather around his new body, whole and eternal.

I return to the clinic, but the doctor has left to attend an animal rights rally.

I LEAVE THE present carnage, and yet I do not. It stays with me, in the very essence of myself. There will always be other such slaughter-houses, and righteous people trying to block the entrances, trying to stem the murderous tide *any way they can!*

If laws must be broken, then it is better to do that, to grind humankind's pitiable legal machinations into the transient dust, better indeed *that* than to ignore what God Himself has mandated. It should be noted that if angelkind, of which I am a member, were of flesh and blood, they would be sitting with the protesters. About this there can be no doubt.

I pause for a moment, watching Operation Rescue loyalists. I hear their hymns. I see their determination. I realize the Father is rejoicing with eternal pride over what they are doing, as well as other groups of like mind and soul.

Do not give up, I encourage them, though they will not hear my words, yet knowing that I must say what I say for myself, if no other. *Defy the law. Trash its precepts. Resist those who enforce it. It is not holy law, from the mind of God. It is debased and corrupt. Throw it off like dirty, ragged clothes.*

Someone stands.

A woman.

Looking about as though she has heard me.

I go up to her, puzzled briefly, and then it is clear, as I see her face, the pale skin, eyes blood-shot, the thin, frail frame. She should be at home or in a hospital, preparing for death, but she is not. She is possessed of a singular mission, and for a special reason, she cannot concentrate on herself while innocent ones die at the hands of an industry that is one of the most profitable in the United States.

"You have come for me?" she says, others around her thinking that she is indeed quite delirious.

"I had not intended to do so," I admit, "but that may well be the Father's will, and I am prepared."

"So am I," she adds. "This life is nothing to me anymore. It has been cheapened. It can be snuffed out with the twist of a doctor's hand on a tiny, tiny neck. We protest against infamy, and *we* are the ones who are imprisoned."

"There is no sense to that," I say. "But then, we must understand, the world is in the grip of evil."

"Evil? Yes, yes, I agree. Demons run to and fro, seeking the unsaved."

"I have seen it many, many times, dear sister."

"I prayed that . . . that . . ." she stutters.

"Yes?" I ask, "Tell me the best way you can."

Her eyes widen, her features brighten.

"I prayed, oh, how I *dreamed* in the course of those many nights when I could sleep without hearing *their* screams all around me, I prayed that the Lord would accord me a certain task in Heaven."

"What task is that?"

"To hold each infant that ascends, to hold them, and present them in love to Him, to my blessed Lord, to say that I did my best, that I was willing to die for them if that had to be so."

All attention in that crowd is fixed on her. Even the police stand motionless, quiet, listening to what she is saying. . . .

"And, later," she adds, "to watch them . . . grow. Is that the way it is? Is there growth in Heaven?"

"There is," I tell her. "They come as babies. They mature as adults. But then the process stops. They do not grow old. They do not start to—"

"Praise God, praise God, praise God!" she says, rejoicing, interrupting me, though I do not mind at all.

Someone pulls at her leg at last, asking her to sit down, but she does not. She continues to stand. In less than a minute, it will be over for her as a pain develops in her chest, the last pain she will ever know, and she topples over, but just before she does, she tells them in a voice of clarity, strength, "Don't give up. It is worth everything, what you are doing. God knows. God supports you. The angels attend our way!"

I hold her hand, then, not an old, withered hand, the hand dotted with age, but the hand of a new form, a new body, born from the old, and she steps out of that now exhausted human shell, and she looks up.

"Jesus, it's Jesus!" she exclaims. "And so many angels! What is that they all are holding? *So very tiny!*"

It takes only an instant for her to know, as she approaches the head of that line of angels, and the first one holds out a pure, healthy baby to her, and she takes the soft little form in her strong new hands.

A little infant boy looks up at her.

"He was going to be a scientist, wasn't he?" she says, not quite certain how this insight comes to her.

The angel nods.

"And would have found a vaccine for the disease his mother eventually died of," he says with irony.

"She and hundreds of others, I suspect," the woman muses over that striking likelihood.

"Hundreds of *thousands*, dear one," the same angel tells her, "truly a vast multitude."

On and on she goes, stopping at each angel, a triumphant choral accompaniment in the background, as she receives each baby, learning what it could have been, what it could have done.

Finally she is at the end, she stands before the One, before the ruddy form He is embracing to Himself.

His voice is commanding, as always it is.

"A president," He tells her in a voice of infinite tenderness. "This one would have been a president able to rally the country and stop the slaughter . . . a man people could accept and support."

There is a hint of pain in His voice, pain of the spirit, as He adds, "Good men, good women these here, who could have blessed My creations, could have eased their suffering, their hunger, could have eased the curse of Eden. . . ."

His voice trails away, as images coalesce, images in a holy mind knowing completely the beginning and the end, and all else, images of what could have been forcing even the Savior into silence.

She looks into His face, His loving face, and then down again at the baby's, now mirroring the same peace, the same all-encompassing love.

Just at that moment, a boy steps into view, stands at the side of his Master, this one older, strong-looking, smiling.

Jesus turns the baby He had been holding over to a nearby angel eager to please Him, and puts His hand on the boy's strong young shoulder.

"Your son," He says. "He has been waiting for you."

All these years!

This dear one can scarcely believe what is happening.

She had yearned for Heaven, prayed for the moment to come quickly, believed a vibrant and redeeming faith, but she had cast out of her mind any hope that her son, gone so long at the hand of a hired assassin—and there could be no other description for the one who pulled him from her—any hope indeed that her son would be standing without hate before her, reaching out his hand to take her own.

More angels come forward, gathering around. The woman feels nurtured by the finest love, the most complete love she has ever known.

"How can you all treat me in this manner?" she asks, wanting to cast the last fragments aside. "How can you love me the way you are loving me? How can my son look up at me with such warmth, such joy? Will he never stand before me and ask, 'Dearest, dearest Mother, why did you allow this? Why did you deny me what I could have been?' How can You forgive what I did? How can this my flesh, my blood do the same?"

I see what she does not, a constant flood of unfallen angels, streaming up from earth to Heaven, each carrying, with exquisite tenderness, the soul of an aborted baby . . . the multitude around us, already so massive, being swelled by the new arrivals, their faces initially fearful, remembering the suffering but this turning to relief and a quiet trust, trust that no longer will be violated. . . .

"These are the ones you tried to save," the gathered multitude says in a single, glorious voice. "They are more your children than the children of the mothers who consented to their doom."

She looks at Jesus, her eyes searching His face.

He nods.

"It is true," He tells her. "They are the ones you gave your own life for . . . but they are not alone. Because you have been dedicated to this cause for a very long time, there are many more who wish to express their love."

An even larger group now can be seen coming from every distant part of Heaven, some still quite young and needing to be carried by angels . . . some of an age that they can walk on their own, many haltingly, not quite accustomed to the use of their legs . . . but others with full strength, approaching her proudly, and she can hear faintly, then louder, so much louder that it would seem a sudden thunderclap on earth, she can hear just a few words, but enough, she can hear, "Bless you for caring, bless you for trying to stop those who took life from us."

"Those many moments when you stood and protested their murder, *that* was when you earned their devotion for eternity," Jesus says. "They could not tell you so before. There was no time, and, helpless, they had no voice. But it is now different, sweet servant, it is now that they stand before you, as do I, and give you this place to belong, and us as your companions time without end."

Yet still this woman hesitates, clinging even now to the last remnants of her oppressing guilt, for it can be said that no other kind of guilt in all of humanity is quite so deep as what she has suffered. I know that is true. I have seen it often, whether in those who are escorted to Heaven by me or others of my kind, souls hungering for release from what Satan has managed to manipulate throughout their imperfect lives, or, else, those dragged to Hell by demonkind, where that guilt becomes the chief foundation for their torment, aching, tearing, unholy torment that never, never ends.

"I *want* to let go," she says to the continually swelling multitude, which is now millions strong. "I want to leave *everything* back there with my dead, cold flesh. But how can it be for me that I am *ever* forgiven so devilish a decision as to destroy my own helpless, dependent baby's life, my very flesh, my very blood? *For, truly, and how it has torn at me, truly I am one of those mothers your angels have just condemned!"*

Jesus the Christ smiles then, as do the rest of those ringed in a giant circle around her. He has no sorrow on His face, nor do they, nor is there a hint of lingering anger, nothing but pure love, as He holds out His hands to her, pierced palms upward, giving this redeemed soul the only answer that could ever matter.

$\mathcal{M}$ERCY-KILLING ALSO has been given a familiar "turn" by the media, just as abortion had been before
Roe vs. Wade.

Television docudramas with "sensitive" depictions.
Well-planted news stories. Very emotional case histories.

A typical campaign by the hidden forces of darkness.

To me, though, they are not hidden at all. I see them as
I enter hospitals, hovering as they are before the dying,
eager to grab the souls of those who are going to be lost
for eternity.

Mercy-killing. . . .

That travesty is going on a few rooms down the
corridor.

Her name is Norita.

She is in a coma. She has been in a coma for weeks.

Doctors have conferred. They now advise her husband
to stop the life-support system.

"There is no hope," he is told. "Your wife is being
sustained artificially. Her body itself is incapable of
taking over. She will never pull out of the coma. We feel
quite certain about that."

Shawn, the husband, does not decide immediately. He
ponders the responsibility.

If I wait, how can I ever be certain when my beloved will regain consciousness from the darkness?

If I don't wait, how will I ever know—?

He could not finish the thought. He was lost in memories of what their relationship once had been like. *Norita. . . .*

He would never hold her again, he would never touch her lips with his own, he would never watch her smile as a sunset was reflected off her white, pure skin, he would never hear her voice whispering into his ear, "I love you, Shawn, I love you so much."

He owes her something. He owes her as little pain as possible. The doctors say that they couldn't be sure about the so-called "pain factor." Is she in oblivion? Is there nothing but nothing?

Or is his beloved actually being tormented by agony while seeming to be free of it?

*If there is the slightest chance—*he starts to tell himself.

He knows he has to eliminate that possibility by eliminating the woman who means so very much to him.

How can I say that? How can I conjure up even the remotest chance?

So quickly their lives had changed. Less than a year after their beautiful island honeymoon. The other driver was not even hurt. Alcohol. The courts let him off with a stiff sentence and a large fine, but that was all. Norita never even knew what hit her.

I prayed and prayed. I begged God to touch your body and heal it. I wrote letters to men on TV and my envelopes were included in piles over which they prayed. Nothing worked. And now the doctors say she'll never wake up. . . .

To see Norita so pale, to see the tubes in her nose and down her throat, to see the chest moving up, falling back, then up, then back, kept going only by ingenious devices that had nothing to do with life but generated a grotesque caricature of it, like those people who had their pets stuffed and then placed on mantels or tables or elsewhere, often holding them in their laps and patting them as though nothing had happened, the only difference being that the stuffed remnant in each case didn't have an air hose stuck through its mouth so that the sides could be pushed out, then drop back, then out, furthering the illusion.

It cannot go on, he decides. *It has to stop.* He has to ignore a thin little wisp of a voice that seemed to be saying, *Wait. Please wait. Don't anticipate the actions of a Holy God. You must wait.*

He buries those words under the immediacy of the moment.

Hours later, Shawn stands again by Norita's side. He has told the doctor that he wants to be there, by her side, when the machines are unplugged.

But he cannot stay. The tubes are being taken away. He feels a great, drowning surge of sorrow. He has to leave before he changes his mind, before he tells them, *No, no, it's wrong. Put everything back. Please, I don't want to—*

Shawn turns, pauses for a moment in the doorway to her room.

"Shawn . . . I don't want to . . . die . . ."

He assumes he has imagined those whispered words, that they had crept to the surface of his mind from a corner of wishful thinking, idle fantasies.

He turns, in any event, and sees Norita's eyes closing, those attending her frantically trying to reconnect the life-support system. A single tear slides down her left cheek, and she is gone.

They have to sedate him to stop the screams.

Can there be any question why my kind hungers after the new Heaven and the new earth? Though we be as insubstantial as mist, we think, and we feel, and we listen to the screams of a man who has realized what he has done to his beloved, we listen, oh, that we do, my comrades and I, and we shiver from the impact. We almost give up. We beg Almighty God to keep us in His Kingdom, to give us the peace, the joy with which He has graced redeemed human beings for thousands of years.

That must not be, we know.

For if He were to grant us what we craved, He would deny countless numbers of men, women, and children that which we can give them from time to time. For if we were to be allowed only Heaven, then God Himself, to be consistent—and He is never less than that—would have to abandon the world for all time, and in that case, He, like us, then would be insulated from the pain, for it is that insulation which we oft crave and cannot be granted for the sake of humankind.

*S*OMETIMES UNFALLEN ANGELS can take human form.

Satan was jealous even of this, knowing that neither he nor his demons had a similar power, so he started the practice of possession, taking over an *existing* man, woman, or child.

I myself have been in human form, but not all angels are allowed to do this—only those on special missions.

I remember a midwestern family with a devoted relationship to a little poodle named Gigi. Eight-year-old Chad especially loved Gigi. He had some emotional disorders and would often withdraw, seeming to lose touch with the world around him. But he was different when he was with Gigi. A special rapport existed between them from the beginning. The two were, in a real sense, in communion constantly.

Then the dog contracted cirrhosis of the liver, which led to a liver shunt condition causing waste products to be diverted into the bloodstream.

A painful two-year battle for Gigi's survival began.

The last night of Gigi's life, Chad was holding her in his arms, rocking her back and forth. They had all been taking turns with her throughout the night . . . first, the father, then the mother, then Chad's two sisters.

For the past two years, Chad had been slipping back more and more frequently into his internalized world. As Gigi's life faded, so it seemed to be with Chad.

But that night, Chad was drawn back into reality. He asked if he could be the next one to hold his friend.

"She'll know it's me," he told his parents. "She'll be calmer. Oh, please, she needs me now."

When his mother or his father had been holding Gigi, she would go through periods of intense, sudden jerking motions as though spasms of pain were tearing through her. Then she would seem to relax a bit, but later, another awful moment of abrupt movement—yet there were no sounds except a vague little whimpering.

Chad had overheard them talking about putting Gigi to sleep.

"No!" he begged. "You can't do that. I . . . I prayed that God would take her home to Him. Let Him do that. I want her to follow Him into Heaven when she's in my arms."

They looked at one another, and said nothing further. They were skeptical of the idea that animals had an afterlife. And they didn't want to fill their son with false ideas. Yet his expression then, tears in his eyes, conveyed such desperation that they felt they could not destroy that hope of his, and they decided to let Chad hold his beloved Gigi for the next shift between them.

It was a warm summer night, and Chad took her outside.

They had played a lot together in that same yard. Briefly Gigi opened her eyes, and looked at him. There was no pain in them, just simple trust, for it was enough that he held her, thus enabling her to ignore the torment being experienced by her tiny, frail body.

I took on a form then, for only a few minutes, my

appearance that of an old, old man, and I entered the yard, and stood there looking at the boy, gently holding his dog.

Chad's eyes widened.

"Are you—?" he started to ask.

"God?"

Chad nodded.

"No," I smiled. "Just someone who cares about you very much."

"Me?"

"Yes, Chad, and your pal there, Gigi."

"Have you come to take her from me?"

"I have, son, I have."

"But I don't want her to go yet. I love her so very much."

"You had some wonderful times together, didn't you?"

Chad smiled broadly then.

"You know?"

"Yes, Chad, I was there."

"When she warned me about the snake?"

"I was there."

And he talked about other times, times when Gigi helped, if only by being with him, resting her head on his lap, and trying to reassure him by her presence that he was loved, truly, truly loved.

"And now I won't have her anymore," he said.

"She'll be safely in God's hands."

"You mean—?"

I looked at him through my human form.

"You're smiling?" Chad said.

"I am, yes, I am."

"But why?"

"It's time."

"*No!*"

He held Gigi close to him but as he did so, she groaned.

"Pain," I said. "She's tired of the pain."

He heard little sounds escape from her emaciated body.

"Goodbye . . ." he whispered.

For an instant, Gigi's eyes were open again just as he had spoken.

"She's looking at me," Chad cried. "She—"

"Not at you, Chad. She's looking beyond you."

Just then, Gigi let out a gasp. Her body grew limp.

Chad bowed his head, unable to hold back the sobs.

"Is she—?" he asked.

He looked up when I did not answer.

"Sir?" he said. "Sir, where are you?"

As Chad stood, a puzzled frown on his forehead, with the lifeless apricot-colored form in his arms, and went back inside, we waited and watched for a moment, Gigi and I, spirit both of us, and then her Master called her home.

Being involved in such moments does truly keep me going. Being with human beings governed by love is so beautiful. Being with animals for which love is all that matters makes me yearn even more for the old days of Eden when it was always so.

Cruelty is another story. I cannot abide it. Animals seem incapable of indulging in cruelty.

But not humankind, truly not them. . . .

$\mathcal{D}$IETRICH BURHANS.

His death was a shock to the community of Wheaton, Illinois, where he had lived and worked for several decades as a financial analyst.

He died at home, with his large family gathered around his bed.

He spoke just two words before his ravaged body twitched a couple of times and then was still.

"The Jews! The Jews!"

At the time no one knew what he meant. And in the wave of sorrow that followed his death, Dietrich Burhans's final "statement" was overlooked.

Even though an atheist, he had maintained good relationships among the evangelical community that dominated Wheaton, the "Protestant Vatican," many thinking they would be the Lord's instrument in bringing him to a redemptive faith, others as much concerned with his favorable impact upon their financial health as anything else.

He never did change. He died an atheist. Yet Wheaton was at a standstill until the day of his funeral. His impact upon the community was felt among too many families for him to be ignored.

The minister delivered an impassioned eulogy as he spoke of Burhans' humanitarianism, expressed through outreaches he funded to reach a variety of worthy recipients around the world: starving children, AIDS researchers, many more.

His three daughters and two sons each gave their own brief remarks, speaking of a devoted and generous father. They all would find that their financial concerns would be nonexistent for the rest of their own lives. His widow, who met Burhans not long after he came to the United States from his native Germany, caused tears to flow more freely than any of the other speakers when she told the assemblage how very much her husband meant to her.

I thought of everything I knew about this man, based upon many years of being near him, of seeing what he was like, of wishing he would come to Christ, and knowing how many, many times he had rejected the Savior.

You fool! I would shout with words he never heard. *You have a good life. You think that this is enough. You are certain you will never have to pay an eternal price for your stubborn rejection.*

I liked Dietrich Burhans, despite his atheism.

I liked this man with such a kind heart that it seemed to *compel* him to do whatever he could that was benevolent. He died wealthy, with a mansion as a home and seven family cars, but far less so than would have been the case if he had proved significantly more selfish with his money.

I had met far too many Christians who hoarded their money, who forgot that it was only being loaned to them, and that they had no right to hold onto it with a kind of zeal that would have better served the cause of Christ if it had been directed toward the Great Commission as opposed to their individual bank accounts.

Not Dietrich.

I had gotten to know him well enough as a young man, and traveled with him as he made his way to the United States. I did not stay with him permanently, for I had others to minister to but he seemed especially in need of help, a man fleeing his own country's horrors and trying to construct a new world for himself. But, he appeared, after a fashion, to be remarkably self-sufficient, and yet so stubborn in matters spiritual. I remember one time in particular, when he came very close to death after a car accident.

He sensed my presence without knowing what or where I was.

I could see him consciously pushing that awareness away, denying its existence.

"But how can you do this again and again?" I asked, hoping that *something* would get through to the man.

"There is *nothing* that I hear now. It is a voice in my mind, some silly fragment from the past."

"It is not, Dietrich, it is not that at all. You *know* that I am standing right next to you."

As he lay in that hospital bed, he brought his hands to his ears, trying to shut out my voice.

"You pretend that I am nothing because your belief system has no place for me, for my kind. If you admitted that I existed, then you would have to stop denying so much of what you really believe."

He spoke softly then, almost a whisper.

"There are so many things I do not want to face."

Dietrich's eyes widened. I could see tears slipping from them onto the pillow beneath his head.

His mouth opened and closed, and he seemed to be saying something but what it was could not be heard.

Abruptly another angel appeared in the hospital room. Observer.

I was on Dietrich's right side, and Observer was on his left.

"You cannot have this man," I said.

"My master has already prepared a place for him," my former comrade-in-Heaven replied.

"It matters not. God can overturn Satan's machinations in an instant."

"Not with this one."

I knew he was wrong, of course. God could snatch Dietrich from the arch deceiver at any time—but Dietrich needed to change from his atheism to acceptance of the Savior, whose very existence he had been denying.

He would not. But I did not know that to be the case when I was contending with Observer. Only God had the ability to tell the future.

So I continued what would prove to be fruitless while Observer tried to come back in rebuttal.

Finally, defeated on the theological level, he simply looked at me, quite sadly in fact, and said, "You do not know everything, Stedfast."

He was gone then, the faint sound of dancing flames accompanying him.

The eulogy had ended. The minister was about to step from the podium.

"No!" an elderly man, thin, pale, screamed from where he had been sitting in a pew at the back of the church.

He stood, holding up his right wrist.

I could see numbers tattooed on it.

This old one was in the aisle now, walking toward the open coffin in the front of the church.

"How can you *do* this?" he asked as he passed row after row of astonished gazes. "How can you pay homage to that—?"

He finally reached the mahogany coffin, and before anyone could restrain him, he managed, despite his frail appearance, to kick out from under it the stand on which it had been resting.

The coffin crashed over onto the floor, and the body of Dietrich Burhans toppled out, which sent screams of shock through the gathered mourners.

"Remember Maidanek?" the old man shouted at the lifeless body. "Remember the 1.5 million who died there? Remember the coarse sound of your laughter as you watched them drop, often at your very feet?"

He spat on the body, and then strode with uncommon vigor from the sanctuary.

I liked this man with such a kind heart that it seemed to compel him to do whatever he could that was benevolent.

I leave the mourners a short while later, having found reaffirmed another truth among many through the centuries of my existence.

Angels do not know everything. . . .

$\mathcal{K}$ARL LEEMHUIS WAS a Dutch billionaire who had become fed up with what was happening in his native country, epitomized by the influx of drug peddlers and sex merchants turning such a beautiful urban area as Amsterdam into a place of filth, filth of one sort or another, with drug deals in the square in the center of that city, with prostitutes in picture windows along the polluted canals, and, in general, a sense of absolute moral and spiritual decadence that had caused many travelers to change their plans and spend far less time there than originally anticipated.

So Karl moved to the United States, and built an isolated estate in the mountains of Colorado. He hired locals to make up his household staff and bought everything he needed—food, clothes, furniture—entirely from the local merchants. By himself, even with such immense wealth at his disposal, he couldn't have been responsible for turning around the depressed economy. But the very fact that he had given the location such a vote of confidence drew in other individuals, along with the companies over which they had charge. He became a hero to the people of that town.

Five years later, his doctors delivered the news he had
secretly suspected for some time.

"I have five billion dollars," he told a very special
friend, "but I cannot buy a cure for this cancer. I can fund
a dozen hospitals but I have no power to turn back—"

Interrupting himself, he stood and walked over to the
large window in his office on the second floor of his vast
house, twenty thousand square feet of glass and timber
and concrete set in the midst of fifty acres of alpine
meadows and fir trees. For a few moments he gazed
silently at the beauty of his mountain estate.

"From the beginning, I liked this spot because of the
elevation," he said. "I can see for miles in every direction."

He chuckled as he added, "I didn't think, when I moved
here, that I would be able to see the end of my life so
soon, and just as clearly."

Then he confided in his friend what he intended to do.
He did this because it seemed natural to tell her, for he
trusted this woman more than he trusted himself. She
listened to his plans, every word of what he was saying,
loving him even more for the mixture of compassion and
wisdom that he was showing.

When Karl had finished, she sat without speaking for
several minutes, then started weeping.

"They will hate you," she said honestly.

"Oh, at first, yes, I agree," he replied. "But the alternative is that if I don't act while I still can, they will end
up hating each other. Can you imagine the squabbling,
dear, dear Colette?"

That she could, indeed she could.

Karl had five children. None of them was pleased that
he moved to the United States. It seemed that he was
deserting them as well as his country. But, finally, they
each followed him to America, however reluctantly.
When he told them, five years later, that he had fallen in

love, they found that somehow as difficult to accept as the move from one country to another.

"I tried to make them understand that when their mother died, my life changed," he went on. "But they never did. They're children of wealth, Colette. They have always had full bellies and dressed in the most expensive clothes. I've never denied them anything, I'm afraid."

Years of regret danced across his face on leaden feet of despair.

"They couldn't even exist on their own," Karl said with a husky voice. "Whether they would admit it to themselves or not, they *had* to go where Papa was, where the money would be banked. Each one is drawing a salary from my corporation but none is working, not really, none, that is, except—"

"Rebekkah?" Colette finished for him. "It *is* Rebekkah, isn't it?"

Karl nodded.

"You are perceptive, as always, dear," he told her. "The rest . . . ah, they're all betting that you and I are sleeping together, you know."

She blushed at that remark.

"I know how you feel," he said. "But—"

"You're a Christian, and you cannot have sex with me unless we're married," she mimicked amusedly. Then her expression changed to one of concern. "But surely, now that you're—"

"Dying? You think that would make a difference?"

She was blushing a deeper red this time.

"You think God would understand?" he said. "You think He would give us this final pleasure before I go? I agree. He would want the two of us to be happy."

She shot to her feet.

"Oh, Karl!" she said joyously. "I *know* God wants nothing else for us."

She started to embrace him, but he held her at arm's length very briefly.

"That is why," he told her slowly, passionately, "I am now asking you to be my wife, Colette. Would you consent to marry a dying old man?"

Colette and Karl were married a few days later. The wedding was not an elaborate one; there had been little time for preparation. Karl was wise—if they had waited any longer, the children surely would have mounted frantic opposition to it. But now they had no maneuvering room whatsoever; they could only sit back in cold, bitter acquiescence.

After their father and new stepmother went on their honeymoon, they fumed among themselves, calling Colette a tramp, this bright, beautiful, middle-aged woman who married someone twenty years older than she, someone who was obviously in bad health. It could scarcely have been for reasons of sexual fulfillment, they surmised.

"She's after only one thing," commented Erika Leemhuis. "And once she gets hold of *our* money, we'll have to come crawling to *her* for every penny. She doesn't have hands, she's got claws, and once they dig in, they'll stay there, sure enough. You can bet she won't be pried loose from *anything* that has our family name on it!"

"Father must have a few remaining fantasies, whether he can ever realize them or not," remarked Hans. "He might well just want to prove to himself that he still can attract a beautiful woman—"

"What's he going to do with her?" interrupted Anna, another of the Leemhuis offspring.

They all broke out laughing.

All except Rebekkah, though her brother Peter had since joined in with the others. She felt uncomfortable with this ridicule even if she had initially resisted the idea of a father she knew was dying suddenly getting married.

"But what if they're happy, *really* happy?" she said finally as they all sat in the large dining room of that massive house.

The others turned to her, almost in unison.

"Of course *she's* happy," Erika pointed out. "What would you *expect*? After all, she'll soon be included among the beneficiaries of our father's fortune. A hundred-million-dollar pot is sure to make *anybody* happy! I tell you this: Colette won't let go of our father. Once she's got hold of him, she won't let go."

Grumbling, they pushed back from the table and left the room. Rebekkah remained seated for a few moments, lightly caressing the polished wood of the huge table where she had joined her father for many, many meals.

Then she stood and walked into the hallway. Everybody was heading outside.

Hans turned around, asked, "Are you coming, Rebekkah? We're heading into town for the music festival."

She smiled, thanked him, declined the offer, then walked upstairs to her bedroom, and sat down in a large leather chair, holding an envelope her father had given her a couple of days earlier. He had wanted her to read it sometime in the future, maybe years hence, because specific instructions were written on the front: "To be opened only after I have died."

"Please forgive me, dearest father," she said out loud, as she could no longer restrain herself.

She gasped as she read the contents:

I am writing this to you because you are the only one of my children with whom I can feel any rapport at all, dear Rebekkah.

The others have taken my worst tendencies and magnified these while discarding all of the good ones, anything that could be called right and proper, yes, I must say, that which is Christ-honoring.

They want only that which is material—more money, more cars, more diamonds and clothes and real estate holdings and trips abroad, and they want this from the labors of another, and not their own. "What is the point of having a rich father if we have to work for a living?" they ask.

They do not know that they can get along perfectly well on a great deal less. They do not know that money spent to help others brings with it the most profound blessings of all.

But they will find out, my dear Rebekkah, and they will find out quite soon. I have provided enough money in my will so that they will not starve, of course, but nothing beyond that. They will have to earn anything else with their own labors. They will have to continue my business dealings in a profitable manner for them to be able to continue anywhere near their accustomed standard of living. Yet, dear daughter, once they do, they will learn, in the process, not to throw away money as they have been doing. They will learn that the finest sports car means little if there is no peace deep down in their souls. I know, Rebekkah, that they do not have that peace now because their joy, as transitory as it is, is based upon their possessions, and their insecurity arises from the nagging fear that they might somehow have to give up that which has been the very foundation of their existence.

As for you, fair child, I am secretly leaving you more than I have your siblings. Because I know your heart, and I know what you will do with it. All the rest of my fortune will be put in a foundation, a foundation to fund the spread of the gospel of Jesus Christ throughout the world. I want you to head that foundation, because I want it to be run by someone for whom the salvation of otherwise lost souls will be a magnificent compulsion.

As for Colette, she is to receive no more than the others. This is, by the way, at her request, for she knows well enough what they think of her.

Goodbye, dearest child.

Your father

P.S. I want to encourage you to study more about angels. I have sensed one by my side.

Rebekkah pressed the pages to her chest and wept.

As soon as the tears stopped, she knew what she would do. She would go to where her father and his new wife were honeymooning, she would go there, indeed she would, and beg them both to forgive her for acting just like the others, and then she would return, keeping the secret as though it was something holy.

I went with Rebekkah, though, naturally, she was not at all aware of this. I went with her to that cabin beside a clear and beautiful lake where her father and her new stepmother had spent hours sitting happily on the shore, watching the fish swim in water so clear that their multicolored bodies could be seen without squinting, listening to birds calling, and—

The air.

Yes, just inhaling it into their lungs, its sweet purity radiating throughout their frail, tired bodies.

I know. I was there with them earlier, before I went back to their house, before I sat with Rebekkah as she read her father's letter.

Before—

That moment came as they were walking inside.

"Colette?" he said. "Did you see that?"

She smiled.

"Yes, my dearest," she told him. "He's quite astonishing, isn't he?"

"So beautiful, dear, so—"

He stumbled then, fell into her arms, his body nearly lifeless, as his soul reached out to me.

Colette managed to sit down on the front porch of that little cabin, and wrap her arms around his chest, and rock him gently, singing softly in his ear.

"Thank you, dearest," he said with infinite tenderness, the last words of his life as I took him to his awaiting Father.

Colette sat there, still rocking him, even as he gasped—not from pain, she knew, no, not pain, but from what he saw, and what he heard, and the glory of it.

"Save a place for me, my beloved," she whispered as his body became limp, the life gone, but only from there.

They were still like that when Rebekkah arrived, Colette holding the lifeless body, her head pressed next to his, lips touching his cheek in one last kiss, her back resting against the closed front door.

None of the children knew that Colette had been dying, too. Not even Karl had known. She had had her reasons, very personal, very fine. She simply told no one, and since angels cannot read minds, I could not tell either. There was some speculation in days following that the shock of having Karl die like that, as she held him, was perhaps the final link in a chain, compounding her heart problems.

Rebekkah stood there and waited while paramedics tried to pry them apart. Colette had been firm in her hold, as though afraid to relinquish his body.

The words came hauntingly back to Rebekkah from

that awful meeting with her brothers and sisters, words that made her shed tears in front of strangers.

Colette won't let go of our father. Once she's got hold of him, she won't let go. . . .

She didn't.

I HAVE BEEN present at innumerable funerals. I have heard the eulogies, seen the tears of mourning, appeared in human form to give a word of consolation to those for whom grief threatens its own kind of death.

True grief or remorse can reshape even the cruelest of human temperaments.

I think of Heinrich Himmler, who was one of the worst human monsters in history; he lived that way more than a decade—but it is quite possible that he did not die the same man who was one of the principal architects of the Final Solution.

No man, woman, child, or angel can mourn the passing of one such as this. Every Jew can breath a sigh of relief, except those—perhaps the majority—who would have preferred that he had been captured, put on trial at Nuremburg, and then hanged.

That was not to be the case. Most of the top Nazis—Hitler, Himmler, Goering, Goebbels—committed suicide. All but Himmler did so to avoid the ultimate defeat: being executed by their enemies.

Yet that is why the world believes Himmler took cyanide.

But I know otherwise. I was with this man when he

died. He poisoned himself out of guilt, guilt that crushed him from the first and only time he visited one of the concentration camps that were his brainchild.

"I sentenced millions to death," he said, his voice getting weaker and weaker. "I saw the bodies of thousands littering more than one battlefield. But it was not until Auschwitz that the *reality* of an intellectual *principle*—"

He was nearly gone, and began to ramble.

"Those pathetic bodies, skeletons covered by flesh . . . they should have been dead, skeletons do not live . . . but these did . . . they were moving, they were breathing, their mouths opened, closed, opened, closed . . . and they looked at me, some with anger, some with resignation, others with pity . . . they were pitying *me* . . . I approached one, and he reached out a hand . . . my guard raised his rifle butt . . . I waved him back . . . that bony hand, the veins pronounced, the skin touched with jaundiced yellow, touched my chest."

I remembered. The man had whispered. "I go from this hell to the Lord's Heaven, I escape it, but not you, Herr Himmler, not your kind. There will be no escape from the Hell that awaits *you!*"

He knew fear then, along with the pity that he felt for this abandoned human being.

Abandoned. . . .

He shivered, for an instant, hoping that no one saw this. The same guard roughly brushed the prisoner aside, and Himmler came very close to reprimanding him for doing so.

That night, he had the first of many foul and terrifying dreams. He saw the man who had spoken to him die. He saw the frail, ravaged body thrown into a ditch. He saw lime poured over that body and a hundred others.

And he woke up screaming.

"I had not been to one of the camps before that

day . . . I used a pen to seal the doom of six million men, women, and children—but this was a *simple* act, you know, ink flowing from my pen onto the appropriate sheet of paper. Even the dead on the battlefields of that war could not have prepared me for Auschwitz. There is a vast gulf between a soldier valiantly giving up his life and an old, tired Jew, barely alive, but alive just the same, *being shoved into an oven!*"

It is interesting, though few men have made the connection, that Heinrich Himmler henceforth was known to have favored the dismantling of the death camps.

"If we win this war, we want to win the world along with it," he had said. "If we lose this war, we do not want the world to view us as barbarians."

He was blind to the fact that the world knew *everything* by then, that Himmler and the other creatures with him would never, under any circumstance, be viewed with other than the rawest loathing.

And so he pushed ahead with the possibility of razing the camps. But the change in Heinrich Himmler did not stop with that. He befriended countless numbers of Jews, sending them secretly into Switzerland, or redirecting them to camps where there were no ovens or gas chambers—though this hardly protected them from the cruelty of the guards themselves.

It was the children, I think, children who looked like their own little dolls but with the stuffing sucked out of them, so pale, so afraid, so ill.

The children were being shoveled into the ovens, two or three bodies per enclosure—more if tiny babies were involved, a practice to which Himmler put an immediate stop at Auschwitz and other camps.

The cries of boys and girls dying in the awful heat!!!

He bolted up straight from where he lay, his eyes bloodshot, the poison throughout his system.

"Oh God!" he cried. "You could never forgive me!"

Yes, I tell him. Yes, you can be forgiven. You were once a devout Catholic. Take your words beyond words and let them reflect the yearnings of your very soul.

"Oh, please," he begged, tears streaming. "Please help me."

Then take the hand of the Savior who is reaching out for you now. . . .

Himmler started to do so, reaching up physically as well as spiritually, to grasp the hand of this Messiah, this *Jewish* Messiah.

He fell back on his deathbed, the years of anti-Semitism making him withdraw at the last instant, a sob escaping him, encrusted Nazi dogma pulling him down to a furnace unlike any in Auschwitz.

True grief or remorse can reshape even the cruelest of human temperaments. . . .

I cannot say that "reshape" is the most accurate designation for a Heinrich Himmler. But I also cannot deny that even he was capable of something approaching kindness, if only as an effort to drown those cries of anguish at night.

In the end, this was not enough for Heinrich Himmler. The thought of reaching out to a Man who was incarnated two thousand years before as an itinerant Jew, a hated Jew, was impossible for him to accept, and he threw away salvation because of this.

Coming close is not enough. . . .

*T*HERE IS SOMETHING else about grief. It confuses matters. It screams out the word "tragedy" and applies this to the deceased when it is better used to describe the survivors.

In a Christian context, grief is not for the dead husband or wife or mother or father or daughter or son. Grief is the realization that those left behind are now going to have to get used to living life without someone very important still around, someone who has meant a great deal to them.

That really is the essence of grief. As such, grief is a bit dishonest, a kind of charade, if the dead person is a Christian and as soon as death has claimed him or her, their soul is ushered by my kind into eternity. Grief wails and moans about the tragedy of someone so young dying, while so much of their life remained unlived.

Why is it a tragedy for *them* if they live again, instead, by the Father's side, in the company of angels, and walk streets of gold?

If they have died, that is, in their mortal bodies, if they have died through a long illness, an illness that caused continual pain, that took life from them with slow agony, and then, brain dead, heart no longer beating, lungs stopped, they are transformed into a body very much like an angel's, and now have entered Heaven where such will never afflict them again—*where is the tragedy?*

If death comes through a murder, if life is torn from them by another human being for anger or money or whatever the insane reason might be, or even accidental death as in an automobile accident—then the tragedy is still not for the one who is dead, if dead can ever be the right word for somebody who has accepted Jesus Christ as Savior and Lord. The tragedy is for humanity itself, for what this shows as to the depths of the perversity of "mere" carelessness of human nature. And, yes, as accurately as before, perhaps more so for those left behind, for the wife and mother whose husband has been taken from her and who now must raise a family quite, quite alone, for the husband whose beloved marital partner has been raped and murdered, and who is thrust into the dual role of father-and-mother to their three children—yes, again, this is where the essence of the tragedy is found. But not, no, not for the victim who is beyond fear of what the night holds on the terror-stricken streets of cities and towns, around the world.

Here, however, is the true tragedy, the tragedy that transcends all others. . . .

If the victim is not a Christian, if they have rejected Christ as Savior and Lord, and death whisks them away instead to damnation, their opportunity for salvation gone forever—*this is the tragedy!*

Picture a young, intelligent, attractive woman with a future in her profession, always busy, always planning the next "campaign" for a promotion. For this individual, for this woman, accepting Christ as Savior and Lord is a decision akin to that of an oft-delayed mammogram, something she knows she must *do* someday—yet not now, for she is far too busy, but later, for sure later. And then, later, the good intentions blow up in her face in a dark alley, her clothes shredded, her body violated, her soul leaving its dead, cold mass, surrounded by demons as she is dragged, screaming, into the abyss of flames.

But then she is hardly alone. Others, men and women both, who tend to put off, put off, put off everything ranging from raising a family to tests for cancer to a personal relationship with the Savior face the possibility—and the longer it goes on, face the *probability*—that they will never do what *must* be done if they are to survive pain in this life and in the life just beyond.

This is where grief, for this woman, for that man, for them and a thousand, a million, a hundred million others, for those left on this planet who find such souls torn *forever* from their presence, this is where talk of true tragedy is right on the mark. For the only way there can be a reunion with loved ones is if they, too, are damned. Yet, in one of the ghastly ironies that have followed the sin of Adam and Eve, it is a truth, a pathetic but unchangeable truth, that in the punishment of Hell, love dies, has no place—love goes up in smoke, you might say.

GRIEF IS CAPABLE of doing something else for which it is seldom given credit. It takes hold of memories and transforms them.

Dying can take a very long time. I know this all too well. I have been with thousands of dying men, women, and children over the centuries. I have personally guided many, many of these into Heaven as they take off that which is corruptible and put on that which is incorruptible, immortal.

Some of the people with whom I have grown close during the final days or weeks of their lives have seen their senses sharpened as they come closer and closer to the end. I remember one old woman named Dottie.

"I never knew the air could be so clear," she said that final day as she sat on the front porch of the home she had occupied for half a century.

"It is the same as before," I told her. "It hasn't changed."

"But I have, haven't I?" she said, understanding.

"It happens, Dottie."

"I would think that coming so close to death would cloud my mind, put me in some kind of befuddled fog."

"It is that way often. But that occurs mostly with those in great pain."

"The Lord gives them His own kind of sedative."

"You could say that, Dottie."

She sighed, and smiled.

"I see you sometimes," she told me. "I see you all shimmering and iridescent, lit up with a hundred colors."

"And then—?" I probed.

"Other times I don't see you at all."

"The life force ebbs and flows. One minute you are a bit closer to death, another a bit further away."

"Like a river?"

"Somewhat, dear Dottie."

"You call me dear. Surely all of us blend together at some point in your memory, indistinguishable from one another. You couldn't possibly remember *everyone* you have been with."

This time I was indeed visible. She could see a smile on my glowing face.

"I do," I replied. "We are children of God, Dottie. We are extensions of Him. We remember just as He remembers."

"If there are a hundred million people over the years, a hundred million *identities* that you have comforted, you can recall *all* of them?"

"All hundred million."

She stopped rocking.

"What an amazing thought," she said softly.

She turned and looked at me, studying me carefully.

"How many like you are there?" she asked.

"How many grains of sand are on a beach, Dottie?"

She gasped then.

"So vast a multitude!" she exclaimed. "And you know each one of them, too?"

"I do."

"What about the third that rebelled and were cast out, along with Satan?"

"Them as well."

"What a mind you must have!"

"The same humankind was meant to possess."

"And sin in Eden shut off all that as well?"

"It did, Dottie, it did."

She rubbed her forehead.

"I hate forgetting," she said, "and I *do* forget so much."

"There is a purpose even to that."

She sat up straight, waiting for me to explain, eager to have this newest of revelations explained to her.

"What you remember is often filled with pain, Dottie. What you remember is carnal more often than not. When you shed your fleshly body, when your soul is freed for the journey ahead, you shed many of the memories as well, the sad ones, the sinful ones, gone in an instant."

"I won't remember *people?*"

"The best people, Dottie, the kind ones, the ones who have added much joy to your life."

"The ones who are in heaven ahead of me or will follow after me."

"*Those* people, Dottie, yes."

Her mind went back to her husband.

"It was quite awful with Harold," she said. "He became very ill, you know. He would wake up in the middle of the night, screaming, and thrashing about."

She was shivering.

"I feel so cold now," Dottie remarked. "Is it going to be warm in Heaven?"

"It will be," I told her, "truly the sweetest, the most total warmth you have ever known."

She started talking about Harold again.

"Just after he died, I looked back at our life together, and all that pain, all that suffering of those last few weeks were, can it be, almost forgotten as I concentrated on the good times, the moments when he had his appetite, and he could control himself in various ways, and . . . and—"

She brought her hand to her mouth.

"Harold was so very embarrassed," she said. "He had been so strong, able to do *everything* on his own, you know and, yet, now I had to change his diapers, I had to force spoons of food into his mouth, I had to sit by the hour, and hold his hand, and talk to him, or sing to him, hoping, oh, how I hoped that I could calm him down, that I could quiet that low, awful moaning that seemed to go on and on and on."

After wiping her eyes with a lace-edged handkerchief, she added, "But that's not how I usually think of Harold, you know. I see him water-skiing in his youth. I see him rocking our baby daughter to sleep or playing tennis with our son and so much else. The dying part of it almost never intrudes."

"Death will do that, Dottie. It will transform your memories."

"Just as Heaven transforms so many things, is that it?"

"A little like that, Dottie, just a little."

"How much longer?" she asked.

"Soon," I replied as gently as I could.

"Soon?" she repeated. "It's coming—?"

She fell back on her chair.

"I'm frightened all of a sudden," she said as she closed her eyes for a moment or two. "Please, help me."

"Dottie?"

"Yes?"

"Open your eyes, dear lady."

"Will it be soon?" she repeated.

"Oh, Dottie, it already *is!*"

She did as I asked, and saw, then, ten thousand like me standing before her. Their colors glistened under a radiance quite unlike anything cast by any sun in galaxy after galaxy.

"Harold?" she asked, her own face aglow.

The angels stepped aside.

Ahead she saw a white throne, and a Figure sitting on it, and kneeling in worship and adoration before that Figure was someone familiar yet transformed, who now stood and turned in her direction.

"Bless you, Stedfast," she said, "bless you, dear angel, for being by my side Down There."

"And here as well, sweet friend. We will never leave you."

"You call me friend," she said, a bit puzzled.

"I have known you for many decades," I told her, recalling in a kaleidoscopic surge moments that we had shared without her ever knowing this was so.

She could scarcely comprehend that.

"So long," she mumbled.

"Only the beginning," I smiled, "only the tiniest beginning."

Her new hand touched my ancient hand, for just an instant, but enough so that I knew how she felt, and she stepped forward, briefly hesitant, then more confident as she experienced, in that transcendent moment, what eternity was all about.

This is a good time, I decide, for me to visit True at Eden, which I do periodically, passing on from one assignment to another. It has been centuries since I was with him, and he must surely need some encouragement after so long. . . .

I AM AT the entrance to Eden, guarded as always by my comrade. True has remained there for thousands of years, alone much of the time except when ones of my kind have been able to pay our friend a visit, to talk with him, to tell him what has been going on in the world.

"There have been so many tragedies," I say, my mind swirling with the history that has elapsed since the last time.

"I can understand that," True replies. "I remember the awful darkness that fell upon this place just after Adam and Eve left in shame."

His radiance dims momentarily, a sign of intense sadness.

"Oh, what they gave up, Stedfast, what they gave up," he says, his sorrow almost palpable.

"And what they brought upon the world!" I remind him, though "remind" is scarcely the right word, for he could never have forgotten.

"How *can* the Father forgive them?" he asks. "How can even mercy itself be so merciful with such as those two? I have been told by others about Calvary, of course, I know all about it—but Stedfast, the sacrifice the Father underwent!"

True's presence shines with extraordinary brightness at the mention of Jesus.

"I love Him so very much," he says.

"As do I. That is why we serve Him with such loyalty," I reply. "Actually, I have talked with Him quite recently."

"You have? It has been so long for me."

"He admires you a great deal, True," I remark. "You have certain qualities far beyond what most of us possess."

"*They* liked Lucifer as well, Stedfast."

That was accurate, of course, which was why Lucifer had been the highest expression of the Trinity's desire to have beings such as us populate the Holy Kingdom.

"But there is a reason, True, a reason why *you* are so adored," I tell him. "Can you imagine what that is?"

"I do not know the answer. Please, please tell me."

"They *knew*, Father, Son, and Holy Spirit. They knew."

"Knew what? No riddles now, Stedfast."

"Knew that you were the *only* angel who could endure staying here until the end of time."

True looks at me, believing my words because no unfallen angel is capable of lying. He is astonished by what I have just told him.

"Out of so many, *I* was the only one?" he asks.

"That is my understanding."

The weariness that had attended him a moment ago seems somewhat dissipated now. I sense that he is looking at himself through a kind of mental mirror, and, in memory, at the multitude of angels to whom he had belonged before being called to duty at the entrance to Eden, trying to cope with the singular mission which he, above all others, had been assigned.

He turns toward the interior of the Garden.

"Smell the scents, Stedfast," he says, a curious note in his speech. "Are they not as strong as ever?"

I do what he has asked, and I lend my agreement to his words.

"The same," I tell him, "the same as before."

I shiver, gossamer strands of light coming from me.

"It has been thousands of years since I walked its path," I say, musing.

"Do you want to enter?" True asks.

I nod, embarrassed that I seem so obvious.

"Go, then, my kindred spirit," he urges me.

And that I do, not quite sure why the impulse gains my attention, nor why I succumb to it.

I step into Eden after millenniums away from it, this my first visit, which I am ashamed to admit to myself because of the sense of deserting my friend that it suggests.

It is not the same. It is far, far different from that which I left. It was once a place of lush life, the very sounds of life, the color of it, the scents.

No longer.

Dead.

Everything has died, at least that is what seems so upon first glance. The trees have become dead husks of what they once were.

"How can that be?" I ask out loud, puzzled, knowing what I detected before entry.

I hear True in back of me.

"Your memories of Eden are so powerful and you anticipated something so strongly that—" he says.

"—that I made it so, in images that no longer have any basis in reality," I finish the sentence for him. "There are no scents except of decay."

True cannot leave the entrance to Eden but his mind connects with mine, born as we were from the same Father's mind, retaining a measure of His consciousness in our very selves, as does Satan—which makes the tragedy of what he became all the more pathetic, since he is still "connected" to the Trinity, and yet still rejects everything that They are.

No glory left in Eden.

All is dust. The remnants of gray and brown and black where there once had been pink and blue and orange—a vast array of other colors signaling vibrant life.

So sad, Stedfast, so very sad.

I know that True has been there throughout the process of deterioration.

It was not all at once, was it, dear friend?

A pause.

No, Stedfast, it came gradually, through the centuries, as sin abounded more and more in the world. The greater the sin, the quicker the collapse of Eden.

Until the Flood.

That cleansed the world, for a time.

What happened then, True? Can you tell me?

Another pause.

I feel from True a wave of exaltation that is quickly overcome by despair.

Eden bloomed again. Dying animals revived. . . .

I am startled. True senses this.

Quite so, Stedfast. Not all died the instant Adam and Eve left. Eden was a haven for those that remained, animal and plant and bird and fish alike. They thrived . . . for a while.

But Eden became corrupted by the world around it!

The flood stemmed the process for a time, but a cleansed world saw men and women with their sin natures intact going back into it and beginning the infestation all over again, blind to the lessons of history.

Those that were left . . . oh, Stedfast . . . they died with agonizing slowness . . . enduring pain that puzzled them, unaccustomed as they had been to it . . . I saw them go before my eyes . . . I heard them as they came to me, and begged for mercy, begged for—

The funeral atmosphere in Eden seemed to grow stronger as images flooded my mind.

A bird . . . and another, and another, falling dead just like the one I had encountered directly after Adam and Eve lost Eden.

Lizards . . . they took a much longer time than did the birds, which tended to go all at once. The lizards became white-toned, vibrant green shades no longer apparent, their little eyes bloodshot, their sides collapsing, their tongues protruding.

The fish . . . yes, the fish! The clear streams of Eden became polluted because they were still connected to the outside world. The fish died more recently than other creatures since the problem of contamination accelerated only with the advent of the Industrial and, later, the Nuclear Age.

Suddenly I hear movement!

How could that be? Life no longer exists here.

Wrong, Stedfast, terribly wrong! Some small fragments of life have remained. But those clouds, those ghastly clouds—!

"From the oil fires set during the last war?" I ask out loud, forgetting myself.

"Yes, my comrade, yes, that is the cause," True replies out loud. "This monster succeeded in his attempt to devastate, to ravage at least part of the earth."

I turn and see him there, next to me.

"You have left the entrance!" I exclaim.

"I still guard Eden, Stedfast, even if I am a few feet from that usual spot."

His expression is gentle, concerned.

"Our Creator is loving, merciful, understanding," True adds. "He knows that you will truly need me by your side when the last living creatures of Eden come into view."

And come they did . . . a rodent, a single large bird, a

gorilla-like specimen, others, but not many, considering the vast numbers that once populated the Garden.

All are ill.

"Of the air," True says, "the poison comes invisibly. Of the water, burning their throats even as they need it so desperately. Of the soil, sending up twisted fruit that must be eaten even though it destroys them."

He walks forward, and they gather around him.

"At least they have not lost that!" he says. "At least that is something."

He refers to the sensitivity between such creatures and the angels.

"Even when the last dog contracted rabies," True tells me, "he went about snapping at others, grabbing a poor squirrel, attacking his own body—but he stopped as I came upon him. He sat before me, whimpering, the pain throughout his little form so great that the madness seemed almost a blessing since, at the last, he did not know what he was doing, could not have known when he bit at his own flesh in an uncomprehending outburst."

He looks at them, and I sense the sadness in his spirit. True must fight emotions, for all angels have emotions. . . . as Almighty God, as the only begotten Son, as the Comforter . . . as *they* also have emotions . . . these emotions every bit as traumatic to angels as any experienced by humankind.

Most profoundly, my dear friend feels pity for those in our presence who will not be alive another earthly season. All have existed since Eden was first created. All are thousands of years old, since this was to have been a place of eternal life, as much as in heaven. None have sins, animals being incapable of that, but all have been affected—*even in this place!*

"Think of the years!" True exclaims. "This must be one reason why I guard Eden, and do naught else."

"I would agree," I say in confirmation. "If sinful man

were to discover this spot, were to realize what these creatures represent, it would be a carnival overnight."

"I have heard the stories from others," True replies.

"A carnival," I add sadly. "The Protestants have water from the Jordan and the Catholics have water blessed by the pope, all sold at a premium. There have always been people who profited from simple faith sold for much money."

"It is amazing what a thousand years will do to an angel," True remarks. "When you were last here, you were not quite so cynical."

"Your task is to guard Eden," I remind my friend. "My own is to guard human beings. Here you have the remains of sinless perfection. Out there, just a few miles from where we stand at this very moment, a mad man, the latest of many in this region, is slaughtering anyone who opposes him, and the opposers' families along with him.

"I can stand *anywhere* in the world and feel the nearness of Satan's armada, True. I can feel them waiting, always waiting for an opportunity to grab another soul away from me, waiting for me to be less than diligent even for an instant, and then, without hesitating, they move in."

Screeching. . . .

"If I had blood, True," I continue, "it would freeze within me the moment I hear that screeching."

"Yes, yes," True nods, knowingly. "I have detected it, too. They would like to get into Eden, dismember every portion of it, hold up the pieces in front of us, and announce that they will be victorious in the end, as they were in the beginning."

"If you were not here, that would happen."

"I feel so weak sometimes, Stedfast."

"I will stay with you this day, my friend."

"Bless you, Stedfast."

I smile.

"Stedfast and True," I say, "as it was meant to be."

I stayed with my fellow angel for a while. In eternal terms, it was not long. In finite ones, it spanned decades perhaps. We watched the last of the animals die, the last links with the original creation of Eden. They died horribly, the sins of the world at last literally crushing life from them through diseases, through poisons, through the ravages brought on by man.

Each came to True, or to me, and flopped down before us, sighing audibly before it died.

I remember the rabbit, no longer fat and white but thin and splotched with dirt and a hint of caked blood. It seemed to be smiling, if animals can smile, as it looked up at me, and said, in words clear and strong, humanlike indeed, "The pain has vanished. I feel no pain." It closed its eyes, tilted its head, and then was gone, truly gone from that once-paradise.

I AM OFTEN in the company of people consumed by regret. They regret past deeds. They regret the present. They stand and face the future with little but anxiety. Everything is a source of worry, of fear, of endless speculation.

But some of the regrets are understandable.

I am now with a middle-aged couple who have come to visit the husband's quite elderly parents.

"What a bore!" he says. "I wish we didn't have to do this."

"It's only once a month," she replies, "sometimes not even that."

They are sitting in their family car, outside the same home in which he had grown up many years before.

"I wonder why they never left," he says. "I guess they just felt so comfortable."

"The tyranny of the familiar," she muses.

"No, no, it's not that. Some people find comfort in life that is predictable, the same rooms, the same pictures on the walls, the same furniture. It's almost a tragedy when something wears out and just *has* to be replaced."

She leans back against the front seat.

"Wears out . . ." she whispers.

"It's such a strain on them to pick out something new. You'd think they'd lost a dear friend instead of an old rug."

She closes her eyes.

"Are you feeling badly?" he asks.

She shakes her head.

"It's not that," she tells him. "I'm just remembering. . . ."

"Remembering what?"

"My own parents."

"I'm really sorry they died before we met each other. Both of heart attacks the same day, wasn't that it?"

"My father died that way. Not my mother."

"How did she die?"

"Slowly. Some blood disease."

"Leukemia?"

"Probably."

"You never knew before then that she was sick?"

"Mother kept it from me. Father apparently felt I should know, but she was the one to say what happened."

She says no more, for a moment, thinking of that single funeral years earlier, the dark, cold trip as she came home from college, realizing that if she had known, she would never have left. She would have been willing to give up her education, or at least delay it, just to be with her mother, just to whisper the kindest, the most loving words to her.

"Just to hold her hand before . . . before—" the wife tries to say.

The husband reaches out and touches her shoulder.

"You were spared—" he starts to tell her.

"Spared?" she responds a bit angrily, pulling away. "I wouldn't have described it as being spared."

"I didn't mean—" he says, genuinely sorry.

The wife smiles.

"I know," she tells him. "I know. I still have a few lingering fragments of guilt left, despite—"

"Despite what?" the husband asks.

"Despite what they told me."

"They?"

"Yes, their doctor. He's a family friend, still alive, still practicing."

"What did he say?"

"That—"

She brings a hand to her mouth, trying desperately to force back the tears. In all these years, she had never really discussed her parents with her husband. She preferred to keep her emotions in a neat little box somewhere deep within her.

"You don't have to—" the husband remarks.

"I know that," she says, her voice trembling. "If not now, then later. It comes back periodically, you know, it sneaks up on me and announces its arrival, along with the memories, all those memories."

Until what that doctor told her is recalled, for it had, over the years, helped. And now, in another moment of reliving that brief interlude. . . .

"They weren't themselves," this dear, caring man had said, gently, his eyes misting over.

Then, the doctor cleared his throat as the two of them sat on the front porch of her parents' house.

"Your mother had lost so much weight. That dear lady was just a network of bones, with a little skin stretched over it. She was nearly blind. She—"

"In just six months?"

"Oh, yes."

"But they never said anything. When I was home the last time, I saw that she seemed a bit pale, I asked if she was feeling all right. She just looked up at me and said, 'I'm feeling as good as I can expect.'"

"And she was being truthful."

"But there was a hidden meaning to those words, wasn't there?"

"Yes, there was. She knew even as she said them. She didn't believe in lying, so she said nothing that was not true. She felt as good as she could expect."

"But how could she feel good at all, knowing what was wrong with her?"

"She talked a lot about the Lord's gentle touch. When there was any pain, even very severe pain—"

I, Stedfast, was there, you know, by her side, as she came closer to death, her guardian angel, her ministering spirit, and she sensed my presence, smiled contentedly even as her friends visited and saw the edges of pain reflected in her bloodshot eyes and whispered among themselves about her courage. . . .

"But I could have been a comfort. I *should* have been a comfort."

The doctor looked at her with compassion.

"Then, perhaps, but you could not have endured the ugliest part."

"You mean Mother losing weight, is that what you're saying? Am I so weak that I could not—"

He put his fingers to her lips.

"She was nasty, and loud. She threw things. She became what she was not. She could not hold any food in her stomach. She—"

"Please no!" she said in a loud voice. "I don't want to hear—"

"—any of the details? That's right. You don't. You needn't. But how could you have *experienced* any of it if you cannot bear to *hear* any of it?"

She was silent. They sat quietly, both of them, a slight breeze dancing across their faces and weaving gently through their hair.

"I missed seeing a mother I would have not recognized,

a mother who became someone altogether different," she finally offered.

The doctor sighed as he said, "That *is* what you missed, my dear. She had lost control of everything, her mind, her emotions, every function of her body."

"She had been so strong. . . ."

"At the end, just a couple of minutes before she died, she had regained some measure of that strength, of spirit if not body, and she took your father's hand, and she smiled."

My hand, also, the hand of an angel . . . just for a moment, holding onto a man she had loved for most of her life, not wanting to leave him, and, as well, being lifted from her body by someone else, then to meet, a gossamer moment later, yet Someone else.

"He said he could feel her leave," the doctor went on. "Your father said he could see his beloved turn for an instant and look back at him, and some creature of inexpressibly bright and shiny countenance by her side."

"In his imagination, of course?" she asked. "He couldn't really have seen anything, isn't that right?"

He saw us, he saw this sweet reborn child of the King because he had already begun dying himself. . . .

"I can't say," the doctor replied. "But delusion or glimpse into the other side, whatever it was, your father was comforted. He left that room, and sat down in his favorite old chair in the living room and, a short while later, when I went out to check on him, he too had gone."

The doctor handed her a sheet of paper that she unfolded and read aloud from.

Do not be sad, Sweetheart. Your love was here. Thoughts of you were here. We talked by phone. We wrote letters. Your spirit was here, brought on the wings of an angel who knew how much the writing of your hand and the sound of your voice filled your mother and me with the greatest joy we could ever experience. Rest easy, my child. The same angel now attends you. He does so with our love as a gift eternal, to whisper into your ear when you think of us as you stand someday before your own family and give yourself to them.

She reread those words, then glanced at the doctor. She found it so very difficult to speak but managed somehow, somehow.

"How did he realize this?" she asked.

I know, child. I know. I have the answer. I am the answer, sweet child.

A voice intrudes that reverie.

Her husband.

"You weren't here for awhile, were you?" he asks.

She nods. "Back in those days, that day."

"Did it help?"

"Yes, yes it did. Let's go inside."

"Boring day ahead of us, honey."

She reaches out and grabs his shoulders, but gently so.

"Don't *ever* say that," she admonishes him.

"But they're old, they're failing, they can hardly hear, I have to keep repeating things. That's a hassle."

She smiles with love, with understanding risen from the memories.

"But they're here," she says. "You can hug them. You can eat your mother's cooking. You can sit back and reminisce with your father. And you can say goodbye, knowing that it's not the last time."

She leans forward to kiss him.

"That's everything, my love. It *is* everything, you know."

They embrace, and then get out of the car and walk up the path to the front door. The husband knocks, and his mother answers, after a few seconds, and for an instant she doesn't quite recognize either of them.

"Mother?" he says with sudden warmth, with love. "It's us. We're here to visit, remember?"

She comes back to awareness just as quickly as it had left her, and she reaches out to hug her son, her daughter-in-law.

The wife looks at her husband, wondering if he is as irritated and uncomfortable as usual.

His tears are his answer.

*T*HE OLD MAN named Thomas had been a lighthouse keeper most of his adult life. He and his wife had
built their entire existence around the requirements of
that job. Not far away was the cottage they had shared.

But no children.

They had wanted boys and girls to hold, to laugh with,
children for whom they could wipe away tears and to
whom they could be a source of strength.

It was never Your will, Lord, Thomas thought as dusk
dropped around him, and he stood just outside the
whitewashed lighthouse. *But my beloved and I got along
because we had each other. And we had the presence of
the Holy Spirit within us.*

And me, good Thomas, and me.

I said that not defensively but lovingly. I enjoyed being
with Amy and Thomas. They had separated themselves
from the world, and while that may or may not have been
the full intent of the Father for all Christians, it indeed
worked for this couple. They had no television. There
was one radio in the cottage and one other in the
lighthouse. They got all their news from these, for they
subscribed to no newspapers or magazines. When they

573

had each other, they had no need for anything or anyone else.

Succumbing to a severe case of pneumonia, Amy had passed away several years earlier. Thomas had buried her himself after having a coffin delivered from a town which was ten miles or so away, the same community where he got his food and other essentials. Several people offered to help out, but he politely refused.

So he laid out his Amy in her favorite dress, and gingerly applied makeup on her face, and combed her hair as she would have liked it to be. During the last few months of her life, she was too weak to do anything for herself, and he had had considerable practice taking care of dressing her, making her up, holding a mirror in front of her and asking, "Amy, is this the way you want to look?"

She would nod, and smile weakly, and say in a hoarse voice, "Thank you, Thomas. I wish—"

He would put two fingers gently on her pale, thin lips and say, "We are here to help one another. You mean so much to me, beloved. How could I ever do less?"

She would start crying, and he would dab away the tears from her cheeks. And then he would get into the bed beside her, and she would lean against him, and he could feel her slow, uncertain breathing.

Thomas' beloved died like that, just a little after sunrise one October morning, leaning against him, that breathing suddenly ended, her body limp. He didn't move at first, afraid that he might be wrong, afraid that her heart might still be beating, and he hated to disturb her rest.

Even after he could no longer deny it, he remained like that for nearly an hour longer. Finally, he moved slowly, and her body fell over on the bed, and he stood, and bowed his head, and sobbed until he nearly passed out from the effort, every muscle in his body tortured by the strain.

Then he started to pull a blanket up to her neck, stopped a moment, looking into that sweet, familiar face.

"It's as though you are still looking at me, dearest one," he whispered. "There is almost a smile on your face."

It is indeed a smile, dear Thomas. Your Amy was leaving that body just then, and she had been looking into the face of the Savior in whom you both had believed for more than half a century. . . .

Thomas turned and left their bedroom. He used an ancient telephone to call into town.

A day later, he was taking care of her for the last time. He slipped into the coffin a bottle of her favorite cologne, Chantilly, which she had been using ever since he first met her, its gentle scent much like Amy herself.

The grave had been dug with a slope at one end so that one man could carefully slide it down to the bottom.

One shovelful at a time, he piled dirt on top. Thomas was very tired by the time he had finished, and he went back into the cottage and fell down on their bed. Closing his eyes, he prayed that the next time he opened them he would see Amy standing at the gates of Heaven, waiting for him.

But when he awoke, that had not happened. He was still in that bed, and when he got up and walked to the front door and looked outside, he saw the lighthouse still there, standing as it had for more than a century.

Nothing had changed, except that now Thomas was alone. Or so he thought.

Thomas went on, day after day, for weeks, for months, for years.

One morning, though, Thomas was sitting on the beach, just beyond the reach of the surf. A beautiful sunrise had begun.

It is like that every day in His kingdom, I said.

"Is it like this in Your kingdom, Father?" Thomas said out loud, unexpectedly, with much hope reflected in his voice.

Had he heard me, somehow?

"Oh, Lord, when Amy passed unto You, did she see a golden-red hue suffuse all of creation? Was it so fine to her eyes that she smiled at the sight of it, and then was quickly gone?"

Thomas jerked abruptly, feeling a pain in his chest, but that moment passed. He had grown accustomed to the brief spasms, and he always felt fine after them—a little more tired, perhaps, but fine nevertheless.

"Another day of sunrises, Lord, and sunsets?" he asked of the air and the sea and the gentle breezes.

Thomas stood breathing in the age-old scents, and then he walked the distance to Amy's grave.

"What was it like for you today?" he asked, realizing that this foolishness had been going on for years, and always it was the same, only the pounding surf to provide an answer of sorts, whatever that answer was.

Pain again. More severe this time.

He fell to his knees with the severity of it, but then, in a moment or two, it passed, as before, though he had had to shut his eyes for a bit.

He opened them to the sound of children.

"Where are—?" he started to say.

Still on his knees, he looked up.

Six of them were running toward him, joy on their faces.

"Where did you come from?" he asked weakly.

None of them answered. But two did walk over to Thomas, and helped the old man to his feet.

"Thank you, dear ones," he said.

He responded with unmasked joy to that tiny, tiny bit of kindness, perhaps more so since it was evidenced by bright-faced children. That particular region was not overflowing with youngsters, so he had precious little opportunity for fellowship with any of them. Occasionally they could be seen in town, but only two or three at any time—often just one, hanging on the hand of a parent. But never had he experienced so many together, so many intent on him, instead of just passing by on the street. It was a place instead primarily of the elderly, a quiet town and its environs, where people wanted to be isolated, away from neon signs and heavy traffic and, certainly, dirty air.

Thomas asked if the children wanted to join him in the cottage so that he could give them something to eat.

"Are you hungry?"

They shook their heads.

"May I show you the lighthouse, my new young friends? All children seemed to be fascinated by lighthouses."

They nodded.

Thomas walked with surprising energy to the tall, narrow, whitewashed building, and unlocked the door, and went inside, climbing the steps as though he was once again a young man.

He showed his new friends the huge searchlight.

"At night," he spoke proudly, "if I've maintained it properly, this light can be seen for miles out to sea."

By the time he was finished telling them whatever he thought they could grasp, he was tired but happy.

"All these years, Amy and I wanted children. From the beginning we wanted precious little ones, and talked about them, dreamed about them, prayed for them to be given to us, to be able to talk with them as I have been doing with you," Thomas told them. "It's a miracle that you've come all the way here to see me."

A miracle? Good, good Thomas, you really have no idea how much of a miracle all this is. . . .

We looked at him sweetly, my fellow angelic impostors and I, knowing how much he wanted to be with children, thankful that we could give him that momentary little pleasure, though, for him, it was not so inconsequential.

As he smiled at the half dozen of us, Thomas asked, in his ignorance, "Are you all from town?"

We said nothing.

Not the town to which you refer, Thomas. We come from a city, an extraordinary city. You'll be there soon, old man, very soon. . . .

Thomas became weak just then, and had to sit down at the same old desk he had been using for over half a century.

"Forgive me, my young friends, but I feel my age suddenly," he acknowledged. "It means so much to me, though, that you all are here with me. What a blessing you are! Do you know that?"

He started to hang his head, finding little strength to do anything else.

Thomas. . . .

He turned to say something to the children.

The others were gone, on to other missions, and with my gratitude that they had taken the time to help out, but not me, for I had to remain a short while longer, though I continued to be without visibility to his sight.

They were gone.

He scratched his head.

"Am I losing my mind?" he said.

No, Thomas, you are not.

He cocked his head.

"Is someone there?" he asked.

He looked momentarily at the familiar surroundings, the searchlight, the curving steps leading down to the base of the lighthouse, and detected, as so often over time, the odor of carved wood, salt air coming through an open window. He breathed in deeply.

Pain gripped his chest again.

He got to his feet, and walked falteringly down the stairs, and then stepped outside.

No children. Just the bare landscape, every rock familiar to him.

He could no longer stand.

Thomas did not feel the impact as his body hit the hard ground.

Everything—the cloudless day, the old lighthouse, the tiny cottage a short distance away—was spinning in his vision.

"Oh, Lord, is this that moment?" he whispered.

I assumed the form of a small child again and reached out and touched Thomas on the cheek.

He looked into my face.

"You're not really a child, are you?" Thomas asked with wisdom, his expression knowing.

"No, I am not."

"Will there be any children where I am going?"

"We all are children, Thomas," I spoke with warmth, tenderly, to this dying old man. "We all come to our Heavenly Father in the utter simplicity of our faith and pledge to serve Him throughout eternity. Is that not the way, my friend, that things are meant to be?"

Thomas smiled then, the last smile of his life, as he said somewhat tremulously, "Can I see you as you are?"

I gave him that privilege.

"Where is Amy?" Thomas asked, the last words of his life.

Thomas, my beloved, you have come at last!

I stepped aside as the scent of Chantilly and the laughter of children filled the air.

I THINK A lot about animals. I have seen them transform humans into wonderful beings—and I have seen them horribly abused at the hands of the very ones they long to love them. They do not deserve that of which they often find themselves the object, whether in laboratories or city streets or wherever it is that cruelty is inflicted upon them, cruelty elevated to the so-called service of mankind or, simply, the blind and stupid cruelty from children who delight in hearing their victims scream.

These are the obvious manifestations of cruelty, that to which many human beings would raise their voices in protest, cruelty deemed by the media as newsworthy from time to time, especially if some radical group with placards happens to be involved.

And then there are others, occurring daily in every community across the nation, this nation, and others as well.

Simple cruelties, perhaps, but no less hurtful, no less *cruel*.

Love. Love and concern are the catalysts to everything good and pure for most animals, especially the everyday kind.

Having a dog or a cat "around," without allowing it to participate, keeping it "outside," to which I might add, in more ways than one, forcing the animal to live without being totally loved, which is the ultimate cruelty, it seems to me.

Having without giving.

Animals are meant to love, and to be loved in return.

Consider the elderly comforted by their presence, bereft of human companionship but surrounded by the love of a special friend, the purest love—that is the truth of it, you know, love so pure, so dedicated, so unquestioning and total that it stands second only to the love of God Himself, a hint of the love that mandated Calvary, love with total abandon and sacrifice, love filtered through the gaze of gentle brown eyes or the touch of a pink tongue, giving the slightest hint of the love that suffuses the distant corners of Heaven itself, love without spot or wrinkle or, even, motivation except to love.

Sitting there, looking up, eyes wide, body swaying ever so slightly from side-to-side, almost unnoticeable perhaps, eyes closing, a bit, then opening, then—

Human beings love animals, and animals respond with themselves, until the end of their days. On the other hand, God loves human beings, and human beings so often respond with nothing but their rebellion, their rebuke, their sin flung back into the face of the Almighty.

In such instances, which is the lesser creation?

Not the collie. Not this one. All it wanted was to be accepted. All it wanted was to be part of their family. They took him in, true, but only into their home. Their hearts remained closed.

It was the thing to do. In an age of concern for the environment, an age of animal rights activism, they had a pet. They fed him well. They gave him a clean place to rest. When he wanted *attention*, when he wanted *them*, they couldn't be bothered, and turned this backs.

I communicate with animals, you know. I perceive their thoughts. I cannot do this with human beings because the minds of mankind have been off-limits for a very long time, a netherworld into which Satan often intrudes—no, that is wrong, in which he often ventures as an *invited* guest—and yet God, Jehovah, the Almighty, the King of Kings, must wait until Satan is evicted because the two cannot reside together in the corridors of the subconscious.

The collie. . . .

So grand, so devoted, so ignored.

I could perceive his confusion. I knew his question: *I must not be loving them enough. Could that be it?*

I wish I could tell this splendid creature that it had nothing to do with him, but I cannot. I feel impotent, then, often.

. . . not loving them enough.

Oh, never, you are their friend, their companion, their loyal one, though they are too busy among themselves to know it.

There was a blizzard that year. The youngest member of the family was caught out in it, not far from their house.

He got confused, his seven-year-old mind unsure of the direction in which to turn in order to go back home.

He wandered farther and farther away.

By the time the rest of the family was aware of what had happened, the blizzard was so fierce they couldn't go outside. They had to wait until the severity of it lessened.

The boy's mother was hysterical, certain that her son would be dead when they found him.

Hours later, the snow stopped altogether. The boy's parents threw on their heavy coats and hurried outside.

Over a mile away, they found their son, curled up

inside the collie's embrace, in fact, so completely that they thought they had found the collie but not the boy.

They grabbed their son, and started off back toward the house. The father stopped, tears coming to his eyes, and turned back, bending over the nearly dead animal. Then he picked it up and carried it toward home.

The collie looked at him for a moment, eyes wide, heart beating faster, licking his hand several times, and asking—*I know, I heard him*—asking without words, but certain of a response from grateful parents—*Do you love me? Do you love me now?*

I WANT TO pause for a moment. No, that is not quite right. The word is not *want*. The word is *must.* These poignant moments, tears and joy mixed together, these moments being spoken for those who will soon journey from the new Heaven to the new earth, these are preferable to the ones of battle. Spiritual warfare is that, very, very much that—fallen meeting unfallen in the heavenlies and, often, on earth itself. Oh, it happens, it happens often, former comrades contesting against one another for victory. Satan's plan is a multi-layered one; battles in human hearts and souls, battles between nations, battles among the stars, the astronomers seeing what they do not realize they are seeing, an explosion, a flash of light distant through the lens of multi-million-dollar instruments—not a world, like they say . . . something else, collision between evil and divine.

When my Creator has needed me, I have joined Gabriel and the others, out there, standing up to the forces of darkness—but, also, back on earth where the battle is not so spectacular, not between worlds, not amongst the stars, but in awful places, dark alleys, smoke-filled bars, theatres with flickering, obscene images, battles just the same, requiring warriors just the same. . . .

Warrior angels.

Gabriel is one. Michael another.

And sometimes Stedfast. Yes, sometimes me.

What is wonderful, truly so, is that the warriors are often able to minister as well. They go from their battles against forces of darkness, during these occasions, leaving the tumult behind, and perhaps quietly enter the room of a dying child, taking that little one into the Father's presence.

I remember once when Gabriel had just finished defending a group of Christians in Haiti. All the terrors of Satanic voodoo had been called against them, and he was summoned to vanquish the demonic entities. When that was accomplished, he learned that his next mission was helping some Kurdish refugees in Iraq after the government there had violated yet another international guarantee of protection.

"They're starving, Stedfast," he told me just before leaving on that next journey. "They are sick, dying, their bodies dropping by the roadside. Satan is getting at them through their Islamic fundamentalism. They have no hedge of protection. Yet, while what they believe is heretical, I must at least *Try!*"

Gabriel was in great anguish.

"Oh, Stedfast, how I yearn for that day . . ." he said wearily.

"Yes, I know," I replied, "that day when all this will be over. The war will have been won, and our battles far, far behind us."

He was gone, then, off to the Middle East as a ministering angel—after that, surely the role of a warrior was again waiting for him.

I stood watching him leave, proud of my friend, and I realized what I did not often admit.

He yearned to minister.

I yearned to fight.

In those words should be taken up no hint of rebellion against the will of Almighty God. I think, in such moments, that it amounts to something else. I minister because demons have caused pain. I minister because of the sin and the corruption that their master—and he and they are one, just as God and the rest of us are one—has propagated since Eden, because of Eden. I see tears. I see faces contorted with the effects of disease. I see people dragged off to Hell by his debased puppets.

And I want to strike a blow against my former comrade in Heaven. I want to stand before the collective demon-kind and shout, "Enough! I am a gentle angel, I dry tears and sing away the pain, and give light to those in darkness—but now I am in battle mode. Now I am as fierce as any warrior in the rest of God's army. And I declare that you shall *not* gain victory *this* time!"

. . . *our battles far, far behind us.*

Sometimes those words are uttered in anticipated relief as my kind grows weary. Sometimes those words are uttered for an altogether different reason, as we emerge from the cesspool of evil deeds into which we must plunge on our various odysseys and are consumed by a passion, a passion not simply to minister to the *victims* but to strike back at the foul beings responsible.

I change when I go into battle.

I change a great deal.

I am no longer gentle. My kindness is a casualty. I am not seeking to ease suffering. I am committed, in a sense, to inflicting it upon those who brought the necessity of all this into a once-perfect universe, a suffering awaiting them that is of far greater consequence than anything they had been responsible for showering upon mankind.

Is that possible?

The world itself has been called Hell of a kind. And those who view it as such cannot be thought to be irrational, for they are correct. Can there be any other description that does justice to what is visible before one's very eye—if those eyes have not been blinded by the master of deception?

I see, and I become angry, and, often, that is that. Then I move on to the task at hand, doing what I can to ease the pain of a hundred million demonized lives. That number is a modest one, considering the billions alive on this planet.

But I am not alone. There are other unfallen ones such as myself. Sometimes we meet on our journey. We communicate and commiserate and anticipate the new Heaven, the new earth.

"No more tears!" Samaritan told me once, thinking of what was to be. "No more absorbing their suffering into our very beings so that we can become better able to do what has been our mission for so very long."

The eyes confused . . . the flies landing on parts of the tiny body, the parts where there was more flesh than bones . . . the stomach puffing up with gases, poisons, disease . . . the last cry, "Yamma, yamma!"

"Yes, good comrade," I replied to this special angel, my thoughts becoming verbal. "And what you say is especially sad when it involves the hunger of a dying, malnourished, quite innocent baby."

"Ah, you are thinking of Ethiopia."

"No, I am thinking of the Sudan. I have not been there, but I have heard the reports about what happened."

"Of course! The Muslim leaders decreeing genocide for people in the southern part of the country."

"Simply because those people are not Islamic fundamentalists."

"A sad and terrible situation it is," Samaritan acknowledges. "I have been there with some of the babies, Stedfast."

"I did not know," I told him, with deepest empathy. "You must have faced such devastating sorrow."

"It weighs so heavily on me, Stedfast. Would you be at all willing to listen, my friend?"

"Of course, I would," I said, sensing his need to talk at that moment. "Please . . . go ahead."

"They are so confused. Their mothers cannot provide for them. Their fathers as well are impotent in this regard. So they lay back on the warm sand, and insects gorge on their blood, and the days stretch on and on until—"

Oh, how they change when they see me! There is a smile on each face, faint at first because they are still trapped in a ravaged body of flesh. But gradually the flesh is shed, the smile is broader, deeper, more wonderful. There is peace within it, lighting up their countenance. I extend my hand, and each one of the children takes it in his own, and one by one I lift them to Heaven, I lift them into their Father's presence, and He looks at me, and says the words that I treasure so much, so much. He says to me, "Well done, thou good and faithful servant."

"Oh, Stedfast," Samaritan continued. "We are hardly empty will-of-the wisp phantoms, just flukes of nature, as some will say—the unbelievers, you know—we are so much more."

I looked at him, and knew that this moment would soon pass, and the Father's enabling strength once again would take over. But then—then, Samaritan seemed more like a human child, looking out at the world around him, seeing the evil, the darkness, and not wanting to step out into it.

"As I go from one bedside to another," my friend said, "one battlefield to the next—and not always a battlefield of rockets and tanks. . . ."

"—but one of the soul?" I offered.

"Yes, of the soul, often enough, it is truly that—and I am dealing with a teenager who is about to stick yet another needle into yet another vein, and he is desperately searching for one that has not collapsed . . . and . . . and I whisper to that soul, I whisper, 'Stop, stop, you must stop,' and he hesitates, and I think I may be gaining a victory, Stedfast, I may be the Master's instrument in keeping that soul from the flames. But then the needle is plunged into the flesh yet again, the victim's eyes close, fleeting ecstasy filling his body, while bringing him yet closer to death, to Hell. They are so blind— Stedfast, they are so blind, and I have failed yet again!"

It is not difficult for us to be concerned with failure, and it is not difficult for us to think that the failure is our own.

It is not.

It is not the Father's.

Failure comes through the choices made by men and women every second of every hour of all the time of history.

People fail. Divinity does not.

Judas was the betrayer of Christ. Christ was not the one to sell *him* for thirty pieces of silver.

We know this, the other unfallen and I. We know it very well. And we know that when a soul goes off, screaming to Hell, we are not to blame.

But we feel it, you know. We feel as though we have failed without ever having failed at all. A single question rears up at us: Were we not wise enough, strong enough, present enough to *do* something?

Yet there is one source of consolation for us. Humans have other humans; they have family, they have friends, they have clergymen, they have so many sources of comfort and encouragement.

But not us, not the angels who refused to rebel.

We have one source of consolation.

I smile whenever I think of that, whenever the demonic gloom threatens to overwhelm even me, unfallen that I am.

I smile because of what we have, because of where we obtain that which we all do need.

Where, yea . . . and from Whom.

How could we, ever, ask for more?

$\mathcal{R}$OB ME NOT of my joy. . . .

There are people who delight, it would seem, in taking joy from others and grinding it as dust at their feet. They live miserably themselves. They have seldom experienced a lightness of heart that lifts the spirit to levels of sublime fulfillment that are a glimmer of what is awaiting any who accept Christ as Savior and Lord, and, thereby, gain entrance into Heaven where there is joy unbounded, unencumbered by the sorrows of the flesh, by the twists and turns of moods that afflict every human being at one time or another.

For such individuals, those twists and turns are not from happiness into despair but, rather, from depression into greater depression, from a melancholic outlook on life to one that is near-suicidal.

They seem to be saying, *I am not happy; therefore, I won't allow those around me to be happy. I will enrage them, offend them, disturb them in any way I can, because in a perverse and awful way, I derive some modicum of pleasure from THAT!*

When people of such disposition are by themselves, at least the rest of the world can distance itself from them, as it usually tries to do. But when they are in a temporarily pleasant mood, and they meet a member of the opposite sex, and there is, soon, a marriage, with some children later, it *seems* that joy has supplanted the dark side of their nature or—perhaps, held it at bay.

Not for long.

I tried very hard to help one such individual, a man who was a prominent and talented attorney for the public defender's office. I on the outside tried to do so in concert with the Holy Spirit on the inside—and, yes, let me interject, what I have just mentioned *is* surprising. Can a Christian, with the Holy Spirit indwelling him, ever be so dismal a person as this one? How is that possible? Shouldn't the joy of the Lord be on the throne of his life, displacing all else?

The Holy Spirit has taken up residence in Albert, but He is not in *control*. This member of the Trinity is a boarder. He rents a room, He has the key to the front door, but that is that. Albert's sin nature still holds the deed, still pays the bills.

You see the validity of my analogy?

While Albert was indeed a Christian, he seldom proved a proper witness. Oh, theologically he might have held his own, he might have been able to defend the faith in corridors of intellect, perhaps. But where everyday living came into play, he was at best inept, at worst someone who repelled others from the faith.

Including his wife. His son. His daughter.

"Why do you think so ill of everyone?" his wife would often ask. "There *are* some good people left in this world. Not everyone is out to commit a crime of some sort, against you or another."

Albert's reaction to the latter point was understandably shaped by his days in court.

. . . *not everyone is out to commit a crime of some sort.*

"Are you so sure?" he would reply. "Can you be certain

that there is not the psyche of a criminal in each one of us? The Bible calls it our sin nature. How can you dispute that?"

Yesterday he came to the end of a trial during which he defended a man guilty of murder. He was so good, so clever. He succeeded in getting his client acquitted. That man is now free, and may kill again, not stopping at one more victim. Albert, hired to see that justice was served, perpetuated infamy. Where is the justice in that?

"But there are good people, good deeds in Scripture in addition to those that illustrate what you suggest," his wife retorted. "Consider one of the thieves on that cross next to Christ. He repented. The Lord recognized this, and accepted him into the Kingdom."

"That thief had little choice. After all, he was at the end of his life. He might as well have."

"What about the Good Samaritan?"

"What about those who ignored the man that he eventually helped? Their number was greater."

"The apostles gave up everything for Jesus."

"Peter was certainly an apostle. Look at his threefold denial that he even knew his Master."

"But he wasn't a criminal," she pointed out.

"You're right. He was instead a coward. Is that necessarily better?" Albert replied. "A coward in battle can cause the deaths of his own comrades. So in reality, isn't such a man no more than a murderer as well?"

She became exasperated, as usual, unable to talk any longer, unable to break through to the man she loved.

Eventually she left him, along with his son, his daughter.

Months became years. Albert never remarried. But he went on to become a nationally known attorney. More often than not, he was assigned to defend serial killers, *mafioso* dons, discredited political figures, and many others of that caliber—though, judging by numbers, these types comprised the smallest number of his clients.

It might have been deemed inevitable that his personal outlook would become even more cynical than it was. Could it have been otherwise?

Yes. . . .

Albert could have refused cases involving criminals, those where no doubt existed in his mind that such men were not interested in *justice* as much as in manipulating the justice *system*. They merely wanted Albert to see to it that they would either never be punished for their crimes or, at least, get a much lighter sentence.

Justice has a price, he would tell himself again and again. *It is yet another commodity in this country, available to people with money and clever attorneys.*

The spillover from Albert's courtroom behavior crept more and more into his personal life. Though a Christian, he got further and further away from anything resembling a strong, Christ-centered testimony. The ethics of many of his clients subliminally worked their way into his own makeup. He discovered that he could make more money leaving the public defender's office and hanging out his own shingle. Soon Albert found himself catering more and more to these high-paying but questionable characters.

It was only a matter of time before Albert ended up being on trial himself.

For extortion.

It involved one of his corporate clients. A less polite word would have been blackmail.

He lost that case.

And he was imprisoned for five years.

Finally, after being released, he went back to a life that could not be reconstructed the way it had been. Though barred from ever practicing law again, Albert was far from being penniless. He had no financial worries.

But he had no one.

No, that wasn't quite right. The people he associated with were like those he had been with in prison, the same type, but not behind bars, men and women pursuing their schemes in absolute disregard of ethics and morality.

I am a Christian, he told himself one afternoon. *I indeed AM a Christian. So what am I doing with the swine, instead of being in the Master's house?*

He had fallen to the very bottom of the abyss in his soul, and he no longer could tolerate the cold despair.

My wife, my children, he thought. *Surely I can go back to them. They will greet me with love, despite all that has happened.*

But he had to find them. He hadn't had any contact with them for five years.

It took him several weeks.

But he did find his wife, his son, his daughter.

He found the grave where his wife had been buried. She had committed suicide. She had become infested with his own outlook, and this was spread to their children. When both turned to drugs, she could not endure the struggle to keep the remaining part of the family together. So she split it apart forever.

. . . beyond redemption.

No individual is beyond redemption until the moment he dies, because he has until then to stop rejecting Jesus Christ as Savior and Lord, and, finally, to accept Him into his very soul.

But some relationships cannot truly be redeemed. They have become buried, suffocated under a pile of harsh words and unfortunate acts. There is nothing that can be done to resurrect them, except by a miracle of the Holy Spirit.

That did not happen with Albert.

His wife was buried, and he stood before the tombstone on which had been carved her name.

I dug your grave myself, he admitted. *I placed you in it just as surely as if I—*

He remembered her face when she could still tolerate the sight of him. He enjoyed the feeling of her hair through his fingers.

Now . . . now only the children were left.

He knew he had to find them.

He did.

But what he found showed him the bankruptcy of the way he had been living. He found his son and his daughter in the same drug rehabilitation center.

"They are among the toughest cases we've ever encountered," one of the doctors told him.

"But why?" Albert asked plaintively, still not quite comprehending.

The two men were standing in a corridor.

"Would you come with me to my office, please?" the doctor asked.

Albert followed him. A few doors down the corridor, they stepped into the doctor's well-appointed, wood-panelled office.

After both were sitting down, the doctor looked quite seriously at Albert and said, "You see, they feel there is no hope for them."

"But what were they looking for in drugs?"

"Not hope, sir."

"What could it have been?"

"Oblivion."

Albert leaned back in the chair, his hands starting to tremble.

"But they had so much," he said, "nothing but luxury from the moment they were born."

"A fine suit of clothes is worthless if the one who wears it is filled with pain," the doctor said.

"Because of me—that's it, isn't it?" Albert guessed.

The doctor nodded sadly.

"Look at what you are," he said. "You have already admitted becoming like the clients you represented, absorbing their values, their outlook. Is it so impossible to understand that this is precisely what happened with your own children?"

"I don't know what you—"

"Forgive me, but I have to be frank, however difficult this will be for you. According to your children, if you saw a sunny day, you would wonder how long it would last, rather than be grateful for its warmth, its light *at that moment*. If you earned a six-figure salary one year, you would worry about the next, hoping your income wouldn't drop. If you—"

"—if I read of Heaven, I would worry about Hell. If I saw a smile on their mother's face, I would be consumed with the fear that an hour later there might be pain on it."

"Exactly what I am trying to tell you, sir."

"But there are good people, good deeds in Scripture in addition to those that illustrate what you suggest," his wife retorted. *"Consider one of the thieves on that cross next to Christ. He repented. The Lord recognized this, and accepted him into the Kingdom."*

"That thief had little choice. After all, he was at the end of his life. He might as well have."

"What about the Good Samaritan?"

"What about those who ignored the man that he eventually helped? Their number was greater."

Albert glanced at the doctor.

"Rob me not of my joy," he said.

"That is surely appropriate. Who said it?"

"I did."

"You?"

"Yes, I wrote it during my college years."

"Why?"

"Because everything was going so well. And I became worried—"

"Dominated perhaps?"

"Yes, that's more accurate. I became dominated by the fear that my joy would slip away between my fingers like tiny grains of sand."

"And you guaranteed that that would be so by making it a self-fulfilling prophecy."

"My wife, my children," Albert sobbed, "sacrificed at the altar of my own insecurities."

"And from those insecurities were born a life-view that placed trust in no one, that portrayed everyone as evil."

"The Bible says that is so."

"How easily you raise your Christianity before me when it is convenient, sir."

"But it is what I believe."

"No, what you believe, sir, is not true Christianity. You accept the *evil* of others, while ignoring the possibility of their *redemption*. You have accepted it for yourself while denying its validity for others."

"You cannot compare me to the swine that I have represented."

"Consider this: How many of them, the swine to which you refer, and accurately, I suspect, have wives who remain loyal to them, have children who are loving and have never taken drugs, and who eagerly await the opportunity each day to welcome their fathers home?"

"I don't see the point," Albert said.

"That you don't *is* the point, sir."

. . . *wives who remain loyal . . . children who are loving.*

He *had* seen the point, yes, but he pushed it aside, not quite able to deal with it, not wanting to face even more pain.

"But how can they, being evil, send forth good fruit?" Albert mused.

"No one is completely evil."

"You speak as a Christian."

"I *am* a Christian."

"How is it possible that a mobster who may have been responsible for the death of dozens of human beings, how is it possible for such an individual to be worthy of anything but condemnation?"

"When it comes to family, when it comes to those depending upon him for his unfettered love, such a man was *more* worthy, sir, than you. What is the value of the gift of prophecy or tongues or teaching or any such gift if there is no love?"

"It is empty, it is cold, it is stale, it is—"

Albert could not go on.

"You *did* give them yourself," the doctor went on, "but it was that part of yourself that you would now like to exorcise. . . ."

Albert continued his silence.

"Do you wish to see your children?" the doctor asked after several minutes.

My children. . . .

"Do you *really* want to see them?" the doctor added.

I must. I must tell them how sorry I am. I must tell them that I love them, that I love with every bit of my mind, my heart, my very soul.

"Yes . . ." Albert said.

The doctor stood, and Albert followed him. The children, Martin and Julienne, now teenagers, were in a special section of the hospital.

"Constant care," the doctor said.

"Constant?"

"Oh, yes. We could keep them in strait-jackets continually, but that has its limitations. So we stay with them nearly every moment."

"But why? They're both locked up, aren't they?"

"You have no idea how violent they can become."

"Violent!" Albert started. "Even my little daughter?"

"Neither of your offspring is little anymore."

It has been a very long time, Albert, I whispered in my wordless way, the Holy Spirit prodding him to listen through his emotions, through a tap on his soul, a gentle touch saying, *Try to understand. Try to—*

"But you can help them, right?" Albert asked confidently.

The doctor shook his head.

"Neither will ever be anything more than a ticking human bomb, set to explode at the slightest provocation. Their brain cells have been severely affected by the years of drug abuse. And I'm afraid it won't get better. Brain cells cannot regenerate as others in the body can."

Albert's shoulders drooped. His voice shook as he asked, "You're saying they're doomed?"

"I would like to be able to put it in a gentler fashion, sir, but that is exactly what this amounts to, I'm afraid."

Albert felt perspiration covering his body.

I'm a Christian, Lord, how could this have happened? he whispered to the air around him.

That was my chance! He had reached out.

Because you have Christ as Savior, but not Lord!

He could not hear me in the normal sense. But he could sense something, something nudging his conscience, the Holy Spirit and I together in this. Albert could still be put under conviction, moment by moment by moment.

And he listened, to me, to the Spirit, inside himself.

Yet it seemed too late for his children, too late for their flesh-and-blood bodies as well as their souls. Surely he had lost them, lost them forever. He was convinced of this as soon as he saw his son, and then his daughter.

They were just human shells. They could barely speak.

All over the visible parts of their bodies, the flesh had sunk in pathetically where the veins had collapsed from constant puncturing, from the unholy wrenching de-

mands of injection after injection, always a search for a
fresh vein, a vein that could still do the job their
addiction had forced upon them.

They had escaped AIDS, and that seemed a miracle in
itself—but AIDS, as nightmarish as it was, could not
have ravaged them any more than had been the case
already by other means.

So thin.

Albert reached out to touch his daughter's cheek. She
pulled back in that padded cell of hers and screamed at
him.

"Don't!" she said. "It's so sore, Father, Father, it's so
very sore. I couldn't stand anyone—"

Father! Father!

Albert rejoiced that she recognized him.

But then he heard the other words coming from her.

"—touching me. Please stop this man, whoever he is.
You promised to help me whenever I needed you. *Get
this man out of here!*"

Albert left, and went down the corridor to his son's
room, which also was padded. The boy did not move
when he entered. There was no indication that he even
knew he had a visitor. He just stayed on the floor in a
fetal position, as though he were dead already.

"Son, son, I never knew what I was doing to you,"
Albert said, barely able to speak for the emotion that had
been building up. "I was so concerned about the pain of
life, the rotten people, the corruption—I could never give
to you any joy because I did not have it myself. There was
nothing but venom, nothing but hatred, nothing but
suspicions, nothing but the darkness."

His son's eyes opened for just a moment, only that, and
he turned to his father and asked, "But, Dad, the light—
what about the light?"

And then he fell back into that inner world that had
captured him so completely.

Albert thanked the doctor and left, stepping outside the hospital.

What about the light?

He sat down on a bench on the front lawn and bowed his head.

"They're headed for Hell because of me," he said out loud, weeping at the same time. "They're lost forever now."

A voice intruded.

"Sir, forgive me for this, but I think it is more correct to say that nobody's lost until God says that they are. Wouldn't you agree with that?"

Albert looked up.

No old man. No wavering phantom.

A beautiful red-haired nurse.

"I'm . . . I'm sorry," Albert said, his face nearly the color of her hair.

"That's all right," she replied. "Tears are cleansing."

"There's just so much sorrow in life."

"But that isn't all. You've got to realize that. You've got to grab hold of what is good and decent and loving and never let go."

"But my kids . . . they're here. They're dying."

"You don't know that for certain."

"But they look so pale, so weak."

"So does a neglected flower until it is watered. Your young ones are thirsty, sir, thirsty for *your love.* God loved you enough to give you the gift of salvation through the sacrifice of His beloved Son. You accepted this a long time ago. Why do you turn your back on the rest?"

"You mean the peace that passes understanding, that sort of thing?"

"I do. Exactly that."

"If only I could—"

"Your life had too many 'if onlys.' Give up this one.

Banish it. Tell yourself, 'I *can* go back. I *can* stand with my loved ones. I *can* be the Lord's instrument for whatever He hungers to give to them.'"

"If only—" Albert repeated, out of habit.

"No more!" the nurse told him, undoubtedly louder than intended.

"You really believe it's not too late?"

"I *know* it isn't. Go, sir! Give them yourself, that loving side of you. Wipe away their tears. Tell your son about the light. Tell him, sir. Tell him about the light of the world. Leave the darkness in our Father's hands."

Albert nodded, stood, thanked the nurse, and turned toward the hospital.

. . . *tell your son about the light.*

"Hey, how did you—?"

He spun around.

But I was gone.

Ultimately there was victory, even in such a hard and stubborn soul. And that is something over which we all rejoice.

But another of my encounters during my odyssey shows victory of another sort, victory that is as wonderful, as touching, as grand as any I can remember. . . .

CRAIG WANTED TO be in the Olympics as a pole-vaulter.

He had dreamed of this ever since he was a small boy.

"I pray that the Lord will make me strong enough," he said again and again to anyone who would listen. "I'm working on my legs. My arms are pretty good, but my legs need some work."

The family garage had been converted into a gym. Craig was there every day, after school and on weekends. By the time he had become a teenager, he had managed to break away on occasion, make some friends through social activities, go on a few dates—but, always, the *primary* focus had to be his physical conditioning. Few other activities could be allowed to intrude.

While pole-vaulting was the center of his attention, Craig proved to be a top athlete in two other areas of high school competition: wrestling and basketball. Even though he was a bit short, he nevertheless did well because he had a special characteristic that some of his many Jewish friends described rather colorfully in Yiddish.

Craig was young, good-looking, strong, popular. He had many opportunities for witnessing for Christ.

This young man was what I would have wanted to be if I had been of flesh and blood.

I was assigned to stay with Craig during those final months of his life. That sounds sudden, to say it like that, yes, I know that it does, but the Holy Spirit felt that this young man would be particularly sensitive to demonic oppression since he had been given so much in his life, and it seemed that the tragedy, from a human standpoint, that occurred had the potential to peel away some part of his faithfulness like a movie studio façade.

Satan did attack. He did not assign any of his demons. He wanted to devastate this young man directly, without any puppets, heaping discouragement on him, trying to break his will, waiting for a fist raised against Almighty God. He would fail, this leader of the fallen ones, he would fail, and yet he would not stop trying, no matter how often he was rebuked.

Craig was diagnosed as having a particularly severe bone disease. In time there would be not only pain but something else, a byproduct as much of drug treatment as the disease itself.

Craig's bones would lose their firmness. They would become almost elastic, like somewhat hardened rubber bands, and when they could no longer support his body, he would die.

One week before that happened, Craig spoke at his high school commencement ceremony. He was too weak for crutches. There was no wheelchair to carry him up to the podium.

A sack.

Oh, it was a bit more elaborate than that, but it still could be accurately described as a sack. His father and mother carried Craig in it, and then, when they reached the podium, as three thousand students and family members were seated inside the auditorium, his father held his son's head up so that it wouldn't flop to one side, like a rag doll. Craig spoke, his voice so weak that the sound system had to be turned up nearly to full volume.

"I love Jesus!" he said. "I love Him as much now as when I first accepted Him as my Savior, my Lord. He wanted all of me: my mind, my body, my soul. I don't have much of a body to give Him now—"

As tears started to stream down his cheeks, and his father's and mother's, rugged football heroes and geeks and cheerleaders and a very tough principal and every teacher in the school shed their own.

"—but I won't have this for long, you know," Craig continued. "It's gonna go. I'll discard it like the useless thing it's become. And you know what? The Lord has promised me a replacement, one better than the original, because never again will I have to face disease or pain or even a cold. All that will be in the past, over, ended, *finished forever!*"

There was surprising strength in his voice then. The microphone let out a high-pitched squeal.

"Don't go sobbing around about how all this could happen, me a Christian and all. I never made it to the Olympics, but I think—"

He turned his head slightly, trying to whisper something to his father. The words came through the microphone, "Dad, will you wipe my eyes for me?"

As he faced the audience again, Craig was smiling.

"—I *know* that I will be doing something better in His kingdom. I will run without getting tired. I will jump as high as—"

He just couldn't stop the tears, he just couldn't, and he was terribly embarrassed that this was so, yet through the emotion, the remaining words somehow came through.

"as . . . high . . . as . . . the . . . stars!"

Craig had no strength left after that. His parents carried him off the podium, and down the center aisle. Before the three of them had gotten past the first row, the entire audience stood and applauded. One girl broke away from the rest and hurried to the piano on stage, and sat before it, and started playing, "On Christ the Solid Rock I Stand." Those in the audience who knew the words, and not many of them did, sang along with her; those who didn't hummed the melody.

Craig asked that they stop for a few seconds before leaving the auditorium altogether. He whispered something into his mother's ear.

She turned toward the gathered faculty and students, and, raising her voice through her own tears, she said, "My son wants me to tell you that he loves you all."

She brought a hand to her mouth, her own strength wavering, and in her mind she said, over and over, *Precious Jesus, precious Jesus, help me now, dear, dear Lord, help me!*

She lowered that hand, and tilted her head back slightly as she added, "Because Christ first loved him! And . . . and Craig has tried so hard to share that love with others."

Satan was there, though no one knew it except me. He stood at the entrance to the large auditorium, his wings drooping, his head tilted sadly to one side.

"You could have inspired acts like that, if you had not done all that you have done over the centuries of time," I reminded my former comrade.

"I know, Stedfast, I know," he replied.

"Can you offer anything that comes even close to what that one frail young man has done?"

Satan the Deceiver turned and looked at me, an expression of regret and shame on his repulsive face.

"You are so beautiful," he said with surprising softness.

"As you once were. The ugliness is of your own making."

He shrugged, layers of pus and slime shaken from his

awful countenance, and then he went outside, observing the teenager's parents as they carefully put him in the back seat of the family sedan.

"I wanted him, Stedfast," Satan admitted. "I wanted to tear him apart, and feast on him in Hell."

"You lost," I said. "This one rejected your doctrine of hate, and surrounded himself with love."

"Yes . . . as with so many others, Stedfast . . . so many."

And then Lucifer the once-Magnificent was gone from that place.

That was on a Friday. By Wednesday of the next week, Craig's earthly life had ended. He died at home, in his room, the walls lined with photographs and certificates, the shelves stuffed with trophies. Every empty spot was filled with flowers.

One arrangement had come from his coach. On the card attached to it was a brief message: "Dear Craig, please forgive me for pushing you so hard."

Craig's mother, at his request, wrote a note back to the man. It read, simply: "No harder than the Lord, sir. God bless you. . . ."

People were camped outside on the front lawn, and on the walkway leading up to the front door. Only his parents were in his room with him when his spirit soared.

And I.

He was mumbling briefly, nothing that they could understand, but I heard his words fully.

"There really isn't any pain, is there?" he asked, amazed that he was at last truly free of it.

"None at all," I told this remarkable young man. "Pain is of the flesh, banished as the spirit takes over for those—"

"Jesus," he said, only a breath or two left.

Waiting for him at the gates.

"My Lord," he said. "He's holding something. It . . . it looks like—"

"Go to Him, Craig," I said with joy. "Gather your new strong legs and jump."

He did, always the athlete, jumping without a pole to guide him, vaulting beyond the confines of corruptible flesh and blood and bone, and reaching for the flaming Olympic torch that his beloved Savior held out for him.

$\mathcal{A}$DAM AND EVE were close to God before sin entered their lives. Every human being since then has been closer or further away from Him in direct proportion to the extent to which they let their sin nature hold sway. Never again will there be the kind of spiritual union that once existed in Eden, at least not until the new Heaven and earth—but, glimpses, yes, there will be glimpses of what once was, very muted, even nearly nonexistent, and every now and then, much stronger.

Mother Teresa can experience a closeness that is not shared by a Donald Trump. That may be stating the obvious, but it is indeed quite true. This is not because of her works, for true spirituality cannot be built on a works-oriented foundation. Rather, her spirituality comes from the redemptive faith that has motivated her to serve Him in the only way that she knows how. When she gets down on her knees and says to her Lord, "I am giving You all that I am, all that I have, all that I will ever be in the flesh, and yet I wish, dear Jesus, there was more that I could offer to You," she receives, in that moment, a glimpse of what once was in Eden.

Contrast that spirit of sacrifice with another sort of spirit altogether, a spirit that is rampant in the Body of

Christ, a spirit that makes demands of Him—prosperity, health—a spirit that postulates the heresy that it is more important to maneuver Almighty God into serving the human race than His creations feeling compelled to serve Him.

We should please God so that He will give us the desires of our heart. . . .

I have heard that, oh, I have, though I would have wished that I had not. It is part of the gathering storm, a storm that will sweep over Christendom, that will subvert whole congregations, though some members still may be saved, that will add the symbol of the dollar to that of the cross, the two intertwined in the minds of many.

When I see the flash-and-dash of so much of what passes for Christian service by the leaders of the faith, I know that the Rapture is not far off. I know that my Creator cannot tolerate the travesties much longer, that He must take true believers out of a world, especially a Christian world, that threatens to collapse of its increasingly virulent hypocrisy, pulling all but the elect down in the process.

And I think of the children, especially the retarded children.

If the adults around them only knew. . . .

So often, retardation in one form or another is given as a justification for abortion. Slaughter the babies before they enter a world in which they will be miserable, in which they will inflict so much suffering on others, in addition to their own—for isn't that the kinder act in the long run, the more merciful, a few seconds of pain, perhaps, rather than ten or twenty years of shambling disability?

If a baby cannot possibly measure up to society's standards, then how can there be happiness?

And yet the proponents of this carnage deny intellec-

tual elitism! They scoff at comparisons with the Aryan mentality of the Third Reich. But their very words condemn them. They say it stops at the unborn and cannot possibly be a forerunner to eradication of the elderly.

They lie. . . .

Severely retarded children cannot lie, you know. They cannot lust. They cannot murder, or steal. But, most striking of all, they cannot deny their Creator.

A body of twenty years that houses the brain of a small child is that of a human being forever without the *will* and, really, the *opportunity* to sin in ways that are acquired through the years of the lives of "normal" youngsters.

It is true that Scripture indicates human beings are born to sin or perhaps born into sin. But when there is severe retardation, that *tendency* to sin is blocked off.

No such youngsters can ever be reached by Satan or his emissaries. Oh, he has tried again and again, but he cannot get into their minds, their souls. He fails each and every time.

And for the most beautiful, the most wondrous of reasons.

If those who want to snuff out these children knew the truth, they would never be able to deal with the guilt.

The truth?

I said it was beautiful, I said it was wondrous.

It is, every bit that, every, every bit.

For you see, each retarded child is in a state quite similar to what Adam and Eve experienced in Eden—but even more blessed. Adam and Eve went on to sin. Those severely retarded simply do not have the capacity to do so. Perhaps they will seem to have a bit of temper, but it is actually more a sense of frustration than anything else.

They will never strike another human being. They will never kill or rob or maim or rape.

They *cannot!*

A retarded child would never have taken of the fruit of the tree of the knowledge of good and evil because—and this is the wondrous part—he would never have considered disobeying his Creator.

There is a why to this, a sublime why.

Ones such as these have a bond with Almighty God that no one else can approach. If sin is essentially separation from Him, then they have never been separated.

I have seen retarded children sitting by themselves, laughing. I have heard adults look at them with pity and say, "Poor child! He's off in a world of his own."

Precisely!

It *is* a different world, that it is.

They walk with angels. There is no barrier between us. Unlike the rest of mankind, they do not have to wait until they are dying.

They are not lonely.

They may be alone. They may sit quietly by themselves and seem to be looking into space. But they are not looking into nothingness.

They see . . . you see.

They see a great deal.

We give them glimpses, my kind and I. We give them glimpses of the new Eden, which will be the entire earth. We run a kind of cosmic movie projector and on a kind of cosmic screen we show them what will be. They see thinking, reasoning, handsome adults playing with lions, lions licking lambs, lambs without need of a shepherd because there is no longer any danger.

"Who is that?" some will ask.

"You, dear child," I or another will say.

"Me?" responds a tiny voice, with beautiful eyes flashing brightly.

"You," I tell the child. "You, as you were meant to be, as you will always be in that fine day."

Sometimes they cry. Sometimes they just sit, uncomprehending. Sometimes they are scared and they ask me to hold them, and I say that I cannot, not just yet.

I love having the privilege of escorting them to heaven. Even as they die, they reach out to father, mother, brother, sister, and they smile, nothing more than that, but enough it is, a smile of love, of joy, a smile that says as much as words themselves, "Thank you for loving me. Thank you for taking care of me. God will take over now."

I remember so many occasions when I would sit with a mentally handicapped child and talk with that sweetly innocent one about what awaits him in the new Heaven, the new Earth. Mentally handicapped, yes. Spiritually handicapped, no.

"You will sing," I said to one boy as he played quietly with another child.

"Mmmm," he hummed in the only way he knew how, in the only way he could, since he had never been able to speak more than that.

"You will stand before the hosts of Heaven, and you will sing a great ballad," I continued. "You will stand with your friend here, and the two of you will delight precious Jesus Himself."

His playmate was also retarded. In addition, she had been born without fingers on either of her hands.

Her eyes told me that she wanted to know what *she* would be doing there, by her friend's side.

"You will be playing a guitar," I told her, "right in the midst of a whole new existence, first in Heaven and then in Eden."

She understood, for she held up those fingerless hands and studied them, then started crying.

"Mmmm," the boy put his arm around her and their heads touched, temple-to-temple.

He wanted to say a great deal, but the confines of the flesh gave him no words.

These two would be among the children caught up in the Rapture, and would not see death. I know the moment. Angels are not given glimpses of everything by our Creator, but this one He allowed, this one indeed.

Home.

They would be in their family homes, not in an institution like so many other children of their sort. The boy would be sitting on his father's lap, his mother running her fingers through his soft golden hair.

"Mmmm," the boy would hum as usual.

But his parents would sense something different this time, for he knew sooner than they, his sweet, sweet Jesus even then leaving Heaven and coming to earth and reaching out His arms.

They would look at their child, and smile.

And they both would reach out and touch him, each a different cheek, feeling the so-soft skin.

"It's time, Mother," he would say, turning to his mother, and to his father, "It's time, Father," and then to the two of them, "Blessed Jesus is here."

At that moment, they would be the ones without words.

Only a block away, the little girl would be in her bedroom, her parents in the kitchen washing dishes. Jesus the Christ would call her first and give her the fingers she never had, and a brightly shining guitar, and she would use it without human training, and she would call to her parents by a melody all her own, and dishes would fall to the floor as her beloved ones were caught up to be with her, together, taken unto glory, with a robust voice instantly joining in, the voice of a dear young friend, the two of them singing and playing to the delight of all throughout eternity.

Children. . . .

The defenseless ones, subject to the desires of another generation, in or out of the womb.

Children reach out so often in their lives, for love, for help in dealing with pain, loneliness, hunger. What of the anguish of a starving mother who cannot give her starving child the food for which that child has been crying all day, all night, many days, many nights? The child knows little of this. The child simply reaches out for the only human being he or she can trust, and even though there is no food in return, even though there is no water, the child sinks back into that deep pit of suffering without blaming the mother, somehow sensing that she has done the very best she can, and there is no more which she can provide. At least—though no food, no liquid, nothing but slow death—the child has love.

But in countries where sustenance is not a problem, where there is plenty of meat and potatoes and beans, where there is plenty of clear, satisfying water—children still have other needs, the need to love, the need to belong, the need to laugh.

*T*HE CLOWN HAD brought joy to so many bright faces over the years. Now, he had one more show that he wanted to make.

"I've spent my life out there," he told a friend who hovered over his bed. "I just can't leave this world without one final appearance under the big top."

His name was Sammy . . . Sammy the Clown.

He had given his life to his craft. He had embraced it mind, body, and soul. There was little else for him, little else he knew.

He was in the business of laughter.

He made little children laugh. He made their parents laugh. He brought joy to the sick and to the elderly.

He was the best clown there ever was, the most famous, the most loved.

And he was dying.

"I'm going to die in the center ring," he once told an interviewer for a midwestern newspaper. "The sawdust will be under me, the canvas will be above me, the smell of horses and elephants will fill my nostrils, and in the background I'll go out of this world on the laughter of the crowd."

"They will laugh at your death?" the other man asked.

"You don't understand. They'll think it's just part of the act because I'll be very funny even then."

Tears came to his eyes.

"I will miss it all so much," he admitted. "There can never be anything like what I do."

"You don't know what will await you on the other side," the other man pointed out. "Maybe it'll be something better."

"If there's anything at all. I may end up as nothing."

. . . as nothing.

Those words stayed in his mind, repeated in lonely moments after one stint closed and the circus moved on to another location somewhere else across the nation, times when he was looking out through a rain-streaked car window at the unfamiliar places through which he passed, at the strangers who walked by.

Sammy ran away from home when he was fourteen, and never saw his parents again. His brief marriage had failed miserably. But he still had a family. One brother was a dwarf. Another brother ate fire. One sister rode elephants. A third brother trained lions and tigers. Circus people—they were his brothers, his sisters.

"It's hard to believe," one had said years before.

"What's hard to believe?" Sammy had asked.

"That someday those often raging beasts will actually be resting side by side without a whip to tame them, or a sharp voice to direct them, and a lamb will wander by and see them, and sit down with them."

"You're dreaming!" Sammy scoffed.

"No, my friend, it's been promised."

"Who's the screwball who did that?"

The animal trainer looked at him sadly as he said, "Sammy, Sammy, Almighty God has promised this."

Sammy shrugged and walked off.

Sammy's version of Heaven was the big top. Sammy's

version of Hell was anytime he didn't happen to be in a ring, performing.

The animal trainer would talk again and again with him about spiritual things, about redemption and damnation and the rest.

And always Sammy's reply would be along the same lines, if not in the same words, then in the meaning behind them.

"I've known Heaven, I've known Hell already," he would say. "Your religion can't give me a thing I've not experienced here and now."

"But, Sammy, you need to be prepared."

"You can't mean that! For something that is nothing more than a mere game played on the gullible? A few magician's tricks? You forget; I've been a magician as well. I just like being a clown better."

The animal trainer would walk away, shaking his head regretfully, praying for another opportunity to witness to this man.

And so it went.

Sammy had his circus, he had his family—the animal trainer, the dwarfs, the giant, the others. Most had been with him for decades. There was no other life, as far as he was concerned.

But Sammy started to outlive them all.

One by one, his adopted brothers and his adopted sisters died. One by one, new faces replaced them, strangers with whom he felt not at all at ease. Then there were new owners. The circus became a business; it ceased being a way of life, as it had been to Sammy for more than fifty years.

Sammy was losing his heaven. The alternative for him was hell.

I've spent my life out there, he thought to himself as he struggled to sit up in his bed. *I just can't leave this world without one final appearance under the big top.*

And he made it.

The audience really enjoyed Sammy that night. As he finished, a six-year-old child broke away from her mother and ran up to him, and put her arms around his left leg, and hugged him.

"I love you," she murmured.

He picked her up and kissed her on the cheek, and then, after returning the child to her mother, he told the crowd that this was his farewell performance.

"Ladies and gentlemen, I am a very tired clown," he said. "This will be my last performance."

A gasp of shock arose from the onlookers, and a chorus started shouting, "No, no, no!"

He shook his head sadly, and added, "I wish you all were right. But, you see, my blood is messed up. It's because of years of breathing this sawdust. It's like the condition a coal-miner gets. Sometimes it settles in the blood, sometimes in the lungs."

His shoulders slumped as he walked out of the center ring and toward the back of the tent to the secluded dressing areas.

The crowd forgot him soon enough, turning their fervent attention to the beautiful prancing ponies and their sequin-collared canine riders.

That night, after everyone else in the circus was asleep, Sammy found himself tossing and turning.

He slipped on a heavy robe, opened the creaky door to his trailer, and walked outside.

My last night. . . .

He didn't know how he could tell that. It wasn't a premonition. The soon-to-die often feel the life force weakening somehow.

I startled him as I stood there, having assumed the form of a man every bit as old as Sammy himself.

"I . . . I mean . . . where did you come from?" he asked, his deeply-lined face pale in the moonlight.

"It's been quite a distance, Sammy," I told him.

"How is it, sir, that you know who I am?"

"I indeed know many things about you."

"But how could that be?"

"I've been with you more than you know, Sammy."

"Where? When? Stop these games!"

"I do not play games."

"Then answer me!"

"When you were divorced, Sammy . . . I was there."

"Did you work for the attorney?"

"No, Sammy, I worked for his boss."

"Oh. . . ."

"You gave up your wife for the circus."

"I had been raised under the big top. What was I to do?"

"She tried to live the life you wanted, but she couldn't. She wasn't emotionally capable of shouldering the burdens you placed upon her."

"But she wanted me to give up everything I had ever known, everything I had grown up with!"

"As you wanted her to do."

"But she pledged in her marriage vows to let nothing separate us."

"Those were vows you took as well, Sammy."

He turned toward the huge tent.

"That has been my home for fifty years," he said. "How could I just—?"

"It is but a thing of painted canvas and rope and metal poles, Sammy. Nothing more than that."

"I've had my greatest triumphs in there."

"And you will carry its legacy to your grave."

He turned away from me.

"Do not . . . torment a dying . . . old man," he said, his voice broken, weak.

"Your torment is in there, Sammy, not out here with me."

He became angry then, and swung around to face me. *Gone.*

To his physical sight, I was gone, even though in spirit I remained.

"Where did you—?" he started to ask.

He was very confused at that point, worried that his ailing body was affecting his mind, as well.

Suddenly he felt the need to walk over to the big top.

His gait was slow and painful, but once inside, he looked at the empty seats, the "dome" of the tent, and smiled.

"My cathedral," he whispered to himself, lost in memories.

"And you have worshiped well, Sammy," a voice abruptly interrupted his random thoughts.

Three clowns were standing, together, in the center ring.

"How did you get in here?" Sammy demanded.

"None of that is important," the tallest, most garishly-painted of the three told him. "The fact is that we *are* here."

The clown next to him, shorter, less flamboyant, added, "You said this has been your cathedral. You speak the truth. For it is here that you have found your gods."

Sammy chuckled.

"You make more of my simple comment than I ever intended," he said.

"That is not so," commented the third clown, shorter than the tall one but taller than the short one, and with almost no paint at all. "You have given your *life* to this temple. You have fallen at the pedestal of your own conceit."

"Meaningless piffle," Sammy grunted.

"You call it such because it accuses, it entraps you, old man," the third clown added darkly.

"Please don't misunderstand us," the first one interpolated. "We are delighted, more than you will perhaps ever know, that you have done what you have done, Sammy the Clown."

Sammy felt a chill then.

"Delighted?" he repeated. "Why are you delighted if what you say is true? For what you paint is a picture of a vain old man who—"

His eyes widened.

"Do you now see a measure of the truth, Sammy?" the first clown asked. "You gave up your family for the circus. But you also ignored Someone else."

"I ignored only those who would come between me and my—"

"Passion, Sammy? Isn't that what you should be saying?"

"No, no, *obsession!*" the second clown interrupted. "It is not bad to have a passion in life. But it is otherwise to have an obsession."

"I stand corrected," the first clown agreed. "Your obsession, Sammy, has come between you and anyone not connected with this enterprise."

A gloved hand swung around, indicating the big tent.

We are delighted, more than you will perhaps ever know, that you have done what you have done. . . .

Sammy felt another chill as he recalled those words so recently spoken. He turned to go, intending to walk as rapidly as his old legs would carry him.

"It is not so easy as that," one of the clowns called to him.

"What do you mean?" Sammy shouted back.

"You *know* you cannot possibly leave this place, you funny old clown. *You love it all too much!*"

Sammy was scared, scared of the clowns, scared of

what they were saying to him, scared of what he sensed about them.

You love it all too much!

But there, in that single statement, they had hit upon the truth. They had pointed out to him a singular fact of his very insular life.

And now that my life is almost over, what does it all mean? he thought. *I gave my last performance tonight. There will be no more cheering or clapping for me. What would I be giving up if I just continued on my way? I am too old, too ill to exert myself again. I can stop now of my own accord. It is not that difficult. I can spend whatever time I have left, quietly, feasting on my memories. I will no longer have to arise at five o'clock each morning to help feed the animals or to move on to another town.*

I spoke to Sammy then, after he had put some distance between himself and those three clowns.

I was not a clown, as I did, but a middle-aged man, someone who had seen Sammy many, many times. That was not a lie, you know. The God of Truth would not allow us to lie. Indeed I had seen Sammy often, though he had never been aware of my presence when I was purely spirit. Only when I became a child hoisted up on his knee was he able to see me, albeit in another form.

A flash of insight, inexplicable, fled across his ancient face.

"We have met before, haven't we?" he stated.

"We have, Sammy. You wiped away my tears."

Sammy's eyes widened with sudden realization.

"You were that little boy, weren't you?" Sammy asked, somehow aware, though not sure why this was so.

I nodded.

The little boy rushed out to the center ring more than thirty years earlier. Sammy grabbed him gently and lifted the child up onto his left knee.

"And what can I do for you, child?" he asked.

At first I did not answer but simply looked at him. Tears began streaming down the cheeks of that adopted body.

"Why are you crying?" Sammy asked as he reached out to wipe the tears away. "You are too young to be crying like this."

"For you," I replied through the voice of a seven year old.

"For me? Why is that so? I am very happy. Why are you crying for me, a clown, a stranger?"

Sammy's attention was distracted then, the next act ready to enter the ring. He took the little boy off his knee, patted him on the head, and walked off. . . .

"Can you answer me now?" Sammy asked urgently, never having forgotten that singular incident. "Can you tell me what this is all about?

"There is your answer," I said, pointing to the three clowns behind him who beckoned from the canvas tent doorway.

"They're evil, aren't they?" he asked.

"Yes, they are."

"Why do they want me to go back there? I performed tonight for the last time. What could they possibly offer?"

"They want you. And they will try anything."

"They want this old, dying, stooped over body? Why? It's a wreck. They'd be getting damaged merchandise."

"It isn't your body, Sammy."

He pretended not to understand, but he knew well enough.

"Why should I side with you? Why should I not at least hear what they have to offer?"

"Because having heard, you will accept."

"Accept what?"

"One more night, Sammy."

"One more night in the center ring?"

"That is what they will claim."

"But that's impossible. I don't have the energy any longer."

I looked at Sammy, his eyes and mine locked into a gaze that he could not break for a moment or two. My human form shed tears, just as it had so many years earlier, tears for the same clown, now so old and frail.

"Are you sure that you would not give up *everything* for one more night, Sammy? The crowds cheering, the music playing, the smell of the sawdust in your nostrils? Are you so sure?"

"I have already done it," he said matter-of-factly. "This *was* my final performance."

"Only because you thought that it *had* to be, that there was no other course of action open to you, as you came face to face with your physical limitations."

"I can scarcely walk now. I'm far too tired to give even one more performance."

"*They* would speak to the contrary, Sammy."

"I don't care."

Sammy smiled defiantly.

"Will you join me in my trailer?" he asked. "There are some things I'd like to show you."

Sammy!

Shrill, insistent voices were calling to him from the big top, night-time sirens beckoning him.

Sammy the Clown turned quickly startled to hear his name shouted in such an eerie manner.

He shivered with the cold, but he smiled at me again, though with much less certainty than a moment before.

"They sound so confident, don't they?"

"Yes, they do," I agreed.

Just listen to what we have to say. What can you lose, Sammy?

He looked at me sheepishly.

"Come on," he said. "A nice hot cup of tea can do wonders for the cold."

Sammy the Clown walked to the trailer, oblivious to the fact that I was no longer with him, for I knew, with an awful sense of pure-white clarity, that I could do nothing more for this old man, this lost soul.

He stopped momentarily at the metal doorway, turned, and said, "Hey, mister, I've got a scrapbook of my—"

There was nothing except the dust his arthritic old feet had kicked up, scattered about for an instant by a slight, passing breeze, and then gone altogether, as though it had never been, like everything else in life.

The circus tent was full.

The media were there, regional as well as national.

World-renowned Sammy the Clown had been convinced to give one more show, even after that so-called "last" performance.

Word spread from household to household, children to adults . . . one more night with the master clown, one more night with Sammy.

Three minutes into his act, he died of a heart attack.

Three other clowns carried him off.

A trapeze artist reported later that he had never seen them before, since Sammy was the only clown that circus had ever had.

"Another odd thing," he said to the television newscaster interviewing him.

"What was that?"

"Look, I'll be the first one to admit how crazy this will sound, but, well, I heard some pretty weird noises, mister."

"Noises?" the reporter asked. "Can you be more specific?"

"Crazy stuff . . . yeah, very strange . . . coming from the four of them as they all disappeared outside."

"What kinds of sounds?"

"Weeping."

"Weeping?"

"Yes . . . weeping and . . . and gnashing of teeth. Isn't that crazy?"

End of
the Odyssey

I CANNOT SAY how it is that I know but know I do that I do know.

The wind perhaps? A strange new wind from the east?

Does it carry the echoes of hapless demons with it, as they realize they will soon be dealt the destiny that had been foretold for so long?

I hear cries, I think, from Hell itself. Somehow, damned souls know what is on the verge of happening, the event which they chose to ignore or dispute. They who turned their backs on the Savior—their only source of escape from what they are now experiencing, and *will* experience forever—their cries are far worse than any I had heard before, even as I stood at the brink of Hell and pulled Darien from it, cries not only of torment but salvation lost, salvation pushed aside and spat upon, and now they know it is as real as the very flames around them.

I sit at the top of a tall mountain, high above the clouds. The sky is without blemish. The world below is shrouded under a blanket of soft whiteness.

Another sound supersedes that first, that wail. This is different, and familiar. I have heard it often in Heaven my home, the sound of many wings—a million wings, ten million, more perhaps—beating together, wings of spirit, like threads of shaped mist, all coming from above. I stand as tall as I can, looking upward.

Most mortals below will never know, not those left behind. They will turn around and find a brother, a sister, a spouse, a friend, a co-worker *gone*.

They will assume any number of explanations: a gigantic world-wide terrorist conspiracy . . . mere coincidence involving a number of disappearances at the same time . . . some fundamentalist religious charade . . . on and on . . . without opening their eyes and grappling with the *truth*.

I see blessed Jesus now, coming through the clouds, His arms outstretched, a single word from his lips, a word that connects with the souls of millions, forming an immediate, irresistible link, pulling them upward.

I leave that mountain and scurry about the planet, eager to witness those precious moments of rapturing in every place that I can. I move quickly, before these have all passed by, before that instant, tragic and foretold for so long, when I must leave as a consequence, along with all other angels, leave those humans now standing in their puzzled unbelief, leave them behind in the grip of Satan more completely than ever before.

After a pleasant luncheon, a man walking from London's Simpson's-in-the-Strand to Trafalgar Square is taken just as he is pulling his coat more tightly around himself. He forgets everything, this man does, the chill London air, the traffic sounds, the paper vendor calling out the latest headline, the ancient odors that set London apart from any other city in the world. Yes, he forgets because he is looking into eyes, now, that are beyond any he has ever encountered, for they offer peace unimaginable in his finite frame, a frame that slips away even as the body itself is transformed, incorruptible from corruptible, words of joy escaping from his mouth as he is helped into everlasting life.

Helped into everlasting life. . . .

That is a description of what it is like in Heaven with which some theologians perhaps might well take issue. After all, as they would point out, those in Hell also have everlasting life.

Up to a point, I must say in reply, adding that being in Hell is hardly "life" as it was envisioned in the mind of a holy God, hardly life that is worth living. No, I would have to say everlasting *life* is only for the redeemed. The damned have something else altogether.

I come next to a Planned Parenthood clinic. I wonder how they have gotten away with assigning *parenthood* to the name of an organization whose founder's original purpose was to concentrate on the *annihilation* of blacks, a clever weapon to rid the world of as many of them as possible

I go inside. There is confusion.

Babies are disappearing! Some as they are being scraped from their mother's wombs, others as they have been temporarily tossed onto a cold metal table.

Gone!

Nurses are screaming. Doctors are trying to calm them. Mothers recoil in terror.

I wish I could capture the moments that I now am seeing, capture these on video tape and show them to a society that *might* change its ways with such evidence before it.

I wish I could, but I cannot. What I see is for myself and, hopefully, for the conscience of other witnesses.

I see a baby who has been aborted whole, one who is supposedly dead, yet continues to live. I see a doctor order a nurse to "dispose" of the "thing." The nurse looks at him, and then at the living miniature human form in front of her, and she hesitates, wanting to obey her boss, the man who controls her livelihood, but not quite able to take her hands, put them around the baby boy's neck, and twist. Or shovel him into the oven on premises. *(Heil Hitler, eh!)*

Grumbling, the doctor pushes the nurse aside. As he is reaching for the tiny form, the baby is raptured—the baby is taken up, but not instantaneously. There is a transitory moment in time when he turns toward the doctor who would be his slayer, turns toward this man intent on atrocity, and possessed of a growing wisdom, wisdom that stems from He Who is calling him, from that child issue forth the final tears of his brief existence, the last shreds of what he once was. Now there is only love in the tiny eyes, love mixed with pity—hence, the tears—love so supreme, so unconditional, so undeserved that the doctor breaks into uncontrollable sobs as he reaches upwards toward the child, and the child down toward him. But it is too late, too late for conscience or regret. There is no more time. There is nothing for the child but the loving arms of His Savior and nothing for the doctor but the sharp talons of his own master as he runs screaming from the room to collapse in the corridor outside, not propelled by a vision of incalculable horror, but of a baby's blind, beautiful love beyond reason itself, a deep and total forgiveness he can scarce imagine, and never abide. That is why he can say only, "It cannot be, it cannot be, oh, God, it cannot be," again and again until the clutching darkness has him in judgment unassailable.

There are others in that cruel mausoleum owned and operated by Planned Parenthood. They call it a clinic. It is hardly that, for a clinic, as originally intended centuries before, was to be a place purely of the treatment of diseases, of the curing of ills. And yet an alarming percentage of what Planned Parenthood has dispensed is the aiding and the abetting of infamy of the most despicable sort—but wearing a reassuringly professional face with civil rights statutes rolled up in one hand and some surgical instruments in the other, with a mouth spouting procedures couched in innocuous words that taste like honey and burn the gut like arsenic. They are a Trojan horse of horrors, these human devils, smiling and so very helpful and more than a little efficient in the process, and yet deserving only the most pitiless judgment, the kind that surely will be served up to these vile servants of a mocking maestro dripping with the evil of himself.

The babies are raptured, yet the advocates of their "termination" are left behind to continue wallowing in their hellish practices, practices now become part of the fabric of a society, a world increasingly given over to the very same Prince of Darkness with whom they have been cavorting for so long. The Holy Spirit and all angels and all redeemed human beings are now gone . . . there is nothing left to stem the terrible foul tide.

Who said there is no justice anymore?

*I*T IS NEARLY completed now, this my sojourn on earth, as well as the Rapture. I see others going to the Savior in the air. The elderly, once gripped by pain, suddenly find that it has left them. Those men, women, and children dying of cancer are taken, the ravages of that killer disease eliminated all over the world. The retarded have regained all their faculties as they reach their hands high, and He calls them home. Women suffering through the trauma that has followed rape are now completely at peace as they leave the ground, and He gives them a security that will never pass away.

So many. . . .

Millions are saying goodbye to sin, to disease, to fear, to despair, to loneliness.

To *doubt,* indeed that—in its place the reality that faith all along had been telling them were true.

True!

I have not seen True. Could my comrade still be there at the entrance to Eden? But why? Surely he must know. How could he *not* know?

I go to the Garden, and do find him as I had suspected, exactly where he was when I last left him.

"It is the Rapture, True," I tell him. "We all can leave now. There is no more place for us in this world."

He shakes his head sadly.

"All but me," he says. "My task is not yet ended."

"But there is no more need—" I start to reply, then stop myself, for I had been about to say, "But there is no need to stand guard."

He smiles, seeing my expression.

"You understand, do you not?" he remarks. "There is more need than ever that I, the last of angelkind here on this planet, be twice as vigilant, twice as strong, calling upon everything with which the Creator has fortified me."

"And you will need all of that, dear friend," I agree now that I understand that he must remain, what he must face.

For there is to be a wave of evil so intense that it will sweep over everyone who is left. Some will resist. Some will come to a saving knowledge of Jesus Christ. But most will not, seduced by Satan in this climactic bid for supremacy.

"I have heard them planning, Stedfast," True says.

He shivers then, as though the memories are shaking him to the very core of himself.

"I have heard what they will be doing with the living," he continues. "There will be more and more manifestations, you know, appearances by demonic entities as the veil between Hell and this planet is rent asunder. And mortals will not be able to cope. Many will be driven mad, you know. Many will take their own lives. Others will fall in slavish devotion to the new gods of this age. They will become as one with the evil one, and follow him on the path to damnation."

He pauses, then: "Devilwalk! That is what I have heard it called. That is surely what it is."

Together we shiver at that thought.

. . . the veil between Hell and this planet is rent asunder.

No angels in keep it in place, no Holy Spirit to hold back the onslaught.

"Pure evil, Stedfast," angel True says. "And I will be the only one of unfallen creation in the midst of it."

There seems to be fear in his manner at that moment, but if that is what it is, it is gone in a millisecond. And now he stands, his presence emboldened by a special determination, a divine valor.

"I can take it," he remarks. "I can take whatever offenses they fling at me, whatever foul tricks they might try."

"I will stay with you," I offer.

"You *cannot*. That would displease the Father, I am sure. He has given me my holy charge and I shall not dishonor Him by shifting responsibility to another."

True is being what he could never cease being. His nature did not permit disobeying the Father.

"I will come back, True," I said. "I will come back, and we shall walk side by side through a restored Eden."

For a moment, images of the original Eden consume me. For a moment, I stand there, anxious for the future.

I hear True calling to me, "I will be here, Stedfast. I will be waiting. Trust on that. Believe it!"

And I am gone elsewhere on earth.

*T*HE LAST MAN to be raptured is named Jonathan, and he is very old. He walks at sunrise in a green English meadow with his beloved black-gray-white tabby by his side.

They have been together for sixteen years.

"It's a beautiful morning," Jonathan says. "Smell the heather, Boy-Boy?"

He thinks the cat can understand, and in some respects, he is right. This one does understand that he has spoken, and even if the sense of his words is lost on the animal, merely the sound of his master's voice is enough to set Boy-Boy apurring.

"It's been a rough four months, my dear friend," Jonathan continues. "First, there was that hernia operation. It was hard to recuperate at home. I still think they rushed me out of the hospital too quickly. And with Jessie gone, I—I—"

He hasn't stuttered for a long time. He did when his wife Jessie's heart failed, and he tried to revive her somehow, and cried out for her not to leave him. But that was a long time ago.

He reaches out and pats Boy-Boy, who digs his claws into the soft earth, a sign of momentary contentment.

"You were so faithful," he recalls, "always stretched out in bed right smack up against my right leg. Whenever I would groan with pain, you would look up at me, and it was almost as though you were asking if there was anything you could do to help."

This unusual companion had shown the loyalty and devotion of a dog. There was a great deal that Boy-Boy did to show his unconditional love. He would greet Jonathan and Jessie at the front door as they came in from a bicycling jaunt through the countryside, and fall down in front of them, and roll over on his back because he knew that that pleased them. And if they were pleased, he, too, felt happy.

When Jessie was in bed, that horrible arthritic pain constant for her, and Jonathan found it necessary to go into town to get a refill of some medicine, Boy-Boy would set himself on the pillow next to her and comfort her in ways that helped, that really helped. Once, after finding some relief from the pain in a deep sleep, she woke to find that Boy-Boy had wrapped his four legs around her and was resting his head in the palm of her hand, his warmth radiating through her, soothing her tired spirit.

"You mean so much to me," Jonathan says as he looks down at his side, and finds that Boy-Boy has crawled some yards away, and is now standing uncertainly, his legs very weak.

"*No!*" the old man cries as he struggles to his feet, and rushes over to the cat, sitting down beside him, and taking his friend in his arms.

"Come on, Boy-Boy, you can make it," Jonathan begs. "We've been together so long. I can't bear to be without you, too. Losing Jessie was so bad, and you helped me more than you can know. Please, Boy-Boy, hang on a while longer."

But the cat has no more strength. He had been close to death three times over the past four months, as a siege of tremors had racked his body, each making him more and more weak.

Now, as his beloved master holds him, he opens his eyes wide, and looks at the man he loves with all his being, and tries to tell him what he has just now seen, something bright and beautiful, sparkling light and music, and, yes, the woman, the woman he also loved, waiting, her arms reaching out to take him.

Boy-Boy's chest vibrates for a few moments.

"How can you be purring now?" Jonathan asks. "How can you—?"

Then the cat reaches out, and does something then that he had done often through the years, he folds his front paws around Jonathan's wrist, and pulls that hand closer to him, closer to his fur. How he enjoyed the feel of human flesh against him, and he sends forth for the last time a surge of warmth from his body.

But that is it. He has nothing more to give. His body sags as though with relief, but he is not quite gone. Some small spark of him lingers.

"I can't let you go!" Jonathan screams. "I need you just a little while longer!"

It is time for me now, time for me to appear before this old man.

"Let him go from that body," I say. "Let him put aside what is now of no use to him. It does not function anymore, you know, that earthly body is—"

"No, stranger!" Jonathan interrupts. "No, do not say it. It cannot *be!* I need him. I *do* need him."

"And your friend, your very good friend needs you to say that it is time now. He *must* go, for his sake. Release him, Jonathan. I know that you love him far too much to ask him to suffer another moment for *your* sake."

"But I'll be alone," Jonathan retorts. "I'll have no one."

"You will have *me*," I reply. "I will stay with you."

"But for how long? How long will you be with me?"

I am about to speak when he interrupts me.

"You have just arrived here. I knew Boy-Boy for sixteen years, Jessie for many more than that. Why should I expect a stranger to comfort me?"

"Listen, Jonathan, listen please."

He does that, he listens as Boy-Boy lets out a sigh, the body now limp, a slight breeze stirring through the soft, beautiful fur.

"I can't bury him," Jonathan tells me desperately. "My hands, my fingers, the arthritis!"

"It's okay. Just put him down on the ground," I say.

"But there must be a grave," he protests. "My beloved Jessie is buried only a few yards from here."

"No more graves, Jonathan, no more dying."

With great tenderness, Jonathan lays the still, thin body on the cold rocky ground.

I pause, smiling, and then say, "Now look up, old man."

He does. In an instant his tears are gone.

"You are the last one," I say, "the very last one."

Even for me the emotions are too strong, and I must stop. I realize that it is all over, this phase of God's plan for the ages, and what Jonathan and I will leave behind is not a world in which we could ever want to remain for a single additional moment.

"I promised to stay with you, Jonathan," I finally tell him. "I will do that. You asked for how long? I can tell you now."

"No need," he whispers with awe. "I know."

There is the sound of a final beckoning trumpet. No longer bound by age or ailments or grief, Jonathan is swept up from the earth, and I with him, beneath us the grave of the woman he loved for fifty years. Nearby lay a black-gray-white body as useless as hers had become. But above, ah, above, someone familiar, her arms outstretched, her smile the very light of Heaven's own radiance, and, waiting, at her feet, loyal, loving, beyond flesh itself, a familiar friend, a special gift from the Creator, now returned to them both, to be enjoyed again. No more parting, no more waiting for sweet devotion to be jerked away by dark death.

How long, Jonathan? You asked me, now you know. How long will I be by your side, and so many others I have come to know and to love with a measure of the love of God Himself? Isn't the answer truly, truly wonderful? Isn't it?

That is why the Father, my blessed, blessed Creator, called me by the name that He did in that ageless instant when I came into being, for it was to be the purpose of my life, the sole and holy reason for my very existence.

That is why I am what I am, and will always be, long after the lion lies down once again with the lamb.

Stedfast . . . as ever.

True's *Epilogue*

I *WATCHED THAT FIRST* couple go, their naked-
ness covered, their shame exposed. They left as a storm
arose and swept over the whole of the earth. The first
murder in the history of the human race followed, one
son killing another. . . .

It is peaceful now. The sky is clear. The air is warm,
dry.

I await their return.

I have been waiting for thousands of years. Every epoch
of human history has passed by.

And there have been visitors, human and demonic.
They have stumbled upon this place, but none have
gotten past me.

I have been capable for this my assignment. I need no
food. I need no water. My sustenance comes from the
Father of all.

I feel His power. I need His power. I am but one angel,
and yet hordes from Hell have stood about, taunting me.

They have stayed with me for long periods of time,
have talked about the old days of unblemished fellowship
in Heaven before they followed Lucifer.

"For us, there is no boredom," one said. "We go where

we please. We do what we want. We have no restrictions. We are *free*, True, and that *is* true."

I recalled the times when we walked the streets of gold, when we were in harmony, when the world below was untainted.

"You left," I replied. "I did not."

"To be in service to a new master."

"A pretender to the throne."

"The rightful heir—big difference."

"Deceit. Lucifer is the master of *that*, and nothing else."

They cannot tempt me, cannot seduce me into their perversion.

And always they went away, though always they returned, with some new taunt, some foul breath of deviltry.

Once, just once, it was Lucifer himself, not his underlings, not the duped spirits of a rejected Heaven.

Lucifer.

My once-comrade.

That is truly how it was. It was Lucifer, Stedfast, Darien, and True. Close in Heaven, close to one another, close to our Creator.

To have him leave, to have him turn into what he became was like wrenching a piece of myself away and throwing it into some eternal sea. But I healed. So did the others. Even so, we retained the memories.

And the memories were what Lucifer tried to use against me.

"You are lonely," he said.

"No, I am not. I am alone. But I have visitors. And I can call out to the Father anytime I wish."

"So said Another. And yet even He was driven to cry, 'My God, my God, why hast Thou forsaken me?' Remember those words, True. Remember them during those nights when there is no one, when there is nothing but darkness, and you are alone with the memories of what we once had, what we once were."

This fallen being named Lucifer knew what to say. He knew how to say it. He had, after all, persuaded a third of all my kind to join with him in his rebellion in Heaven.

But I was called True from the beginning. And that has never changed. My name is not Inconsistent. Or Wavering. Or Weak. *I am True*, and so I shall be to my Father, and to myself, and are these not one and the same?

Lucifer lost his veneer of propriety.

"You are stupid, True," he screamed.

"And *you* are false, is *that* not true? You reek with deceit. You shroud yourself with treachery. I serve the Almighty Father. You are the father of nothing but the foul deeds of your compliant demonkind. You stand before the human race and offer yourself as a messiah. Yet you are the very voice of Hell. *You offer nothing but damnation!*"

That got him, I think, at least for the moment.

Lucifer had no immediate reply. I thought he was going to leave, but he turned at the last moment, and looked back at me, beyond me, to the hint behind me of what Eden had become.

"Once so beautiful," Lucifer said. "Once so alive. . . ."

His voice trailed off, and he bowed his loathsome head as though regretting—as much as he was capable of anything of the sort—what he had wrought through the ages of time, epitomized by this dead, dusty, melancholy place.

Something happened then, one of the last remaining creatures made its way to the gate where we stood, a tall creature, rather like a young giraffe, born to be free and proud of its beauty, born to live without disease, born to last forever, without death to take it away into the dark night.

It had aged inexorably. It had become ill, contracting some sort of repugnant disease that reduced its colors to pale blotches and its gait to a pitiable shadow of what once had been.

Then it fell past the gate at the feet of its executioner, at the feet of Satan—and just as it died, it looked up into his face, and there were tears in its eyes. It groaned once, and that was all. There was nothing more. It was gone.

That was ages ago, centuries past. There are no more creatures left, the husk of once-Eden shriveled and ugly, and I continue to be alone. I have seen no demons for a very long time. Perhaps they have gathered together for Armageddon.

Is that music I hear? Has someone slipped past me after all my efforts and broken into that which I have tried to guard for so very long?

I turn for a moment, to look beyond the entrance into that place.

I am startled.

A flower is blooming, looking much like an orchid. I enter Eden and stand beside it. I drink deeply of the scent it offers.

How can that be?

In a nearby stream, I hear the trickling of water over rocks at the bottom.

And swimming just below the surface are silver and gold fish.

Life!

I turn, and see green leaves unfurl on a tree that had been dead for five thousand years.

On one of the branches are two birds.

Singing! They have returned to Eden, and they are singing their joy!

A bush is green. The soil is rich and brown.

That music I hear . . . again . . . so beautiful!

I turn around and around. Before me, in an instant, Eden is coming to life, its own resurrection ascendant at this very moment.

I walk almost numbly to the entrance. I look up at the sky.

I see heavenly hosts descending. I see my fellow beings forming a glorious river of light and life.

I see the Son. He stands before me. He smiles as He reaches out and touches me.

I kneel before Him in adoration, my head bowed, my wings—

Two voices!

I look up.

Oh, Lord, how many times has there been temptation? How many times have I been asked by demons to turn aside? But I did not. I stayed, Holy One. I stayed for Thee.

"Hello, dear, dear True," the woman says.

"It has been a long time," the man adds.

They are changed these two, cleansed, as radiant as the angels accompanying them.

"Will you give us entrance, True?" the couple inquires of me.

I say nothing, I can say nothing. Words are useless when souls are united.

I step aside for the first time since sin entered creation.

The two stop just beyond the entrance, beauty surrounding them, life shouting its emergence in calls of living creatures from the trees, from the ground—everywhere are sounds and scents and rebirth.

They walk in awe, this first couple. The woman pauses before a flower of remarkable beauty. She bends down, pressing her nose quietly among the petals, and takes in what these have to offer to her. Then she stands straight, realizing that nothing has changed—if anything the garden is more beautiful than at the beginning—yea, nothing has changed, except centuries of pain, of disease, of turmoil for the entire human race.

"And all because of me, and my man," she says out loud.

But I go to her, more like Stedfast than True, and I remind her that none of that matters, that she has been forgiven, that her man has shared in this forgiveness.

She smiles.

"Dear friend," she says, "I said that not in melancholy or regret any longer but in rejoicing that our Father can forgive so much, that He can welcome even us into His Kingdom.

She reaches out to touch the flower.

"And now we are back," she remarks softly. "Praise His holy name, He has allowed us to return."

I leave them to their walk along familiar paths amidst resurgent majesty. Soon they will come to the spot where the Tree of the Knowledge of Good and Evil once stood.

No longer.

It is gone. In its place stand angels at their station, angels who, like me, will be with them time without end.

"What now, Lord?" I ask as I stand outside.

"Be with them, True," He tells me. "Be by their side, but not as the guardian of this place."

"But as what, blessed Jesus?"

I hear a chorus then, a celebration among ten thousand upon ten thousand of my kind.

"Be with them, True . . . as their dear friend," Jesus the Christ proclaims.

Sin has been banished forever!

I think, for a moment, of my former comrade-in-Heaven, of Lucifer suffering amidst the flames for what he has done, that for which he has been judged. I think of his guilt, his shame. But nowhere is there his repentance.

It never came. He clung to his abominations and could not, would not, did not let go.

Then I turn and enter Eden, and, in the midst of life as it was meant to be, I think of him no more.

Finis